CATCHING A WITCH

CATCHING A WITCH

A Novel of Loyalty, Deception,
and Superstition

HEIDI ELJARBO

Published by TCK Publishing

www.TCKPublishing.com

Get discounts and special deals on books at

www.tckpublishing.com/bookdeals

For Arnfinn, who always believes in me.

THE PROLOGUE

Toomber's Cottage, Rossby, Norway

Summer 1658

~~~

*I*was not there the day the gravedigger injured his foot, but the *account was passed on even decades later...*

It was a misty day when the air was full of water but did not let go enough to make it rain. Toomber was preparing new graves in the cemetery. He was always a step ahead of the dying. A ready grave meant quick business to him. He had visited the Laursen family that same morning because they had a sickly child. Surely, they would want a grave ready in case the child passed on within the next few days? Then he had crossed the marsh to speak with an elderly couple who lived in the woods close to the abbey. He had convinced them it would be disastrous
~~~

if they died, and no one would bury them. "Buy in advance," he'd said. "Buy while you can still pay."

When he next awoke, it took him a while to recollect what had happened. His first thought was that there would be no breaking up earth in the cemetery for the rest of that day. That made him irritated, and he tried to sit up. He looked around the room and saw her standing by the table.

"Wretched woman!" he grunted, but all his strength was gone. He fell back onto the straw-stuffed mattress.

Even lying down, he felt as if the room was spinning, going around and around, and he wanted it to stop. He tried to lift his upper body again, but the woman put a hand on his shoulder and gently pushed him back down. He wanted to protest, which was something he was good at. He was his own master, the minister had said; no one told him what to do. No one was worth listening to except the minister; but he was long gone now.

Toomber was confused and could not plainly remember what had happened. The ground in the southeast corner of the cemetery was full of clay, and he had been using an iron lever and had stabbed the unwilling soil with all his strength. At one point, he must have hit his right foot hard, as that was where the pain was. Then he must have fainted.

"Please, lie down, Toomber," the woman said quietly.

She was small of stature but had a firm grip and a determined look on her face. Her green eyes looked straight at him and showed no fear, which confused him even more. Most people avoided him, and he wanted to ask her why she had come but did not want to start a conversation.

Toomber knew who she was. He knew what she was known for and what she could do. He knew the people in Rossby needed her but did not want to be her friend. They feared what they did not understand and were jealous because she descended from a line of independent, strong women. Women who acted as midwives in the villages, who cured ailments and diseases by administering potions and warm beverages made of herbs and plants. The villagers feared women such as those and believed the power over life and death belonged to God Almighty, not inferior females.

Toomber watched the woman try to move his leg, so it would not slip off the edge of the bed. He groaned loudly. It felt as if he was being tortured. His thoughts would not turn into words. It was too much effort and too bewildering.

"We have to try to save your foot. You've lost so much blood, but I'll do what I can," the woman continued.

With all the strength he could muster, the gravedigger lifted up his head to see what was going on. His foot was a distorted mess. The force of the iron rod had shattered his tarsal bones, leaving his foot bent like the broken neck of a chicken and had torn through an artery. Swollen and caked in dirt and blood, it was a certain recipe for a bad infection. The pain was excruciating. Then he went unconscious again.

The woman worked quickly. She knew what she had to do. The cottage had two rooms, one small room for working-tools and Toomber's treasures. Old pieces of rope, a copper kettle without a handle, an old, wrought-iron cross with the initials E.J. inscribed. The other larger room functioned as everything else—kitchen, living room, and bedroom, all in one. The furniture was a mixture of homemade, wooden crates and half-elegant pieces that had previously decorated finer homes. The windows were small and thick and without curtains. The wooden floor was muddy with dried grass and sand. Common to the whole setting was that it had not seen soap and water for ages. Cleanliness was not a priority in Toomber's life.

The woman made a fire with some twigs in the open hearth, filled up the kettle with water from a small barrel in the corner, and hung it on an iron rod sticking out from the stonework over the flames. Out of a black leather bag she pulled out anise, chamomile, sage, and horsetail. The herbs left a sweet aroma in the dust-covered room. Using rags soaked in the aromatic liquid to clean the wound would help heal the sores and tame the infection.

Trying to hurry before he came to, the woman rinsed the foot with the soaked rags, picking out small stones and pieces of grass and leaves. She had to work fast. There was no time to spare.

"What happened?" Toomber muttered.

"You injured your foot by the large oak tree near the Laursen family grave and pulled yourself along the ground by your elbows. There was a

trail of blood along the path to the east gate of the cemetery and about a hundred meters farther toward the hill by the marsh and the cottage. That's where I found you unconscious."

The woman told him how she had pulled him toward his little cottage. Even though she was strong and used to hard work, he was a large man to move. The small hill down, she could handle, but getting him through the cottage door had seemed an impossible task.

As he'd come to and had seen her standing over him, he'd uttered, "What are you doing? Get your hands off of me!"

But she was both firm and gentle and did not scare easily. "Toomber, help me out here, she'd said. "Try to stand on your left foot, so we can get you in the door."

"We are not getting me anywhere! Get away from me!"

"I understand you don't want anyone in your cottage, but you are in a terrible state. This is something you cannot do alone right now."

She had pushed and pulled and raised him into a half-standing position, and they had stumbled toward his bed, where he had fallen like a large tree being axed down. The bed cracked and creaked, but luckily it was built to hold his long and heavy body. As he had drifted off again, she had run back to the cemetery to pick up her black leather bag containing her herbs and potions. Because she was a cunning woman. She was a healer.

"Wretched woman!" The gravedigger's voice was deep and hoarse. The words coming out of his gaping mouth were imprecise, as if he had chewed thorny twigs, leaving his throat scraped and wounded and his half-open mouth unable to close.

After she had cleaned his foot and given him some warm gruel with honey for nourishment and rest, she put stinging nettles in and around his pillow and at the foot of the bed, hoping to drive away some of the many fleas and lice that bred there.

～

The gravedigger was in his own bed, and he had been fed and nursed. He looked up as he saw the evening sun hit her head of unruly copper-colored hair in the open doorway.

"I'll be back tomorrow, Toomber. I'll come at midday."

The cunning woman came back the next day and the day after that. And so it went on a dozen or more days, maybe weeks. She would enter unannounced in her hooded cloak, carrying that black leather bag with funny plants and strange-tasting remedies in it. She gave him drink and food and sang to him. She even brought the wee child bound on her back by a long piece of cloth. He was surprised she never expected anything in return, and he certainly never offered it. His comments were unfriendly and harsh. Pretending she did not hear his rude and offending remarks, she nursed him just the same.

"Foolish woman!"

He would never have done anything for anyone without getting paid in return. His services in the village were important, because people were always dying. He would never be out of a job. They needed him.

One day, she pronounced him well enough. The foot was suitably healed. He would have a limp, but it was a limp in a leg that still had a foot attached to it. She had tidied up his room, humming tunes he might have heard before, and had filled his cupboard with berry preserves, bread, and half a dozen apples. On the small table was a pewter cup with field flowers in cheerful colors.

"We're off, then, Toomber. Take care of yourself," she said.

She carried the child out—a little girl with curls the same copper glow as her mother's hair. It would be the last he'd see of them for a while. Finally, he would get some peace and quiet in the cottage. He still did not need anyone.

My father, the minister, had told Toomber to be in charge of his own life. No one should tell him what to do.

He limped out the front door, lifted his chin, and drew a deep breath. Well, he thought. Good riddance to her and her black leather bag. There are things to do, folks to bury, payments for coffins and graves to collect.

He would be his own master.

~

Clara pushed her journal to the right and put down the pen. The window drapes blocked the view of the blossoming hillside. She leaned forward and pulled them aside to let the morning light flood in.

Images of the small, Norwegian, seaside town of Rossby and its impressionable inhabitants danced vividly in her mind. She licked her lips and imagined the taste of salt from the ocean mist. She looked at the clouds coming in and believed she heard seagulls crying, looking for fish. The chatter of people waiting for fishing boats to arrive sounded familiar. The feeling was tangible enough, that if she stretched out her hand, she could touch the folks of Rossby on their shoulders, and one by one, they turned around and looked into her eyes. Their stare opened up a passage, and she saw into their souls.

It had not always been like this. At first, she had not known the townspeople, nor had she comprehended their ways and why they had reacted the way they did. Time, experience, and dealings with the Rossbyans had helped her understand.

Clara wiped her hand across her wrinkled cheek and stared at the books on the shelves next to the writing desk. Unforgettable tales of heroism and voyagers' quests, natural philosophies of Isaac Newton, and thought-provoking writings of faith she had read and pondered. Though she was in the autumn of her life, she felt she still observed. She still learned.

"Nothing compares to life itself," she said and picked up an old piece of paper on the desk. The corners of her lips turned up as she remembered Bess. Clara leaned back in her chair, clutched the letter to her chest, and closed her tired eyes.

Every story is like a prism. When light hits the prism, it breaks into a rainbow, causing an array of magical colors. And so it is with this tale, like light that travels with varying swiftness through a prism, the words of this story can only be revealed at a certain pace and at different angles. Summers have come and gone, but these reflections are mine to tell.

"Just for a moment," she whispered. "A few minutes of rest and then I will write this story. It needs to be told."

Reflections in her mind formed into words and comprehensible sentences. They brought her back to a time when her wavy hair had a deep, flaxen glow and witch-hunting was nothing more than a distant fable.

1

The Arrival, May 1660

~

Clara grabbed the edge of the seat with both hands as the carriage wheels hit large pot-holes in the road. The letter she'd been holding flew down onto the floor. She picked it up quickly, so it would not become even more stained. It was already torn in places where she had folded it over and over again and showed evidence of having been read a number of times.

"I wish you could come and see us," she read. *"It would be nice to have you here again."*

The note was signed "Bess" and written in large, firm letters. Blotches of ink were spilled in places. Words were scratched where mistakes had been made. Clara had spent afternoons teaching her friend the skills of reading and writing. Bess had been a child of nature, hardworking and occupied with chores. She had become a woman you noticed as she entered the room, with her flaming copper hair and a keen look in her green eyes. She harvested herbs, fruits, and berries, tended the sheep, and showed charity. The written word was not a pastime she was interested in, but she needed to learn in order to keep up her family's traditions.

Clara folded the letter and slipped it into a side pocket on her frock. It must have taken forever to be delivered, months of safekeeping from carriage to carriage, on a cargo-trading vessel, and finally handed over by an Irish missionary named Peter, who frequently made the journey between continents, trading goods along the way and bringing with him both wares and news.

As Clara gazed out of the small, carriage window, the landscape seemed to put on a more familiar view with every passing bend of the road. The well-known places of her childhood and early youth were still all there. Not much had changed, except for some open spaces where trees had been cut down. The small brook still bubbled cheerfully alongside the dirt road, and she could see the yellow marsh-marigold, their sunny faces clinging on the banks of the stream. It was spring, her favorite season.

For the last ten years, Clara had lived in a climate unknown to the northern people. The premature death of her mother left her father, the minister of Rossby, so lonely, he had packed up Clara and her older brother Nathanael and had left his beloved parishioners to start a new life as a missionary in the Far East. The family had travelled for months and had finally found a home in the mission of the Ryukyu Islands. On Okinawa, they labored and learned to love the hardworking and honorable people there.

As the carriage came out of the thicket of trees and rolled over the last hill, the landscape opened up before her, and she smiled. There were fields and homesteads, and down around the bend she could see the village of Rossby with the open sea beyond.

Sticking her head out the window, Clara tried to get the attention of the coachman.

"Excuse me. Do you know if Mr. Hansen still runs the inn?"

The coachman slowed the horses. Communication would no doubt be easier that way.

"Oh, yes, Miss Clara. He is nearly seventy summers old now but still takes care of the folks coming in or going out of Rossby."

"That should keep him busy."

"Yes, Miss Clara, but he is also a councilman. A man can hardly blow his nose without the innkeeper finding out about it."

"Goodness, sounds like I need to watch my step." She chuckled and pretended to blow her nose.

"In your father's time there was proper respect for authority, miss," the coachman continued. "Now it has been replaced with fear. The present parson is good and kind, but the members of the town council don't include him as they did your father."

"I'm sorry to hear that." Clara leaned back in her seat. She was not sure what to make of this information and decided to find out for herself after she had met the villagers once again.

The coachman called out again from his perch atop the carriage. "Are you staying at the parsonage, Miss Clara?"

"I hope so, but right now I want to take in all the first impressions of coming home. I'd like to walk the rest of the way. Could you deliver my luggage to the inn for me? I need to savor this view a bit longer."

"All right, miss," he answered then pulled the reigns and called the horses to a halt.

Clara opened up the carriage door, stepped out, and stood there for a while. Dressed in a double-breasted box coat, the coachman leaned stiffly over the edge of his seat and reached out his hand. The heavy clothing was necessary, exposed to all kinds of weather as he was. She placed a coin in his open hand and added an extra coin for delivering the luggage.

"Thank you, miss. You may ask for me at the Watering House should you need my services again."

With a nod, Clara pulled the woolen kerchief tighter around her neck and watched the dust from the dirt road whirl up as the carriage continued down the hill toward the village and the ocean.

She took a deep breath and let the crisp spring air open up her senses and memories, and a smile spread across her face. The open sea in the distance reminded her of talks with her father.

Are the sky and water melted together? Why does it look like they become one where they meet?

Her father had answered all questions patiently, be they deep and important or silly and nonsensical. He'd awakened the interest innate within her to understand the arts and the beauty of nature. She was constantly inquisitive and strove to comprehend and learn esthetics, but the longing for answers had been triggered in the early days here in familiar surroundings.

She knew she was blessed. The opportunity to travel with her father had been an education in itself. So much could be learned from observing people and places, but now she was home again, and it felt good.

With a satchel on a string around her wrist, she took hold of the long gown and petticoat above the knees and pulled them up slightly, so she could jump with ease from the dirt road and over the small brook without getting the gown wet. The carriage was already down the hill, and she decided to cross the field toward Frue Farm to surprise Bess.

The field showed off small, fragrant flowers, and birds sang in the bushes by the edge of the forest ahead. She could tell it was May by the color of the leaves on birch, willow, and rowan. The light-yellowish-green of the new leaves had a golden glow about them, and she could easily pick out the leaf trees from the pine from a good distance away. Later in summer, the leaves would darken, and subdued colors would blend in with the evergreens.

About half an hour after the coachman had left her on the hill, she arrived at Frue Farm. It was a scene of bustling springtime, with lambs jumping happily around their mothers, and fruit trees south of the main cottage blossoming in the shy warmth of sunshine. A bushy dog ran toward her. He barked to alarm his flock that a visitor had arrived. A tall man followed behind the dog, and she recognized him right away.

"Uncle Samuel." Clara opened her arms and ran toward him.

"My goodness. Clara? Is that really you?" His eyes widened, and his arms closed around her body like those of a bear.

Samuel was not Clara's uncle, but he had taken care of the women of Frue Farm for as long as she could remember. Bess's mother had been widowed in her early twenties, right after her daughter was born, and Samuel, her elder brother, had come to help out with the farm. He was a military man, disciplined and strong, who always had a smile and a hug ready for anyone in need of comfort or a word or two of wisdom. He took hold of Clara's shoulders and held her at arm's length.

"Look at you, Clara," he finally said. "When did you arrive?"

"Just now. I came with a friend. Well, he accompanied me and brought me safely to this land. Oh, it's a long story. Can we discuss this later? I'm here now and plan to stay for a while. Where is Bess?"

"Bess? Oh, yes, Bess," he said, "I'm still taken aback. Bess went to Rossby to get some supplies. She and Lucia rode the old mare. They left a couple hours ago."

"Lucia? Her daughter? I can't wait to meet them. After traveling for so long, I don't want to wait another minute."

Uncle Samuel laughed and pointed toward the thicket of trees. "You remember the way, don't you? Take the path through the woods, and stay on it until you reach the road that takes you to Main Street. It's not far."

"I remember." She gave him another hug and turned around to hasten through the flowering orchard toward the path to town.

Before long, she walked the familiar Main Street of Rossby, the small town named for the Old Norse words for *horse* and *town*. The village nestled on a shelf on a slanting hill above sea level. The open sea hugged the shores to the west, and roads going to farms and homesteads and eventually other neighboring towns spread out like fingers on the land around the town itself.

The heart of Rossby was a large village square surrounded by different shops and trades. There was a blacksmith, a butcher's shop, and a bakery, and blocking the view toward the sea was the long cream-colored brick Town Hall, which, in addition to the offices and court room, also housed a festive banquet hall and a prison. Clara had always wondered why those places were all in one building with pain and pleasure next to each other. The more she had thought about it, she had decided it was like life itself, sorrow and happiness walking hand in hand, not knowing which one comes next. It was a way to accommodate a variety of occasions within four walls and a roof.

A man with a wet beard and one shoe stumbled out of the Watering House and tumbled over. *A little early for that*, Clara thought. She did not partake of strong drink, having seen too many with clogged notions, who couldn't even remember their own name. A large woman stood in the doorway of the Watering House and threw the second shoe after the man. He crawled over to pick it up and sat down on the ground while he fumbled with a shoe and a foot that did not want to cooperate.

Horses tied up outside the Watering House stared into space. Wagons that had been brought to the square earlier that morning were now empty of their wares. The coach had arrived, the trunks on the roof gone, already taken in to the inn. The coachman would most likely stay at the Watering House for the night. The rooms upstairs were cheaper than Mr. Hansen's inn.

The square was like an anthill. People ran to and fro, traded commodities, and made conversation. Clara nodded to people she passed, seeking out familiar faces of friends and neighbors from her childhood. Men stared, and women put hands to mouths and leaned toward friends as she walked by. Young and old were going about their daily routines. It had been ten summers since she'd last walked the main street of Rossby. Shy and a little anxious to be back, she was not ready to approach every familiar face to make conversation.

The hint of fresh fish as she passed the local seafood stand reminded her of Sunday dinners at the parsonage. The cook had seemed to know a hundred different ways to prepare the delicacies of the nearby sea. Not all her recipes were favorites of Minister Dahl's children at the time, but Clara had enjoyed the cook's version of steamed cod with boiled carrots and cream gravy.

A mangy dog barked outside the butcher's shop, hoping for a bone or scrap to run away with. The large-bellied butcher with fat, bloody hands finally appeared in the doorway and threw a small bone. His stockings were gathered around his narrow ankles, his breeches too wide around the knees, unable to hold them up. A few dogs rummaged through the piles of waste by the door, too busy to go after the mongrel with the bone. It ran off to a secluded place to delight in the luxury. Customers arrived, and the butcher put on a fake smile to welcome them into his shop.

Clara tried to listen to conversations as she slowly walked across the square. It seemed as though they talked about anything and nothing, everyday chitchat and greetings. There were new faces but some she recognized.

Sitting on the stairs outside the bakery was an elderly woman Clara remembered. She looked the same as she always had, no coif on her white hair that hung in thin strands down her back, her teasing eyes bracketed by tiny wrinkles that showed a sweet disposition to life. The minister's family used to buy honey from Old Magda and sometimes bought her homemade honey cakes. They were delicious and tempting and impossible to stop at only one.

"Hello, Magda," Clara said and sat next to her on the stairs.

The woman looked up, her expression perplexed at first, then the lively eyes lit up, and a welcoming countenance framed a grin showing several front teeth gone. Clara lowered her shoulders and smiled back.

"Yes, it's me, Clara. Clara Dahl. How are you?"

"Clara?" She leaned over to offer a hug. "You have been gone many summers. Where have you been?"

"I have been with my father and brother in a land far from here, but I am back to visit for a while."

"Wonderful."

Clara liked that about Magda. She did not always say much, but the words she uttered were usually nice and uplifting. They lingered for a while and talked about Magda's bees and her work at the cottage in the woods.

"Do you still make honey cakes?" Clara asked. "They were my favorite as a child."

"Oh, you like those, do you?" Magda answered teasingly. "I sell them to the bakery now. Bring some in every week. I have a couple left in my basket. Would you like one?"

Out of her basket she pulled a small, golden-brown cake, freshly baked. The scent of baked honey cake was scrumptious.

Clara nodded. "I would indeed," she said. Water ran in her mouth, and she thought about summer evenings as a child, sitting on the porch, eating Magda's honey cakes. She sank her teeth into the golden delicacy. "Mmm. You make the best cakes, Magda. Thank you."

Clara made no narration about life in Okinawa or her father's illness and passing. It was enough to say he was gone. Magda was not a Sunday worshipper and did not have that kind of relationship with Clara's father as a minister anyway. But as part of his duties to his parish, he had often visited her in the cottage by the woods south of the parsonage. He cared for everyone within the community, no matter what their beliefs were.

"I need to find Bess now. I hope to see you soon, Magda."

"Oh, yes, Bess. Find Bess," Magda said and waved goodbye.

Clara continued up Main Street and passed Laura, great with child, another two or three little ones hanging on to her skirts. She had cleaned house at the parsonage, and Clara remembered Laura as being friendly and upright. Today, she seemed to be in a hurry, and Clara let her pass by. The people in Rossby did not know she was due back, and so no one expected to see her. There would be plenty of opportunities to greet old friends later.

The inn was the last house on the left side. It was the first house the coaches arrived at coming downhill from the opposite direction. Right across the street from the inn was the Lands' residence, an attractive building with a large store on the main floor and a spacious apartment for the family upstairs. The windows were framed with ornate cutouts in a deeper shade of blue, which made this building different from the rest. The door had a smaller window made with colored glass. Not even Town Hall was as richly decorated as the Lands' store.

As she made her observations the door opened, and over the threshold with a hop and a skip came a small, curly-headed child followed by a woman with thick, copper-colored hair that flowed past her shoulders. Clara noticed the hair looked as if it was just as difficult to keep in place as she remembered. There seemed to be no interest in linen coifs to keep the tresses in place. Clara hurried across the street to greet her friend.

"Bess. Bess."

For a minute, the woman stared, looking as if she had seen a ghost, but she recovered quickly and hugged Clara long and firmly.

They wept, hugged, and laughed together. It was as if they had never been apart, even though there would be much to talk about and many stories to tell. The child was Lucia, Bess's first born. Clara had read about the child in the letter. The girl looked a lot like her mother, though Clara could tell there was something calmer about her.

"You are with child," Clara exclaimed. She held both Bess's hands, took a step back, and looked at her. "How wonderful; it becomes you."

Bess beamed in a way that made her whole face light up and twirled around to show off her small, protruding stomach.

"I feel double life," she said. "The child kicks within my living belly."

Lucia skipped around the women, drawing pictures on the ground with a stick.

Clara hooked her arm through Bess's. "Come, I need to see if my bags have arrived safely at the inn."

"You can stay at Frue Farm, Clara. We have room for you. Mychel, my good husband, is a fisherman and away at sea for the next few weeks."

"That's kind, but I need to be at the parsonage. I have written a letter to the parson, asking if I can stay in the cottage for a while."

An eerie squeaking noise sounded as Clara pushed on the door of the inn. She lifted her eyebrows and looked at Bess as the three of them entered. Inside, Clara's two trunks sat in the corner of the dark front room. Satisfied, she nodded.

Bess giggled. "You don't exactly travel light, do you? That's my Clara. So many things to do, so hectic. Oh, I have missed you so much." She walked over and stroked the tops of the trunks with her fingertips. "What do you keep in them?"

"Those are my books and some clothing. That one has spices and treasures from Okinawa." Clara pointed and laughed. "Well, they are treasures to me, anyway."

"You still have more books than clothing and other things?"

"Of course, I don't think I could live without my books."

"Well, you and these books need to get to the parsonage. I'll be expecting you at Frue Farm for supper this evening. We have so much to catch up on."

From behind a nearby desk, an older man with chin-length, gray hair and oversized clothes hanging on his thin body cleared his throat. It was Innkeeper and Councilman Hansen, reminding Clara he had a business to run. He did not greet her but extended an open hand toward her. Clara crossed the room and paid him a coin for taking care of her luggage and another for having allowed it to be delivered at the parsonage. The innkeeper grabbed the coins and stared suspiciously.

Clara remembered what the coachman had told her and decided to act diplomatically. "Thank you, Innkeeper Hansen," she said and curtsied.

Before she turned to walk out, the innkeeper reached under the desk and grabbed a notebook and dipped a quill pen into a pot of ink.

Clara pushed Bess gently on the back. "Let's go out and enjoy the sunshine."

As Bess opened the door, Clara stopped for a moment and looked over her shoulder. She could not help but wonder what he was up to.

2

The Rossby Council

Innkeeper Hansen grabbed his tall-crowned hat and made his way down Main Street toward Town Hall. He strode straight ahead and pointed his walking cane in front of him, making a path as he went along. He walked this direction several times every day. If townspeople got in his way, he would hit them with the cane.

The innkeeper demanded respect without earning it because of his father's involvement in building Town Hall. He took pride in being a significant citizen with responsibilities in the town council, and the townspeople ought to clear the road when he was on his way to important affairs.

He climbed the stairs and nodded to the two guards outside the blue double door of Town Hall. Inside he pulled off his hat and handed it to a maid, then entered the large council office on the left. The meeting had just begun.

"Good day, Hansen." The mayor stood by his chair at the end of the long table, flanked by Councilmen Dr. Bing-Olsen, Land, and a few others. The mayor bid them all sit down. The League was in session.

The mayor cleared his throat and lifted up a document, squinting as if he had a difficult time reading it. His solid stature was evidence of a life filled with good meals and sitting still in meetings. Walking up the stairs to his well-furnished residence above his office, the rooms for council meetings and court sessions was strenuous enough, and he sometimes had to stop halfway up to rest.

"I address the council today," he said and cleared his voice once more, "with a question. Do we need to pass a law in view of the recent burglary at the mill?"

Dr. Bing-Olsen was first. He stretched out his long legs and leaned back in his chair. "We all know there is a problem with the country folks concerning the mill," he said.

The other men nodded and made concurring noises around the table. Dr. Bing-Olsen took a loose strand of hair and placed it behind his ear. He pulled on the ribbon holding the locks in place at the back of his neck.

"There must be a dozen different tales of elves or fairies visiting that mill. The farmers refuse to go near there at night. They say it is protected. But it is built at the head of tidewater on the south creek, an excellent location for transporting the milled flour and boards up to the harbor at Rossby. Easy access for Mr. Land, upon whose wares we are all so dependent."

Bing-Olsen looked over at the storekeeper, who nodded solemnly, obviously proud to be an essential player in the life of the Rossbyans.

"And an imperative focal point for our community," the doctor concluded.

Dr. Bing-Olsen always loves hearing his own voice, the innkeeper thought, *though what he says is not always significant to the discussion.*

"What I mean is," the mayor continued, "do we need a new law protecting the miller and his goods?"

Innkeeper Hansen raised a finger in the air. "This is not a matter of protecting the miller but of protecting the people from fairies, gnomes, and the like," he said.

"The country folks believe in unnatural beings and little people," the mayor stated. "There have been enough stories around Rossby. Now, the question is, do we believe these accounts to be true?"

The mayor lifted his hand to signal the maid at the door. It was time for refreshments. She left the room at once.

The innkeeper raised his finger again. "The influence of evil is in all places; not even Rossby is exempt."

He looked around the room. The members of the council were nodding to each other.

"I have heard tales," one member said.

"We have all heard them," another added. "My wife has seen evidence of fairies in the woods."

A councilman sitting on the far end hit his fist on the table. "Even if we don't all believe in little people, they are real in the minds of our inhabitants," he said.

"Yes, this is true," the mayor concluded. "But what do we do about it? And what do we do about the recent thefts at the mill? Even if it is common opinion that fairies work the mill at night, efficient as they are said to be with forces of nature, water, fire, and power of the mills turning its wheels" — he wiped his brow — "we need to protect every man's possessions by law. People should feel safe in our town and its surroundings."

"C'est vrai, c'est vrai," Dr. Bing-Olsen uttered.

He enjoyed the opportunity to impress the council with his French vocabulary and flipped his head to throw back another loose strand of his misbehaving hair. The refreshments arrived, and he helped himself to the largest piece of cake.

"I will look into the matter and report at our next council meeting," the storekeeper said. "After all, I have contact with the miller every week. I will bring a man or two along and visit him. Maybe the miller can shed some light on the matter, and we can be better prepared for which action to take."

"Very good," the mayor said.

Innkeeper Hansen was pleased. They were actually making progress. He often felt the content of the council meetings was gossip and idle talk. The mayor had often said he wanted to help to the

Rossbyans, but pointless talk did not improve the life of the townspeople. Now the mayor pointed at the cake.

"Help yourselves," he said cheerfully. "It is freshly baked this morning."

The innkeeper was still on the matter about the mill. "I have made some inquiries," he said slowly, while the others had their mouths full of cake. He put both elbows on the table and squeezed his hands together. "We may believe in things out of the ordinary, or we may not. The truth is there are things we do not understand. Powers beyond our understanding are spreading. We really have to do something about the grave matter that evil is lurking around the corner of Rossby. It is there. Do I have permission to make further investigation into what should be done about it?"

Hansen knew their leader enjoyed cake more than lengthy discussions.

The mayor looked at the innkeeper, his mouth full of cake. "Yes, yes, you may take care of that." He then looked around at the faces of the men sitting at the table. "Our innkeeper is always diligent, going straight to the heart of the matter."

Innkeeper Hansen was pleased. He was unable to remember true happiness but found satisfaction in pursuing goals he believed in. He had chosen a solitary life in the shadows many summers ago when the young woman he intended to marry had left town.

"If we are done here, I need to get back," he said and picked up his walking stick and notebook.

The mayor bowed his head and whispered to himself, "Opinionated and cynical."

Hansen frowned but pretended he had not heard.

"What was that?" Dr. Bing-Olsen asked.

"Nothing, I was just thinking out loud." With a flip of his wrist he added, "Yes, Hansen, you may go." He stared at his empty plate. "Is there more cake?"

The innkeeper nodded to the council and turned on his heel. The guard opened the door and let him out into the hallway, where the maid waited with his tall-crowned hat.

On the street, he stuck his hand in his breast pocket and pulled out a letter. He looked at it and smiled, sniffed it, then put it back into his pocket. A dirty boy with an outstretched hand begged for a coin, but the innkeeper kicked him in the shin and walked on.

"This town is filled with fools and idiots," he mumbled. The letter in his pocket would bring about a commotion. Hopefully, a change for himself and a chance to prove his position as indispensable to the people of Rossby.

3

The Roots

~~

Eager to see her childhood haven, Clara started up the road toward the parsonage. Dew still blanketed the grass in the shadow of large pine trees, and birds with little ones in their nests chirped loudly to chase her away. Her mind drifted to memories of lying in the meadow, staring at clouds, making out shapes of various animals. Bess would say, "Look, there's a goat." Clara would find a pig, and both had laughed and rolled down the pasture until they nearly hit the poor sheep grazing below. With wreaths of field flowers on their heads they checked their reflections in a windowpane to see how lovely they were. A third wreath they brought to Frue Farm to adorn Bess's mother's hair. She hardly ever wore a coif, and the flowers suited her perfectly.

The parsonage was just as Clara remembered it. She opened the gate and ambled toward the large, circular flowerbed. The first flowers were already in bloom, and others were budding or waiting for even warmer summer days. As a child, she had spent hours amongst the flowers, collecting ladybugs and watching butterflies and bees. It always amazed her how noisy bumblebees were. They could never sneak up on anyone because they made so much noise once they moved. She used to imagine butterflies whispering to each other, but bumblebees could only nod and wink at each other whilst standing still. The memories made her smile.

To the right stood the main house, a white two-story with a large field behind that stretched down toward Rossby. Straight ahead were the barn and stables, and to the left was a red-painted wooden *stabbur* for the storage of food. When she was a child, the place had fascinated her, as it was the only building—with exception of the main house— that had a locked door. Now and again, she had joined the maid to fetch food for special events at the parsonage. Large slabs of smoked and dried meat hung from hooks along the walls. Barrels filled with brine preserved fish and meat. There was a ladder to a loft holding grains and flour. Clara especially liked the way the four corners were raised from the ground on pillars and flat stones, to prevent mice and rats from sharing their storage. Stepping across the space from the large, flat stone outside and into the *stabbur* had seemed scary when she was little. She thought she would fall down and hurt herself, but the maid had held her hand and had led Clara across, telling her to come and help carry the food.

The whole area nestled in a grove of birch trees with the wooden church and cemetery on the left side beyond the fence. This had been the dwelling of clerical families for a long time. Clara's father had been the beloved minister of the church in Rossby, and the parish had provided well for their family. Clara had been born here, as was her older brother Nathanael. They grew up playing in the fields and woods around the farm and had learned to love books and art from their mother's heritage and the pleasure of serving others from their father.

Before she could knock on the front door, it opened, and the current parson, Herr Christopher, appeared. Clara stated her name, and his face lit up. He smiled and grabbed her outstretched hand in both of his, shaking it vigorously.

"What an honor," he said. "Sara and I are pleased to have you come and stay at the homestead attached to the parsonage. We received your letter this spring. I am sorry to hear about the passing of your father. He was a most respectable man."

The parson's wife appeared behind him. She was his equal, energetic and friendly. They made an interesting couple. Herr Christopher was tall and thin next to his little but quite round wife. It crossed Clara's mind that they might have problems kissing. Maybe Sara stood on a small stool to reach up?

"Come in and meet our family." Herr Christopher introduced each one of the children and added that number five was due late summer. That explained the total roundness of Sara's form.

Entering the sitting room brought a rush of emotions. Clara looked around at the familiar walls and floor. She let her hand slide over the same furniture and picked up a small, wooden chest from the buffet, remembering how she and Nathanael had put secret messages inside the little box. The window had a view of the back field, and beyond that field lay Rossby. The road downhill toward town and the rooftops of the closest houses were just beyond the road.

As she turned to walk back to the others, her eyes beheld a small painting on the wall above the settee. It was one of her mother's. Tears trickled down her cheeks as she looked at it. Her mother had been a lover of art and also an accomplished painter herself. She painted things she loved. This painting depicted flowers in the garden.

"Are you all right?" Sara asked and put a gentle hand on Clara's shoulder.

"Yes, perfectly. I didn't realize how much I missed this painting. We only took a few items when we left." She wiped her cheeks. "Honestly, I am pleased to be here, to see all of this again and to meet you."

A kitchen maid rang a small bell to announce a meal of bread and meats. Clara's eyes went wide with surprise, and Sara laughed.

"Don't be alarmed, Clara. This is the best way for us to gather all the children. When they hear the meal bell, they hurry."

Clara understood why her father had repeatedly mentioned he had left his dearly loved parish in good hands. She enjoyed the liveliness and naive joy of the children as they told about their adventures that day. No one was too young or too old for the whole family to pay attention to.

"You must be eager to see your new home," Herr Christopher said after a while. "No one has lived there for a while. It might need some cleaning up. There's furniture in the house and water in the well outside. Let me take you down there now."

Sara came to the door. "Take this to the cottage," she said and placed the painting of the garden flowers in Clara's hands.

"But it belongs in the parsonage," Clara said.

"No, it belongs to you. Besides, the cottage needs cheering up. I want you to have it."

Clara felt a bond with Sara already. She put her arms around her then followed Herr Christopher out the door.

The path between the birch forest and the fenced-in paddock led to the small cottage built within the boundaries of the rectory. Families connected to the parsonage had dwelled there over the course of the last decade.

"I am not a practical man," Herr Christopher stated suddenly as they passed the grazing horses. "Animals need feeding and fields tending. I employed a couple of families to take care of farm work. The people of Rossby are my vocation. I am useless in the barn or out in the fields. We built a couple of cottages for the families behind the *stabbur*."

Clara breathed in every view and every scent of home. Not much had changed.

"Well, here we are. I see your trunks have arrived," Herr Christopher said as they passed the second fence, and the small cottage came into view in the sunshine. He handed Clara the key, so she could open the door herself then helped her with the trunks.

The old homestead was empty and quiet. Thin sheets covered the windows and gave the rooms a murky gloom. Clara pulled them off and put them on a chair. Cobwebs hung in the corners, and furniture was partly covered with hemp sacks. The dust lay so thick she could blow minor sand storms through the air. She sneezed as she noticed a fat, little white mouse run across the floor.

Herr Christopher started laughing. "You'll need a cat, Clara."

"I'll put it on my list," she said, "along with soap and a broom."

"It's not much I have to offer. Your father has done so much for our family. I wish I could give you more."

"Thank you, Herr Christopher. This is all I need and want. It means a lot to stay here."

"You mentioned in your letter that you like to teach," he said, helping her uncover a couple of chairs by the window. He handed Clara a hemp sack.

"I would," Clara said and nodded. "I enjoy teaching and believe I am qualified."

"You are more than qualified, Clara. Although, knowledge of French, English, and Japanese are not what the Rossbyans need. The sons of farmers, hunters, and fishermen, may not have a great interest in learning, but they would benefit from being able to read and write. We have had teachers here earlier, but the schoolhouse has been empty since the end of last year."

"No teachers for half a year? Why the shortage?"

"The school masters move from place to place. When we've had teachers, a few young boys show up. Most families keep their girls home to help with the chores."

"But there must be some who want their daughters to receive at least some degree of education?"

"Mrs. Land is one, but she wants her twin girls tutored in their home. The problem is, not every teacher can handle those girls."

"Ah, Mrs. Land," Clara said. She folded the sheet and put it aside. "So she still likes things done her way."

"Yes, she walks a little above the common folks of Rossby. My job is to treat everyone the same."

"That's good policy. We should all treat others with respect, no matter who they are."

"That reminds me, I need to get back. I have a sermon to prepare for Sunday."

"Oh, and one more thing, Herr Christopher, I want to encourage girls to come."

"I will see what I can do about it. The Rossbyans will first need to be convinced that a woman is capable of teaching."

Clara thanked him and bid him farewell. The room seemed to beckon to her to get started. It would take a while to get the place livable. Home was here now, for however far now took her.

Visiting Herr Christopher and his family had unlocked a room inside of Clara, a place where memories of her mother were safely kept. Mother, who passed away giving birth to a second son. Both were lost one rainy night. Clara had been too young to understand what had gone on but felt the sorrow and hopelessness that enveloped their home for a long time afterward. Her father's grief saturated both family life and sermons at church. Nothing could make up for not having her in their lives.

Clara unlocked one of the trunks and found a small, leather pouch containing a wooden amulet from her Okinawan mama-san. Sacred powers of life flowed from the talisman. At least that's what the mama-san believed.

Clara placed the pouch on the table. Bess was expecting Clara for dinner; unpacking the trunks could wait.

The fields had a golden glow against the woodland as she walked the path to Frue Farm. She found Bess inside the house, stirring soup in the iron pot above the fireplace with a large wooden spoon.

"I brought you something," Clara said and put a wrapped parcel on the table.

"A gift for me?" Bess's eyes had that excited look, the one she'd often had when they had played in ditches as little girls and found frogs, or discovered herbs in the woods to surprise her mother.

She sat down on a chair with the gift in her lap, turning it over and shaking it gently before unwrapping.

"It's a notebook from Okinawa. Isn't the white cover beautiful?"

"Yes, it's lovely. It's covered with material." Bess caressed the soft surface.

"It's silk," Clara said.

"What does it say? You know I can't decipher these letters."

Clara smiled and took the book out of Bess's hands to show her. "Look here, Bess. It's a book about herbs. When I decided to come home to see you, I wanted to bring you something special. This book depicts some of the medicinal plants of the Far East. Peter wrote it."

"Peter?" The word glided out of her mouth, slow as thick honey and ascending like an upward hill.

"Yes, my friend Peter, an Irish missionary. He is knowledgeable in the use of herbs and plants. I asked him to put pen to paper and describe their function."

Bess looked with a sideways glance and grinned.

Clara pretended to ignore her, though she smiled bashfully. Bess had always teased her about boys, saying Clara needed to loosen up. "In fact, he accompanied me," Clara explained. "He travels and trades for the mission, and I needed a companion for the trip. He stayed behind in Christiania while I came here." She shrugged nonchalantly, still ignoring Bess's facial expression.

"Well, Clara, I won't bother you…for now, that is."

Bess giggled and tickled Clara, who squealed and moved out of Bess's reach.

"Clara has an Irish friend who knows herbs? Hmm, interesting."

"Silly you," Clara said. "He's just a friend. Look here." She flipped pages in the book and showed simple drawings and explanations. "You should be glad Peter wrote it, Bess. He writes in the English language. The Japanese signs are not my forte. This book I can translate for you."

Bess pointed at the drawings and smiled. "I know this one and that, but not that one."

Bess had never buried her nose in books as Clara did, but she thought the little herbal notebook could complement Bess's family's recipe book.

"Thank you, Clara, I will treasure it for life," Bess said, clutching it to her bosom.

Clara looked out the small window at the orchard. "Let's go outside," she said. "I have missed these sunlit evenings and the warm glow the light sky leaves on the landscape.

"I know. Some evenings I just don't want to go to bed."

They exited the cottage, and Bess sat down on a bench by a red currant bush and pulled Lucia onto her lap. The little girl yawned and closed her eyes.

Clara gently stroked the petals of upright flowers next to the bench. "Your garden is certainly like a beautiful piece of jewelry," she said. "Are these tulips?"

Bess smiled and nodded. "I love working here, like my mother and her mother before her. It pleases me that somebody else can also see the beauty here. The produce from this orchard, the herbs, and the vegetable plot is our livelihood."

"There is no other garden like it around here. The only one that compares is at the abbey."

"Oh, I agree. Sister Birgitta and I have some serious discussions about seeds and plants and their uses. We both know our gardens are not for show only. Most importantly, they are full of herbs and medicinal plants."

Bess leaned down and picked a blooming daffodil and placed it behind Lucia's ear. The little girl twisted her head back and forth for them to see.

"I know you two have a lot in common," Clara said. "Have you been out to visit anyone lately?"

"All the time. People around here get stomach pains, toothaches, blisters, coughs, cuts, and bruises like everywhere else. If they cannot find the good doctor in, they call for me. I have probably delivered more children than the doctor. It's the errand I like best."

"I remember your mother said the same. She loved her midwifery duties."

"She did." Bess paused for a moment, gazing out on the garden. Slowly, she removed her shawl and draped it around her daughter's shoulders.

"A couple of weeks ago, I had an experience I wish I had never had," she said and wrapped her arms around Lucia to keep her warm.

"What happened?"

"Do you remember Welam, the Swede who lived in the woods behind the abbey, the skipper?"

"Yes, of course, he married a local girl. They had several daughters."

"That's the one. His wife came for me one day, asked me to heal him."

"What was wrong with him?"

"He was already dying with a serious case of scurvy. He had been away at sea most of his life, long voyages with little food. His body had become weak, he had open wounds, and most of his teeth had fallen out. By the time I saw him, he'd already had a fever for a while. You should have seen him, bruised and pale. He bled inside."

"What did you do?"

"I brought him produce from my garden, herbs to strengthen him, and applied clean dressings to his wounds, but it was already too late. The illness had weakened him to a state of depression and fatigue beyond return."

"But that happens, Bess. You can't heal everyone."

"I know. The problem was his wife blamed me for his death. Gossip spread. Soon, the whole town was talking about it, holding me responsible. Helping others sometimes feels like walking into a lion's den," she said with a dose of sarcasm.

"I'm so sorry. It will pass, don't you think? Few people hold grudges forever."

Bess smiled, no doubt in an attempt to bring the graveness of the conversation to a lighter level. "Most people will hold grudges forever, is more like it. But I will continue to help them anyway. If they desire my assistance, I will go."

"I see that has not changed since I have been gone," Clara said teasingly.

"What's that?"

"Your stubbornness, your perseverance in fighting for what you know is good and true."

"Of course, if not, I would not be true to life, would I?"

Her optimism made Clara smile. "Of course not, Bess," she said. The evening had brought on a mild chill, and she hugged her arms. "Can we go back inside? It's still not warm enough in the evenings to sit out all night."

Lucia had fallen asleep on her mother's lap, and Bess carried her up the ladder to bed. The woodland birds were still singing, happy about the approaching summer and quiet shelter behind leaves on the trees. Uncle Samuel ended his chores for the day and sat down to visit. Clara stayed a while longer, telling stories of life on the Ryukyu Islands and their experiences there. She told about *sakura*, the cherry trees blossoming in the beginning of the year, about family honor and dignity, about the straight black hair and dark eyes of the people, and how she and Nathanael were always the targets of stares because they were different. Bess and Samuel laughed as Clara told them about graves cut into stone walls and caves made from mountain rocks, and how the oldest daughter of the family entered the cave every year to dust the bones and put flowers and food at the grave site.

"Sounds like your red curls would get attention there, Bess," Uncle Samuel said.

Clara grinned. "There were times in Okinawa when someone got their knife out to cut some of our blonde curls off. Nothing dangerous, they were just curious."

"What about your father's work there?" Uncle Samuel asked.

He put his feet up on a chest on the floor then stretched out his arms and rubbed his eyes. Clara looked at him. He was not a young man anymore, and she imagined his legs must hurt after a long day of work.

"You know, that's an interesting story," Clara began. "Christianity is not welcomed anymore in Japan. Missionaries and foreign traders are often put to death right on the Japanese shores as they arrive, without being given a trial nor a chance to explain the purpose of their visit. We landed on the coast of Okinawa, which is part of the Ryukyu Islands. Even though the island has relationships with Japan and China, they are a prosperous little trading nation. Their culture is flourishing, and they cultivate interesting foods and spices unknown to us here in the north."

"How were you received then?" Uncle Samuel, who had seen much of the world as a military man, was genuinely interested in learning about other places.

"Father's goal was always to be a preacher, to help others feel good about the Christian faith the way he did. But in order to stay there and have any influence over the islanders, he had to be careful and progress slowly. They were taught how to be Christian without even knowing it. We worked the land and the rice fields. We traded and established a small infirmary. Besides all of that, he was a wonderful missionary in my eyes." Clara stared into space as she thought about her father and the great influence he had on her life. She was proud to be his daughter.

"And Nathanael?" Bess asked and walked over to fetch some cheese and bread to nibble on.

"My brother followed in father's footsteps. I am happy for him. He likes it there and is well accepted by the Okinawans."

Clara looked out the window. "I forget how light the evenings are here. I am really tired and need to get back to the cottage." She thanked them both for a lovely evening and started on her way home.

～～

Mrs. Land stood rigidly behind the counter as Clara entered Lands' store the next morning. Clara had prepared a note to remember all the things she needed but had left it on the table at the cottage.

"Typical me," she said and searched the satchel in her basket. "How can I be so systematically disorganized?" She stood there for a minute, racking her brains, trying to recall the items she had jotted down on her list as the shop mistress came over to talk to her.

"Hello, Clara. My, you have grown into a young woman. Where are you staying? Are you back for good? Where are your father and brother?"

So many questions rolled up into one, Clara thought. She tried to answer without giving away too much information. Mrs. Land was not known for keeping things to herself, and stories were often changed into something more entertaining the moment they passed her lips. Clara concentrated on thinking of her as a dog with scabies, safer to meet with a friendly greeting from a distance.

"Mrs. Land," she began and put the basket on the counter. "I am here for the time being and happy about it. Can you please assist me in bringing to mind the items I need for my household? I am staying in the cottage at the parsonage, and it's ever so empty."

The invitation kept Mrs. Land occupied for the longest time, convincing Clara, whom Mrs. Land saw as a profitable customer, of all the things Clara could not live without. Clara modified the register, as she knew that even though the cupboards were empty, she did not need to stock them with every article available.

"And I need a cat," Clara said with a broad smile, trying to finish off the shopping extravaganza.

"A cat." Mrs. Land snorted. "I do not keep live animals, Clara. What would people say? Too dirty, you know."

"Yes, I know," Clara said and curtsied. She grabbed the filled-up basket and asked if the rest of the merchandise could be delivered to the cottage.

As she walked out the door, Mrs. Land followed.

"Oh, Clara, Anna, your friend who works at Town Hall has a feline with a litter. If you want a kitten, go ask her."

"I will. Where can I find her?"

"Down Main Street. Third house on the left."

"Thank you, Mrs. Land."

Clara found the door leading to Anna's upstairs dwelling. She knocked, hoping to find her friend at home. A window opened above Clara's head, and a friendly voice called out.

"Hello, may I help you?" A dark-haired woman looked down.

Clara beamed a smile when she saw who it was.

"Anna, it's me, Clara Dahl. Can I come see you?"

"What a surprise. Yes, it's the door on your right when you get up the stairs. Come, come."

Clara climbed the stairs and found Anna at the top, arms open and a welcoming face. The place was small but pleasantly furnished. Anna said she was still unmarried and earning her keep with odd jobs at Town Hall.

"I'm a maid," she said, "but after a long time of working there, I have been given more responsibility. I meet interesting people and can take leftover meals home. It works out well for me."

"Sounds good, Anna, and I'm glad I found you at home. I won't keep you from your demanding agenda. I have a question for you; do you have a litter of kittens?"

A big smile lit up Anna's face. Clara and Bess had always imagined Anna would be the first to marry, considering her feminine good looks and sweet personality.

"I do, and I don't work before later this afternoon. Let me introduce you to my furry, little friends."

It did not take long to choose a favorite, a black charmer with a white chest.

"I will name him Ami," Clara said. "I need a friend at the cottage, and his French name will remind me that he is exactly that."

Clara's mother had a French background and had wanted her children to learn the language. She had hired Nanette, a French governess, to take care of her children. Teachers were constantly at the parsonage, opportunities to learn and grow always at hand. Nathanael was eventually sent to schools in Copenhagen and Strasbourg, while Clara was tutored at home. Nanette stayed at the parsonage until the family left for the Far East, and not having her in their lives any longer had left Clara and her brother with a motherly void.

Clara had loved to hear her father tell stories about what her mother was like. It was clear he loved her dearly and missed her even more.

The little furry bundle meowed all the way back to the parsonage. Clara knocked on the door of the main house to show the children the new family member. They were delighted the way only children can be and waved goodbye as Clara gingerly carried the kitten to the cottage and introduced him to their new abode.

"Ami, we need curtains," Clara said and started unpacking the trunks. She shook the clothes and hung them loosely across the back of a chair and put books on a wooden shelf.

The Okinawan homes were plain and simple with no excess decoration. Lines were straight and rigid, and open spaces had legless seats and beds on the floor. Clara had appreciated that when she was there but now remembered how she had craved colors and ornamentation.

"In a few days, I will go see if Mrs. Land has some material I can use."

She sat down to stroke Ami's back. He rolled up into a soft ball by her feet and purred.

"Ami, why am I really here?" she asked the kitten. Insecurity approached her again. Feelings of uncertainty as to what her purpose in life was. Being on her own and learning to communicate with people outside her comfort zone frightened her. She had forced herself to make this journey. She needed to find her roots, get to know the Rossbyans, and be with Bess again.

The sound of twigs breaking outside startled her. She lifted her chin and peered toward the north window. A shadow moved outside, and she hurried across the room to look out. There was nothing. She opened the door and called out, but no one answered.

"Probably a deer," she said to comfort herself more than the kitten.

4

The Birthing

꘎

A quill pen, barely visible between fur needles and twigs, caught Clara's eye next day as she hurried down the path between the cottage and the parsonage. She picked it up and turned it over. It was not hers, but she put it in her satchel for safekeeping. Maybe the owner would come and ask for it later. Bess had expected Clara at Frue Farm after the noonday meal. Clara found her friend in the garden.

"You must be happy here." Clara kneeled on the ground and started pulling weeds from the herbal patch.

"Happy?" Bess wiped the hair out of her face with the back of a dirty hand. Streaks of soil smudged her forehead. "Yes, I would not want to be anywhere else. This has been the home of my family ever since my great-grandparents cleared land at Frue Farm."

Clara handed Bess a basket filled with blossoming milfoil. "Here, I have picked the ones on this side of the bed. You have a lot of these. What are they for?" She put one in her mouth to taste the flavor.

Bess took the basket and placed it with several others on a bench. "You can eat all you want if it is that time of the month for you," she said, giggling. "It is actually one of my most versatile herbs. Soldiers even carry it in their sacks and apply it to wounds and cuts. I sometimes put milfoil in boiling water, cool it off, and then I use it to rinse my hair."

She flipped her hair with her hand and gave Clara a coy, sideways glance, batting her eyelashes.

"As if your hair needs more encouragement, Bess, Lady of Frue Farm," Clara said. "And why is this place called Frue Farm? Who came up with that name?"

"That was my great-grandfather's suggestion. He saw how the women of the family he had married into helped people, took them in when they were sick or needed a place to stay, and comforted them when necessary. He saw his wife and her mother and sisters organize aid and give of themselves."

"I see. He thought Frue, the word for the married women in the family, was appropriate as a name for the dwelling as well?"

Bess laughed. "Yes, I suppose so. He noticed women ran the place, and in fact, he did not mind. He saw the work they did was good. They treated him respectfully. He liked the arrangement, or so I've been told."

"Owning your own place must give you a good feeling."

"I don't see it as owning. We seem to claim responsibility for each other, the land and I. The good earth gives me fruit, berries and greens for both nourishment and healing. I replant the things I harvest and make sure it is well tended. It's a blessed circle."

"What a wonderful way to appreciate life. I learn so much from you, Bess."

"You learn from me?" She pointed her finger at Clara then at herself. "You are the clever and intelligent Clara."

Clara smiled and handed Bess another basket to put the weeds in. "Well, let's agree that you and I claim responsibility for each other. If we learn from each other, we'll be ready for anything."

"Silly you, Clara. Very well, I agree." Bess looked up as drops of summer rain fell on her face, and after a little while it poured down, warm and refreshing.

She got up and looked over to where the dog, Binna, and Lucia were playing.

"Lucia," she called, "bring the dog, and hurry inside."

The little girl ran toward her mother, poppet under one arm, and pushing the dog along with the other. Bess patted the furry dog vigorously as they passed her. With her bushy coat, Binna lived up to the name for a mother bear.

Uncle Samuel was away for the afternoon, and the three of them pulled off their gowns and huddled together in their chemises, feet up, sipping warm, blueberry tea. Binna fell asleep on the floor and snored, kicking her back leg a little, no doubt dreaming puppy dreams about pastures and hunting.

"I am a little confused as to where home is now," Clara said and put her empty cup on the table. "The parsonage is now the home of Herr Christopher and his family, my brother is still in Okinawa, and I live in the cottage with a cat."

"You make it sound sad."

"No, I am not sad. I have been to many places, and now I am back here with you. It's a little confusing."

"Well, we are thrilled to have Aunt Clara here, aren't we, Lucia?" She pulled the little girl closer and hugged her.

They were Clara's family, true without bloodlines or genealogical traces, but they had an inseparable bond, and she was grateful for it.

"So, Clara, any handsome men in that land far away? Anyone special? What about Peter?" Bess had that teasing look in her eyes again.

"The Okinawans are handsome, and I love the way they honor their families and their forefathers. They are a proud people, in a good way. But I am not attached to Peter or any of them, if that's what you mean."

"Attached? Funny you. Just you wait, Clara Dahl; you'll be attached one of these days."

It was getting late. Uncle Samuel returned from his errands and found all three properly dressed and preparing supper. The rain had not subsided. Bess opened the door to let the dog out. Binna took one look at the downpour and immediately backed away from the door.

"Out you go, Binna," Bess said, pushing the dog gently outside.

A man on horseback emerged through the darkness and rain and galloped toward the cottage. He brought the horse to a sudden halt by the steps right in front of Bess. It was Mathias from the lake by Nord Hill.

"It's Laura," he managed to say, sounding out of breath. "The doctor is out of town. It's different this time. I believe the baby is breech. She's in so much pain. You have to come, Bess. You're the only one I know who can help her."

"I will come straight away," Bess answered. "Let me go inside and get my bag and coat and make sure Lucia is all right. I'll be back soon."

She ran into the house past Clara in the doorway who had heard the din outside and wondered what she could do to help.

"Can you get my uncle," Bess answered. "I need him to watch Lucia. I want you to come with me. I may need some help. And, Clara, ask him to saddle up the horses."

"But can you ride? What about the baby?"

"I'm used to it. I'm pregnant, not sick," she said with a grin.

A few minutes later, they were on their way with Mathias. They found Laura on a bloodstained blanket on the floor in front of the fireplace. She was definitely in labor. She looked at Bess, but she was obviously too worn out to speak. Bess asked Mathias to fetch some hot water and clean sheets, giving him things to do as she saw how worried he was.

Bess leaned over and whispered in Clara's ear, "The waters have broken, and the baby's bottom is visible. I need to make a small incision. Her pelvis may not be large enough to give birth this way, but fortunately, this is her fourth. The child should be turned around, like we do with the animals, but I'm afraid there is not enough time. We cannot lose both Laura and the child, so we are going to help her deliver this baby by having her kneel on all fours."

With Bess instructing, Clara fetched a chair and a pillow and helped Laura get up on her knees and lean forward, arms resting on the chair in front of her. The pillow propped up her arms and aided in supporting her upper body. It was as comfortable as they could make it.

Bess placed her hands on Laura's heavy belly and said the movements of her hands would, hopefully, make the child within move along and eventually kick his or her little legs out first.

Laura moaned and cursed anyone in her presence.

"I know you're exhausted, Laura," Bess said and stroked her hair, "but bear with me; we'll get this child safely home." She asked Clara to hold Laura's hips to support her movements. "Move with me, Laura. Back and forth, back and forth, that's it."

Laura screamed in pain, and Mathias dropped the pail of hot water onto the floor as he jumped forward. His eyes were wild, like those of a boar charging through the forest. He salvaged the bucket before all the water spilled and continued toward his wife. The little ones, who had been told to stay in the large bed and wait, started calling for their mother. Bess flung out her arm to stop Mathias from coming closer.

"Mathias, go and stay with the children. Keep them calm. Let us do our job here."

He wiped his brow and lumbered backward into a chair that tumbled over. Clara watched him stumble then turn around to embrace his children and calm their frightened sobs.

"Back and forth, back and forth," Bess continued to say as she wiped Laura's forehead and patted her cheek. "Good girl, Laura, you are doing well." She gave Clara a worried look. It was not over yet.

"I see the feet," Clara said. "What now?"

"We need to get the infant out as quickly as possible." Bess pressed her hand in next to the little feet. "This child is early."

"How can you tell?"

"It's not as large as I had expected."

Laura moaned and cried out as she collapsed. "I cannot," she said. Her voice was hoarse and short of breath.

Clara helped her back up onto her knees. "Almost there, Laura, hold on." She looked at Bess and hoped she had told the truth.

Bess held the infant's feet in one hand and tried to find the arms with the other.

"There may be complications," Bess whispered into Clara's ear. "Pressure on the cord could injure the child. I don't know why, but I have witnessed several deaths that way. If the infant dies in the womb now, we have little hope of saving Laura."

She straightened up and smiled at Laura. "You are doing well. Not long now," she said.

With her hand, Bess gently found the little arms and moved them toward the child's chest. The head was large, and if the arms were extended alongside the head, it would be difficult to get the infant out.

"Laura, I need you to push with all your might now," Bess said. "That's it. Come on, Laura. You can do this."

A few minutes later, a little girl was born feet first. Bess had saved both mother and child. Laura was completely worn out but alive, and with some rest she would recover beautifully.

Bess placed the child into Laura's arms. Clara covered mother and child with a clean blanket. The tension left the room, leaving Clara feeling as if she had escaped a fierce winter's storm and stepped over the threshold into a warm house.

"Come see your little daughter, Mathias," Bess called out.

The father, tears rolling down his rugged cheeks, entered the scene. The three young ones, eyes wide open, hugged his legs then crawled on the edge of the blanket to meet their new sister.

Before leaving, Bess had some instructions for Mathias. Laura had lost a great amount of blood and was weak. "Feed her dandelion leaves and stinging nettles. They will give her strength," Bess told him. "Red beets are also good for her, and make her some thyme tea. I'll bring you some tomorrow. I have plenty of dried thyme at home, and I'll leave you some hops."

Bess took out a small linen pouch from her bag, and Mathias started laughing.

She read his thoughts and said, "No, Mathias, not for brewing beer. Make tea with the hops and some dried chamomile. It will help Laura sleep, so she can get some deserved rest."

As they walked out the door, Mathias held Bess's arm, looked at her, and said, "We will name the little girl Bess if you don't mind."

Bess smiled and nodded affirmatively. She gave Mathias a hug and told him to take good care of Laura and little Bess.

It felt good going home that night. The rain had subsided, and moon glow shone on the wet grass and stony path. Branches spreading their fingers toward the horses sparkled as the moonbeams filtered through the woodland and hit the drops of rain still clinging to the bark. It was tranquil and reverent. A lonesome, hooting owl was the only proof of life other than the two tired but contented travelers. By the time they reached Frue Farm, the night was nearly gone, and it was far too late for Clara to return to the cottage at the parsonage. They snuggled in Bess's bed, lying on either side of a warm, little Lucia. The sun was beginning to rise already, and Clara closed her heavy eyelids and drifted off into a pleasant dream. Having another person named after you was an honor, and Clara knew Bess would be a fine example and not let her little namesake down.

∿

Clara woke up a few hours later as Bess came in the front door. With eyes like narrow slits, Clara climbed down the ladder. She was unsteady and tried not to step into thin air.

"Good morning," Bess whispered. "Did you sleep well?"

"Have you been out already? I know the sun has been up for a while, but the sheep have not woken up yet." Clara rubbed her eyes. "What have you been doing?"

"I woke up," Bess answered. "It must have been a couple of hours ago. I felt wide awake and in high spirits."

She was bare-footed, only wearing her night-shift. Her hair hung down her back like a messy tangle. Clara thought it possible that untangling the tresses could take all morning. Surely, even the hairdresser in Rossby might get nightmares from a wild mane like that.

"Could you not have dreamed a cheerful dream instead of wandering about alone? Remember, you have chores to do today," Clara said. She tried to sound serious behind the chuckles.

"I know, I know, but I was so happy, I could not help myself. I ran out barefoot in my sleeping gown and ended up at the clearing in the woods out yonder. The birds were up, Clara. You would have liked it, you and your birds." She giggled. The joyous feelings had obviously not subsided. "I thought about the baby born last night and the child I carry inside. It made me dance with delight. I danced and skipped and—"

She twirled around the room, almost toppling.

Clara laughed with her, imagining Bess dancing in the clearing with only birds and trees as spectators.

Right then, Uncle Samuel entered the front room. He had to bend over practically double, so as not to hit all the sprigs of parsley and peppermint hanging from the wooden beam above the door. As he straightened his back, sprigs of drying herbs clung to his navy-blue felt hat. He had a rabbit slung across his shoulder and dumped it on the table.

"Supper," he said and continued over to a corner of the room, where he pulled off his hat and placed his hunting gear on a chair. The large, muddy boots he placed by the door.

The catch of the day would make a good stew, enough to feed the family for the next few days.

"Mmm," Bess said and smacked her lips. "I have some lentils and vegetables. Thank you, Uncle Samuel."

He smiled tenderly back at her.

Clara had seen his service when she was younger. He still served and seemed to be happy with his life, taking care of his family at Frue Farm.

Clara picked off some of the herbal decorations on his shoulder and one sleeve. "Uncle Samuel, you are a sweet-smelling hunter." She giggled and turned to Bess. "Do you think you have hung enough bouquets to dry in the front room? Your poor uncle can hardly get through the door without being attacked by scented greenery."

"The town fair is barely a week away," Bess said as she helped a sleepy Lucia down the ladder. "We are going to be busy as ants in the anthill behind the stables, aren't we, Lucia?"

The little girl braided stems of dandelions and daisies into a wreath. Clara sat down next to the child, whose little fingers twisted and turned the stalks. The wreath kept falling apart.

"Here, Lucia, can I help you?"

The child nodded and let out a long sigh.

Bess put a pot of gruel on the table. "Later, Lucia," she said sweetly. "Now we eat."

She pushed the flowers to the side. They lay on the table, rootless and droopy.

Clara looked at the wilted plants, thinking her Okinawan mama-san would have said they showed a presage of things to come.

5

The Abbey

The day after the Sabbath, Clara walked up the long, windy lane to the abbey to visit Sister Birgitta, a friend from childhood. The abbey sisters had taken Birgitta into their care when she was orphaned at a young age.

Birgitta's green fingers and knowledge of gardening and herbal remedies were widely known. Clara found her friend, sleeves rolled up and head down. Birgitta was kneeling in a patch of vegetables, weeding. An old, straw hat, yellowed by the sun's rays, sat on Birgitta's head to shade her eyes from the strong light of midday. An apron, smothered in dirt and grass, was tied around her narrow waist.

"Good day, Birgitta, I see you keep the gardens flawless, just like I remember them."

The sister arose, wiped her forehead, and pushed strands of hair back in place under her hat. She squeezed her eyes a little and stared hard at Clara before her face broke into a lovely smile.

"I heard you were back at the parsonage."

Birgitta threw her arms around Clara, who almost fell over and had to take a step to the side so as not to lose her balance.

"Yes, I'm back. At least for the time being," Clara said, amused. She straightened up. "It's good to see you again."

Birgitta's face took on a more serious expression. "How is your family?"

"My father caught a fever this past year. It was during the rainy season in Okinawa in the Far East. The skies open up every afternoon, and it pours down as if someone sits up there, throwing buckets of water at you. Father lay in his bed, listening to the rain. You remember him; he had so much he wanted to accomplish, people he wished to serve and help. He fell asleep one evening as the moon peeked forth from behind a heavy cloud and shone on his coverlet. He never woke again."

Birgitta's eyebrows drew together, and she bit her lower lip. She looked at Clara with empathy in her eyes. "I'm sorry," she said, her voice filled with what sounded like genuine sadness. "I hope he didn't suffer." She paused for a moment and continued. "And how are you faring? What is it like there? I would love to travel and see other lands with you. Is it different from here?"

A dozen images of Okinawa flashed through Clara's mind and she said, "It is another world, but I love it. The people there work diligently, like you, and they have honor and integrity. My brother, Nathanael, is running the mission now."

Birgitta smiled and shook her head. It was not easy for Clara to describe the sights and smells of the Orient. The feeling had to be experienced.

"Come, walk with me," Birgitta said.

They strolled down the path toward the gray walls of the abbey. Clara stopped for a moment and looked at an area of green herbs outside the front entrance.

"What is that?" she asked and slid her fingers across the leaves.

"Smell your fingers now," Birgitta started. "It's called oregano. Smells wonderful, doesn't it? The monks planted it there to protect the abbey from evil and witchcraft. Can you believe it? I chew it when my tooth aches."

"I recognize the fragrance," Clara said. "I have eaten food cooked with this herb. It's delicious."

"Are you hungry?" Birgitta asked. "It's nearly mealtime."

Clara nodded and followed her down the garden path and opened the heavy gate by the stone fence, as Birgitta's hands were occupied carrying two large baskets and a shovel. Even with dirt on her face and hands and dressed in soiled work clothes, she was beautiful. Her long blonde curls were tied loosely in a knot on the back of her head. Ringlets of flaxen hair had fallen out of the hat and danced next to her ears as she walked. Her eyes were the color of the ocean on a clear summer's day.

"I must commend you for your good work," Clara said. "You have always helped others with your knowledge of herbs and useful plants. Bess tells me how much service you do. Still, you are free to leave here. You are not one of the sisters. Any suitors, Birgitta?"

"No, not yet," she replied with a smile. "Maybe the handsome men out there are unaware of my existence." She untied the ribbons on her work apron and folded it neatly on top of the chair by the door.

"Some women used to come here to find a safe haven and someone to take care of them in their old age," she continued. "They transferred the rights to both their land and inheritance to the convent. It's not like that anymore. And even if it were a convent, I would probably be a worker here, not a nun. I would not have taken any vows. Celibacy is not for me." She widened her eyes.

"Why are the abbey women unmarried?" Clara asked as they walked down the long corridor, along which hung several large oil paintings in decorated wooden frames. They showed a male saint being baptized, administered to by angels, and finally stigmatized.

Clara stared at the canvases.

"Bernard of Claivaux," Birgitta explained.

"Who?"

"The saint in the paintings on the wall. He was a French abbot who inspired the former order here. His perception of women and their role influenced the Catholic Church for centuries."

"But you're not part of that now, are you? The order of the sisterhood was shut down with the Reformation more than a century ago."

"Yes, that's true. But even though the statues of St. Mary are gone and the relics and icons of holy saints have disappeared, the good work here continues. The sisters tend the lovely gardens and help sick and poor neighbors. They even learn to read and write."

"I know my father welcomed all of you to church."

"He did. And the Rossbyans leave us alone for the most part as long as we portray a Protestant way of life."

"It's funny how you are still called sisters. Religion is not the same as it once was within these walls, is it?"

"No, not really, but habitually the women here still live the way they have always done. St. Bernard taught that women should be submissive, as they were by nature morally weaker than the men."

"What?" Clara interrupted. "Did he actually meet normal men in the towns?"

Birgitta stared at the paintings and fingered the cross around her neck. "He instructed the church of his day that nuns were brides of Christ and also Mary's successors," she said. "Virgins were the ideal, as if they were on a more superior level than other human beings."

"I understand," Clara admitted. "It's not easy to break habits and teachings, is it?"

"No, it's not." Birgitta folded her hands in front and lifted her shoulders. "I don't feel I am of little worth because I am a woman, but there are plenty of men who believe it's so."

She continued walking down the hallway toward the dining hall. Other than the paintings on the walls there was little ornamentation, except for a tall table with a vase of summer flowers, which stood next to the door and gave color to the lifeless room.

"Someone will find you, Birgitta," Clara said and put an arm around her friend's shoulder. "Maybe a nobleman or a prince?"

"I don't need a prince," Birgitta said, "but I want a man who is kind."

Clara nodded. Birgitta's statements triggered thoughts Clara had often pondered. Women's workloads were heavy. In addition to giving birth every other year, some had employment outside of the home to supplement the family's income. If she were a widow, she could hope for charity from the church or the town council. There was no guarantee for this, however, even though it was both preached and legislated. And there were widows in the town of Rossby, like everywhere else. Fishermen, soldiers, and sickly men often left this world at a young age, leaving their families to fend for themselves. That the women should be considered to be of less worth was unjust and wrong, and it angered Clara.

The abbey seemed unchanged. Clara had often been here with Bess when they were younger and had listened to Bess and Birgitta discuss everything from how to strengthen the chest with warm drink made of sap from the buds of fir trees and honey from the beehives in the corner of the orchard, anise seeds, and thyme for breathing, or why liquid from the dandelion made warts disappear.

The dining room had windows with a view of the road down below. Three long, birch-wood tables with benches on either side were set with simple plates and cups. A dozen and a half women, ranging from rosy-cheeked young girls to a few older, hunchbacked sisters, were getting ready to sit down. Their habits were plain but sensible, made of un-dyed wool in colors such as nearly white, gray, and brown. The former wimple had evolved into a simple white kerchief to cover the hair, and most of them had a narrow, leather band tied around their waist. A few more sisters came out from the kitchen, carrying bowls of warm lentil and onion soup. The smell of fresh bread filled the room, and Clara suddenly noticed how famished she was.

"Come, sit," Birgitta said and motioned to an empty space on a nearby bench.

They bowed their heads as an older sister who seemed to be in charge of the abbey said a blessing on the food. Her gray hair coiled neatly at the back of her neck, and her eyebrows were bushy; her chin even had a few misplaced strands of hair. The kind but determined look in her eyes gave the impression of a firm and good leader. A small gold cross hung from a cord around her neck. Clara had a little knife on her belt that she used for mealtime and was about to pull it out to cut a slice of bread when the older sister knocked on the table with her wrinkled fist.

"Sisters, sisters," she called out. "We had a visitor earlier today. Innkeeper Hansen from the town council came by and asked questions about several of you."

The sisters turned and looked at each other, perplexed and curious as to what that could mean.

"He probed and inquired about the most peculiar things," the head sister continued. "Sister Leah, have you prevented cows from giving milk or hens from laying eggs lately?" She had a sober look on her face. This was a serious matter.

"What? No, I have done no such thing," Sister Leah answered, her eyes wide. She appeared a little embarrassed by the odd question.

Some of the other sisters giggled and leaned over and whispered to one another.

The head sister knocked her fist on the table again.

"Quiet. Quiet. What about you, Sister Elisabeth? Have you raised any storms this last year?"

A couple of the younger sisters started laughing, commenting on how on Earth anyone, except the Savior himself, could cause the weather to change.

"I know it sounds ridiculous, but these are grave accusations," the head sister said, looking around at the sisters with a stern but concerned expression in her eyes. "Of course, I don't believe it, but I am nevertheless alarmed we are being examined in such a manner. I admonish you to tell me if anyone has queries that seem out of the ordinary. And if that happens, don't let them frighten you into deception. Now, please eat your soup. It's getting cold."

Clara decided to keep quiet for the time being, but it was clear the town council had Innkeeper Hansen inspecting the area for witches, searching to see if there was anything out of the ordinary in Rossby and its surroundings. She did not want to admit that witch hunting had reached the idyllic haven by the sea. The thought made her heart and her shoulders ache, as if she had been bound with heavy ropes. She could only hope nothing more came of it.

Birgitta must have noticed Clara's discomfort and eyed her as if expecting an explanation.

"I'm well," Clara said. "I have a slight headache, but I am sure you know what to do about that." It was true. She had not slept well the night before, and her head felt heavy. It was best not to stir up any emotions until she had more proof.

Birgitta ran into the kitchen and fetched a small pouch with a piece of ginger root. "Here. Make some tea when you get home." Then she added cheerfully, "Don't drink too much, or you'll be the one chasing princes."

Clara got up and put the small pouch in her pocket. "I need to go. I have some things I need to do this afternoon."

Outside, Birgitta picked a violet flower and stretched out her hand. It was Clara's favorite color. Her friend had remembered.

"The town fair is tomorrow," Birgitta said. "You'll be there, won't you?"

"Yes, I know," Clara answered. "I am looking forward to it."

Clara thanked Birgitta for the flower and then continued on the road south of Rossby. She wanted to visit some of the homes in the outskirts to see if they had any children who could attend school. The first farmhouse was close to the dirt road. A middle-aged man stood alone in the field, sleeves rolled up and sweat running down his unshaven face.

"We are trying to squeeze another year of harvest from the depleted soil," he said without looking up.

He stuck the shovel into the ground with more force and stepped on it. Clara waited for him to continue.

The farmer lifted his chin and leaned his elbows on the shovel handle. "Miss Clara, we hope for the weather to cooperate one season at a time. We work from sun-up to sun-down and go to bed exhausted."

"I know," Clara said. She felt for him. His family probably slept on coarse canvas mattresses stuffed with dried leaves and moss or piles of straw directly on the dirt floor. She opened her shoulder bag and took out a piece of paper.

"Knowledge can change the life of any person. I know this to be true. Let me help you learn to act on your own." Illiterate peasants and fishermen were vulnerable, and Clara chose her words wisely so as not to upset him. "It will be harder for anyone to take advantage of you if you can read and write."

"I have no use for psalms and biblical words of thunder. I get enough of that on Sundays."

She showed him the document. "But look, you and your children can learn to read things like this. You can learn about who owns the land, how to travel from one place to another, and where to ask for information when you need it."

"I have managed well so far without schooling."

"I am sure you have, and I don't mean to offend you. It's a free offer." She smiled and put the document back in her bag.

"Not free. If my sons waste their days on a chair instead of working the farm, I don't get any further, do I?" He lifted the shovel and stabbed the ground again. The conversation ended.

The next homestead had only daughters. A pregnant woman with one child hanging on her hip and a bucket in one hand stared at Clara.

"My young ones are needed here to help with the chores. My husband is gone at sea for days at a time." She pushed her hair back behind her ears and wiped her nose with a dirty hand.

Clara offered to hold the child, a round-cheeked little girl with a runny nose. "Here, let me help you feed the animals, and I can try to explain how your children will benefit from both books and hard work."

The woman nodded and listened as Clara told her about how the abbey used to give even young women the opportunity to be educated.

"Girls?" The woman frowned and made a forced cackle. "Why would a girl need an education?"

"Everyone can have an advantage in life if they know letters and numbers. Even girls."

"I have four girls."

"You do? That's wonderful. Give them a chance to learn. It can also be useful for you and your husband if they can read." Clara put the child down and placed a hand on the woman's shoulder. "If you plan ahead, maybe you can find a few hours a week for them to come to my school."

"Could be." She turned her back to Clara and wiped her cheek.

Clara continued on her journey along the dirt road, stopping at each home she passed. She met folks whose faces beamed with hope that their descendants might have more opportunities in life than they had experienced themselves. Other parents were indifferent. After the last farmer almost chased her off his land, she decided to turn back.

Clara could not blame the skeptics and remembered having read notes written by the distinguished artist and inventor Leonardo da

Vinci, who claimed that knowledge could only be achieved by putting it into practice. He kept learning all his life, undoubtedly an easier task because of his skills with words and numbers. He was even left-handed as Clara was.

She walked home that evening, satisfied to have eight names on her list. Her guess was that some of them might not show up after all, but others might come unannounced out of curiosity or due to word of mouth.

The discussion at the abbey had disturbed her. Innkeeper Hansen's questions were threatening. Hopefully, it would blow away with the wind.

The sun lingered on, and the northern summer evening was still light and dewy. Clara could easily find her way home. She watched the sides of the road with its tall grass and weeds and heard the grasshoppers sing. The fields were filled with flowers of summer, and a woodpecker could be heard working on a tree trunk.

The sounds and smells made Clara's imagination wander. Tales of fairies filled her mind. Petite elves could be hiding in the bushes. Maybe one climbed a straw and watched her pass. A beautiful elf girl sang and directed an orchestra of bumble bees with tiny violins. Three elves held on to strands of her hair, floating in the air behind as she walked down the road toward the parsonage. They laughed and played in the breeze. Clara flipped the back of her hair to shake them off, and they made summersaults through the air, before landing on the petals and leaves of a flower in the ditch. Her imagination was both a curse and a blessing, and although it kept her entertained, it could also be frightening. Nonetheless, it was part of her, and she was used to it.

People actually believed in the magic of the elves and trolls in the woods, and they often made decisions by considering the ways of fairies and wood creatures. Anything from skin complaints to aching backs and teeth were blamed on the hidden-folk. An infant born with an unhealthy little body was thought to be a changeling, substituted by these wood creatures because they had stolen the newborn and taken it to their hiding place underground. Clara's father had taught her a practical way of thinking and a Christian belief that did not leave much room for superstitions. But her imagination had no boundaries. Just about anything could trigger a story or picture in her mind.

Clara had learned much about superstitions in Okinawa. Hideko, her mama-san, who helped their family around the house, taught her how to step on a *tatami*-mat, so as not to bring bad luck. Hideko had shiny black hair, straight as an arrow when she let it hang loose. Long hair was important to the Okinawan women, and ornaments and talismans in the hair were used for protection.

Hideko-san taught Clara which numbers to avoid and how to treat spiders, animals, and birds. Superstition was a way of life for the Okinawans. Clara tried not to believe in myths but considered her behavior in different situations of everyday life.

Clala-san, she called Clara, unable to pronounce her foreign name.

"Clala-san, where is amulet pouch I gave you. It will protect you. Where you put it?"

She had not stopped asking until Clara found it and hung it around her neck. Hideko-san cared and wanted her safe, so Clara wore it to please the older woman.

"Clala-san, you help me make beds in hospital?"

Clara could be lost in her books, and Hideko-san would gently remind her to help out in the mission's small infirmary wing. It was a long, brown wooden house with a flat red roof, designed with strong winds in mind. The bamboo rolling blinds were fragile during storms, thus another set of wooden shutters covered the windows during typhoon season. Free flow of air between windows and doors helped bedridden patients cope with the high humidity.

Clara made the beds, changed the soiled sheets, and emptied the potties. The beds were numbered one, two, three, five, six—number four meant bad luck and was omitted every time.

As a young girl, Clara sometimes volunteered for other chores than potty duty, such as running errands or keeping the journals updated, hoping her mama-san noticed her talent.

"Clala-san, you go pick up package for your father from tailor at Naha Way 36?"

Hideko-san knew how frustrated Clara got when her mama-san gave her an assignment like that. Hideko-san put a hand in front of her mouth and chuckled before she gave in and told Clara the landmarks and how to find the tailor. Street numbers were never in the right order. The houses were numbered according to the year they were built. Any number could be next to another. Clara found that confusing and learned, like the Okinawans, to use landmarks to navigate around the island.

"Clala-san, go to pink grocery store, go left, then walk down hill and then left again by fountain."

That was a much better road map, and off she had gone to fetch her father's parcel.

Now, anxious to get home, Clara decided to take a shortcut and cross the marshes behind the cemetery. They were dry enough, and she could walk across without getting wet. It was like walking on moss, soft and airy. As a child, she had always been scared of walking there alone. Now she looked for courage to do it, thinking she was an adult, brave and unafraid. Not quite true but she talked herself into doing it. There were two reasons for her hesitation. One, the marshes, when wet, were difficult to walk on, and her legs sank deeply into the weeds. She had heard horror stories about people sinking into a marsh and drowning amongst water, plants, and roots. Those tales had formed images in her mind difficult to erase. Two, Toomber dwelled in the small cottage next to the marshes not far behind the church.

It seemed as if Toomber had lived there forever. He was part of the landscape and for better or worse a part of the history of Rossby. Toomber was the official undertaker, gravedigger, and coffin builder. He took care of everything concerning death in Rossby.

Toomber, or Thomas, if he was ever christened properly, dealt with death every day and seemed to enjoy making a profit on other's misfortune and sorrow.

Clara remembered him well. He certainly looked the part—grim and dirty and standing a head taller than other men in the village. She wondered if the corners of his mouth ever turned up into a genuine smile, but looks could be deceiving. The stench of his filthy clothes, brown teeth, and the permanent grime and dirt on his face and hands did not necessarily make him less likeable or approachable. His countenance and behavior were the traits that gave the impression of someone who preferred a life alone.

As a child, Clara had never ventured alone through the cemetery and down the hill toward the marsh. She had not wanted to chance upon meeting Toomber by herself. Her brother and his friends climbed trees and spied on the gravedigger. Children made snares to trip him, but those same children were long gone by the time he passed by, for fear of being caught. People ridiculed and loathed him in the same breath.

Clara had difficulty imagining Toomber ever being a small child with rounded rosy cheeks, playing happily and carefree. Had he ever thrown skipping stones into the water? Had he ever had a mother who hugged him? Had he ever loved anyone? The thought became remote and unlikely. The Toomber Clara knew was a long-limbed, gangly man who literally walked over corpses. He used every opportunity to make money from other's misfortune and had no sympathy for those who mourned the loss of a loved one. He did his work alone and kept to himself.

Father must have seen something else in Toomber because he did not replace him. Clara had heard Toomber threatened anyone who aspired to take over his job, but her father had treated him respectfully and let him continue his work.

Was he still there? She hurried across the marshes. Her plan was to save time and not meet Toomber on her way. His small, timber cottage with thatched roof looked dark and empty. The tension she had felt gave way to relief. She lowered her shoulders and climbed steadily up the small hill between the marshes and the cemetery. Walking across the lawn with all the graves in the evening did not bother her because she had grown up next to the church and the graveyard, and nothing there frightened Clara. She followed the main path between the headstones and epitaphs and stopped for a minute at her mother's tablet. She heard a noise behind her back. Startled, she turned sharply around, and there he was. Even though she was now a grown woman, he still appeared tall. His greasy, dark hair, now streaked with gray, was tied in a ponytail that hung down his back. His clothes were shabby, covered with dirt and soil. She felt a shiver and knew her opinion of him had not changed. He was a disgusting man who made her feel unwell.

"Toomber," she said. She looked straight at him, pushing away the knotted feeling in her stomach. "Are you still working?"

"Miss Clara," he mumbled. And that was all. He just stood there staring.

Feeling increasingly uneasy, Clara wished she had taken the longer route around the cemetery instead.

"I have to go now," she said.

She tried to leave, but he grabbed her arm. She looked down at his long, filthy fingernails on her sleeve. He just kept staring with a hollow look. The stench of his dirty clothes and body was strong, even outside in the evening air. Clara had never wanted to be this close to him.

She pulled away and said, "It's late. I need to get home."

He let go of her arm, and she walked away, her steps a little quicker and her breath a little shorter. She tried to hear if he followed, not daring to turn around to check, but all was quiet. However, through the thin air she could feel his hollow-eyed gaze trailing her.

As Clara entered the gate of the parsonage, Herr Christopher was outside on the front steps, seemingly speaking to himself. He looked up as she approached.

"Clara, is something wrong? You look like you have seen a ghost."

"I wish I had. I met Toomber in the cemetery a few minutes ago. What is he doing there at this hour?" She sat down next to the parson on the stairs and put her satchel in her lap. Something bit her neck, and she swatted it with her hand, hoping the bite would not keep her awake scratching all night.

"Toomber often works late. He may be many things, but he is not idle. He always has a job to do," Herr Christopher answered, swatting flying insects, now they had discovered them sitting on the stairs.

Clara thought body armor was appropriate just then. She was weary, and the little pests were disturbing the conversation.

"He's the same as he has always been, isn't he?" Clara asked again. "He is a loner, someone who keeps to himself, no friends, no one who cares about him?"

Herr Christopher nodded. "That's true, but he doesn't do much to encourage relationships, either. He has his work and seems to think that is enough."

"I grew up with him around here, but still, I don't trust him."

"I think that's wise, Clara. I don't know him well, but you should probably just leave him be."

He opened his collar in the warm evening air, his feet were without shoes, and he had papers on his lap. Clara thought about this man who had cared for the parish.

"So what are you doing here on the stairs?" she said. "Staring at the sky?"

Herr Christopher chuckled. "Well, I'm pondering... contemplating... thinking." He straightened his back and cleared his throat. "Actually, I'm trying to gather thoughts for my sermon on Sunday. It seems like sitting here under God's lighted blanket helps me think. As you can imagine, it can get pretty noisy inside when everyone is home." He put his papers on the stairs and folded his hands in his lap. "But how did it go today? Did you get any more pupils for your school?"

"Yes, I'm excited. I'll encourage more to come. A few hours of learning each week may provide a security for their future."

"That's wonderful, Clara. I know my children are excited to have you teach them."

"You must be proud of them."

She stood up and pushed the wrinkles down the front of her gown. "Well, I had better get home. I love these long summer evenings in Norway. It's magical when the sun seems to be up forever, but I still need some sleep to function tomorrow. Goodnight, Herr Christopher."

"Goodnight, Clara, and try not to worry."

She walked past the circular flowerbed, taking in the scent of flowers in bloom. Birds and bugs had gone to rest for the evening, but the grasshoppers were happily noisemaking in the tall grass as she walked the path across the field to her home in the cottage.

Ami stood outside the cottage door, wanting to come inside for a midnight treat and some fresh milk before his nightly mouse hunt. Clara opened the door, and he snuck inside past her legs. She had to be careful not to step on him.

Clara prepared some milk and bread for both of them and sat down by the table. Herr Christopher's last words came to mind again and again. She worried about what Toomber was capable of. There were things about him she did not know. Why did he shun friendships? As a child she had avoided him altogether, but her father had always been kind, letting Toomber have his life at the cottage and his livelihood taking care of the cemetery. Yet, as far as she knew, he had never been inside their home. Why, she did not know.

She put her hands on her cheeks and let out a sigh. Some rest would help. Thoughts of Toomber were grinding still as she went to bed. She could not let her imagination take over her senses. She wandered off to sleep and drifted back and forth in a dream, where she was out among the weeds on the marsh, trying not to step on birds sitting beneath the swampy straws. They poked their little beaks up through the moss, squawked, and called for help. Clara bent down and tried to get hold of their bills, so she could pull them up and help them onto dry land. But they were slippery and wet, and some slid out of her grasp. She tried again and pulled out a few birds, using both hands, and threw them onto the edges of the marsh. One bird bit her index finger, which started to bleed. She wiped the blood on her frock and tried again. The little thing hacked at her one more time then slipped away and disappeared into the unknown. She desperately pushed her hand down through the moss and weeds, trying to locate him, but to no avail. Then she looked up and saw Toomber standing on the edge of the marsh. He bent over and picked up little birds that had landed where she had thrown them. He had several of them in his large, dirty hands. Tears rolled down his grimy cheeks.

6

The Midsummer Fair

～

Clara got up the next morning, confused and tired from dreaming about Toomber. She tried to avoid analyzing the events of the night. The last few hours she had been awake, waiting for the large cock to crow. The twitter in the trees and bushes outside sounded more intense the harder she had tried to sleep. Even the porcupines living under the cottage ran around, grunting like tiny pigs.

"This dream, this strange dream," she said to herself, wondering what it could mean. Why would Toomber show emotions? Who were the little birds? She decided to let it go for the time being and get on with her chores and schedule for the day, grateful for a new day and fresh opportunities. It was the morning of the town fair, and she looked out the window on the haze, low on the fields, and remembered a rhyme her mother had taught her:

> *Eventide is red as I go to bed*
> *The morning gray will clear and sun will gather near*
> *If otherwise it be and morning skies be red*

I welcome summer rain that falls upon my head

The sun appeared right behind the gray, ready to brighten up the village of Rossby and its inhabitants. After the morning chores and feeding Ami, Clara walked down the hill toward Rossby. She was not the only one. The townsfolk, farmers and visitors alike, streamed to the square in front of Town Hall.

On the way, she met Uncle Samuel pulling a cart loaded with woolen blankets, furs, and jars of various kinds.

"Hello, Clara. How are you this fine morning?"

"Uncle Samuel. I'm fine, thank you. Look at all the people. I cannot remember the fair being this busy before."

"Well, it has grown into the main event of the year. We have more foreign visitors and people from neighboring villages now than before."

Clara looked at the cart full of sales items and noticed something— or rather someone—missing. She asked, "Where are Bess and Lucia?"

"I brought them down earlier. Bess is setting up a table with wares. I went back to Frue Farm for more then came to pick up some boards for our stand on this side of town."

"Bess has been busy as usual, I see." Clara rummaged through, looking at things he brought on the cart, and held a pair of woolen mittens up in the air.

Uncle Samuel's eyes lit up with pride. "She started preparing the day after last summer's fair. Her handmade items will bring a good income this time, by the looks of it."

"I hope so. I am looking forward to helping her. Just tell me what to do. I have all day."

"Good. Mychel is still away fishing. An extra set of hands will be great help."

At the town square, Uncle Samuel steered the horse and carriage through the crowd of people. Dogs ran around, barking with excitement. One mangy yellow cur had stolen a line of sausages from a peddler, and a young boy with shoulder-length, dark hair chased after the four-legged thief. The peddler wore a short waistcoat and breeches in a colorful material with long crimson tassels by the knees. He stayed put to watch the goods on his stand but gesticulated and called out in a foreign language Clara did not understand. The dog disappeared and enjoyed the tasty meats before anyone had the chance to catch up.

Children darted back and forth between tables, boxes, and sacks. Clara noticed that a couple of boys hid under a table filled with various bows and arrows. They whispered to each other while they tied a rope to one of the wobbly table legs. Before long, they had snuck away and hidden behind a plump woman farther down carrying two young children in her fatty arms. The boys pulled the rope, and the table fell apart, causing arrows, bows, and other wooden sticks to fly in every direction. The bow-maker fumed. Despite his short temper and impatience, he had carefully crafted the bows out of supple limbs, finding just the right branches and tying them with strings of coarse hemp. The time he had spent treating the arcs with beeswax to make the weapons resistant to moisture would not pay off if his merchandise were damaged.

"You cuckoos," he yelled at them. "You worms."

Other indelicate name-callings charged out of his mouth, words not part of Clara's vocabulary. The boys ran off with short, fast legs, while a couple of other hawkers assisted the bow-maker and helped him get his table ready for customers again.

The pale-yellow Town Hall looked magnificent in the morning light. The windows and the large, blue double main doors were decorated with garlands of flowers with bows hanging down. In front of the steps of the main entrance, the town of Rossby presented everything a fair could want and more. Clara planted herself in the middle of the square and slowly moved around in a circle to look at the buildings.

"Let's find Bess," Uncle Samuel said. "I need to unload the cart and take the horse to a shady spot on the north side of the Hall."

Clara followed in the same direction and found Bess placing jars of preserves on a wooden table covered with a pretty piece of cloth. Lucia bounced and skipped toward Clara, who picked her up and swung her around in a loop.

"More, Auntie Clara, more," she squealed.

"Lucia, you're such a pretty little girl this morning, and you have blue ribbons in your hair. Very nice."

Bess looked at Lucia and smiled. Her child's joy was her own joy.

"Clara, look at this weather," Bess said. "Did you pray for this? It's perfect for the fair. Well, if you did, I am grateful. And look at all the people. Bustling, isn't it? It'll be a busy day. I can tell."

"Yes, it's perfect. Let me help you get your stall ready."

They emptied the cart and placed sheep wool, furs, and woven blankets on a couple of large crates. Soon, the table was loaded with Bess's pots and bottles of remedies, herbal concoctions, and dried herbs in tiny bags of cloth. There were jam jars and juices made from berries and fruits, and Uncle Samuel organized dried meat and fish he had prepared with Mychel.

Clara looked around at the stands. Hands had been busy for months, preparing delectable extravagancies and mouth-watering meals. She saw tools, household items, and clothing—both common and fancy—presented for sale. Artisans, craftsmen, and skilled workers alike were in abundance in Rossby this day.

"You should take a walk around the square and look at all the stands. Maybe you will find a treasure or treat to take home," Bess said.

"Very well, I'll be back to help you out. By the way, did you see the tapestry-covered wagon and the man with the enormous mustache selling potions in small, glass bottles? Your competitor?"

"Oh, him. I have spoken to that charlatan several times before. He sells tonics made with water, a little color, and flavor from berries, and a droplet or two of some unknown liquor. It's scary, really. Folks don't know what they are buying. But they believe in him. He's clever with words."

"I guess he has the right to be here and sell his wares, just as everyone else."

"Yes, but if you see customers in doubt, send them over here, will you?"

"I will."

Bustling was the right word to describe the fair. Not only were there people, dogs, stands, and goods everywhere, but Clara could feel the keenness in the air, and anyone with a few extra coins in their purse could enjoy nourishment other than the ordinary, everyday gruel.

Clara hardly knew which way to go first but decided to make a round in a clockwise pattern, weaving back and forth so as not to miss the booths in the center.

A small, thin man with a mustache and a purple hat adorned with two large peacock feathers, paint brush in one hand and palette in the other, stood with his legs wide apart, painting a portrait of a couple of young, twin girls. The girls batted their eyelashes and smiled sweetly, heads tilted. They wore their long blonde hair in ringlets and had ribbons attached on both sides of their heads. They must have been about fourteen summers old and clearly enjoyed the attention of the admiring artist and the people standing around watching them. Clara recognized the girls as Taran and Tilla, the daughters of Mr. Land, the storekeeper and member of the town council. Mrs. Land was standing next to the artist, her head a little back and her eyelids half closed.

"Portray my beauties flawlessly on that canvas," she said in a high-pitched voice.

Though no doubt annoyed with the constant interruptions, the artist kept his tongue and didn't complain.

Clara continued on and heard the loud voice of a man calling people to come and have a go at his betting table. The trickster had three cups turned upside down, which, with his large, working hands, he moved back and forth faster than anyone could follow. The game was to guess which cup had a pea underneath it. His lace collar and cuffs were dirty and a little torn, and his left leather shoe was missing the buckle. As he rapidly moved the cups around the table, he spoke with the speed of a woodpecker and then asked the audience to place their bets. The crowd became boisterous and eager to wager. The large, plump woman Clara had noticed earlier by the bow-maker's stand had placed her young children somewhere else and now carried a small dog under her arm. She was next in line and chose the middle cup, which, when turned over, did not have a pea.

"You cheater," the woman called in a shrilling voice. "I saw you place the pea under that cup. Where is the pea now? I bet you have removed it altogether. Give me my money back."

The crowd became louder and uneasier. *It could continue like this all day*, Clara decided and hastily moved on.

Old Magda had jars of honey collected meticulously from her beehives. Her bees had swarmed in the clover field near her homestead, producing sweet, tasty honey. Clara bought a large jar and asked how Magda managed the work, now she was getting older.

"Oh, I am used to it, you know. But everything goes slower. I am not as limber as I used to be." She pushed some loose strands of hair away from her face and pulled an earthy carrot out of the pocket on her apron. She wiped the carrot on her skirt and took a large bite of it using her left molars, as the right ones were missing.

"Wouldn't you like to move a little closer to town?" Clara asked. "It might make life a little easier, not having to travel so far for supplies, and you would also be closer should you need help."

"I don't need help from townspeople." She chomped away on large bites of carrot and spat on the ground. "I summon my own help in the woods," she answered defensively.

Clara knew Magda differed. She did not come to church often and had her own special ways. The townspeople just let her be, a harmless, old soul.

"Do you want to buy one of my witch boxes?" Magda asked with a crooked smile.

"A witch box? What is that?"

"Oh, it's a special box for protection. Look." Magda pointed to the boxes. "Everyone should have one. It will keep you safe from wolves and bears and such. It will take care of you when the storms of winter come."

Clara looked at the pile of small, wooden boxes with brass fixtures for locks and was curious as to what Old Magda had put inside them. She thought about her mama-san in Okinawa's amulets for good luck.

"What's in the box?" Clara asked again, noticing Magda had scratched the same emblem on all of the lids.

"Oh, magical things, a candle for special occasions, a spell to say when you're in need, things like that. You should buy one. You be alone. You will need it. It will protect your cottage from evil."

"No, thank you, Magda. I ask for help in different ways than you do," Clara said as respectfully as she could.

She put the jar of honey under her arm and said goodbye, hoping people would come to buy Magda's honey and not shun her. She waved, and Clara strolled back to Bess's stand, past sausages stringed on rafters, pottery on tables, and downy chicks in cages. A drunken man who could barely stand straight whistled at Clara as she passed. She did not enjoy the compliment or pay him any attention, as he probably would not remember the next day.

"There you are," Bess said as Clara approached.

A couple paid for a woolen jacket for their daughter, and Bess put the coins in her apron pocket.

Clara went behind the stand and placed her honey jar on the ground. "I saw the Land twins," she said. "They were just little girls when I was here before. Now they are young women, posing for a portrait."

"Well, they must have grown tired of sitting still," Bess said. "They were here a moment ago. I caught them trying to steal pieces of dried beef from the next stand over there."

"What? Why would they do that? They are not in need at all."

"I know, but you should have seen them. One smiled sweetly to get a taste of the delicacies, and the other one slipped the meat in her pocket." Bess shook her head and put more wares up on her table.

Clara frowned. "It must be a game to them. They use their innocent looks to deceive unsuspecting traders and peddlers." She bent down to help Bess lift a crate with jars. "Are you tired, Bess?"

"No, I'm well. It's a wonderful fair, isn't it? I love the different smells and seeing all the merchandise and cheerful people. Besides, Lucia fell asleep, and I can concentrate on my sales."

Clara looked around. "Where is she? I don't see her anywhere."

Bess lifted the corner of the tablecloth. Lucia slept under the table. Her tiny hands rested under her cheek.

"An angel she is." Clara straightened up, ready to greet customers. She cocked her head to the side and squinted to see what was happening by the water trough in the middle of the square.

Bess leaned over. "What are you looking at? You look doubtful."

"It's the innkeeper. He's up to something."

"Oh, don't worry about that now. He's always grumpy and unfriendly."

"But, Bess, look at the way he is eyeing Old Magda. And what is he writing in his notebook?" She opened her satchel and took out the quill pen she had found outside her cottage. "I'll be right back, Bess," she said. "I need to ask him something."

Bess lifted her eyebrows and sighed then turned to a young woman who was looking through small, cloth bags filled with dried herbs.

The innkeeper had moved on by the time Clara reached the water trough. She saw him walk past the ale tent toward the abbey sisters. Clara hurried a different way through the crowd and found Birgitta selling flower wreaths. Clara pulled her over to the side.

"Has Innkeeper Hansen been here to talk with the sisters today?" she asked.

Birgitta shook her head and smiled sweetly. "No, I haven't seen him. Why?"

"Be wary around him. If he asks strange questions, be watchful how you answer."

"Yes, of course. Something amiss, Clara?"

Clara lifted her shoulders. "I'm not sure. I have a bad feeling, that's all." She kissed Birgitta on the cheek, turned around, then walked right into the innkeeper.

"Watch where you are going, Miss Clara Dahl," he said, his mouth limp and curved down.

"Excuse me, my mistake," Clara said. She lifted her hand with the quill pen. "I wondered if this could be yours."

Hansen looked at the quill pen and nodded. "It is. Where did you find it?"

Clara avoided the question. "It's nice. My father used to have a similar one, but I see you have one more." She pointed to the pen and notebook in his hand. "Very good quality."

"Hm, yes, it is an excellent quill pen. Thank you, Miss Dahl." He grabbed the pen and bowed farewell.

Clara lifted the shawl off her shoulders and tied it around her waist. She pulled her sleeves up and wiped her brow. A man with a barrel of apple cider tempted her to buy a jug. She gave in and sat down on a crate and let the beverage run down her throat. She licked her lips.

Out of the corner of her eye, she noticed Taran Land sitting on a merchant's lap. Clara did not intend to eavesdrop but was close enough to hear the conversation.

"Yes, Jacques, we can do that. What would you like us to get for you?" Taran asked.

Jacques rubbed his long, matted beard with its graying edges with one hand, while gesticulating with the other. His heavy, brocade coat with golden tassels down the front fit snugly on his broad shoulders and oversized belly. A dagger with a metal handle and wooden case hung in his belt, supported by a chain. He bent over and spoke closely to Taran's face with a heavy French accent, ale drooling down his beard.

"You use imagination and think...think what is of interest. What is of value? What can we sell? Where do you find these things?"

His voice was deep and his manner controlling. His piercing eyes were fixed intently on the twin girls, switching back and forth between them, and his long, fat arms swung around whilst he spoke.

The twins looked mesmerized, their eyes fixated on the large Frenchman. Taran spoke first.

"What kind of things? How about this? I stole this from one of the stands." She handed him a small, brass bell.

The merchant threw the bell onto the ground and spat on it, then he grabbed both girls by the arms and pulled them close to his bearded face.

Tilla whimpered. "But how can we know what you need?"

Jacques pushed her away and pointed a finger to her forehead. "Use this," he said firmly. His grin exposed yellow teeth, pieces of meat from his last meal stuck in between them. "You will find out. Practice, practice."

"But how do we get it to you?"

The Frenchman rolled his eyes as if he listened to an imbecile. "I leave tomorrow. I will not be back until next summer."

The twins nodded. Clara knew they were too young to understand men. *They are getting in too deep*, she thought. The merchant was obviously a dishonest thief.

Clara put her empty jug down and wiped her mouth. She glanced over at the twins and the French merchant and saw him lean toward the girls.

"Tell no one, or else," he said and made a flat-handed motion across his throat. He grabbed them both by the shoulders and swung them around, then patted them on their behinds and told them to get to work.

Clara's heart sank. *They are up to no good*, she thought.

Bess's table was surrounded with people asking questions and purchasing wares as Clara returned. Lucia had woken up and ran around their legs as Clara continued to help Bess sell goods from the bounty on the table. Uncle Samuel was on the other side of the square and traded furs and dried produce with foreign merchants.

"Clara, can you take Lucia for a walk?" Bess asked after a while. "She is so lively right now. I have a hard time watching her with all the customers here."

Clara took hold of Lucia's hand and took her to see a young boy who presented a game of mouse and maze. His large hat almost covered his eyes. He had midcalf breeches, and bare feet. The game was built like a small, round table with a labyrinth. It had a starting square in the middle and eight ending areas. The table was brightly decorated in a painted pattern of red, gold, and green and had an outer edge to keep the mouse in. Laughter surrounded his table, and Clara decided to try her luck. She handed the boy a coin and placed a bet that the mouse would run to the end at number four.

"I want to see, want to see," Lucia said.

Clara lifted the little sunbeam up in her arms and pointed out the mouse on the table.

"Number four, the lady has number four. Any other bets?" the boy called out and pushed his oversized hat from his forehead.

Others followed and placed bets on numbers three, six, and seven. The boy picked up the mouse with one hand and placed the rodent in the middle square. He quickly slipped the other hand into his pocket then placed his thumb on number eight, opposite from Clara's bet. She was sure the mouse could smell the piece of lard he probably had in his pocket, and she could not help but smile as she saw how eagerly the tiny rodent ran with fast, little legs down the corridor to number eight.

"Sorry, no one wins", the boy called out. "More bets? Who wants to guess where the mouse runs?"

Clara thought it was funny but did not want to waste any more coins. She put Lucia down and held her hand as they headed back toward her mother. A woman with rosy cheeks and bushy eyebrows sold poppets on a stand next to the ale tent. Clara bought one, and her heart melted as Lucia clutched the little doll to her chest.

As Clara and Lucia returned to Bess's table, Clara caught sight of the twins standing there. Taran put her mouth next to her sister's ear. She pointed at Bess. Tilla threw her head back and cackled. Clara sighed.

"A poppet? Did Aunt Clara give that to you? You lucky little girl." Bess picked her up and swung the child around then pointed at a foreign-looking couple at a stand a few paces away. "See the Italian couple there, Clara?"

"Yes, do you know them?"

"They come every summer to the fair and sell beautiful cloth. Her name is Lucia."

"Oh, so is that how you chose your daughter's name?"

"Yes, she is a lovely woman. Lucia means light, you know. I thought it suitable."

Suddenly, she looked at Clara with a mischievous grin and said, "I have an appointment with an arrow now." Then she turned to Uncle Samuel. "Do you mind watching the stand for a while? I want to take Clara over to the game field."

"Go ahead. Enjoy," he said, "I know how much you love a good archery contest."

Ever since Bess was young, Uncle Samuel had taken on the role of her deceased father and taught her how to handle both tools and weapons. He had taken her hunting for meat, thus Bess could handle a bow and arrow as well as any man in Rossby. Teaching Clara had not been as easy. Her arms were not as strong and her aim not nearly as precise.

Clara took hold of Lucia's hand, and all three hurried over to the area where the fair games were being played. The competitions had been going on for hours already, but anyone could come throughout the day and have a go at archery, axe throwing, and rope pulling.

They walked past a colorful juggler, a conjurer with a dwarf assistant, and a white-bearded storyteller. Creativity and talent flourished.

On a small stage, four or five local, masked actors were in the middle of a play. Clothed in colorful costumes with limited but innovative decorative exuberance, they performed a comedy. The spectators cheered. Way into the day, the summer light was a blessing, and people were not at all ready to go home. Clara was not alone in wanting the sweet smell of the season to last longer.

She lifted Lucia up on a stone fence and put an arm around the child's waist, so Lucia could safely watch her mother and the other archers on the grassy field. Beyond that, they could see men throwing axes at a man-sized, straw puppet tied to a solid tree trunk.

With the bow and arrow in position, Bess aimed at the straw target and let go. The arrow flew with the speed of a hawk and pierced into the center position on the target. She tried again and a third time with the same remarkable results. Lucia and Clara cheered and clapped and gave her all the praise they could. A couple of competitors shook their heads. Embarrassment mingled with envy. A woman had no place in the games, no doubt. Bess just smiled sweetly and walked contentedly away.

"We should probably get Lucia home," Bess said as they approached her stand and Uncle Samuel. "It's been a long day, and I am about ready for bed, too."

They started packing up the remaining jars and furs. All in all, it had been a profitable day. The extra income would be helpful during the dark winter months.

This time of day, the ale barrels were emptier, people rowdier and louder, and a few fights popped up around the square. Some felt they were cheated as they either sold something too cheaply or bought something too expensive, but most of all, the general population of Rossby were enjoying themselves.

As they lifted the last box onto the carriage, Tilla came running.

"Please, Miss Bess, Taran is sick, and I can't find Dr. Bing-Olsen. My mother is worried. She sent me to find you. Please, come and help my sister." The words came out disconnected, and she drew shallow breaths.

7

The Missing

~~

Bess put down the box immediately and walked over to Tilla and put a hand on her shoulder. "What has happened? Try to calm down, Tilla."

Tilla stood tensely with her arms straight down and fists clenched. "They carried my sister away," she continued. "She does not speak, just moans and makes strange noises. I think she is in pain."

"Where is she now?"

"Two men took her home. She is in our bed."

"Take me to her." Bess turned around. "Uncle Samuel?"

Her uncle replied before she could finish. "I'll take Lucia and the horse and carriage home, Bess," he said. "Go help the girl."

Bess grabbed her black leather bag and looked at Clara questioningly. Clara nodded and followed her and Tilla down Main Street to the Land residence.

Mrs. Land, the maid behind her, met them at the door.

"Finally, there you are. What took you so long? My daughter is dying." Mrs. Land spoke sternly but in a shrilling voice that sounded as if she were singing an opera.

Bess kept calm and asked, "Where is Taran? Please, take me to her."

They were taken into the twins' bedroom. It was lavish with large curtains all the way to the floor. The lacy bedspread was folded at the foot of the bed, and a pale and whimpering Taran lay propped up with two large, down pillows. Her grimaces showed she was in pain, while her mother fussed and walked back and forth, her opera voice continually asking questions, complaining, and accusing everyone she could think of.

"She won't talk to me," Mrs. Land said. "I don't know why she is like this. Is she dying? Don't let my Taran die."

Placing the black leather bag on the floor, Bess sat down on the edge of the bed and felt the girl's forehead.

Taran seemed to be in and out of consciousness.

"Would you please fetch a damp rag, a small bowl with cold water, and an empty bucket?" Bess asked Mrs. Land, who in turn flipped her hand at the maid and continued nagging at Bess.

The maid curtsied and scurried out the door.

Bess carefully turned the cover down and put her ear to Taran's chest then felt her stomach. Being touched on her abdomen appeared painful to the twin. She twisted her body and whimpered louder.

"You are hurting her," Mrs. Land shouted. "Stop it."

Bess looked over at Mr. Land, who stood by the window, watching but not saying a word.

He walked over to his wife, took her gently by the arm, and said, "Come, dear, we should let the woman help her. We can wait in the next room."

The maid knocked on the door, came in and put the requested items down, curtsied again, and all three of them walked out, closing the door behind them.

Once the parents were out of the room, Bess—grateful to be able to concentrate without Mrs. Land's endless comments—looked over at Tilla and asked, "Now, tell me what you two have been up to."

Tilla stared into space.

"I believe she has eaten something that did not agree with her," Bess said to Clara.

"I saw her with the foreign merchants. Maybe she ate or drank something bad with them?"

"That must be it. Who knows what victuals they had brought in their trunks or the state of their foodstuff? If this is food poisoning, it could be serious."

The contents of a small, dark bottle from the black leather bag was the first thing Bess administered to Taran, small sips at a time, then Bess asked Clara to fetch the bucket and hold it next to the side of the bed. Before long, Taran started gagging. Bess pulled her up by the shoulders, and Clara held the bucket up and let Taran vomit. The procedure was repeated a couple more times, until Taran seemed to calm down.

⁓

"What did you give her?" Clara asked, surprised at the rapid effect the syrup had on Taran.

"It's called Ipecacuanha," Bess answered. "It's a plant from Brazil. I bought it from some traders the last few summers. I use the root to make the syrup." She dipped the rag in cold water, wrung it out, then placed it on Taran's forehead.

"How did you learn about it?" Clara placed the bucket on the floor next to the bed.

"I'm always looking for remedies and spend a lot of time with certain tradesmen who bring plants and extracts. Other countries have plants and roots we don't grow here. I want to learn more, so I can be of more assistance to people around here." She put the lid back on the small, glass bottle and slipped it into her bag. "The syrup is a strong remedy for emptying the stomach. I have administered it to myself several times." She pulled the bed cover to the side. "Now, let's get the fever down. She's still too warm. The syrup will cause her to sweat."

Bess washed the girl's face, arms, and feet with the rag several times and asked Tilla to have the maid boil some water for an herbal remedy.

"Do you know what is ailing her?" Tilla asked, obviously still frightened. Her eyes were large and full of questions.

Clara had a hard time not feeling a little sorry for the girl at that moment, considering Tilla was still a young woman with concern for her twin sister. It almost made Clara forget what had happened that day. But she noticed Bess kept the grieving girl at arm's distance, speaking to her in short sentences and trying to get information out of her. Tilla seemed ready to open up and speak when the mother barged through the door. It was as if Mrs. Land had been leaning on the door, which gave way to the weight of her oversized body. She fell on her knees, clearly embarrassed, and got back up with the help of her husband.

"Well," she said through her teeth. "What is with the poor child? Have you anything to say, Bess? Who has done this to my sweet Taran? Someone has obviously cast a spell on her. I have heard about things like that."

Bess explained in simple terms, but Clara could tell her friend's words fell on deaf ears. Bess gave Mrs. Land a small pouch filled with peppermint, fennel, and chamomile—herbs for soothing an upset stomach—and told her to keep the fever down by washing Taran's face and feet with a cloth dipped in cool water. Bess then grabbed her black bag.

"Come and fetch me if Taran gets worse," she said. "Day or night."

"Will she be well?" Clara asked when they were back on the cobblestone street, heading back to the market. "Mrs. Land could have shown a little gratitude, don't you think?"

"She'll be fine," Bess answered. "Mrs. Land, on the other hand, is suffering from pride, and that's not something to be healed with a slug of syrup." She smiled and hooked her arm in Clara's. "No one will ever take responsibility for their own mischievous behavior or wrongdoings. It's always about blaming someone else for his or her ailments. I hear it time and again."

"I am sure you explain the cause of their ailment to them," Clara said.

"Every time, but a common opinion is hard to change with a few words. It's an ingrown attitude of the community to blame others for their misfortune. Sickness is, in their opinion, a form of God's vengeance, a curse, an inheritance, or simply bad luck. It's anything but a result of their own negligence."

"What about pests and diseases?" Clara absorbed Bess's words and compared them to beliefs and attitudes she had been subjected to, eager to learn more.

"Oh, those are hard to contain and control. But I am certain there are ways. I want to know how to stop disease from spreading. I am working on it."

Bess yawned and stretched her back forward, like a cat after a good nap. "My feet ache," she said.

"Will they pay you for your services today?" Clara asked. She thought about how willingly Bess gave her time—day or night. Knowledge had been passed on through several generations of women in Bess's family, and she had spent her whole life learning about medicinal herbs and remedies. She was called a cunning woman.

"Most people give what they can," she answered. "It can be food, goods from their farm, cloth, a bird or rabbit, sometimes money. One boy gave me a toad after I acted as midwife when his little sister was born. Imagine what I could do with that. Cook it and serve for supper, boil a broth with it to use for ailing folks in Rossby, or breed it, and start a toad farm?"

Both laughed as they walked back to Frue Farm, imagining green toads hopping all around the homestead. The town still swarmed with people packing up their stands, trying to earn a few last coins for entertaining, or merely looking for amusement.

"But Mrs. Land," Bess continued, "she usually chooses Dr. Bing-Olsen to tend to her family. I am a last resort, so to speak. A few times, they have asked for me. Mrs. Land will most likely let me choose a few wares from the shop the next time I come by."

"I am sure she doesn't pay you what your services are worth."

"No, probably not, but I won't let people die, by refusing to help them." Bess quickened her stride. "It's late; why don't you spend the night at Frue Farm? Let's hurry. I want to watch Lucia sleeping."

～

"What's up with the twins?" Clara asked, once they had sunk deep into the comfortable couch at Frue Farm.

Luckily, all the remaining goods were stored away just in time before the weather changed. They sat and listened to the gentle sound of raindrops falling on the barrels outside, like thuds when small mallets hit a drum. The wind played with the leaves on the trees in the orchard outside the window.

"Do they hold a grudge against you, or what is it? Are they just cruel?" Clara let her hair out of the restrictive bun in the back of her neck and let it hang freely down past her shoulders. Even though she liked a clean and neat appearance, she was not an every-hair-in-place kind of woman. Wavy hair like hers had a tendency to go where it pleased, and she did not mind if it did. Uniformity made her feel like a sheep. If she were a sheep, she would probably be the tricolored one, happily grazing, not knowing she was different from the rest.

Bess stared out at the soft gray summer evening. "I actually feel sorry for them."

"Sorry? Whatever for?" Clara wrinkled her forehead.

"Can you imagine growing up with Mrs. Land as a mother? They have been groomed early in lessons of scheming and lying. They've watched their mother deal with people around her. Like most children, they have been told how to act and what to say ever since they were old enough to walk. We can only hope they have some of their father's good personality traits in them as well."

"But he's a pushover. He's kind but not strong enough to stand up for what is right and good. Not even in his family."

"But I've been pondering...I think I know what they hold against me."

"I don't see how anyone could hold anything against you, sweet Bess."

Bess poured two cups of chamomile tea. They needed something to calm down after such an eventful day.

"When I was seventeen and you were in the Far East," she continued, "their brother showed an interest in pursuing me."

Clara pulled a small blanket over her legs. "Oh, I remember him. Thorvald, wasn't it? He was a little older than we are. I haven't seen him around since I returned. Did he move out of the village?"

Bess warmed her hands on the teacup and glanced out the window. The heavy clouds lined the sky like a lid on a cauldron and blocked the setting sun. She sat immovable, quiet for a while, then turned to face Clara.

"Thorvald was different from the other boys in some ways. When he made up his mind, he was as determined as a hunter who has just seen a deer in the forest. Do you remember the large lovage plant on the sunny side of the cottage?"

"I remember. It grew taller than us when we were little."

"It's still there. Lovage is a willing herb and gives wonderful flavor to soup and pottage, besides being good for the stomach. My mother used to tell visiting children funny stories about plants and trees in our garden." Her face broke into a smile. "One time," she continued, "my mother told the children about how lovage was used as a love plant in the olden days. One leaf at night under your pillow was all one needed to find a sweetheart the next day. Traveling salesmen sold tea of lovage as a love potion."

"I enjoyed listening to your mother. Her knowledge about nature was fascinating. She had such a great sense of humor and told stories with a twinkle in her eye."

"I know. She made learning fun. I miss her."

"So what happened to Thorvald?"

"It was at the time of the midsummer fair. I went with my mother. We had prepared soaps, dried herbs, dried meat strips. You know, all the wonderful scents and treats my mother was widely known for."

Clara nodded, reminiscing about visiting Bess and her family as a young girl. Her mother had long, wild hair, hanging loose around her shoulders. It was like fire, just like Bess's, only with streaks of yellowish-gray. She was short and quick in her movements, despite a limping gate caused by a broken ankle healed crooked. The cottage was fragranced with the wonderful aromas of herbs and spices, and Clara was always welcomed with a big hug and an honest smile.

Clara's thoughts went back to Thorvald. "The way I remember him, he was an innocent," she said. "A little slower in thought than his peers. Naïve is probably a good description, wouldn't you say?"

"Yes, he was," Bess added. "He was the opposite of his mother and sisters. I believe he was the joy of his father and the shame of his mother."

"Well, I'm not surprised he noticed you. He wasn't the only one, remember? Most of the boys dropped what they held in their hands when you entered a room."

Bess looked down and smiled. "It was a long time ago, Clara. I remember some were scared, too. A woman of nature with a fierce temper intimidated more than a few."

"But Thorvald wasn't? Intimidated, I mean?"

"No, he wanted a girlfriend. He chose me, and that was that. What I wanted was not even a question in his mind; he just assumed the feeling was mutual. He hovered around the booth at the fair that summer. Toward the evening, as mother and I were packing the remainder of our unsold goods into boxes, he approached me and told me to meet him by the hollow oak after I finished at the fair. I told him I had chores to do and animals to feed, but he would not take no for an answer."

"So you went home after the fair, and he still thought you were meeting him at the hollow oak?"

Bess leaned back on the couch and let out a sad sigh. "Yes. He went there anyway, determined I would show up. He stayed there all night, waiting. The next morning, someone found him dead, hanging from a rope on a large branch of the hollow oak, his pockets filled with lovage leaves."

Clara put her hand over her mouth. "That's awful. The poor lad. He did not even think his feelings were not returned."

"I feel his sisters blame me for his death. They have never forgiven me."

"But you didn't do anything wrong."

Bess got up to refill their cups with more hot water from the kettle by the fireplace. "I think they need to keep up appearances by appearing faultless in public."

"But, Bess, this was a long time ago. Surely, they don't still hang on to old accusations and superstitions."

"Oh, it's pretty much the same around here as it has always been. They keep me at a distance, making hurtful remarks behind my back, whispering in the store when I come to buy my groceries, and so on. Rumors and gossip are easy to spread but much harder to gather back together again. It's like spilling milk in a pile of hay. There's no way of getting it back in the bottle again."

"I am so sorry."

"It doesn't matter. My life is full. I don't need every person in town to be my best friend. One only has time for a few trusted and faithful friends, and that, Clara, is as important as a good meal every day."

She handed Clara another cup of steaming-hot tea. This time she had added peppermint leaves to the dried chamomile, and the aroma was delicious. She sat back down and pulled the woolen cover farther over their laps. The chill in the evening air was noticeable. Outside, the rain came down harder, and they sat and listened to the drops hitting the lid of the barrel on the corner of the cottage. Suddenly, Bess jumped up.

"Oh, wait," she explained. "I just have to remove the lid on that water barrel. The time I can save not having to carry water can be used for other fun activities." She winked and gathered a shawl around her shoulders, opened the door, and went outside.

8

The Crucifix

On the south side of town, Taran was still bedridden the morning after her illness. She woke up late as she had been up half a dozen times during the night with stomach pain. Even though her stomach was empty, she still had convulsing cramps that turned into gags and the urge to vomit. Weak and with an ongoing fever, her slender body ached every time she moved.

The maid had not left her side except to empty the waste bucket, to fetch clean rags, or to brew warm drink from the herbs. Taran had finally fallen asleep in the early hours of the morning.

Suddenly, the twin's eyes flew wide open as if she had an epiphany in her sleep. She gazed over at the sleeping maid, snatched a cup from her nightstand, and thrust it at her. It hit the maid's arm.

"You lazy girl," she said hoarsely. "Can you not see I am awake?"

The maid, confused at being awakened so abruptly, rubbed her face, stood up, and curtsied.

"Good day, Miss Taran," she said a bit groggily. "How are you feeling?"

"What do you think? I am bound to this bed with a sick, sick body. Go fetch my sister."

The maid curtsied again and hurried out the door, returning a few minutes later. Tilla opened the door slightly and stuck her head in. She widened her eyes and smiled as she saw Taran sitting in her bed, propped up with several large, down pillows behind her back.

"There you are, finally," Taran exclaimed and waved at her sister to enter.

Tilla scurried over to the bed and hugged her sister.

"You're awake and so much better."

"Don't crush me," Taran said, annoyed.

"I'm just so delighted to find you well, sister," Tilla said, her pretty smile beaming. "How are you faring?"

Taran fidgeted and lifted the cover up and down to let cooler air grace her body. It had been a difficult night, but the tonics Bess had administered had brought her back to health. She knew it was true but would not admit it.

"I am still feeling poorly," she moaned. "No thanks to Bess. She made me feel worse. Typical of her. I vomited and suffered all night long."

"But I thought she could help you," the younger twin said, worried she had made a mistake. "Dr. Bing-Olsen was out of town and I—"

"No matter." Taran looked around the room. "There, grab that chair, and sit next to me. I have been thinking."

Tilla hurried and fetched the chair by the window. "What have you been thinking?" she asked. "Is there anything I can do?"

"I have come up with something we can give to Jacques, the French merchant, next summer at the fair."

"You have? What?" Tilla giggled and wiggled around on the chair.

"It's perfect, but we need to be smart about it. No one must suspect us, and we need a special hiding place for the item." She waved Tilla closer and put her mouth to her sister's ear.

～～

That afternoon Tilla walked through the village of Rossby to see Albert, a young man of seventeen summers who lived and served in Dr. Bing-Olsen's house north of Town Square. Tilla found him quiet and handsome, he was trusted and liked by everyone, and she had often caught him looking at her when he accompanied the good doctor to the Lands' residence.

Rumors were that Albert's father had left when his wife died giving birth to their only child. Still, Albert seemed optimistic, sometimes talking about what he would do when his father one day returned.

Tilla knocked on his door and tapped her foot for a few seconds before Albert slowly opened. He tilted his head and stared at her.

"Hello, Albert." Her chin was coyly down, her eyes looking straight at him.

He stood motionless. "Miss Tilla," he said.

"Albert, I need your help." She pulled him outside by the arm and made him close the door.

"You need me, Miss Tilla? What for?" He put his hands into his pockets.

She looked around to see if anyone was listening then leaned in and whispered, "I need you to help me get something in the church."

"In the church? I don't understand."

"The church door is always open; you only need to go in and get it. No one will know."

"No one will know what, Tilla? What do you need from inside the church? Did you forget something, your shawl, your purse?"

"No, silly." Tilla let out a girlish giggle then said seriously, "I need you to get the crucifix that hangs on the wall on the left side of the altar."

Albert ran his fingers through his thick brown hair.

"Come on, Albert. You look as if the moon has fallen down in front of you."

He scratched the back of his neck. "Miss Tilla, that means stealing. That crucifix belongs to neither you nor me. It belongs to the king or God or someone. I cannot just go and pick it up."

Tilla spoke slowly, accentuating the words. "But it *does* belong to us, Albert. The church belongs to the people. We go *every* Sunday. My father pays enough for benefits in Rossby and plenty in taxes to the king." Tilla put her hand on Albert's arm and smiled charmingly. "Besides," she said, "who really knows what belongs to anyone in this world? Come on, Albert, how about some adventure? Will you do it for me?" She fluttered her eyelashes shamelessly.

Tilla put her hand on Albert's arm. She needed him to melt like butter in the warm sun.

"What do you want it for, Tilla?"

His voice was soft, and she could tell he was mesmerized.

Tilla looked down and let out an impatient breath. Patience was not a virtue she possessed. She was used to having things her way without having to provide explanations. She realized Albert wanted a reason, a motive for the deed she asked of him. He was probably smarter than she had given him credit for.

"Albert," she said with a feigned smile, "no need to worry. We will hide it in a safe place. It will make *us* rich. Trust me."

Albert straightened up and pushed his shoulders back. "I will do it for you," he said.

"Good." She let out a deep, gratifying sigh. "Now let me tell you about my plan."

She whispered in his ear, revealing Taran's plan in detail, leaving out parts unnecessary to a mere aid. Breathing close to his ear, she let him feel she was more than an acquaintance.

～

Albert waited until dark before he made his way through Main Street and up the hill toward the Rossby church. The doctor was still out of town; the other servants were settling down for the night. Sneaking away had been an easy task.

The Town Square lay hushed between the houses with lights in the windows. Albert seldom came out this late, and if he did, he was often in the company of the good doctor or one of the other servants. He was not one to frequent the alehouses or stay out late with friends. The doctor did not appreciate such behavior. Now Albert hurried across the square, looking straight ahead. A couple of singing drunkards tumbled out from the Watering House. A woman hurried down the street. She carried a basket in one hand, a bird cage in the other. A young couple stood by Town Hall, arms entwined, exchanging adoring glances.

Once at the church, he slowed down and made sure he was alone before entering. He did not want to meet the tall gravedigger. He had heard the man dug graves in the cemetery at all hours. The parsonage had a few lighted windows. Not everyone there had gone to bed yet; he had to be careful.

The door squeaked slightly as he tucked his head inside. The chapel was empty, only a mouse ran across the floor in front of him. An eerie feeling came across him as he tiptoed up the aisle, looking around as if saints from previous generations were lurking in the corners or hiding under the pews, waiting for someone to visit the church late at night. The summer evening's cloudless sky squeezed sufficient light through the narrow windows to trace an adequate path toward the chancel.

Albert slowly climbed the steps to the altar. The crucifix hung on the left wall. He had not seen it up close, as he had never been behind the altar, had only kneeled down below the stairs to partake of the sacrament.

He pondered the value of the old relic, carved wood depicting the crucifixion, a leaf and scroll motif gracing the cross. Maybe it had hung here since the church was built. Perhaps the relic was even older, carried to Rossby by men of long ago. It seemed sacrilegious, removing it from the wall.

His thoughts went back to earlier that day. Tilla had chosen him, and he would do anything for her. He slid his fingers over the crucifix before he removed it from the nail and tucked it under his coat. Deed done, he started back.

Tilla had said she would meet him by the two large oaks on the path toward Frue Farm north of Rossby. He had to hurry; he did not want to keep her waiting.

She appeared suddenly from behind a rock by the oak trees and pulled the hood on her black cloak off her head. The long blonde hair glimmered like strands of silver in the soft moonlight.

"Do you have it?" she asked impatiently.

Albert nodded and pulled out the crucifix he had hidden in his coat. He handed it carefully to the young woman, though in his mind he took it back.

"Yes, yes," she said and snatched the wooden cross out of his hand. She turned it over and smiled. "Look, I brought a piece of cloth to cover it. Now we will hide it, and next summer, we will come back. This ridiculous, little, wooden thing will make us rich. Come, I know where to hide it."

He followed her between tall tree trunks and forest green. Birds were already awake, singing cheerfully high in the trees off the trail. Albert tried to push away the guilty feeling inside as he faithfully followed the golden-haired beauty through the woods.

As they approached Frue Farm, Binna came running. Albert stretched his neck to see if anyone at the farm had heard the dog barking. Tilla threw a bone in front of Binna, and Albert let out a long sigh. They were safe for now.

He got the feeling Tilla had been here before. She seemed so prepared, had even brought a treat for the dog. He pushed the thought aside and followed Tilla over to the corner of Bess's orchard.

Next to the wooden fence by the road, Tilla turned to the Albert and said, "Now we make a blood pact."

She pulled a small kitchen knife from her pocket, clutched his pointer finger, and cut a small incision in it. Albert gasped as the sharp blade slit his skin, and drops of blood trickled forth. She did the same with her finger, not saying a word, and then let a drop from both fingers spill onto the cloth with the crucifix.

"Now promise," she said sternly. "Promise you will not tell a living soul about what we have done."

He nodded again, looked at her face adorned with ringlets like those of a fairy.

"Don't just nod, Albert. Say it. Make the promise," she said.

With a whisper, he pledged and then helped her hide the crucifix. They placed it safely under a stone, easily moved with a wooden branch as a lever, before they returned to Rossby and their seemingly innocent lives.

"Aren't you afraid of being out at night," Albert asked as he walked her back.

"No, not really. Taran and I often go out to explore and discover. We like to find out about things."

"What things?" Albert was still confused why young girls were out alone at night.

"Never mind, we just like to collect information."

He accepted her explanation. It did not clarify his curiosity about her but made him even more fascinated with the girl and her ways. She did not seem afraid of being out in the dark, maybe because hardly anyone else was out at that time.

After he had walked Tilla home, Albert sat for hours on the street. He thought about the theft and tried to push his conscience away.

~

Early the next morning, he skulked back up the hill to the cemetery and saw Toomber in the opposite corner digging a grave. Albert slunk to his mother's gravestone and sat down on the grass. Now and then, he turned his head to make sure the gravedigger did not notice him.

Albert's friend from the northern part of town had just died a few days earlier. The boy had been coughing blood and feeling poorly. One day, he passed on. It looked as if Toomber dug a family grave. From what Albert had heard about Toomber, the gravedigger appreciated the income of digging graves, no matter the age of the deceased.

The large man straightened his back and wiped his forehead with his sleeve. Albert stiffened as Toomber walked toward him. He got to his feet and stumbled behind the grave stone, thinking he was safer there, his eyes wide when he noticed the gravedigger stopped next to him.

"This is not a playground," the giant finally spoke. "Go somewhere else."

"I am not playing," Albert said. "I am trying to find out what to do. I thought talking to my mother would help."

"Your mother is dead."

"I know. It just seems like it helps to talk to her. I do it all the time."

"Get out of here," Toomber said gruffly. "Your mother can't hear you."

"But you can," the boy tried again. "Can I tell you?"

"Why tell me?"

"She made me promise not to tell a living soul. I had to bleed to promise. But you are hardly a living soul. You are always here among the dead."

Toomber grunted and turned away. He put the spade straight in the ground. Albert wondered why he seemed offended.

"I have done something wrong," Albert continued. "I have wronged God."

"Speak to the new parson."

"I don't dare. Listen, Toomber, I have stolen the crucifix from the church. God's vengeance will come over me. I am afraid."

Toomber turned around and stared into Albert's eyes.

"I have hidden it by—"

"Stop." Toomber covered his ears with his large hands.

Albert immediately closed his mouth and just gawked at the gravedigger.

"I don't want to know," Toomber said. "Go away. Go now."

Albert glanced at the windows of the Lands' residence as he passed on his way back home.

～

Taran woke up abruptly as someone had grabbed her shoulders, shaking them vigorously. Taran's face was right in front of her eyes.

"Wake up," Taran said. "I want to know how it went last night? Tell me everything."

Tilla stretched and rubbed her eyes. Her night with gullable Albert had been a success. She gladly told the story.

"That's good," Taran grinned. "Now we need to stay low for a while. If we are to get proper things for Jacques, we need to take some risks."

"I don't like that merchant," Tilla whined. She dropped her legs off the side of the bed and let her feet search for her slippers on the floor.

"I don't, either, sister, but you must admit it's more exciting than snatching honey cakes from stands at the fair. If we can get hold of a few more items like the crucifix, Jacques will be pleased with us and we can have some coins in our pockets."

Tilla had to admit that making money this way sounded tempting. Her twin sister was always inspirational. She orchestrated and Tilla played along.

"Now," Taran said, helping Tilla pull her nightgown off. "I need to continue feeling poorly for a fortnight or so."

"That long?"

"You're right. That would be boring. A couple of days will do. You, of course, will have to accompany me, read to me, and comfort me when I need it."

Tilla giggled. "I think I can do that," she said. "I'm good at sitting still and doing nothing."

"Exactly," Taran said with a devious smile. "This should work really well. The crucifix will stay safe at Frue Farm until the fair next summer. No one will expect it's there."

~~~

A few days later, as planned, Tilla and her seemingly recuperated sister, Taran, stood outside the store eating honey cake. Their thoughts were not on Albert. He was merely a tool, a means to get their hands on the crucifix.

As they lingered on the steps, Laura walked by. The mother carried little Bess and had a couple of children running around her skirts. The twins looked slyly at each other and made their way in between folks bustling to and fro to talk to her.

"Hello Laura, how are you today? We haven't seen you for a while," Taran said, smiling.

"Miss Taran. Miss Tilla." Laura took a step back.

"We just wanted to see your baby. Oh, she is beautiful." Tilla pulled on the blanket to see the infant better.

"What are you doing?" Laura asked. She turned away from the twins and clutched the child in her arms.

"Don't worry, Laura," Taran answered reassuringly, "We just want to look."

Laura faced the twins.

Tilla lifted the blanket aside and found what she was looking for. Little Bess had a mole on her left leg.
~~~

For a moment Tilla forgot herself and said excitedly to her sister, "I knew it. It's there, just like the innkeeper said."

"Innkeeper Hansen? What are you talking about?" Why is my child the talk of the town?"

"The innkeeper came to see father yesterday. We overheard them talking about signs of evil," Taran said with a smug smile.

"My child is not evil, and certainly not important enough to have councilmen make conversation about her." Laura pulled the cover tighter around her young daughter.

Taran laughed. "No, he did not talk about your infant in particular," she said. "They were just discussing possible outcomes and eventual circumstances."

Laura shook her head. "You speak words larger than your understanding," she said. Her face looked worried now. "What do they want with me?"

"Nothing, we think," Taran answered. "We say it's more a problem with the person who acted as midwife. Have you had any other difficulties?"

Laura stood perplexed. "What strange notions are you unfolding?" she asked. "Little Bess has had stomach cramps frequently, more than my other children, but it—"

Taran interrupted her. "Potions and herbal concoctions that perhaps harmed the child? What say you, sister?"

She turned toward Tilla, who grinned and nodded.

Tilla patted Laura gently on the arm. "Why don't you and the children come to our store for some of Old Magda's delicious honey cake?"

Tilla felt the need to cover up for any curious behavior and was pleased with herself as Laura's young ones skipped joyously into the store. The mother followed closely behind, a little more apprehensive.

"Can you believe it?" Taran said in a low voice, her eyes beaming. "Of all the children we checked today, Laura's newborn carries the mark."

Tilla was equally enthusiastic. "Let's go write it down in our journal. I know someone who will be interested in our discovery."

9

The Introduction

~

The days after the fair, Clara walked about the parish and talked with anyone who would take the time to listen. Her attempt at encouraging education and learning skills, such as reading, writing, and numbers, received diverse responses, varied as the clouds above her head. Even though she had gathered enough children to teach once or twice a week, there were more in need of schooling. Boys did better in finding employment if they were literate. Girls were better prepared for widowhood or attaining respect in the community if they were learned, if only a little. She even encouraged grown men and women to come visit her classroom in the small house by the church. The council had agreed to pay her a modest wage for educating the poor and needy, though her class had children from various backgrounds. Mrs. Land, in lack of a tutor at the time, had asked Clara to teach her children twice a week at home. Clara had tried to persuade her to put the twins in the classroom with the rest of the pupils, but Mrs. Land would not hear of it.

"My lovelies will not sit with nitwits and scoundrels who have their hair full of lice and no shoes and socks on their feet," she said. "I will pay you well."

Mrs. Land was used to having her way. Clara thought about it and decided the salary was good, and she might perhaps have an opportunity to teach the twins one or two good things in life.

"Recruiting children for school will be an ever ongoing process," Clara said as she entered the main house at Frue Farm late in the afternoon. She threw the books onto the table and looked around to see where Bess was. She sat in the corner on the floor crying.

"Bess, what is the matter? What has happened?" Clara kneeled down on the floor next to Bess and took her hands.

Bess did not respond.

"Hey, Bess, what is it?" Clara asked tenderly and stroked her friend's flowing hair.

Bess lifted her large green eyes. They were tearful, and her cheeks wet. "I'm sorry, Clara, I just feel sad."

"No need to apologize. Why are you crying, Bess?"

"Mychel. I miss my Mychel. He's been gone too long. We are used to him being at sea for weeks at a time, but he should have been back by now. I am worried."

"When did you expect his return?"

"In time for the fair. He usually helps me out. I missed him being there with us, and I pine for him now." She looked down at her stomach. "I know I'm with child, and I'm sensitive and..."

"No, Bess. You have the right to worry and to grieve. This is me, remember? You don't have to hide your feelings and thoughts."

"I know. Having you here has made the time he is away fly by faster."

Bess started to get up, and Clara pulled her arms to help.

"I weigh as much as a bear now, don't I?" Bess wiped her cheeks and straightened out her apron.

A jar of hyssop with bright-blue flowers sat on the table. Bouquets of the herb had already been picked before blooming, to enhance the remedial outcome. They were hanging from the rafters in the barn to dry. Clara had seen Bess administer the herb to people with breathing problems, also when children lacked the will to eat. Bess aimlessly rearranged the stems in the glass jar then walked across the room to stir the pot above the open fire.

"Yes, you do," Clara said, teasing her. She gathered the books on the table and put them onto a chair. The aroma of Frue Farm cooking floated past, and she knew Bess would want to set the table soon.

"What were you saying as you came in?" Bess asked.

Clara did not want to seem insensitive to her friend's needs but wanted to answer her question. Bess had started chopping an onion, which only made her eyes water even more.

"Earlier today, I walked by the cottages right north of here—you know the ones closer to the ocean," Clara said.

Bess nodded but kept silent. Clara continued.

"There were lots of children there."

"Yes, we call their mothers the fishing widows. All three women lost their husbands a few summers ago."

"What happened?"

"The fishermen were on the same boat. It was a clear day, the ocean calm. They just disappeared."

"Disappeared? What do you think happened?"

"Nobody knows. They never returned. Rumors circulated that they *chose* not to return, that they left their families."

"What do you think?"

"It puzzles me. I didn't know them well, but I don't want to believe that my Mychel chose to leave us." Tears rolled down her cheeks again. She took a deep breath and slowly let go.

Clara got up and hurried over to Bess, wrapping her trembling shoulders in a warm embrace.

"Bess, don't even think for a moment that Mychel would do that. Who could leave you? From what you have told me about your husband, he loves you and Lucia. He will return, Bess. He will be back. You have to believe that."

"Believe?" She pushed her hair back. "That has always come naturally to you, hasn't it? It's as if you were born with a testimony of spiritual matters. I am glad you always remind me of how important faith can be."

"Mychel will be back, Bess," Clara said, trying to comfort her friend. "I will pray for it every day."

"Thank you, Clara."

The wooden floorboards in the loft above creaked. Bess looked up and wiped her tears. Lucia awoke from her afternoon nap. Bess got up to help the child down the ladder.

"Me do," Lucia protested, wanting to make the climb all alone.

Bess reached out her arms in case the child tripped.

Clara grinned. "Just like her mama. You still don't ask for help either, Bess."

"Oh, she can climb down by herself. That's a willful little girl. I have no idea where she got it." Bess rolled her eyes. The corners of her sweet mouth turned up. "It's when she is half awake, like now, I am afraid she could trip and fall. She is not even three summers old, and already we disagree."

Clara shook her head and smiled back. She remembered little Bess, a headstrong instigator, who more than once had gotten them into amusing and sometimes difficult situations. Once trapped, she had always stared at Clara with a serious look and said, "What do we do now?"

Clara helped Bess get the meal on the table. Broth heated in the iron pot hanging over the open flames. Peas, lentils, and onions were added to the warm potage. Lucia whined, and Bess sat down to comfort her daughter, while Clara stirred the soup.

"Tell me more about Mychel, Bess. He must be special to have captured your heart."

Her eyes smiled dreamily. "He smells of fish," she said.

"Smells of fish?" Clara started giggling. "That's the first thing you can think of?"

"It's a good thing, Clara. Don't tease. That smell means he has work, and work means an income. Besides, he is happy with his choice of work. The men in his family have been fishermen for generations."

"What else?"

"He is kind and thoughtful, and for some strange reason loves me for the woman I am. He puts up with me, my temper and all, opinionated and stubborn as I can be."

"You do have one or two sweet qualities, also, you know."

"You're still teasing, Clara. Well, he sees things his way. I don't know, I guess he loves me for loving him."

"Good on you, Bess. You are far better than any of the women in Rossby. Let's be optimistic and plan ahead for your husband's return."

Bess hugged Lucia tightly. "I just want him to come home," she said.

***

The next day, a crow sat right in front of Clara in the middle of the road by Frue Farm. It stared intently, as if looking straight into her soul. Without words, the bird told her about hunger and need, as if it knew she had a small piece of bread in her pocket. She took it out, broke off a morsel, and threw it forward. The crow picked it up and gawked at her with grateful eyes. Then it flew away.

Bess laughed heartily when Clara told her what she had experienced. "So you speak with birds now, do you?" she asked.

Throughout her whole life Clara had loved birds. They were varied and interesting to her. Some were colorful, others rather subdued, almost dull in appearance. There were birds that were predators and hunters; others were funny or cute. The Far East had birds with large beaks, long, thin legs and amazing colors. She wished she could have brought some for Bess to see.

Clara's father spoke in a sermon once about the baptism of Jesus and how the Holy Ghost descended as a dove. She sat mesmerized and listened to how he enlightened the congregation with his simple explanations of the scriptures.

"What is it with you and flying creatures?" Bess asked and narrowed her eyes in amusement. "Let's see, there were stories of fairies when we were little, now stories about crows or any old bird. Next you will want to fly yourself, huh?"

Clara chuckled and flung her arms up and down as she ran around in circles. "Wouldn't that be something? I could fly, Bess, like a bird."

Lightheaded and giddy Clara had to sit down not to fall over. Bess laughed and handed her a large piece of cheese.

Clara took a bite and said, "I also weigh too much, you know. I will have to eat less cheese or I will never get off the ground." She chomped a large bite and enjoyed the flavor of caraway seeds, a specialty of Frue Farm.

"I went to the harbor today," Bess said.

Clara helped her hang up clean laundry on the wash line on the south side of the house. She handed her one of Uncle Samuel's shirts.

"I contacted anyone I thought could have heard about Mychel and his boat, mainly fishermen and sailors," Bess said.

"What did you find out?" Clara spoke with her mouth full of cheese, eager to hear any news.

"Nothing. No one had seen him or heard from him. But there were a few optimistic seamen who told similar stories about the return of fishermen after months away at sea."

"Then that's what we will believe in—his safe return—only a little tardy."

"You are still praying for him, Clara?"

"Every day."

"Good, that comforts me. You know I'm not as good as you about that."

Clara handed her the last shirt and asked, "How about if I help you write a letter to hang up on the docks, requesting information from any boat or trading ship that could have seen Mychel? I could ask if they would consider mentioning it in the town council as well."

"Oh, could you? Anything we can do to find out. He has to come home to us. I am not ready to be a widow with two young children."

Clara put the basket in the corner of the main room and fetched a piece of paper and a quill. Lucia played with her poppet on the floor and Bess sat down next to her.

"Thank you, Clara," Bess said with grateful eyes brimming with tears. "Please, bring a piece of cheese home. There's plenty and I know how much you enjoy it."

Clara hugged her. "I promise I will help you get the word out that Mychel is missing."

As Clara returned home, she met Herr Christopher on his way out of the front gate. With steady paces, as lengthy as his long legs could comfortably handle, he marched forward. He looked determined, his fists clenched, and his brow furrowed. She could not help but ask him what the problem was.

"Herr Christopher, what is wrong?" she asked and put the sack with books and the cheese from Frue Farm on a rock outside the fence.

The parson halted and took a deep breath. "The crucifix is gone. I believe it has been stolen. Who would do that? I have never had anything taken from the church."

"Gone? That's terrible." Clara put her hand to her mouth. "Have you asked around? Are there any witnesses?"

Herr Christopher shook his head. "No, none. I have asked the people here at the parsonage, but no one knows about it."

"Do you have any idea who the culprit is?"

"No, and I don't want to make accusation east and west. I am on my way to Town Hall to let the council know. Holy items should be left alone."

"Is the church still unlocked?"

He nodded. "I want it to stay that way. It should not be necessary to lock up the house of God."

"I agree. I have never heard of anything taken from there before."

"Well, I had better get down there," Herr Christopher concluded. "They are busy men, but they need to hear about this."

"Of course, I hope it turns up soon."

She watched him leave. He looked straight ahead, not taking the time for the customary nod and greeting the parishioners were used to. Clara knew how the townspeople expected clergy to be better than others. It was as if they thought their vocation made them more exalted than the average citizen, not prone to breaking any of the Ten Commandments or even misbehaving. Two women turned their heads as he passed them. Clara noticed their puzzled faces. No doubt, they were curious as to why he did not address them with a warm hello or even respond when they looked him in the face as he approached them.

"Why did he ignore us," the woman with a flat hat, which looked like someone had pulled it too far down over her ears, asked the other. "Herr Christopher should behave like the head of the church in Rossby."

The other woman pointed a finger in the air and said, "That, good woman, is because he is not the head, but rather the *headache* of our town."

They hit their thighs with their palms and threw their heads back and cackled.

Discourteous gossip, Clara thought and turned to walk home. Tomorrow was Sunday. Maybe somebody had news about the stolen crucifix then.

〰

The Sabbath Day was special to Clara. She enjoyed a day different from the rest of the week. Her parents had taught the importance of taking time to smell the flowers. Besides, it gave every person in Rossby a break from the toils and hard work of everyday life.

There is much wisdom in having a day of rest, she thought. God must have known and decided every seventh day should be unlike the rest.

She opened the front door to let Ami in. He had been out hunting all night. Two fat mice lay on the doorstep and he looked proud about it. Clara patted him and noticed how much he had grown lately. He purred and rubbed against her leg like only cats do, before running over to slurp the water she had poured into his bowl by the fireplace.

Clara hurried with breakfast, dressed in her Sunday best, and walked the path to the parsonage. She continued out the front gate and turned right where the old, brick church stood proudly in the morning sun. Bess and Lucia were going to meet her by the church, and Clara did not want to be late. She arrived early and watched the parishioners arriving from near and far, either by foot or by horse and carriage. As she grew up, her father stood on the right side of the stairs in front of the large church door and greeted everyone. He would ask them how they were faring and made sure every person felt welcome. Clara stood on the left side and watched him with others. It was a schooling all on its own. His compassionate way with young and old, his ability to feel empathy, and his wisdom as he offered his advice were all valuable lessons for her. She was shy and loved burying her face in her books, writing stories, or playing at Frue Farm with Bess, but she hoped to be more like her father. Maybe one day…

There was Bess. Uncle Samuel and Lucia were chasing each other around a tall oak. Clara walked up to Bess and kissed her cheek.

"Uncle Samuel is trying to wear Lucia out," Bess said. "Hopefully, she will be more reverent during the sermon."

"Are you sure he won't be the one to fall asleep?" Clara asked, giggling. "He's already panting like a hound on a warm day."

"Let's get those two and go inside. I'm tired just from walking over here today."

"Just wait a few more months, Bess. You'll be as round as a ball of hay and we'll have to carry you around."

She grinned and pushed Clara in front of her on the stairs. They greeted Herr Christopher, and Clara asked him quietly if he had any news about the stolen crucifix. He shook his head and said nothing, so they went inside to find seats on a pew to the left.

Clara turned around to look at the congregation of faces, familiar and unknown. Some were in church with a deep Christian belief and a desire to do what was right. Some came every Sunday to be seen or acknowledged. Others wanted to believe but did not know how. Maybe some did not have a choice.

In the back she spotted Toomber. Her father had taught him to put aside his toil and work to be fed spiritually. Clara had heard the gravedigger did not like being crammed in a room with townspeople, it made him uncomfortable to be crushed and squeezed into a corner like a mouse with an open-jawed, drooling cat. Out of respect for the parson, Toomber came every Sunday but arrived late and stood in the back, right next to the door, ready to escape if anyone came too near. Not that they voluntarily moved too close, anyway. His clothes were dirtier than most, his baths less frequent, his manners less than gratifying. Unless someone needed his services, he was left alone.

She noticed Laura by the door in the back. She had just arrived and let a family pass before she kneeled down on the threshold.

"Look, there's Laura with her new daughter. Has it been forty days already?" Clara leaned over and whispered to Bess.

Bess smiled affectionately. "Little Bess is so sweet. I must admit there's a special place in my heart for all the children I have helped deliver. Forty days, you say? Yes, it must have been that long. Laura is a God-fearing woman. She would not be out in public before her days of cleansing were over."

"The parents probably had the infant home christened. She had a rather rough beginning, remember? They would have wanted her safe from any evil."

"She looks strong now, though," replied Bess proudly.

Just then the organ started playing, and they straightened up in their seats and looked toward the altar and the minister in the front. Lucia pulled on her mother's sleeve, and Bess looked down at her, whilst putting a finger on her smiling lips to teach her daughter reverence in church. The child held the poppet in her lap and started playing with its long, woolen yarn hair as the congregation joined in the singing of the opening psalm.

After the first hymn, Herr Christopher walked back to Laura, who rose and walked with him up the aisle. According to tradition, three women, all close relatives and neighbors, accompanied her. The minister motioned for her to sit next to her husband and children on the fourth pew and then returned to the pulpit to continue the service. The three other women joined their families.

The more Clara had come to know Herr Christopher, the more she liked him and appreciated his work in the parish. She noticed her father's perception of him had been correct. Men of the clergy had often been in and out of their home. She would not call all of them men of God. The ministry paid well, often with a parsonage to live in. A parson was admired by young and old and his opinion revered to and judgment respected. No wonder it attracted different kinds of men. But Herr Christopher, like her father, was a Christian man who served others, not expecting anything in return. Both of them truly loved their parish and their lives were devoted to the well-being of the parishioners.

Lucky town of Rossby, she thought. Other small towns were led by servants of deity who did not put God first.

Herr Christopher's positive philosophy about life and death flourished in his words this Sunday morning. The prayer of gratitude was also a request for blessings and protection of the newborn child of Mathias and Laura as a member of the fold. An affirmative "Amen" came from the congregation. They seemed to feel uplifted and encouraged that doomsday was still a distance away. But there were some who shook their heads. One man had fallen asleep, and a neighbor's elbow nudged him rudely in the side, so he could join in the last amen.

Some women in town brought hyssop to church on Sunday to wave back and forth under their husbands' noses in case they should doze off in the middle of the sermon. Sleeping in church was not looked upon lightly by the fire-and-brimstone devotees.

"We will have a change in the remainder of our program today. Instead of a concluding hymn, we will be privileged to hear a duet from Taran and Tilla Land, accompanied by Lucas on violin." Herr Christopher closed his Holy Bible, placed it carefully on the altar, and sat down on the high-backed, embroidered chair on the left, hands folded in his lap, ready to enjoy the musical performance. He waved to the twins to come forward and stand in front of the pulpit.

Clara enjoyed the performance. The twins had angelic voices, no doubt about that. Their musical perception seemed a rare talent. The utter confusion was how anyone with such a sweet countenance, could actually be so devious and sly.

Mrs. Land watched her daughters, her chin a little higher than most, a satisfied smile on her face. Her proud husband nodded his head to the left and then to the right, and beamed to anyone who might be looking at him.

The twins finished with a curtsy and walked back down to sit with their parents. Mrs. Land, head back and eyes half closed, smiled smugly, while her husband stood up to make room for the girls to sit down.

Herr Christopher then called the congregation to come and partake of the sacrament. Laura and her three followers were among those who went up to partake as part of the initial introduction back into the fold of the church after giving birth. Bess and Clara kept their eyes on Laura.

"I am so grateful we could help Laura and that precious child," Bess said. "Today is a special day."

Laura kneeled down at the altar, opened her mouth, and let Herr Christopher administer the holy sacrament to her. Clara looked over at Mathias, who was busy keeping his little ones reverent.

At the conclusion of the Sunday worship and blessings for a prosperous week, Uncle Samuel lifted Lucia and carried her outside. Bess and Clara sat for a while in the middle of the commotion as everyone prepared to leave.

Clara liked watching people as they left the chapel after the Sunday sermon. Some were happy to have a day to rest and some were looking forward to a meal of meat and potatoes. Others went home to the burdens of everyday life and brought along the words of Herr Christopher, choosing to let his message uplift or frustrate them. Every face had a story, every parishioner a soul, and each person a secret.

They got up to greet Laura and congratulate her. Friends and neighbors surrounded her and Mathias, shaking their hands and welcoming her back. As they approached, Laura suddenly turned her back and pushed her way out amongst the crowd of people, clutching the child in her arms. Bess gently took hold of Mathias's arm to talk to him, but he pulled his arm away from her and walked rapidly out of the church, his children following close behind.

Bess gave Clara a perplexed look, her eyes questioning without saying a word. Clara knew her thoughts, even though they did not understand what was going on or why. In silence they waited, as if an explanation appeared if they wanted it enough. Eventually, Bess hooked her arm in Clara's and walked out. Laura and her family had already left. Clara and Bess started dejectedly on their way back to Frue Farm.

When they were on their own, Clara could not keep quiet any longer. "What happened back there?" she asked.

"I'm not sure. I keep wondering what I could have said or done to offend them in any way." Bess pushed the bonnet off her head and let it hang loose on her back. Her untamed hair flowed out, happy to be free again.

"Bess, I saw how grateful they were when you saved their infant's life. You probably saved Laura's life as well."

"Yes, it was actually much worse than I let them know. We could have lost them both."

"They were so blessed to have you come and help them that night."

"Something has happened, Clara."

"Or someone—"

"Who? What do you mean?"

"I will do some research. There is a reason for such behavior, and I am going to find out. I am certain two angelic church singers have something to do with it."

〜

Ami sat outside the homestead as Clara returned that evening. He proudly presented a dead mouse on the doorstep. Torn between praising his hunting abilities and wanting to scold him for bringing rodents to the front door, Clara patted his head and let him inside. The mouse was lifeless; it would do no harm.

She pulled out some books from the shelves between the windows in the main room. Inherited from her mother she found adventure novels in French, depicting dramatic piracy and maidens in distress. There were comical books, like Cyrano de Bergerac's stories of utopias and magical places, even lands of the sun and the moon. Clara's favorite book from her mother's collection was a French translation of the second part of a Spanish novel about Don Quixote, a chivalrous old man who believes he is a knight and goes out into the world to find adventure, but learns about life's realities, instead.

Her collection of books had grown since she had returned to the parsonage. Herr Christopher had let her go through some of the volumes her father had left behind. She now had copies of plays by the wonderful English author called Shakespeare, sonnets and poems by various poets, even a book of religious poetry by the Danish author Arrebo. Even though Clara loved literature in diverse forms, she was selective and did not want to fill her head with disparaging thoughts. Once in her mind, it was difficult to forget or remove. Choosing learning and uplifting works became a habit, and she enjoyed the challenge.

The old Bible inherited from her father was already on the table. It was printed about thirty summers earlier and named after King Christian IV. She sat down and started flipping pages.

"By their fruits, ye shall know them," she read out loud, trying to understand the wisdom from the scriptures that a good tree could not possibly bring forth bad fruit and vice versa. *Beware of false prophets in sheep's clothing* was another phrase she had marked before, easy to find.

With her head full of words and theories, she put a blanket around her shoulders and decided to go for a walk to the shore.

An owl hooted from the large oak by her fence. It startled her, its immense eyes wide open, breathing the night air, keeping watch in case anyone passed by its tree. The owl was more likely looking for mice and lemmings running unattended in the late hours—or early hours—she didn't know but imagined the owl said, "I'm keeping to myself. I don't want company."

Then why the hooting? she thought. *Why attract any attention at all?*

The moonlight shone from a clear sky throwing beams of soft-glowing light on solid stones and tangling roots. The sun drew nearer. Nights were short and gentle at this time of year.

The waves moved rhythmically and tenderly on the sand and rocks on the beach. Narrow white streaks of foam on their tips reminded Clara of thick cream crowning the buckets of milk from the parsonage cows. She sat down on a large rock, her legs up to keep dry from the never-ending waves that licked the shoreline.

"Where are you, Mychel?" she said, looking out at the sea. "We need you here right now."

Clara pulled the woolen blanket tighter and looked around at the slanted trees and bushes that had witnessed years of storms, clutching their roots in the ground below seaweed and sand. Like these, she had to stay strong, too, and hold on to her roots, her faith, and what was good in life. She fell asleep praying and woke up hours later to the sound of crying seagulls following the incoming fishing boats.

Safely home, Clara found Ami meowing by the door and picked him up. "I'll bring you to school today," she said. "The children will learn to write words like cat, mouse, and hungry. Ami closed his eyes and purred. Clara held him close. "You are such a good little kitten. I'm glad you are here."

～

After school as Clara came around the bend of the road, right by the large rock by the parsonage, she met an old man with a long white beard. He had a walking stick in his hand and a wide-brimmed hat on his head, which made his narrow face seem pointy like a mouse.

"There's a lot of weather today," he said with a cheerful countenance.

"Yes, Clara answered. "It's a little windy, but the air is wonderfully fresh."

The white-bearded man stopped and looked at her, the cheerfulness gone. He planted his walking stick on the hardened dirt road and leaned on it with both hands. "Oh, there's a storm brewing, alright, and it's more than just wind," he went on. "We are in for some stormy days."

Somehow, Clara knew he was not talking about the weather. Typhoons with strong, deafening winds sometimes destroyed coastal villages in the Far East. Then and there, she got the feeling a tempest approached Rossby.

She walked down the last hill into town, passed the bakery, and found her way to Lands' store. A small bell on a metal rod attached above the door announced her arrival as she entered. Mrs. Land appeared from the storage room behind the counter and asked if Clara needed any assistance.

"Hello, Mrs. Land. I need some material for an autumn dress and would like to look at some bolts of fabric to see if you have something similar to what I have pictured in my mind."

Mrs. Land had a table with various pieces laid out in the corner by the window.

"It's for a Sunday dress," Clara said and walked over to look at what was on the table. "Preferably dark blue, if you have some."

"I will go in the back and find some more," Mrs. Land insisted. "I believe I have just what you are looking for, nice cornflower-colored taffeta to bring out the blue in your eyes."

There was much to say about Mrs. Land and her manners or her lack of neighborly kindness. She was a clever storekeeper and knew the trades and ways of a profitable sale. As Clara waited for her return, in came Innkeeper Hansen and Dr. Bing-Olsen eagerly engaged in a conversation with Mr. Land. Clara didn't mean to listen in, unnoticeable as she was in the corner behind the table of fabrics, but they stopped by the counter and were speaking loud enough for anyone to hear. She could not believe her ears. They were discussing the forthcoming arrival of an English witch-finder.

Councilman Hansen spilled the news. "His name is Angus Hill and he was taught in his youth by the eminent Witch-finder General, Matthew Hopkins himself. He is a trained physician, but has put his career on hold to safeguard Christianity and goodly folks."

"A fellow Doctor of Medicine. How appropriate. We will welcome him gladly," Dr. Bing-Olsen stated enthusiastically.

Bing-Olsen was not really an educated physician. There were only four or five holding that title in the whole country, but he liked to present himself as such, having apprenticed in Christiania with a Danish doctor. Titles were important to the men of the town council, and helpful in making a distinguished, if not completely honest, impression.

The innkeeper straightened his thin, little body and put his chin up. "Since our council meeting in May, I have searched diligently to find someone with a good reputation for seeking out witches."

"He sounds like a highly regarded man, Hansen. Well done." Dr. Bing-Olsen, enthusiastic as ever, spoke as if a witch-finder was the answer to any problem in Rossby.

The arrogant look on the innkeeper's face could not be mistaken. Clara could tell he was full of pride for his research and accomplishments, and for having hiring someone to cross the English channel and come northward to their little community.

Mr. Land added, "It will do us all good to finally cleanse out the evil persons from our community."

What in the world? Clara felt her jaw drop and desperately moved rolls of dress material back and forth, pretending to be occupied. The three men must have finally noticed her presence because they started whispering. Too bad. At this point, Clara wanted to hear what else they were saying. She strained her ears to decipher their low voices, but only caught a few scattered words...witches...protect...smoke out...evil...

Mrs. Land came out from the back room and carried a large bolt of beautiful blue material. She was right. It was the color of cornflowers bathed in sunshine. The Okinawan women Clara had seen used color combinations in unconventional ways, in comparison to the strict rules of traditions and dress codes in this colder climate. Narrow silk frocks in analogous hues of yellow, orange, and light red complemented the seasons of flowers and warmth in the sub-tropical climate. The practical women of Rossby were bound by fierce weather changes and cool winds. The colors of everyday wear were subdued and dull in contrast to the kimonos of Okinawa. Clara pulled herself together and tried to concentrate on the purchase.

"This is lovely, Mrs. Land. How much?"

Mrs. Land was good at her job and had an impeccable sense of style and fashion. She especially liked customers who could pay right away. Clara asked her how her daughters were faring in their school work. She grinned proudly and bragged freely about their recent project. You would think, by the way she explained, it was extraordinary that two girls of fourteen summers could read and write. But she was their mother. Boasting was mandatory to her. As a teacher Clara enjoyed the progress of her students, even if she did not agree with their extracurricular activities. She paid for the dress material, some ribbon, and thread, and then bid Mrs. Land farewell.

On the way home Clara could not stop thinking about what she had heard inside the store. She couldn't wait to tell Bess about it, but first, she needed to find Herr Christopher. Had the council forgotten to mention this news to him? The little respect they showed him was pitiful. They were proud and lofty and repeatedly made decisions before they heard the parson's opinion. Herr Christopher was meek and soft-spoken. They stepped on him like a toad in the middle of the road and kicked him into the gutter.

Countries in southern Europe still clung to the faith of the church before the Reformation. The clergy was more controlling, more authoritative. They owned the church, not like here, where king and nobility were the influential factors.

Herr Christopher and Sara sat in the garden under the large oak tree as Clara approached the shady grass. The parson pulled a nearby chair closer and asked her to join them. It was a warm day, and the cool shade with the subdued colors was a refuge to body and soul.

"May I speak freely?" Clara asked as she sat down. She placed her basket and purchases carefully on the ground.

"Asking to speak freely usually means wanting to utter an opinion, most often a contradictory one," Herr Christopher answered.

Sara handed her a glass.

"I am hoping we will have the same opinion about this matter," Clara continued.

"What is ailing you, Clara?"

"Have you heard about the arrival of an English witch-finder here in our town?"

"Yes, I have, just this morning. I have been told he will come by ship Saturday."

"Well? What do you think about it?"

"I don't believe he will find anyone to accuse in Rossby. I know these people. This is a community of good men and women. We don't have any witches."

"But you don't have to be a witch to be condemned by the likes of him."

"What do you mean, Clara? Do you know of this man?"

"I know about his predecessor, Matthew Hopkins. I have a friend, an Irish missionary called Peter. He was a young man in England at the time the Witch-finder General Matthew Hopkins travelled the English countryside condemning innocent people. Peter told me about the hurting, torturing, and killing. Hopkins had followers. Angus Hill was one of them and has learned from him. He is his successor. Do you see what this means?"

Clara was so upset and spoke in brief sentences without pausing. A dozen thoughts ran through her mind, scaring her, worrying her. Herr Christopher sat silent as the grave with his face in his hands.

It was Sara who finally broke the silence. "What can we do to prepare ourselves for this? Christopher, you have to stop them. You must watch over the parish."

"I will speak with this Angus Hill, when he arrives. But first, I will speak with the town council. Surely, they will behave like Christian men."

Clara was not comforted as she walked back to the cottage. The old man with the white, long beard was right. A storm approached. There were unsettled days ahead.

10

The Presage

Saturday morning, Taran snuck into her father's study and opened the middle desk drawer. Paper, pen, and ink were taken out and put into a small bag. Closing the drawer quietly, she tiptoed out of the room, taking a last look to see if everything was left the way it should be. Then she walked down the staircase into the drawing room where her mother sat.

"Mother, Tilla and I are ready to go for honey now," she said sweetly.

"Thank you, my dears." Mrs. Land pulled a few coins out of her pocket and put them into Taran's open hand. "Here you are. Now be careful. Walk properly, like ladies, and come home straight away when you have finished." She tilted her head to the side and smiled at her daughters. "I can send the maid, you know. I don't know why you two always insist on buying the honey every time, but it's good of you."

"Mother, we only want to help. We know how much the servants have to do, besides we like the walk over to Old Magda's place.

"Do you have a bag to carry the honey in?" the mother asked.

"Yes, mother, we are ready, bag and money. Goodbye."

"Goodbye, my dears. Don't lose the money." She kissed them both on the cheeks and went back to her embroidery.

Out on the street, the twins hurried along, up the road past the parsonage and from there toward Magda's homestead in the woods not far from the abbey.

The old woman sat outside the little house when they approached half an hour later. She sorted piles of wooden sticks into different sizes. She stood up when she saw the twins coming.

"There you are again," she said cheerfully. "Need more honey?"

"Yes, Magda, and we thought you needed more help with your writing."

"You are such good girls. Yes, I have need for some more help with my writing. Please, come inside."

The girls went into the cottage. The floorboards creaked and light came in along the base of the left side of the door, where the floor and wall did not meet. It was a welcoming spot for mice, squirrels, and any little forest animal that wanted to find morsels of food to eat or a little shelter on cold winter days.

"Please, come, come." Magda beckoned and showed the girls where they could sit by the table. "You brought the writing stick and paper with you?"

"Yes, we have all we need. Do you want the same words as last time?"

Magda spoke each word slowly and repeated every sentence to make sure they understood correctly. Pleased with the result she said, "I will only be a minute. I have the honey out in the shed."

Tilla, who still had some words to write, looked up at her sister standing next to her.

Taran rolled her eyes and said, "No need to make it pretty. The old hag doesn't know what you are writing anyway. Maybe the people who receive the cards don't even know how to read."

"Well, I still want to do it nicely for my own sake," Tilla responded. "What if someone should find out I wrote it? I would want it to look nice."

"Hopefully no one will." Taran walked around the room and poked her nose into pots and lifted lids on jars sitting on the small table in the corner.

"What are you looking for, Taran?" Tilla asked, finishing up the last words.

"There might be something here we can collect for Jacques." She opened a cupboard and let her hand fly around, touching this and that, searching for something of interest.

"What about this?" Taran asked and placed one of the witch-boxes on the table in front of Tilla.

"Good enough. I'm not sure what we can use it for yet, but I'm sure you'll find out," Tilla said and closed the ink bottle. "Quickly, Taran, put it in the bag, she's coming back."

Old Magda stepped across the threshold carrying four cans of honey. "Same procedure as always?" she asked. "Thank you for writing. It is good trade for me and you, yes?"

"Very much," Taran said with her hand in her pocket, fingering the shiny coins that would not be paid to Magda and never returned to her mother.

The twins bagged up the honey and started on their way back. Clouds had rolled in, and they hurried in case of rain.

As they approached home, they noticed a gathering down by the harbor.

"Look, a foreign ship. Maybe the witch-finder is here, the one Father has talked about," Taran said. "Let's go down and see."

She pulled her sisters arm, and they both ran down the hill just in time to see a thin man in his thirties place his knee-high, spurred boots firmly on the ground, seemingly pleased to be safely ashore. A walking stick, nearly as long as the man himself, was in his right hand. He wore a long cape with numerous buttons on either side. Under the short-crowned, wide-brimmed hat—which Taran thought looked out of fashion at the time—she saw his narrow, weasel face. He had brown, chin-length hair, a slender mustache, accompanied by a narrow, pointed beard.

Taran smiled and nudged her sister. "I told you so," she said. "It's him; the witch-finder. Look how rude and unpleasant he looks."

She rubbed her hands together, already thinking about how she and Tilla could take advantage of his visit to Rossby.

"Who's that behind him, dragging the trunk?" Tilla asked.

Taran thought for a second. "I don't know. There's Father. Let's go and ask him."

They ran up to their father and stood on either side of him, hooking their arms around his.

"Girls, I'm so glad you're here to witness this memorable moment. That's the famous witch-finder Angus Hill and his personal interpreter John Pywell."

~~

The Land family opened their home above the large store for distinguished guests the same evening. Dinner was served in the elegant dining room; tall silver candle sticks and porcelain dishes adorned the long table. Taran and Tilla were allowed in the dining room for the first part of the evening to meet the guests and perform one of their duets.

The twins could hardly wait for the witch-finder to arrive. When Innkeeper Hansen finally arrived with the English visitors, they ran into the hallway.

"This is the eminent witch-finder Angus Hill and his interpreter John Pywell," the innkeeper proudly announced. "They are staying at *my* inn."

Angus stepped right into the middle of the room. "I am not here to make friends," he said in a loud voice. "My vocation is above everyday dialogue with citizens of this village. I am here to help you and save you from destruction."

Taran and Tilla lifted their eyebrows at each other and giggled. Taran knew they had promised to behave and stay out of the way but had a hard time concealing her excitement.

"Look at the innkeeper walking behind Angus Hill, as if he would do anything for him," she whispered to Tilla. "I can't wait to hear the conversation here tonight."

In the dining room, guests were drinking wine from Venetian glasses. Several of the council members were present, including Dr. Bing-Olsen.

Mr. Land clapped his hands.

"My distinguished guests and Mr. Angus Hill, Mrs. Land and I are proud to announce a musical number. We will now have the great pleasure of listening to a duet by Taran and Tilla Land, our daughters."

The twins, in matching white dresses, sang harmoniously. Taran kept her eyes on the witch-finder, smiling sweetly.

After the performance, Angus walked over to the girls, his interpreter following closely.

"Very lovely," he said. "Such talent, such beauty."

Taran coyly bowed her head, batting her eyelashes, making the most out of the moment with an admiring foreigner. She saw her father nodding, reminding his daughters it was time for young girls to leave the adults to their dinner and important discussions. The twins curtsied and left for their room.

"Hurry, we have to sneak back and listen behind the door," Taran said as they walked the hallway to their room. "We don't want to miss out on any of the conversation."

She pulled her sister by the hand. They quickly undressed, put on the shifts laid out on the bed by the maid, and brushed their hair. Soon they were in place behind the half-open door to the dining room, straining their ears and concentrating on every bit of information. Eaves-dropping was a talent they had eagerly developed with practice.

Angus stood encircled by other guests. "General Matthew Hopkins, ah, now there was a man who knew how to uncover evil," he said. "I was a young man, a mere sixteen-year-old when I first met him. He was a lawyer. Oh, yes, an educated and intelligent man."

With his legs firmly planted and hands in his sides he looked around at the circle of men gathered about him while he spoke.

"You call him a general. How did he come about his occupation as a witch-finder?" the mayor asked.

"Ah, but he had a talent you know. A nose for seeking out the unnatural behavior of malevolent people, especially women, one could say. He took me in as an apprentice, and I journeyed through our fine country of England with him, learning to understand the trade of witch-hunting."

"And the testing of witches?" Dr. Bing-Olsen clutched his hands together.

"Yes, also that, but that is all too much for the first evening here. But I will tell you this; his early death was tragic. Tragic, I tell you, a great loss to the salvation of this world. He was so young, not even thirty." He shook his head and looked at the floor.

Mr. Land asked, "What is your target, Angus Hill? What is your aim?"

The Englishman turned his head toward his host and said in a serious voice, "You northern people are already trying my patience. The target is to smoke out the heretics."

The twins looked at each other and grinned. How exhilarating. Their dull days and petty pranks of nonsense could turn into an adventurous pastime with Angus Hill in town. Tilla started giggling, but Taran put a finger to her lips, stretching her neck to hear the conversation in the next room.

Innkeeper Hansen cleared his throat. "Can you guide us, so we may be of assistance to you?" he asked. "For instance, searching for moles and such, I am sure Dr. Bing-Olsen can look for markings as he examines people."

"Oh, there is much to look for. It's a quest in itself, and moles are important signs of having been marked. Imps can suck blood from marked spots on the skin; that's why we have to bring an end to all evil practices."

Taran peeked into the room and saw the men nodding. Angus was an orator. No doubt about that.

"This is exciting," Dr. Bing-Olsen said. "I didn't even know we had witches in Rossby."

Taran was craving to hear more, thirsty like fields after a drought. The maid came down the hallway carrying sheets to put away from the laundry.

Taran scowled at her and hissed, "Not a word. Get away or I will tell our father you have stolen goods from the pantry."

The maid continued down the hallway, and the girls stretched their necks against the door again.

"Think of who you want to get rid of. Now there's a beginning," the witch-hunter concluded. "I will find them. Every community has its share of peculiar people. It does not mean they are witches. But I tell you, without a doubt, I will find the ones who are. A few are acquitted of witchcraft, but many are found guilty and sentenced to banishment or death."

As Taran peeked inside the doorway once more, she shuddered as she heard Angus's next words, spoken in a lowered voice.

"Evil does not only lurk in one place in this world. It's everywhere."

11

The Finding

〜

Clara could only think of derogatory descriptions of Angus Hill. No matter how many sermons she had listened to about forgiveness and brotherly love in church, or however deeply she searched the depths of her heart for a vocabulary of pleasant words, her description of the witch-finder was set in stone. It was hard to find any uplifting characteristics at all about such a man.

Many summers earlier, families were encouraged to come and settle down in order to colonize and build a community in Rossby. They had planted trees and fields for harvesting. They had built houses and a church. Their children had grown up to become farmers, fishermen, storekeepers, and doctors. No one could have foreseen the day when one single man unnoticed could change their peaceful way of life.

Clara felt sad, afraid, and angry all at once. She had to keep busy; too much thinking was detrimental. She hoped the arrival of the witch-finder meant nothing to the little town of Rossby but did not believe it.

Old Magda was a person who had been on Clara's mind a lot lately. From what she knew about the woman, Magda did not read or write. Besides, she sold delicious honey, and Clara was fresh out of that luxury.

The old woman sat on a branch in a tree in front of her cottage. Clara, eyes widened, hurried over to stand under the branch in case Magda fell down. She looked up between greenery, her gaze dodging talismans that reflected the bright sunlight. The breeze made the trinkets tinkle and make music on a light and airy note.

"Magda, what on Earth are you doing up there in that tree?" Clara asked, bewildered.

"Oh, hello, Clara, I want to get closer to the sun," Magda explained cheerfully.

Holding her arms up, Clara tried to guide the old woman safely back down on the ground.

Old Magda came down with a thump, and Clara fell over trying to catch her. Good thing she was a small woman.

"Thank you, Clara, but I would have managed just fine," Magda said. "It's harder to get down in the dark when I talk to the moon."

"Magda, you could break a leg or fall on your neck or bruise yourself severely." Clara warned her.

But Magda refused to hear it.

"Bruises are signs of trolls biting," Magda mumbled. "They don't bite me."

"Let's go into the house," Clara begged, trying to get Magda into the mood for why Clara had arrived in the first place.

Bess had told Clara once that Old Magda suffered from a falling disease, something that made her lose her balance. Climbing trees was probably not the wisest thing to do.

"How is Bess?" Magda asked as they walked the few steps back to the cottage. Her feet dragged, and she tripped on small stones along the way.

"She's well," Clara answered. "The child within her is growing, and she is busy with her garden and animals as usual."

"Powerful she is, that Bess," Magda said, "born on a Tuesday. I remember. A full moon it was that night. I was there and tended her mother. I went out and scraped off yellow moss of the north wall of the house at Frue Farm. I put it in bread dough and baked small rolls that night. The north wall is more potent, you know. I fed her mother the rolls to secure the infant's health. She came out rosy-cheeked and healthy, not yellowish and sickly like some. I held little Bess tightly to my chest to make certain the wee folk would not come and trade her for one of their own. As I gave the child back to the mother, I checked to see that the shoes were pointed away from the bed, to avoid any evil thing jumping into them."

Clara listened, intrigued by Magda's memory of days from long ago, and apprehensive at the superstition controlling her life. The old woman hummed in between the words of her story, and Clara gently plucked a few leaves and twigs out of her white hair.

Magda put her shawl on a chair and started sweeping the floor. "I washed the child gently," she continued. "Her downy hair was red already then, it was. I threw the bathwater out of the door, and took care that no strands of hair were left in the water, nothing the wee folk could use against the child."

Her window on the right side of the front door was open and Clara could see witch-boxes sitting on the sill, candle half burned, and next to it a piece of paper.

"Magda," she asked, "who has written the spells on paper for you? You don't know how to write do you?"

The old woman's face lit up and dozens of tiny wrinkles formed around her mild and cheerful light-blue eyes. "No, I have never learned. Don't need it. The Land twins come by now and then, came by earlier today, they did. They buy honey for their mother; I ask them to help me with my cards for the witch-boxes. I tell them what to write, and they make beautiful scribbles on paper for me. It is good trade." She stirred the pot on the stove. It smelled of lentil soup with onions.

"And do they ask for anything in return?" Clara asked again. Magda called it a trade and she knew the twins were too devious to do favors without a plan.

"Oh, no need to," Old Magda replied. "They get the honey and I receive help with the writing. It's all fair."

Fair to whom? Clara thought. Knowing the twins, the money their mother had sent along as payment for the honey, went into their own pockets. *Who cheats on their own mother?*

Magda fetched several cards with different spells. Clara read a few. The handwriting was precise, though with spelling mistakes and ink spatters.

Clara was still curious, wondering how Magda could deal with pieces of paper with words she could not read herself. "Magda, how do you know which ones to use? How can you tell which ones to sell?"

Magda tilted her head and squinted, causing the wrinkles to reappear around her eyes. "I have marked them," she said. "See the marks in the corner?"

Surely enough, each card had marks. No doubt, she would have an easy time telling them apart.

"I know the spells by heart, of course," she continued. "Always have. My mother taught me."

Old Magda was not interested in being schooled, but Clara could help the old woman in another way. She placed a hand on Magda's shoulder and gave her a concerned look.

"Magda, there is a man in town, an Englishman, he is looking for witches. Please, for your own safety, stay out of his way."

Magda pulled Clara's hand away from her shoulder and laughed. "He can try," she said. "I will cast a spell on him if he gets anywhere close to my home."

It was useless to try to convince her any more. Clara left her there, stirring the lentil soup. She hoped Angus Hill would never know. Old Magda was simple, unlearned, and practiced the ways of nature and superstitious manners of folks of the woods, but Clara knew in her heart that Magda had not cooperated with evil spirits.

~

At midday Angus Hill accepted an invitation to have eggs and ham with the mayor at Town Hall.

"Take me around the village and countryside today," the witch-hunter demanded.

A young maid with a clean apron carried the delicacies between the kitchen and ballroom, where the massive table was set with the abundance of summer. There were fresh dairy products and meat from the best farms in the area, and the mayor had opened a bottle of red from his cherished imported wine collection.

"From the valley of Coucheron," he proudly announced in his broken English and poured the glasses himself. "The taste is magnificent."

"Where exactly is this valley?" Angus Hill inquired. "I have not heard of it before."

"Southern France. There are military officers in our country, with ancestry from there. Persecutions initiated by the French queen Catherine de Medici caused their families to flee that valley almost a hundred summers ago."

"Ah, the Huguenots," Angus Hills said with a sigh, as if he had been there to see the persecutions and uproar himself. "Why would anyone want to persecute good Christian people?"

"Why indeed," the mayor answered and helped himself to another egg. "My friend Wyllem de Coucheron has told me how his forefathers fled northward from that picturesque valley. They eventually ended up in Holland. Captain Coucheron's father even worked for our former king, Christian IV. This wine is a gift from the captain.

He gently showed the bottle with two hands, like a valuable treasure revealing an emblem on the glass. "Look, here is the Coucheron weapon. The red rose on silver is—"

"Hmm, I see," Angus interrupted, not interested in tales of weaponry or family quests. "Very interesting." He wiped the corners of his mouth with a napkin. "What I want to know is if he can be useful to us?"

The mayor hesitated and seemed confused and uncomfortable by the turn of conversation. His eyebrows pushed together as he stared at his food.

"You brag about acquaintances and good wine when we should discuss why I have been invited to Rossby," Angus Hill said.

The mayor cleared his throat and repeated the witch-finder's words with a question. "How can the captain be useful?"

"Well, first of all," Angus Hill said and put his right pointer finger in the air, "military officers have the right to punish their men. It is their duty in the service of educating their staff." The witch-hunter showed two fingers, while nodding his head affirming his own statements.

"Second, military officers are not afraid of using this right." He lowered his hand and continued eating.

"And what are the consequences for our town," the mayor asked. He tapped nervously on the table; his eyes found no rest. "I have heard horror stories of women bewitching innocent people, causing their crops to fail, killing their cattle, even causing newborn children to die." He straightened up. "The safety of Rossby is my responsibility. If evil women roam the countryside and endanger the lives of my townspeople, I will assist in their capture."

The witch-finder grinned. "Where is this captain now," he asked and stuffed his mouth with a large bite of bread.

"I believe Captain Coucheron is occupied with the infantry for the time being."

"Very well." The witch-finder pushed his plate away and added with a grim smile, "We have plenty of work to do, shall we commence?"

***

Angus walked briskly down the stairs outside Town Hall and stepped into the carriage. The coachman continued to hold the door open as the interpreter and the mayor, cane in hand, slowly followed. The innkeeper was already there and squeezed in snugly between the wall of the carriage and the mayor, who took up more than his half of the seat. Hansen put his notebook on his lap and eyed Angus Hill intently.

"I am glad you come prepared," the witch-finder praised him. "I expect you have picked out certain places of interest for us to visit on our rounds today. I would like to scour the area first, get a feel of the atmosphere, so to say."

Two horsemen rode behind, armed guards on duty. From experience, the witch-finder knew that not all witches came willingly. After an hour of combing Rossby and its surroundings, the small surveying group ended up on the road going north of town.

Innkeeper Hansen knocked on the roof and the coachman brought the horses to a halt.

"There's a trail here that leads down the hillside to the ocean," he said and pointed out the small window. "I thought this a good place to start."

"This is perfect," Angus Hill said and stepped out. "Start small. Good idea, Hansen. This will do well, indeed." He stretched his arms and breathed out. "It's such a lovely day."

They started down the steep, rocky path to a shed by the seashore, unprotected from nature's raging storms and without close neighbors.

"I will wait here and admire the view," the mayor called after them.

"The interpreter might confuse these people," the innkeeper said. "Maybe I should lead the investigation?" He rushed forward to aid the witch-finder down the path. Angus loathed being grabbed unannounced and stared at the innkeeper's hand on his arm. Mr. Hansen pulled his hand back and lowered his eyes.

He cleared his throat and repeated the question, "Would you like me to lead the investigation?"

"Lead?" Angus Hill dragged the word out between his teeth. "Well, you may communicate with them. We don't want confusion, do we? You may see this as a learning moment, possibly a future trade for yourself. People will admire you."

"Thank you, Mr. Hill." The innkeeper proudly marched the last steps and knocked on the door.

"Gently, gently, we don't want her running off first thing," Angus Hill whispered to the guards. "Stay behind. No need to scare her away."

A rawboned man in a dirty shirt and wide breeches opened the door slightly. He poked his face out. Messy tangles of hair hung down past his shoulders.

John Pywell placed himself strategically for interpretation between all parties. The witch-finder took a look at the man, wrinkled his nose, and backed away.

"Mr. Hansen, what do you want?" the man asked suspiciously. "We don't owe anything."

"Good day, Lars," the innkeeper said. "We are here to see Hilda, to ask her some questions. May we see her?"

Lars nodded.

"Name?" Angus asked the innkeeper, blowing his nose in a large handkerchief.

"Hilda. The locals call her Hilda by the Sea."

"Well, bring the woman outside, I cannot think in there."

The innkeeper politely asked Lars to bring his wife outside.

Angus was puzzled at how cheery she looked; as if she did not expect any danger. *Her mind is obsessed and not equipped for such thoughts*, he thought.

It was mid-day and no breeze. Hilda sat down on the ground and pulled her shift up to her knees, showing flea-bitten legs and ankles tied with strings of woolen yarn. She held a hand across the brow to shade the brightness of the sun. Her tangled hair was pulled back, and she scratched herself vigorously above the ears.

Angus stepped a little closer. "Ask her what she has on top of her head," he said. "It looks as if she has stems from a plant caught in her hair."

"Me have headache," Hilda answered, toying with a dry twig on her lap.

Lars came to her aid. "She says it eases the pain if you rub some field mint on your head. Hilda likes to leave the stems there. That way she can rub them in whenever her head hurts."

Angus waited for the interpretation and nodded, while staring at Hilda. He rubbed his bearded chin and hoped to be enlightened as to why he had been brought there.

"I am bored," Hilda said. "Can I go?"

The witch-finder looked her up and down. "She has no shadow," he said.

The others looked and confirmed it certainly appeared as if she lacked the common silhouette.

"A clear sign," Angus continued. "What else have we got, Hansen?"

"Well, we have witnesses with evidence of this woman's doings."

"Oh, and what is that evidence, exactly?"

"There is the case of Mrs. Land's bad back."

"Interesting. Yes, come on man, what of it?"

The innkeeper opened his notebook and traced his finger along a couple of written lines.

"The twins explained to me they saw Hilda outside the Lands' store, shooting an invisible arrow at their mother," he said. "The next day her back was worse than ever before. I thought this was a plausible reason for making our trip here today."

"Invisible arrow, you say. Yes, this is a common craft of the unbelievers. The poor girls, having to experience a horrible act like that."

Angus looked out at the open sea and cleared his throat to make a statement. "This woman definitely needs to be brought in; not one sensible word comes out of her mouth. Usually dimwitted women are too stupid to know how to be a witch, but we will test her, nonetheless. Let's proceed directly to a nearby lake. Keep her on the top of the carriage; the smell is unbearable. I certainly do not want to touch them; it is easier if they move on their own for now."

"How do we do that," the innkeeper asked.

"Tell them they are invited to Town hall for dinner with the mayor."

Angus hesitated a moment after the others had started up the path to the road. He looked for a witch's trinket outside the cottage. Not content, he put the handkerchief in front of his nose and entered the small house. His eyes swept across the room and landed on a small knife on the table. He walked over, grabbed it by the handkerchief, and held his breath as he rapidly exited the house. He kept the handkerchief with the knife hidden in his pocket, out of sight.

Angus reached the road as Lars and Hilda were told to take seats on top of the carriage. Lars protested and pulled the innkeeper's arm, begging him to let them go home, but Mr. Hansen shrugged off the man's large hand and spat on the ground.

"You will dine with the mayor," Hansen said. "Now sit still and enjoy the ride."

Hilda was giggling. Lars helped her sit down, held her hand, and said nothing.

"It's been a lengthy afternoon. The mayor looks hungry." Angus threw his head back and laughed.

The mayor wiped his forehead. "We could all need some nourishment," he said quietly.

They made a brief halt outside Town Hall where the mayor requested bread and meat.

Lars tried to get down from the carriage top. "We are invited to dinner," he said and pulled on Hilda's arm, but the guards planted the couple firmly back on their seats.

Anna came out and carried a basket with enough food and drink to keep them occupied all the way to the lake.

Angus and the innkeeper stepped out to stretch their legs.

"Better keep the couple still," Angus said. "Give them something to eat."

He watched Anna hand Lars some of the food wrapped in a piece of cloth. Lars mumbled a *thank you* and placed the bundle on Hilda's lap.

The innkeeper looked at Lars fidgeting in his seat. "Sit still, Lars. This is dinner for now. We need to check something out by the lake."

"Check what?" Lars asked.

But the innkeeper ignored him. He told the driver to continue to the lake and squeezed back down on the bench next to the mayor.

"We will perform the swimming test on this woman," Angus stated promptly, as they arrived at the lake. He walked through the crowd gathered by the water's edge. More were arriving on foot or on horseback.

This happens every time, Angus thought. *Curiosity always brings people together with the speed of a lynx.*

The witch-finder opened his book to check procedures and fees. Next time he would talk with the mayor about his salary, and there would more than likely be a next time.

"Swimming test?" the mayor asked. "Don't we need the victim's permission to do that?"

"Do you believe it's necessary to ask a female witch to make the decisions around here?" Angus Hill asked in return, sourly kicking a rock out of the way. He straightened his back and put on a fake smile, trying to be civil and patient, in spite of the nincompoops surrounding him. "Honorable Mayor, this country still allows swimming tests, from what I understand. And yes, you are correct. In some places, one needs the permission of the target. There was a legal abandonment in England a few summers ago, but not here. No, we will proceed and test the woman here in this very water today." He rubbed his hands together. "I will not charge anything for my services this first time."

The mayor nodded his head then turned away. "I need to speak with my council," he said.

The witch-hunter with John Pywell on his heels, followed the mayor to address the men surrounding him. He liked preaching. It made him feel skillful and in charge.

"A true witch renounces her baptism. If she is a witch, the water will reject her, and she will float. If she is innocent, she will sink," Angus Hill said, speaking with conviction.

12

The Helpless

～

"She has been taken in for questioning," Clara exclaimed panting, as she stormed through the front door at Frue Farm. "Everyone is talking about it. I was shopping for buttons at the Lands' store and heard the news.

"Well, hello to you too, Clara." Bess looked up from her work and smiled. "What are you talking about?"

She was filling pots with soil for planting various herbs inside. The weather was cooler now and the days shorter, and she continued growing her garden in her kitchen. She hummed a tune. Clara recognized the melody as one Bess's mother had sung, a long time ago.

"Angus Hill. He has summoned her...and will question her."

"Who is he? Question who about what?" Bess was preoccupied with her seedlings, humming and talking to them. "It will help them flourish, she said. "I sing to them because they live. It will help them grow stronger and will be better for me to use for medicinal purposes."

"Bess, I'm serious. Angus Hill is an actual witch-finder. He's here in Rossby."

"A witch-finder? What are you talking about?" Bess put the plants down and looked at Clara. "Why is he here?"

"He travels around from place to place, seeking out witches and sorcery."

"But that's silly. We don't have any witches in Rossby. I don't know of any with demonic tendencies or connections. Well, there are a few who blabber about things they shouldn't, but..." She giggled a little. "I have been called—"

Clara interrupted her. "Bess, listen to me. This is not a joke."

"I'm listening, Clara, who has he allegedly taken in for questioning?"

"Hilda, the wife of Lars, you know, the couple who live in the small shed by the ocean. She has been taken to the lake. Anna told me." Clara was so upset, she breathed in and out, while speaking.

"Hilda? Not Hilda by the Sea? She's simple-minded and not clever, but she is certainly no witch. She would not know how to cast a hex on anyone." Bess sat down on a chair and rested her elbows on the table. "Surely this Angus Hill and his company will find out they have been misinformed, and the accusers themselves will be put in the stocks outside Town Hall this coming Sunday. That should be humiliating for them."

"It's not that simple. Angus Hill is a powerful man."

Clara spoke fast and filled Bess in on what she knew about the notorious Witch-finder General Matthew Hopkins and his pupil. "Bess, we need to hasten to the lake," she said.

~~~

They rode swiftly, Uncle Samuel clutched Lucia in front on the large mare. They tied the horses to a tree and ran toward the gathering by the lake. Clara turned to make sure Bess was able to keep up.

"Run, Clara, I'm right behind you," Bess said, holding her round belly, moving a little slower.

Clara struggled to get through the horde of townspeople, Bess and Uncle Samuel with Lucia close behind. Uncle Samuel held Lucia close amidst fists flung up in the air and loud shouts. Above the noise was a
~~~

high pitched screech that went through Clara's marrow. It was Hilda. They reached the water as two guards tossed the woman into the lake.

A sentry seized Clara's arm and held it tightly. She was not strong enough to get away. Bess jumped into the water and started wading toward Hilda. Her gown floated up and made it difficult to move forward with any speed. Someone took hold of her hair and pulled her back. She fell into the water, screaming in pain, her head bobbed under a couple of times as she struggled to get free.

Hilda was on her own in the water, fighting for her life, gasping for air. Even if she had known how to swim, it would not have helped, as she was bound in a fetal position. The crowd watched her slowly sink into the darkness of the deep pond.

"No, no, let me go. Someone save her," Lars yelled. He kicked and scuffled to get free from the guards' firm grip on his arms.

People on dry ground gasped and some called out, "Witch, witch."

Clara and Bess screamed in terror as they watched Hilda go under. The witch-finder, with John Pywell on one side and the innkeeper on the other, stood on the water's edge. Angus held his walking stick in one hand and a book under the other, looking straight ahead at Hilda. The councilmen whispered to each other. In the back Clara could see the twins flirting with some young boys. They arrived just in time for the experiment.

Hilda did not reappear to soar up into air and life. She stayed under, and stillness swept over the lake's shore like a swift plague.

"I have never been this angry in all my life," Clara said when she and Bess were let loose. They ran into the water. Lars was already there, pulling his beloved wife up from the depths. He shook her lifeless body.

"She's gone, Lars," Clara said. "Come, let us help you with her."

"Well, that can happen," Angus said to the bystanders. "Not all women are witches, you now. Now I'd like a warm meal. I'm hungry again."

And with that statement, he turned his back to the commotion on the beach. Since the mayor had already left early, the witch-finder told Dr. Bing-Olsen to bring him and his interpreter back to the inn on Main Street.

"Talk, talk," Clara said and kicked sand, rocks, and anything in her way with her foot. "But what do townspeople do? They gossip and dig holes for each other to fall into."

"They don't know any better," Bess replied quietly. "Maybe witch-hunters actually believe they are being charitable. People have lots of gods if you think about it. There is the god of earthly possessions, the god of nature, the god of food, even a god of yourself. Not everyone can see religion for what it is. I believe in a god who wants us to progress and be happy. I believe he knows us. He's the same god you believe in, Clara."

Clara was happy to hear her say that. Bess's testimony warmed the heart. Despite all of the accusations and spiteful happenings, her friend was still positive and still had her childhood faith.

As Hilda was found innocent to the charges of witchcraft, the councilmen decided she could be buried in Christian soil. Bess and Clara helped Lars get Hilda's lifeless body into Herr Christopher's carriage to bring her to the cemetery. Lars appeared heartbroken and refused comfort. No matter what other people had thought of Hilda, she had been the love of his life.

Herr Christopher had arrived late. Clara saw him come and ran toward him to fill him in on what had happened. He approached councilmen Hansen and Land standing in the crowd of people, knowing they had been spectators to the open-air witch trial, and had done nothing to end Hilda's misery. The usually calm and collected Herr Christopher raised his voice and shouted at them.

"How could this happen?" he said. "You know as well as I do that Hilda was no witch. Why torture an innocent woman of our village? Hilda never hurt a fly. She would not have known how."

The councilmen shrugged. For once they were short of words, and even though it had been a horrifying experience, they did not seem concerned.

Along the beach, men and woman stood and talked about everyday things. A few women were admiring Mrs. Land's new dress. She twirled around in a girlish fashion to show off the pattern of the fabric.

"All the way from France," Clara heard her say.

Some of the women reached forward to touch her dress and feel the richness of the lovely fabric that had travelled so far. They nodded their heads and agreed that it was exquisite. A few young girls giggled as they watched the boys throw skipping stones on the water. It was as if Hilda did not matter.

It has begun, Clara thought. A person had actually been accused of witchcraft in the small town of Rossby, and they had watched her die. Would the townspeople think Hilda was the first and only one Angus Hill would accuse? Would they feel safe in their homes? Would they be more careful, or would they hide?

Clara walked to where Bess stood with her arm around the shoulder of an inconsolable Lars. He was not whole anymore. Hilda's death had left him half a man, with little knowledge of worldly goods and matters and now with a broken heart, as well. As they rode away, Clara turned her head to look at the people on the beach. *They don't worry. Not yet.*

The parson's carriage with Lars and his Hilda followed them to the cemetery to hold a short funeral service. Toomber was already there, coffin ready and eager to discuss the price with Lars. How that brute could smell death a mile away was a mystery.

"I have no money to pay you," Lars sobbed. He wiped his nose and coughed. "Why my Hilda? Why?

Toomber pulled his arm. "You will pay. I don't work for nothing."

Lars turned his back on him and Clara said, "Please, Toomber, not now. Give him a little time to grieve."

"I will come to you tomorrow," the gravedigger said to Lars. "Find something to pay me then."

Lars nodded. He sniffled, removed his hat, and held it close to his chest. Toomber scurried to fetch Hilda to put her into the coffin. Before Clara and Bess could help, the gravedigger had picked Hilda up from the carriage and thrown her over his shoulder. Without effort, he carried her over to the coffin and dumped her in. The limp body landed with a thump in the dirty coffin. Bess and Clara looked at each other. Lucia picked a bouquet of wildflowers, and Bess helped her daughter place it gently on Hilda's chest. Lars put a knitted shawl over her body, as if he thought she might get cold.

Clara accompanied Bess back to Frue farm.

"I think the parson said some nice things about Hilda, Clara said. "She was gentle and uncomplicated, just like he said. Poor Lars. He will be lost without her."

They walked in silence, arm in arm. After a while, Bess broke the silence.

"Who has the authority to decide who should live and who should die?"

Her clothes were still wet and she hugged herself to keep warm. Clouds had gathered, and the evening dew on the grass was cool and damp. Clara put an arm around her friend's shoulder, thinking they both needed warmth both inside and out.

"This is not really about authority," Clara answered, "but more about misguided beliefs and superstitions, even opinions."

"What do you think will happen now?"

"I believe this is only the beginning, although I pray it's not. It may be a small spark in the corner of a dry field, just waiting for a breeze to spread like wildfire."

"We have to try to stop it then. This is our town, our families, our friends and neighbors. Surely a stranger has no weight here."

"If he is who he claims to be, and if the town councilors support him, I'm afraid we will see more atrocities before this is over. Rumors will start, then gossiping among the neighbors, and soon, he will have followers and admirers, even here."

Full of thoughts and worries, Clara decided to walk by the cemetery on her way home. Toomber was at the fresh gravesite. He lifted the coffin up again from the open grave by using strong rope. He did not see her coming at first, and subsequently used a hammer to pull out the nails that fastened the lid to the coffin. He had an iron bar to pry it open at one end, then kicked the wooden casket over sideways. Hilda's body fell out. The stench was already poignant and reached Clara several meters away. He put his boot in the corpse and Hilda dropped lifeless into the open grave, the small bouquet of wildflowers spread all around her. The knitted shawl dropped onto the muddy ground and the gravedigger's large dirty boots stepped on it. He picked up the shawl and tossed it into the open grave, where it landed on Hilda's head.

Clara put a hand in front of her mouth, so that he would not hear her gasping.

Toomber rapidly shoveled the soil to fill up the hole, but then he noticed Clara standing there. He looked up from his work, and his eyes had a wild look about them. Drool hung down from his mouth, and he seemed annoyed at being watched.

"Why are you here?" he grunted.

"I've come from Hilda and Lars's house. The question is rather what you are doing here. The funeral ended hours ago."

Clara tried her best to remain calm and not get him angry, but as she walked a couple of steps closer, she grasped what was going on.

"Toomber, how many funerals has that one coffin seen? Do you remember the Scripture, *Do unto others as—*"

He finished the sentence, "*—as ye would have them do unto you.* I must have slept through that class of catechisms. Besides, why are you preaching unto me? You're not my minister."

Clara took a couple of steps back, mostly because he smelled worse than a pile of dung, combined with sweat and strong drink.

"I look out for people I care about. There are a lot of good people out there and they don't deserve to be deceived by you. Their minds are not as calculating as yours is, Toomber. Not everyone expects to get hit in the head from behind."

He flipped his hand and made a snorting noise. "Aagh, it will all become dust anyway, so what's the difference? I've done it a dozen times already."

"The point is that it is disrespectful and dishonest. You are charging poor widower Lars for that coffin. Don't you think he has suffered enough? Besides he doesn't have much to spare, and you know it."

"Well, it was used for the funeral of his missus, wasn't it? It doesn't hurt either one of them that it's been reused. She's dead; why would she care that someone else can have that coffin for their funeral."

Clara was amazed at how clear his mind acted, even if his words come out slow and sloppy. She backed up a few more steps as he stood up straight and held the shovel in both hands as if he was ready to use it on her. He stood taller than a door and had a look on his face that told Clara he was done chatting.

"Now, get." he said gruffly. "Not a word of this to anyone if you don't want to meet your maker, too. There's room enough for one more in that grave."

Without thinking Clara looked straight at him. "You cannot threaten me. My maker hasn't called for me yet."

And with that statement Clara turned on her heels and walked away from the gravesite. She shook and did not want to turn around to see if he followed her. She had allowed words to come out of her mouth without considering the consequences, without taking into account how strong and utterly ruthless Toomber was. She hurried home, clutching the satchel in front of her, looking straight ahead until she reached the cottage and could close and bolt the door behind.

Safely inside, she fell down on the bed, exhausted. Ami jumped up and lay down next to her, purring. She let the tears frozen behind her eyes explode and cried as if it was her last day on Earth. There was nothing more she could do for Hilda, but Lars could need a friend now.

Testing Hilda for witch-craft by drowning her in the lake showed a fragment of what Angus Hill was capable of.

Peter had told Clara about how Matthew Hopkins legalized the murder of about three hundred women in England. Witch hangings in Ireland were scarce, but their neighbors in England were less fortunate.

If Angus Hill lived up to his predecessor's reputation, he could easily wipe out most of the female population in the small town of Rossby.

13

The Sermon

～

The following day was Sunday and church. Clara was sure Herr Christopher had prepared a sermon to comfort and warn the people of Rossby.

As the parson welcomed the congregation, the large church door opened, and Angus Hill entered. He removed his hat and sat down on the front pew. All eyes were on him, a situation he seemed to thrive on. After the introduction and announcements of the day, he stood up and walked to stand behind the pulpit next to the parson. Herr Christopher took a step back and stared at the witch-finder.

From the congregation, the voice of Dr. Bing-Olsen called out, "Let him speak, Herr Christopher. Let Angus Hill teach us today."

Herr Christopher humbly bowed his head and sat down at a chair next to the pulpit. Angus Hill moved over, his rat-faced little translator following him. Angus placed his pointed black-spurred boots firmly apart and grabbed the front top corners of the pulpit with his white, long-fingered hands. He remained thus for several uncomfortable minutes, squinting and staring into the faces of the soundless parishioners. No one dared move or make a noise. It was as if they had all of a sudden remembered what that man was capable of.

"Exodus chapter twenty-two, verse eighteen: Thou shalt not suffer a witch to live," Angus Hill's non-masculine voice rang loudly through the chapel. "Do not believe it is all well and fine to ignore the matter. Don't think for a moment you can choose to look the other way. Rebellion is as the sin of witchcraft. I quote from the first book of Samuel, chapter fifteen, verse twenty-three. Here you are at church today, sitting there, expecting to be nourished by words from the good book. I tell you, God says to you that he will cut off witchcrafts out of thine hand. Micah chapter five, verse twelve. Oh, Rossbyans, Jezebel and her witchcrafts were many in the olden days. Do you want peace and growth in your town? Then you must carefully weed your parish. Jezebels are hiding. Where are they? Where are they?"

Clara looked around at the awestruck congregation. For the first time in the history of their little church, not one member of the parish had dozed off. All eyes were fixed on the foreigner; even children must have noticed the tension. Not even a whimper could be heard. Herr Christopher looked afraid. His mouth was half opened and he could not keep his nervous hands still in his lap. Innkeeper Hansen looked pleased, as did the other council members. The mayor was not in his regular place. Perhaps he was still feeling unwell from the events of the previous day.

The witch-finder's voice went up and down, loud and soft, catching everyone's attention as planned. Citations from the Holy Bible were obviously learned by heart for the occasion.

"Beware, I tell you, sorcerers shall have their part in the lake which burneth with fire and brimstone. Revelation chapter twenty-one, verse eight."

This last sentence he yelled out so loud that a mother on the first pew held her hands in front of her small son's ears. People were now starting to fidget in their seats, looking at each other and mumbling sounds Clara could not make out.

His voice become soft again as he leaned over the pulpit and almost whispered, "Did you know a healer can be condemned to death? Do you remember what the father of our faith, namely Martin Luther, has said? He said witches shall be burned." He straightened his back and spoke firmly, while pointing around at different people in the pews. "Well, I have an admonition for you today. Look around; look in your neighborhood. Are there witches hiding among you? I say again, look. Who is missing services today? Who is a liar, a thief, a troublemaker? Is there a lone woman among you who is unstable, mouthy, unpredictable? A woman who yells and quarrels reveals herself as a troll-woman. Don't be deceived. They are out there."

He stretched out his arm and pointed toward the door.

"Now, what does your parson do about this? Nothing. He has not worked among the people of Rossby to find out who is possessed and who has sold their soul to evil. No, I say. He has not."

He turned around and looked at Herr Christopher, who sat breathing uneasily like a rabbit hiding under a bush when a fox passes by. Clara felt sorry for him because she knew he was a good man, dedicated to preaching the word of God. Like her father, the parson looked for the good in people, not the bad, although Herr Christopher at times ignored the fact that the latter existed altogether. Parishioners from all walks of life needed a good parson.

"I will see that you get a proper court for trying witches. I hoped Rossby was exempted from evil, but alas, evil has made his way even here in this picturesque little town."

Angus Hill turned to Herr Christopher with a fake smile, flicked his hand, and said nicely, "Please, continue, let us hear what the good parson has prepared for us today."

There was not much more to say. Clara looked at Herr Christopher and felt his despair. The taunting remarks had momentarily cut out his tongue. She walked outside with the crowd and tried to hear people's reaction to the witch-finders message.

The response was much the same as she paid attention left and right. Some agreed, not thinking they could ever be a target or in any danger. Everyone wanted a safe community. As in any situation where blame could be distributed, fingers pointed in any direction but toward themselves. Clara went back inside to see if Herr Christopher was alright.

"Surely, you don't expect anyone to tell on their neighbor or friends here in Rossby?" the parson asked the witch-finder as the chapel cleared out. He was nervous and had a hard time keeping his long legs still. His left fist churned in his cupped right hand, as if he ground dried herbs in a mortar.

"Ha ha ha." Angus Hill snorted his numb, staccato-like laughter. "You don't understand. After I am done with them, they will give away their own grandmother if they have to. They will soon understand the importance of separating the chaff from the wheat. Not every citizen is innocent. You know that. Obviously, you are not a fool."

"You cannot compare the words by John the Baptist and how our Lord will judge his people to this atrocity you so generously fold out in our community."

"I will and I shall." the witch-finder fumed back. "It is exactly the same thing."

"There's a difference between being innocent or guilty and plainly being accused of crimes you have not committed." Herr Christopher's normally calm and collected behavior obviously steamed inside.

Clara was proud of his courage. The last words she heard before she left and joined Bess and her family on the way back to Frue Farm was him politely telling the witch-finder to leave the chapel.

"I am not worried," Bess said stubbornly, staring out of the window of her kitchen, as if determined that a decision had been made about her state of mind.

"For the sake of Heaven," Clara blurted out, "you have to worry. Look at what's happening. Look at what happened to Hilda. You certainly have a lot more things to worry about than she did, and she was tried and found guilty of goodness knows what."

"I have things to do," Bess said, still staring. She walked over to the large, iron pot cooking over the open fireplace and gave it a good stir.

Her recipe book was on the kitchen table. Clara reverently picked it up and carefully turned the pages. The paper was old and yellowed. Dried leaves from pressed flowers and herbs adorned the sides, and various efforts of writing explained the use of plants for remedies and medicinal purposes. For this reason had Bess learned to write. She needed to keep up her family's tradition. The women of Frue Farm were midwives, healers, cunning women. Bess's great-grandmother had come to Frue Farm with her husband more than a hundred summers earlier. She used the few words she could write and diligently searched for ways to help others through her knowledge of restoring health. She had been taught by her mother before her, and she passed the skills on to her own daughter in return. Dutiful and diligent were words to describe these women. Clara had seen how Bess carried the traditions further by teaching little Lucia about the rewards of their garden and the surrounding woodland. The women of Frue Farm had been, and still were, gifted in their skill, and Clara had the highest respect for their hard work and goodness in sharing their wisdom with others around them.

The several authors of the old recipe book inspired Clara to want to do things better, to help others more, and choose the good things in life.

The tension from their conversation about Angus Hill and his attempt to conquer evil in Rossby was hard to release. The horrible Sunday sermon and the recent funeral for Hilda, kept them silent for a while.

"Would you help me write something down today?" Bess asked quietly. "I have discovered a good use for a small herb in my garden."

"Of course, but you can write well now, Bess. You don't need me."

"But I do, Clara, it will be better with your help."

Clara felt she meant more than just writing. They needed each other. There was comfort in a good friend, especially then.

"What is it like to be smart?" Bess asked. "You are a combination of bookish learning and the word of God. What is it like?"

"I don't know how to answer that. That's how smart I am." Clara tickled her and laughed, and they both felt a little lighter. No matter how much they grieved for Hilda, mourning would not bring her back. They could only live to prevent any more episodes involving Angus Hill.

Bess's recipe book was usually kept in the kitchen cabinet, the silken notebook on top of it. Clara turned the sides to find a blank page, imagining the generations of women who had written down their thoughts and acquired knowledge. Like the inventor Leonardo da Vinci, they also tried, proved, and learned for themselves how to do things, and their mission was to cure illnesses and to be of use to others.

Clara picked up the pen. "Now, tell me what to write."

Bess described the leaves, stem, and root of a certain herb, and how it could be prepared as a treatment for coughs and chest pains. Clara wrote exactly what she was told, pleased to learn from Bess, happy to be her friend.

〜

Despite the strict sermon and harsh words, Angus Hill and his interpreter seemed to be well liked among the parishioners. The common man and woman admired the knowledgeable Englishman. He was the talk of the town at both the Watering House and the inn, for better and for worse. The higher-standing Rossbyans, such as Mr. and Mrs. Land, invited him over for dinner now and then, often in the company of the innkeeper.

Clara saw them enter the Land residence one evening as she passed on her way home from Frue Farm. The twins stood in the doorway, charmingly welcoming their parents' guests.

Clara did not like the look of it. The witch-finder got under the skin of the people in Rossby. A clever orator, he used persuasive conversations and arguments to turn heads and certainly change opinions and beliefs. His influence and entertaining ways of presenting himself and his message were in fact admirable. Speaking in public, daring to have opinions, confessing to know the truth about magic and witchcraft, all this drew people toward him like Old Magda's bees around an open jar of honey.

14

The Sisterhood

After the midday meal, Herr Christopher showed up on the threshold of the school house.

"Dr. Bing-Olsen came by and said you are expected at Town Hall without further ado," he explained.

The doctor had not been given any reason other than that Clara was to come directly.

The children questioned their teacher, wondering why their school day was interrupted; but as she packed her books into the shoulder bag, they realized school finished for the day. Some were elated and grabbed their chalkboards and ran out. A couple of little girls lingered and asked if they could help tidy the classroom, but Clara nudged them out the door and told them they could finish later.

Clara was not sure what the hurry was but had an uneasy feeling as she hastened down the hill. Close to the town square, she heard loud voices and shouts and noticed the sound came from an assembly of townsfolk standing by the large steps of the entrance of the Hall.

Several guards were on the steps, trying to calm the crowd and make sure no one passed through. She pushed her way through the throng but got no further than the bottom of the stairs as a watchman blocked the access with his weapon.

"What is your errand?"

"I am Clara Dahl. I have been summoned," she explained. "I was told to report forthwith."

"Wait here," he replied, his voice a few pitches deeper than normal. He disappeared through the large, blue double door at the top of the stairs.

Clara stood there, looking at the crowd of people. Some seemed upset and others were clearly there out of curiosity.

Why can't sentinels speak as normal people? Clara wondered as he reappeared. They always had to prove superiority and instill fear in others by sounding menacing and showing intimidating behavior.

"Miss Dahl, this way."

The man had the patience of a fly. It was not easy to get through more people crowding the stairs trying to get information from other guardsmen.

She finally slipped past the last one and entered the infamous blue double door. Surely, the town council and the mayor walked through these doors all the time, as did Anna, the other maids, and the watchmen. But it was also the entrance of thieves and murderers. Folks had stepped across that threshold and many fates had been decided inside that building.

A guard showed Clara into the conference room on the left. She took a deep breath as she entered and noticed the council, the mayor, and Angus Hill had their eyes on her. What they wanted, she still did not know. She felt nervous and worried, although she tried not to show it.

"Miss Dahl. Approach the table. Sit down". The mayor was proper and to the point, as usual. He was not known for having a flourishing language or for sweet-talking people. She sat down on an empty chair opposite the mayor and tried not to look at Angus Hill, who was standing to the mayor's left.

"We have an important council meeting under the direction of Mr. Angus Hill," the mayor continued. "There will be a witch trial this afternoon. Mr. Angus Hill's interpreter is out of town for the day, and we need you to act as translator and assistant. The inhabitants of Rossby do not understand English. We need you to bridge the language barrier between our honorable witch-finder and the people of this town."

Clara's jaw dropped and she was about to protest, but he noticed and quickly continued.

"This is not a request, Clara. You have no choice. Angus Hill may sentence anyone who goes against his methods for being a witch supporter, and then you, my young lady, will be in danger yourself."

"Who has he pointed out this time? Which innocent person has fallen under your suspicious eyes?" She kept staring straight ahead at the mayor.

He hesitated a moment before he cleared his throat and said, "Sister Birgitta."

Clara jumped out of the chair and placed her hands on the large oak table. "What? Sister Birgitta? You cannot be serious. No, I will not assist in any such thing. Mr. Mayor, in all honesty, you cannot believe there's any substance in accusing Sister Birgitta? Please."

"Be careful, Clara. Keep it down," the mayor almost whispered. "The witch-finder has ears and eyes, even if he does not understand our tongue, he can discern body language and the sound of your voice. The innkeeper speaks some English, as do I, but you are most proficient in several languages. Dr. Bing-Olsen speaks some French but not sufficiently for such a grave matter. Until the interpreter returns tomorrow, we require your services."

Clara was surprised at how the mayor spoke to her. Never before had she heard him be so deliberate. She sat down and decided not to fight it; only then would she have the chance of saving her friend Birgitta. Only then could she raise a voice against the evil ways of Angus Hill and his accomplices. The witch-finder's gaze was straight at her, penetrating and cold. Clara was not ready to look him straight in the face and concentrated on staring first at the mayor, then toward Dr. Bing-Olsen's satisfied face, and back at the mayor again. She tried to gather her thoughts systematically in order to find any logic in this nonsensical situation.

In other countries, when matters of the state were of the utmost importance, interpreters had been beheaded for rendering incorrectly. Clara worried about the translating part, but most of all, she dreaded standing next to—and actually assisting—Angus Hill in his labor of horror in the community.

"Where's Sister Birgitta now?" Clara asked as she made an effort to sound calm, still trying to avoid the witch-finder's stare. He said nothing, but Clara noticed how he looked her up and down with his weasel eyes, as if he were putting together a personality profile about her. Uncomfortable, she did her best not to show her disgust and worry.

"She's in the waiting chamber, brought in this morning."

The mayor still headed the conversation, with the rest of the council as solemn bystanders, nodding and making grunting noises to show they were of the same mind.

"What? She's here? Can I see her?"

"No one sees the prisoner," the innkeeper interrupted.

"Prisoner?" Clara paused a moment, silently praying she might find something intelligent to say which could help her get an audience with Birgitta. She struggled to stay calm and not reveal her true feelings. Inside, she desperately tried to work out how she could hinder a guilty verdict. Of what she had seen of witch-hunting and trials in other countries, and what she had heard about the Witch-finder General Matthew Hopkins, she knew the chances for aiding an alleged witch were slim. She had to be careful.

"It might help the translation, if I can meet the…prisoner", Clara said.

There was safety in friendship. It was like refuge from the storm, help in time of need, an assurance for things to come. Birgitta was Clara's friend, but being a friend could be dangerous, as well, and she was careful and thought before she spoke and pondered before she acted. Nevertheless, whatever she could do to help Birgitta, she would do.

The mayor requested Clara's company in the carriage with himself and his wife. The innkeeper was glued to the witch-finder. They had a carriage of their own, along with a few of the other council members. Not having to sit in a closed coach with Angus Hill was something

Clara was grateful for, amidst all the trouble. In the last coach with barred windows, Birgitta sat.

Clara paid a boy to run over to Frue Farm to try to find Bess and asked him to hurry, as she needed Bess. Birgitta needed Bess. The boy put the coin in his pocket and ran off.

By the time they reached the pond, a score of people had already gathered to watch the witch testing. Words about the event had again flown on eagle's wings to every corner of Rossby, and those who believed the reality of a real witch-trial wanted to be there.

Without a word, the mayor nodded. With a hand gesture, he let Clara know she should accompany Angus Hill to the area where they had watched Hilda's drowning, not many days earlier.

Clara needed to get on with the uncomfortable task of translating for the Englishman. She tried to see it as an opportunity to liberate her friend, but it was not painless.

"Mr. Hill, what do you see happening here today?" Clara asked him, standing a few paces away from him. "What does this mean to you?"

"Oh, I am a most humble servant," he said, flipping through a note book and a few loose documents.

One piece of paper flew out of his hands and landed on the ground. He did not move, but looked at Clara. She had no desire to be his lackey and stared back, but before Angus Hill could make a comment, the innkeeper had bent down and passed him the document.

The witch-finder continued turning pages and sat down on a wooden chair brought by the innkeeper for Angus's comfort and said, "I give my days—my life, in fact—to the cleansing of evil and making this world a better and safer place to live in. I charge but a small fee for my services, paid in coins. I do not want wares."

He opened up his brown hide bag and pulled out a piece of paper, presumably the one he had been searching for. It was torn and stained and had obviously been presented on several occasions and in various places. He handed it to the mayor, who looked upon the document and nodded his head.

"Yes, this is satisfactory," the mayor said. "It is fair indeed. We certainly want a safe and God-fearing village. You will be recompensed accordingly."

The mayor passed the document to Clara. It was a detailed list describing the trade of witch-finding. She looked at it and sensed a darkness enveloping her as she read one impiety after another:

Fee for the Seeking out a Wytche	*1 Copper Schilling*
Fee for the Gathering of Evidence	*1 Copper Schilling*
Fee for the Distinguishing of an Imp	*1 Copper Schilling*
Fee for the Interrogation of a Wytche	*2 Copper Schillings*
Fee for the Testing of a Wytche	*2 Copper Schillings*
Fee for the Controlling of Execution	*1 Copper Schilling*

It was signed, *Doctor Angus Hill, Wytche Finder Executive.*

What was Clara to think? It might have been a sensible plan, had the land been flooded with witches flying around the countryside, cursing people and casting evil spells.

But Sister Birgitta? If she could fly, it would be by angelic wings, not on a broomstick. And Rossby, well, there were problems, but the inhabitants were basically the salt of the earth, or so Clara thought.

She stared at the witch-finder and saw a man possessed with his quest for seeking out inequity. His clothes bore witness of a solid income, and the look in his eyes showed he thought himself proud and an important citizen, even a savior. She was not sure if he was just after money and recognition, or if he actually believed in what he preached. Either way, he was misled.

"She has a cross around her neck," Angus Hill commented to the mayor.

Clara interpreted.

"Have someone take it off and bring it to me. We don't want her wearing it for the trial."

"This is not a trial, Mr. Hill," Clara said. "A trial would let the accused have a chance to prove her innocence and have someone defend her. This is not fair." She could not let him believe he was all knowing.

"Fair? Do witches deserve fairness?" His face became angry, his eyes mean.

"Mr. Hill, you must give Birgitta a chance. Let her speak."

"I will interrogate her in a minute. She will be given the chance to speak."

"You cannot make the decision alone. There should be a court session and a fair trial with witnesses and an impartial judge."

"Watch your tongue, Miss Clara Dahl." The witch-finder stood legs apart, his hands on his back, and chin up. "You can be assured I have been told of your heritage." He hesitated then continued while he rubbed his thumb against his fingertips in front of Clara's eyes. "And your inheritance. You are an upright and faithful Christian woman. You are gifted and learned, but do not test my patience, Miss Dahl. Do not shake the conviction that you are the respected female the mayor claims you to be."

"Yes, inheritance is great, Mr. Hill," Clara said, "but heritage is better."

She tried to quote scriptures about forgiveness and loving thy neighbor to the Englishman, but to no avail. Even the well-known phrase that all men and women are equal in the eyes of God was a waste of time as it came across as insignificant words, unrewarded in terms of hoping for understanding.

It dawned on Clara that Angus Hill was not a learned man of the cloth. He had memorized a few scriptures from the Holy Bible, but she could tell by his indifference to spiritual matters how narrow-minded his opinion of faith, hope, and charity was.

The barred carriage door was opened at the back and Birgitta dragged out. She fell on the ground and as she lifted her head, Clara could tell she was exhausted.

"A most effective way to start the testing," Angus Hill ranted.

He must have noticed Clara's surprise at the way Birgitta looked.

"Sleep deprivation. Yes, helpful to me. You may think my job is simple, Miss Dahl, but it is intricate and demanding."

Oh, the words that man uses, Clara thought. *He truly believes himself to be unique.*

A middle-aged woman with large lips and hair enough for two people approached the witch-finder and asked in an endearing way if she could be of assistance. A couple of men from the woods came, requesting the same. Clara translated the words and wondered how people could have changed. Or had they changed? Had they been like this all along, only she had not noticed? She was gullible and believed well of her fellow beings. Maybe new thoughts and fresh ideas blossomed into new-fangled opinions, and love and neighborly friendship changed to disgust and hatred? Friendships needed nurturing, but misunderstandings could easily alter the way people behaved. She assumed that perhaps the problem was they had not thought it through properly.

It turned out Angus had kept Birgitta awake in a cell all through the night, piercing and stabbing her delicate skin with a needle called a witch-pricker, trying to discern whether she had invisible markings on her body. No wonder she looked worn-out and in a sad state.

Angus put his boot out in front of Clara as she tried to run toward her friend on the ground.

"Your place is here," he said sternly. "Now stay put and do your job."

Clara's heart went out to Birgitta. She gained eye contact and tried to let her know how she felt. Birgitta looked back with her large innocent eyes but said nothing.

"This calls for a different test," Angus had Clara inform the town council as he faced Sister Birgitta.

She had been placed on a large stone with her hands tied behind her back and two sentinels holding her arms.

Suddenly, Bess came running. Clara would have thought her a lunatic, had she not known Bess; hair friend's hair was unkempt, her frock dirty from working in the garden, and a wild look in her wide-open green eyes.

"Clara, I came as soon as I heard," Bess said, breathing hard. "What is happening? What are they doing with Birgitta?"

Clara shook her head as the witch-finder still informed her on scriptures, medical procedures, and witches. He stood there as a model of a man, attempting to accumulate more power by applying each factor of his learning to fit his own needs.

"What is he saying, Clara? What is going on?" No doubt frustrated by the language barrier, Bess paced around in circles.

As the witch-finder stepped away for a moment to study the surroundings, Clara informed Bess of what had happened.

"No, not Birgitta." Bess cried out.

She had become aware of her friend sitting on the stone and ran toward her. Before she could reach Birgitta, the sentinels pushed her away and she fell to the ground. Clara gasped as she thought about the child Bess carried, but Bess got up right away, brushed the dirt and small stones off her hands, and went at it again. Once more they pushed her away.

"Strength of the arm doesn't make it right to hold her down," Bess yelled at the guards holding Birgitta's arms. "You are restraining an innocent. No job is worth hurting another fellow citizen who has done nothing to deserve it. Look at her. She has done nothing wrong."

Bess looked furious. She paced between Dr. Bing-Olsen and the innkeeper, trying to convince them how ludicrous the situation was.

"What is the purpose of this?" Bess shouted at the innkeeper. "Who is this so-called witch-finder who thinks he is free to pick and choose innocent inhabitants of our town to torture and kill? What is wrong with all of you? Why doesn't anybody stop him? You all know Sister Birgitta. Surely, you must know she is no witch. In your hearts, you must know how wrong this is. She has spent her life helping people."

She looked around at the crowd that had gathered. "How many of you have benefitted from her services?"

The men and women assembled looked at each other, some mumbled into their neighbor's ears, and others snorted. Herr Christopher stood to the right side, holding his Bible with both hands, eyes closed, obviously praying.

"Herr Christopher," please stop this.

Bess pulled the parson's arm, but he stood still.

"Bess, please calm down," he said. "Come pray with me. There's not much else we can do."

"No, I have to try." Then she faced the small group of men from Town Hall, her voice raised and angry, and said, "Has she not healed you from stomach ache, Mr. Hansen? Or you, Mr. Land, I know Birgitta has traded herbs in your store more than once."

The councilmen ignored her pleas. They pushed Bess aside and had the guards from Town Hall make a human fence to keep spectators away from the witch-testing area.

Two guards grabbed Bess and dragged her away screaming and kicking from the scene and over to the side.

The innkeeper commanded, "Silence that woman and tie her down. We don't have time for this."

Clara ran forward. "Mr. Hansen, please, she's with child."

"She's disorderly, Miss Dahl. I will not have that woman make a spectacle here. She's disturbing the witch-trial." He flipped his hand to the guards. "Proceed," he said.

A piece of cloth was ripped off the hem of Bess's gown and pushed into her mouth. Two more guards assisted in tying her legs and arms, which was not an easy task with someone who struggled like a wild wolf in a net.

Clara called out, "Please, be careful with her."

One of the guards shook his head and stuttered back, "Sh—sh—she should be careful her—her—herself."

Clara felt as if she was bound as well. Angus had returned and continually spoke about practice he had attained fighting witches. She peeked over at Bess and thought it safer for her to be restrained under the circumstances. Clara did not want her anywhere in line behind Birgitta.

"Present your case, Mr. Hansen," Angus Hill said firmly through Clara. Even with his thin voice, he demanded authority. "What are we confronted with here today? Let the crowd offer their evidence as well."

A horde of accusations from this and that bystander flew toward Angus, like arrows on their way to a target. They were ridiculous charges, blaming Birgitta for turning their milk sour, causing a man to fall from a tree and break his leg, after he had set his eyes on her. There was also a story about killing someone's goat and another about conjuring up a storm on a day their wash hung out to dry.

Clara's shoulders stiffened, and her neck hurt. She reluctantly interpreted the townspeople's stories. Every time she hesitated, the innkeeper poked her with his walking stick, telling her to continue and to do it correctly.

"This is pointless finger-pointing," Clara said and took hold of the witch-finder's arm. "You must see there is no substance to what they are saying. These silly things happen. It does not make Birgitta a witch."

He looked down on his arm and removed Clara's hand with his long white fingers. "This is all adding to the one allegation every guilty witch admits to. You'll see."

"I don't believe you," Clara spoke, not minding that she sounded angry and unladylike. "There's nothing she could have done to upset the people of Rossby."

"There is and she has." He looked Clara in the eyes.

She stared back, even though it was uncomfortable.

He leaned toward her and said, almost in a whisper, "During the night's questioning, she admitted to being under evil pacts and influence." Then he looked at the crowd and repeated the same words, loudly and clearly.

"No, no, no," Clara said.

But he pushed her away and concluded. "The evidence is overwhelming. Translate the words, Miss Dahl. Each one."

Clara breathed hard a few times then translated the accusing words.

Angus Hill turned around in a circle, swinging his cape and looking dramatic. "This is a witch if ever I saw one. Build a fire."

Clara gasped. A fire? No, it could not be. "Mr. Hill," she said pleadingly, "surely you need more evidence. Won't you let Birgitta have a word. Won't you have someone plead her case?"

"Well, Miss Dahl, you are certainly trying, aren't you?" the witch-finder said sarcastically. "No, I have heard enough. No need for any more opinions or wasted explanations." He flung his hand up in the air and called out, "Build the fire."

The innkeeper recognized the command and seemed impatient with Clara's delay. He called out the translation himself.

Clara looked desperately from Birgitta to Bess and to the engaged crowd of Rossbyans. She had been so trusting. How could the townspeople turn on their own neighbor? She stared at the witch-finder with tears in her eyes.

"Mr. Hill, please, there is much evidence of how Sister Birgitta has helped the people of Rossby. She has healed, cared for, and done good deeds all her life. She is filled with compassion. Never done any harm to anyone." The words came out in short, sputtering sequences. "Mr. Hill, if you could speak with the people she has—"

The witch-finder put his palm up in front of Clara's face. "Stop there," he said. "No use, Miss Dahl. Don't play soft with me. My decision is unmistakable. That woman is a witch; no doubt about it."

Clara saw Uncle Samuel leave with Lucia as a long pole was placed in a deep hole, rocks supporting the base. Logs, dried grass, and drift wood were piled on top. She imagined that being burned alive was horrible and hoped Birgitta blacked out from the smoke and heat before the pain of the hot flames licking the human flesh set in. But when she saw the innkeeper bring a ladder, she shuddered with horror.

He threw the ladder on the ground in front of Birgitta and said triumphantly, "Do it properly."

Being tied to a ladder and then thrown into the fire was far worse than being tied to the pole. Angus had rambled on about different methods and had mentioned that the ladder method was more painful, thus punishing evil even more. Besides, in order to cleanse away all evil, one had to make sure the witch burned to death, suffocation was not enough. At this point, it did not comfort Clara that Angus Hill had proclaimed burning as a way to cleanse away evil, hence giving the witch a chance of redemption in the next life. Birgitta was not a witch.

Bess sat and looked at Clara with pleading, wet eyes. She squirmed and whimpered noisily with the cloth still in her mouth.

"Changing the weather or even causing a goat to die or cows to produce sour milk are not necessarily criminal acts that can be punishable by death," Angus said while he flipped the pages of his handbook, probably planning how much he earned from the day's witch hunt.

For a moment, Clara thought he had come to his senses, if only a little, until he continued.

"Although when they actually admit to having—"

"She didn't," Clara pleaded, tears rolling down her cheeks. "Mr. Hill, she never—"

"Oh, but she did, Miss Dahl. She has admitted to such a pact. I saw her nodding. Speaking is difficult, under the circumstances, for these poor women who are without will and without power over their own self. They have sold their soul."

"Birgitta would not sell her soul, why would—?" Clara said again.

But he cut her off once more. He placed a hand on Clara's shoulder, and it felt as if an ice pick had been stabbed into her flesh. The man was gruesome, and it hurt just to be in his presence.

"She would," he said, "and she has. It was done in exchange for diabolical favors. Now we will help her get free from this evil. The fire will cleanse her soul."

He walked a couple of paces away and called out to Clara to ask the innkeeper how the fire came along. It needed to be blazing hot.

Clara curled her arms over her head and moaned. The blessings of knowing several languages felt like a curse, and her body shook with anguish as she gave the innkeeper the message.

As the flames intensified into a smoldering fire, Birgitta was pulled up off the rock she sat on. She battled for her life as two guards tied her arms and legs to the ladder. She begged them to let her go. Bess was still held tight and could only make grunting noises because of the cloth in her mouth. Clara stepped forward, but the witch-hunter thrust his arm out and placed his walking stick in front of her belly. Herr Christopher walked up to Birgitta and waved his right hand in front of her to bless her. The innkeeper told him to leave, and the parson bowed his head and staggered back into the crowd of spectators.

The guards pulled the ladder on the ground toward the fire. Birgitta struggled all the while, calling out names of people she saw in the crowd and beckoning God's help. The sisters from the abbey were held back as they tried to get to her. They shoved the guards, but all their attempts failed.

The ladder was held upright as close to the hot flames as the men could muster. Clara saw Birgitta look up into the heavens but could not hear the words she uttered before the guards moved the ladder forward into the blaze. Clara could not look anymore. She turned her head but could not block out Birgitta's scream. It seemed to pierce her skin and penetrate her soul.

People were staring and hiding children behind them. Some children watched, and some threw twigs onto the fire for more flames. Clara pleaded with them, but some just turned their backs, hiding their face in their hands, while others held their nose or even covered their ears so as not to hear the screams of both Birgitta and people in the surrounding crowd.

Black smoke filled the air, the smell of burnt flesh and cloth carried along with the gusts of wind that only encouraged the flames to burn more fiercely. A group of bystanders called out, "Witch, witch, witch." Even children joined in the chanting.

Much like the tension among the spectators, most of the heated flames eventually turned into glowing embers. The townspeople turned and walked home.

Bess was let loose after the burning and caused a stir by walking back and forth, yelling and spitting at the council members. Angus Hill had left only moments before. *Probably hungry again,* Clara thought.

"Calm down, Bess", Dr. Bing-Olsen said sternly. "No need for such an outrageous display of theatrical emotions."

"What?" Bess yelled back. "No, I won't calm down. Do you know what you have done? Birgitta is dead. I can't believe you're telling me to calm down. You legalized the murder of another innocent woman. And to what cause? I know you and I don't always agree on your methods of healing the sick, but we both work to save lives, not take them."

The doctor snorted, turned away, and walked back to the waiting carriage.

The mayor was still on the shore, looking at the last of the flames. Clara knew she needed to try one last time before returning home, even though her hopeless desire to stop iniquity did not bear any fruits. She approached the town leader as respectfully as she could handle.

"Mr. Mayor," Clara said. "Please, this is barbarious. You cannot try people without a proper trial. You need to let the prisoners speak. This is not England. Let the accused have a chance to testify, to go to court. You cannot let Angus Hill make all the decisions by a pond. The town of Rossby cannot be guilty of burning and drowning innocent folks without a trial."

The mayor looked at her with sad eyes. He was not in any state to give a lengthy speech. "Go home, Clara," he said. "Go home."

Bess and Clara walked the horses back, their arms around each other's waists, sobbing, hurting, and trying to make some sense of the madness. They parted by the inn, and Bess continued down Main Street and on to Frue Farm. There were people everywhere in town. You would think it was a festival. There was laughter and playful behavior, but Clara could sense that some were downhearted by what happened at the lake.

Conversation with the witch-finder at the lake spun through Clara's mind. She was surprised how blunt she had been, how brave in speaking her mind to a stranger. He was a dangerous man, and she had told him her opinion, even contradicted him. She was usually shy and a little timid with unfamiliar persons. What made her do it? Insecurity overwhelmed her now, and she feared she might have said something to endanger other women in Rossby.

As she walked through the gate of the parsonage, Sara came running toward her.

"Clara, Clara, I have been waiting for you. Laura was here just now. She talked about Bess. She told me stories I did not want to hear."

"Now, Sara, catch your breath. What is going on? What kind of stories?"

"I don't believe them. I just need to let you know. People are talking. There's gossip going around about Bess."

"What kind of gossip? Tell me, Sara."

"Come inside, Clara. I need to feed the baby. I'll tell you all about it."

They walked in and sat down in the parlor. Sara fetched the newborn child from the cradle and put him to her breast. Clara sat bewildered and curious but also worried about what Sara was going to tell her. Sara politely asked her older children to go outside to play, although she let a toddler stand and hold onto the chair where she sat.

Clara stared at her. "What is it, Sara?"

Sara informed Clara of episodes she knew well that had been twisted in a way to harm Bess. Some of the gossip happened by the lake and Clara could see how it was easy to coil the words and make them come out with a different meaning, especially with Angus Hill adding dry wood to the fire.

How was it possible that gossip returned home faster than Clara did? How could Clara be confronted with something she had been a witness to before she reached her own doorstep? How could it spread so fast? Did people run between houses? Did they ride a horse 'til the animal nearly passed out just to tell a story? Did they send messages with pigeons? Did they put a note in a bottle and send it downstream?

Clara was angry and frustrated. What had happened to friends and neighbors in Rossby?

15

The Chase

Uncle Samuel had gone hunting the morning they came for Bess. He had taken Binna with him and enough supplies to last for a few days, then he headed for the hills at the break of dawn. The other hunters, who preferred company in the lone hills and dark woods, called him the hermit hunter. There was no telling which direction he had gone or when he would return. He knew every cub hole, nesting area, and hibernating cave, and he never followed the seasonal paths of the common hunter's ground.

Bess and Lucia were in the orchard, pruning the plum trees when the men arrived. The fruit had been harvested and preserves made. September was a good month for cutting back the eager branches stretching sky high at their own will.

Seven or eight riders and a horse-drawn, open cart squeezed out of the narrow, wooded path and trotted into the clearing. There was no Binna to guard the property and alarm the family of intruders, but

Bess had heard the noise of horses' hooves before the men appeared in the thicket.

"Lucia, look at mamma," she had said gently, trying to stay calm.

The little girl looked trustingly into her mother's green eyes. "Lucia, please pick up your poppet, and hurry to the place behind the barn where we play hide and seek. Can you do that for Mamma? Please wait there for a while. Will you play that game with me?"

Lucia nodded and skipped across the yard. As she watched her go, Bess put a hand in front of her mouth to calm the breathing. She had hoped this day would never come, and although she had felt it inevitable for a while, there was no proper way of being prepared for the arrival of a witch-finder. She walked back into the garden and continued pruning the trees.

The men were close enough for Bess to hear their voices. "Look at where she lives," Angus said. The interpreter, John Pywell, had returned from his errand and trailed behind the witch-finder, a little less enthusiastic. Bess peeked through the branches and saw them approach the farm.

Angus Hill looked wound-up and walked ahead. He looked left and right with eyes like those of a child, waiting for a surprise.

"Her house is next to a definite cross in the road," he said, "a sure sign of a magical place."

The innkeeper trailed behind and pulled out his book to make notes of everything the witch-finder said. "Cross...in...the road," he said slowly and stopped to scribble the words down.

In her heart, she knew and expected Angus Hill and the innkeeper would come calling at Frue Farm. She braced herself. She would let them hear her opinion of what they were doing to the people of Rossby.

"A witch is a strange creature," the witch-finder said. He made a hand gesture and gazed philosophically into the air. "She may appear in another shape or form. Beware of running mice or flying birds. It could be her, trying to escape."

Bess wrinkled her forehead and shook her head. *I would definitely be something fiercer than a mouse or little bird had I known you were coming,* she thought. She wished Uncle Samuel would return from hunting and appear at any moment.

The witch-finder motioned his hand forward and spoke as the horses slowly trotted through the open gate.

"Look for anything out of the usual," he said.

Angus spotted Bess in the orchard as soon as they entered the farm. She wiped her hands on her apron and put the basket on the ground.

"Bess of Frue Farm?" the witch-finder asked. He looked up and down at her working habit.

"Yes, I am she." Bess put her hands on her hips and frowned. "I know who you are. What do you want?"

Angus Hill did not answer, but walked around the orchard and looked at the abundance of trees and bushes. The fruits, berries, and vegetables were a result of hard work and knowing ways of generations of women at Frue Farm. He stopped by a tall tree with black berries, not yet fully ripe.

"I see you have an elder tree in your garden."

"Of course, the sap is wonderful and healthy for—"

"Yes, I'm sure you know of some uses." He pulled off a cluster of berries and put them under his nose before discarding them onto the ground.

Bess looked at the unripe berries on the ground, and her heart ached. She disliked wasting vital food and medicine.

"I do," she said meekly. "My grandmother traded the sap for— "

He cut her off again. "You reveal more than you know, woman. Every witch has an elder tree in her garden, but you are aware of that, I'm sure."

"You twist and turn every—"

"I am not interested in what you have to say, woman. The court will decide what to do with you. The league has now officially set up witch-trials at Town Hall. Are you satisfied with that? Your friend will be satisfied, I'm sure. She has approached the council several times to request indoor courts for witch-trials, not that it makes a difference." He pulled out a handkerchief from his pocket and blew his nose, a long trumpet-sounding noise.

"I'm not satisfied. I will not go to court. You have no authority here. This is my place. Get off my land."

The guards came closer, and Bess felt trapped. She put her arms around a tree and called the witch-finder names. She would not go easily and kept looking across the yard to see if Lucia was still out of sight, trying not to alarm her daughter. There was also the child in her belly to consider. She had to be careful.

"This is not the first time we've had to silence you, woman," Angus Hill said. He flung his hand out to a couple of the guards. "Take her. Bind her to the carriage, and gag her loud mouth. I've had enough of this wild animal."

Four guards were needed to hold Bess down. She kicked her legs and bit a guard's hand as he tried to tie her hands. As they gagged her mouth she looked longingly toward the barn. Lucia was still hiding, and Bess had done everything to keep her away from the witch-finders grasp. She tried to protect her belly with her tied hands as they threw her with a thump on the back of the open carriage. Her head hit the side of the cart, and she felt faint and shaky. The last thing she noticed was how a rope was tied around her feet connecting her to the side of the cart, to make sure she could not escape. Then she lost consciousness.

<p style="text-align:center">~~~</p>

Angus Hill stomped toward the cart, his interpreter close on his heels. "Now look what you have done." he said. He grunted and hit his fist on the side of the cart. "I need her to tell me where her almanac is."

"Her what? What are we looking for?" The men were apparently at a loss.

"You imbeciles. Do I have to spell everything out for you in little details? Find her recipe book."

Obviously puzzled, the guards and councilmen looked at each other. The innkeeper placed himself next to the witch-finder, hands in his sides. Angus was appalled at the ignorance of these country folks. How was it possible to make progress with ill-prepared men like the Rossbyans? He took a long, deep breath and hoped his efforts made them learn and understand.

"Her recipe book." The words came out like pouring thick gruel, and he hit his head with his hands. "The book she writes her spells and curses and what-nots in. Every valid witch has one." He increased the sound of his voice and said loudly, "Find it. It must be destroyed."

The witch-finder walked with long paces toward the house and inside the front door, clutching Birgitta's cross in his hand. The innkeeper followed close on his heels, and a few more of the men came in behind him.

They searched in cupboards, under the straw mattresses upstairs, in between wool, yarn, and fresh produce. It was easier to find than they had thought. Bess's recipe book was on her kitchen table.

"That's it. Here, give it to me." Angus grabbed the book out of the sentry's hand and immediately started going through the pages, eager to see if it was what he expected. He lowered his eyelids and looked out through little slits. His mouth pulled into a thin smile.

"This is magnificent. Harvest, plants, herbs, and medicines. And it looks old, probably written by generations of witches."

"There's one more here," the sentry said, holding out his hand with a white, silk book.

The witch-finder grabbed the book and looked inside, but shook his head when he read the heading. "Peter," he mumbled, and looked at a few more pages. "Peter, who? No, this is written by someone else. Just leave it for now." He held the recipe book of the Frue Farm women high. "This is what I want. I am pleased we found it so easily."

"Do you want us to bring the evidence to Town Hall, Mr. Hill?" the sentry asked, holding out his hand toward the recipe book.

"No need. I will take care of it."

"What about the child? We have not seen her around today."

"The child?" Angus Hill lifted his eyebrows and lowered them again. "Oh, yes, exactly, there is a young daughter. What is her name?"

"Lucia."

The witch-finder now smiled broadly. "This gets better all the time," he said. He held the recipe book in his hands and caressed it like a small pet. "Lucia, you say. She actually named her firstborn after the father of all lies." He turned and walked toward the carriage. "No, leave the child. We don't need her at this point. The old man will return. He'll tend to her. We can get the child later. Let's go back."

He walked with steadfast paces back to his carriage, passing the open cart. He paused for a moment and looked at the woman tied to the cart and out cold. She was not like the rest, and yet he needed to be well prepared for her trial at court. This was one witch he did not want to let go.

16

The Closed Door

Grinding thoughts did not leave Clara alone all morning as she taught the children in the school house at the parsonage. Only three children showed up, but that was no reason to postpone the lesson. She kept thinking about Bess, sensed something was wrong, and was impatient to get to Frue Farm to see her.

Main Street was full of peddlers and everyone going about their business as usual. But as Clara drew closer to Town Hall, she saw a crowd by the stairs.

A woman who passed her said, "They brought your friend in."

Clara started running. She held up the front of her gown and tried to avoid holes between the cobblestones on the street. Her greatest fear had become reality.

Uncle Samuel with Lucia in his arms stood on the steps in front of the double blue door, yelling at the guards. They refused him entry and pushed him back down the stairs. Protecting Lucia, he turned his back to them but did not give up. When he saw Clara, he handed her the child and ran back up the stairs to try to get inside the door. This time, they hit him and pushed him hard. Uncle Samuel fell down but got up again and limped toward where Clara stood with the child.

"I can't get in," he said angry and tearful. "They came for her. Lucia was all alone when I arrived at the farm. Good thing I returned earlier than planned. They must have just taken Bess right before I returned." He swallowed hard and wiped his runny nose. "How can we get to Bess, Clara?"

"Here, hold Lucia," Clara said. "Let me try."

Clara pressed her way through the throng of people and addressed the stone-faced guards. "Please, let me in to see Bess of Frue Farm. She's with child and has a young daughter who needs her mother. Please, let me by."

"We can't do that, Miss. No one gets in, orders of the mayor and Mr. Hill."

"But, please—"

One of the men pushed Clara away, making her trip down the stairs. She looked up at him, but he just shook his bearded face and looked at her with stern, determined eyes.

Uncle Samuel took hold of Clara's arm and helped her back to her feet. They were both at a loss for words. Lucia asked for her mother. Clara had to swallow twice before coming up with a suitable answer for the copper-headed angel.

All day Clara sat outside on the stairs of Town Hall. When the shadows became long and the Rossbyans returned home, Clara sat there still. The blue double door was opened only when a couple of the council members went home for the day. She tried to ask them about Bess. They ignored her and walked on. Clara looked up and saw the mayor in the window of his upstairs apartment. When he disappeared from view, she felt so alone. A drunk gentleman with a cane and new clothes came toward her and asked if she needed help. Clara thanked him, but knew there was nothing he could do in his state; besides, she did not know if she could trust him.

Clara looked up again as she heard the upstairs window open. The mayor looked out and called her name.

"Clara, what are you still doing there? It's late. You have been there all day."

"I have, Mr. Mayor. I don't know what has happened to Bess. Please, I would like to see her. Can you let me in?"

"It's late, Clara. Go home. Come back tomorrow."

~

Clara cancelled school and went back early the next day. The town square looked as if nothing had happened. Life went on as usual; no one seemed to worry that Bess was locked up inside the prison. Clara spent another day on the stairs, waiting, crying, hoping for someone to come by—anyone who with the authority to open the doors would let her in to see how Bess fared.

On the south end of Main Street, a carriage pulled up in front of the Land's store. Out strode Angus Hill. His pointed black boots hit a puddle as he stepped out. He frowned and wiggled his feet to shake off the water. Facing the front door, he straightened his back, rolled his shoulders, and pulled up his chin. With a fake grin, he cleared his throat and knocked on the door with his walking stick. The maid opened and curtsied, before she showed him and his interpreter into the parlor.

"Mr. Hill, how nice to see you." Mrs. Land stretched out her hand.

The witch-finder requested the twins' company on an important errand. "They are always so helpful," he said. "They seem to have a certain flare when it comes to seeking out suspicious women of the area."

Flattery worked well with Mrs. Land. "Of course, they may come with you, as long as they are well taken care of," she said. "I don't want any harm to come to my beauties. If there are witches about, I don't want them near."

"I will guard them carefully, Mrs. Land." The witch-finder removed his large hat, gallantly swung his arm and in a welcoming manner bowed, inviting the girls to join him and the innkeeper in the carriage. As always, several horses with guardsmen would follow closely behind.

On the way out the witch-finder comforted the worried mother. "I'm so sorry for all the twins have had to go through. Being spokespersons for such a grave matter, and at such a young age is beyond description. I only hope they will recover well and be able to move on with their good lives."

Mrs. Land nodded and put a lace handkerchief up to her mouth and made a sniffling sound. She waved the handkerchief to her daughters and called out, "Goodbye, my dears. Take care."

Old Magda lived just beyond the abbey. They would return in time for their midday meal. The innkeeper reluctantly climbed on top of the carriage as Angus Hill needed his interpreter near, in order to have further conversation with the Land twins. Never before had the witch-finder met anyone so full of information and thoroughly beneficial to his important work.

As they passed the church, they saw Toomber carrying wooden planks from one pile to another.

"Who is that tall man?" Angus Hill asked and pointed out the window.

Taran poked her head out to look. "Oh, that's Toomber. He takes care of the cemetery in Rossby."

"What do you know about him? Does he have a family?"

The twins started giggling.

Tilla said, "Toomber, a family? No, who would want to marry him? He lives by himself in the small cottage by the marsh on the hill behind the church and the cemetery."

"I have seen him around." Angus Hill nodded his head and made mental notes of the conversation. "I saw him in church and also on Main Street carrying heavy loads. He looks strong."

"Oh, that he is. He could probably lift both Tilla and me at the same time," Taran said. "But don't go near him, Mr. Hill. He smells terribly bad."

The twins giggled, and the witch-finder sat and stared at their lovely smiles and perfect teeth. They were so young and innocent, without worldly worries and knowledge of wickedness in the adult world. And yet, they were helpful to him in his effort to free the Rossbyans from evil.

They drove past the gray stone abbey and saw several of the sisters busy at work outside the large building. Some were in the orchard picking apples from the trees. Angus Hill got the twins attention by pointing out the window on the other side of the carriage. He wanted to safeguard them from the scary memories they might have, thinking a witch had actually lived there at the abbey just a few days earlier. But now she was gone and he had been the instrument in God's hands in protecting both young and old in the quaint, little town of Rossby.

Close by Magda's cottage they halted, and the guardsmen tied up their horses and stayed a little behind, a procedure they had gotten used to now. Angus always snuck up on his victims, not wanting to cause a stir from the beginning.

The cottage was without neighbors and nestled behind trees, not easily seen from the road. Angus Hill stepped out of the carriage and breathed in the fresh air of the woods.

"I have learned from my studies," he said as he sauntered toward the small house, "that when a woman thinks alone, she thinks evil."

"Hear, hear," the innkeeper added, as always two paces behind Angus.

"Come, come, girls," the witch-finder beckoned. "Don't be afraid. I'm here and will not let her harm you." He turned around and gently held out his hand toward the twins, summoning them to come closer.

The twins were hesitant but took small, ladylike steps toward him, turning around now and then.

"Who is it that bewitches you," he asked kindly. "What are you afraid of?"

The girls pointed to the cottage and slowly moved further along.

"What have you experienced here that is so horrible? What is so difficult for you to talk about?"

"She has witch-boxes," Taran said. "She has eight or ten in her house, with spells written on paper and items to do witchcraft."

The talismans hanging from the tree in front of the cottage played a soft tune in the gentle, late summer breeze. Charms of unripe rowan berries hung from the lower branches to dry. Angus studied them as he heard a sweet voice from the door of the cottage call out.

"Keeps them fairies away, they do. Do you want to buy one?"

Angus grinned when he heard the translation. He turned his head, intrigued by the welcome. Their visit would be much easier than he had expected.

"Good morning," he said, "and you are?"

Old Magda frowned. "Don't understand gibberish talk," she said and looked back and forth at the men. "Makes my head spin."

Angus stepped closer. "You were asking us something?"

"I asked if you wanted to buy a charm. I also have St. John's wort and four-leaf clovers, if you prefer those. They are useful for the same matter, you know."

Angus Hill was fascinated. This was an excellent witch's specimen and he was pleased, but had to move slowly and make sure he understood the signs and processed the proof properly.

The little woman with the kind eyes and large toothless grin was pleasing enough, but that was often how real witches deceived their fellow beings. He listened to her go on about how cock's crows drove fairies away, about remedies protecting someone from trolls and gnomes, and how to chase away aches and pains.

"Poor Hilda's leg ached with cramps," she said suddenly.

Angus Hill widened his eyes and thought the day could not have gotten any better. The old woman even related stories about other witch friends.

"I tied woolen strings around her legs to help her," Old Magda continued. "Not much good it does her now, poor Hilda, my dear."

"So that's why that first smelly woman by the sea had woolen threads around her legs," the witch-finder whispered to his interpreter. "I could not remember what that was for. This witch is revealing much more than we could have hoped for."

She invited him in and offered him and the other guests a cup of cider and some pine resin for chewing. The resin had a strange consistency and strong flavor, but after some meticulous chewing, Angus Hill nodded his head and affirmed it was actually quite good.

"This is typical," Angus Hill said and turned to the innkeeper, who eagerly awaited results of the day's hunt, "a woman with no man to take care of her, who needs and wants male protection, becomes desperate and joins in with evil, practicing the ways of darkness and making pacts, in order to find refuge. This one has gone all the way, just like the last witch. Take her in. We will give her a trial and keep her safely out of the way. She will not have any influence on anyone anymore."

He turned to the twins, who followed him around. "Girls, you don't need to be afraid anymore. I will take care of this. Thank you for warning me. You were right in doing so. Now go outside, as this could become ugly."

When Old Magda found out they were taking her precious freedom away, forcing her to go to town with them, she screamed like a banshee.

"Women who scold, reveal themselves as a witch," Angus said loud enough for Magda to hear, even if she did not understand. "Her tongue is like poison."

He looked out of the door and called for guards to come and take hold of the situation. He did not want to be scratched up by a filthy witch's fingernails or have her bite him. He took a couple of steps back and let the sentries do what they were good at.

"You two," he instructed, pointing at two of the guards, "go outside, and see if there's anything that could be known as her familiar, an imp, who serves her and stays here on the grounds. Be careful; you don't know what it is. It could be a black cat or a large toad. Be gone with you, and hurry. I don't want to spend the afternoon here listening to this woman's screams."

The little old woman rattled off one curse after another, looking directly at the witch-finder, who by now had turned his glance away from her. He knew well what she did, even though the language was foreign to him.

They brought the woman outside and dragged her toward the carriage. Her voice seemed to penetrate the soul, and even the twins waiting outside had to hold their ears as the guards finally lifted the kicking and screaming Old Magda up and carried her the rest of the way.

"I will just finish up in here," Angus Hill told the innkeeper. "You go on and join the others; I will be there shortly. I will look to see if there is anything else we have missed here. At least this witch kept a clean house."

He walked around the small room, opening up the drawers of a chest and looking under the bed in the corner. In a vase on the small bedside table, he found a ring. He slipped it into his pocket and walked out to join the others, closing the door behind him.

"Any finds?" he asked the guards.

They shook their heads.

"Very well, let's take her into town."

It was a noisy trip going back. Old Magda recited all the curses and spells she knew, and seemed to make up the rest.

Angus leaned back in the carriage seat, his chest puffed out. He glanced out of the window and let out a long, gratifying sigh.

17

The Snake Pit

~~

Who really knows a person or what he is going through in life, but the person himself and God? Clara had been aware of Old Magda's activities and had not done anything about it. Maybe she had not taken it seriously enough. Magda had her own sort of religion, and even though Clara belonged to a preaching family, she did not always know how to be a missionary. Her father told her once that a missionary is someone who teaches a principle through good deeds wrought out of the goodness of one's heart.

Even though Clara was used to spending time alone, she felt the need to discuss her feelings and thoughts as never before. Other than Uncle Samuel, she felt she could trust the parson and his wife.

"You look worn out," Sara said.

Clara came by after she had spent another day in front of Town Hall.

"I'm well," Clara answered.

She rubbed her eyes and shook her head when Sara asked if she was hungry.

"How can we get them to release Bess?" Clara asked. "I have tried and tried but can't get in to see her."

Herr Christopher stared at the floor.

"He feels outnumbered," Sara said. "The council and people in town are with Angus Hill. We love Rossby, but our hearts ache with what it has become, a witch-hunting town where no one can be sure about a neighbor."

"I know," Clara said. "But what can we do? How can we influence for good?"

"There are parishioners who come to me for solace," Herr Christopher said and folded his hands in his lap. "Some are afraid and seek direction, but for the most part, they choose to follow the excitement of the hunt."

Clara hung her head low as she walked back to her cottage. She wished Mychel was home at Frue Farm and her father and brother at the parsonage. She needed Peter. He was always a good listener and saw solutions when Clara saw challenges as problems. *They all would have known what to do*, she thought.

~~~

In the early morning light, she decided to pick blueberries for a cobbler. Lucia's third birthday approached and Clara wanted to bring her and Uncle Samuel something in the midst of all the difficulties.

Clara found a hilly area with bushes of luscious berries with a deep blue color. She put the basket down and started picking when suddenly a snake slithered through the berry bushes right in front of her hand. She turned stiff from fright and slowly moved her hand back and watched where the snake headed. Luckily it was either eager to get away or too occupied to care.

"If you stick your hand in dangerous places, you risk getting bitten," Peter said one time when Clara wanted to explore a rocky area by the mission home in Okinawa.

She was curious about everything and unaccustomed to dangerous and poisonous wildlife.
~~~

"Beware of *mother habu*," the *papasan* who took care of the mission garden warned. "Very venomous snake, not afraid of you and will strike if sense heat. Sometimes get into house if door open, even climb trees."

Clara continued picking blueberries. She could risk sharing the woods with the occasional snake but never grab it by the tail or encourage a confrontation. She thought about the trial. She was afraid of exactly that. By appearing in the courtroom, she stepped into a nest of snakes to confront the witch-finder himself. She would have to be careful not to say or do anything to expose his fangs and worsen Bess's status.

Thank goodness for Uncle Samuel. He was a tower of strength and kept his calm, so Lucia stayed happy, even though she missed her mother. The day he returned from hunting, he had found Lucia asleep on a pile of hay behind the barn, hungry and asking for her mother. Since the day Clara had met him outside Town Hall, he had kept watch at Frue Farm and stayed away from town and meddlesome people.

Uncle Samuel worked the farm more than ever before. He became quieter, almost silent at times. She could tell he grieved. It was the reaction of a disciplined man, used to putting words to action, used to following plans and orders. His situation now was unbearable. His beard became wild and unkempt and his eyes hollow from sleepless, tormenting nights.

Clara asked him if she should take Lucia to her cottage, but he just shook his head.

"Lucia needs to be here when her mother returns," he explained. "The child needs to stay put and I have to make her days as normal as possible."

She knew he was right, as he had helped take care of Lucia since she was born. His company was her safe harbor.

Four days had passed since they had taken Bess. Clara heard people talk. Angus Hill collected witches now, and the first two witch-trials had only served as an illustration of what was to come. At least he would try the women in court, even though Clara heard that he had agreed to court trials to save time. The first hearing was set for a couple of days later.

The night before the first trial, Clara tossed and turned. When she finally drifted off to sleep, she dreamt she could fly like a bird high above the tree tops. She knew she could float in the air, gather the breeze under her wings, and enjoy the view. She had the ability to fly weightlessly and carefree, but her body felt heavy, and it was as if the soles of her feet were covered with heavy syrup that stuck to the ground like glue. She simply could not lift herself off the ground and felt powerless.

As the cock crowed the next morning, she felt even more tired than when she had gone to bed the previous evening. Dreaming sometimes drained her strength.

"You lead an exciting life," her father used to say when she told him about dreams she could remember. "You have two lives—one during the day and one when you dream at night. No wonder you get tired."

Nevertheless, there was no time to moan or be tired. Clara had to get to Town Hall. It was unbearable, but she had no choice in the matter. She prayed she might help Bess in some way. The dream the previous night was a reminder of how feeble she felt.

Outside Town Hall young and old gathered. Some were let in the blue double door and shown a seat in the courtroom set up for witch-trials, others were allowed to stand in the back as space permitted.

There were still people waiting in the town square as Clara walked inside to find a seat. The twins with bouncing curls tied with ribbons and lace satchels in their hands, sat with their mother on the front row. Next to them, a solemn Herr Christopher and his wife Sara, who sat with her legs wide apart and rested her hands on her overdue pregnant belly. Clara saw Mathias with Laura, who held little Bess, serious and content at the same time. It was hard for Clara to guess let alone understand what they were thinking.

A couple of the sisters from the abbey had shown up, and Anna had kindly saved Clara a seat on the front row. There were many Clara did not know, but she recognized Margit, Skipper Welam's wife, whom Bess had told her about, and in the crowd in the back of the court room was young Albert. He chewed nervously on a twig and stared intently at Tilla on the front row.

Toomber was not there, nor Uncle Samuel, as it was best that he kept Lucia safe.

It was a gray day outside, and although the room had several large windows, candles were lit in stakes on the walls, and the curtains were pushed all the way to the side.

There was a large table in front of the room with a scribe sitting on one end, ready for work with paper, ink, and quill laid out in front of him. Chairs were set up behind the table for the town council members on the right, the mayor in the middle, and Angus Hill and his interpreter, John Pywell, on the left.

There was much talk in the room, but when the mayor hit his mallet on the table with some force, it became silent as the grave.

Old Magda was brought out first.

"Do you have any helpers, any associates?" Angus Hill was effective and devious in trying to smoke out the witches of Rossby as quickly as possible. "Who do you work with?"

"No one. I never work with anyone. I do my things and Bess does hers. We both—"

Angus Hill turned quickly as he heard the last sentence in his own language. "Bess, you say. Bess of Frue Farm? What about her?"

"There isn't anyone in Rossby as powerful as Bess," Magda continued. "Eyes the color of fairy-eyes, she has. If she wanted to, she could fly into town on stems of ragwort or perhaps on the back of a bird. I am not surprised if she shape-shifts either."

This is not helping anyone, Clara thought. *Old Magda has no idea what she is doing. Poor, old woman, she probably thinks she's bragging about Bess, not hurting her.*

She remembered how Magda had told her stories about Bess. But the damage was done and Clara could tell how eager the witch-hunter became by this bit of information. While John Pywell translated, she saw Angus Hill make notes on a paper in his hand. Clara's shoulders tensed up as he continued with the interrogation.

"Could you tell us about townspeople you have *helped*?" The last word he said sarcastically. He looked at the audience and showed his disgust.

"I am always helping, and it's not a burden or a drudge. It's how I live, and it makes me happy. I want you to let me go now, so I can continue doing just that."

"Oh, we cannot possibly let you go yet. Tell us examples."

She told the court about how Laura had come to her house just recently, asking her what to do to protect her infant from evil. Old Magda had placed a piece of bread in the child's blanket. She also told the court about herbal mixtures, honey cakes, and witch-boxes sold at the fair.

Clara's mouth went dry. She could only imagine what Angus Hill could do with the information Magda offered and had experienced firsthand how skilled he was in how to ensnare a person with their own words. She said a silent prayer for Magda.

"Have you sold your soul?" the witch-finder finally asked.

Mumbling and loud whispers filled the room as the spectators anxiously awaited the outcome of the trial.

Clara could not hold her tongue any longer. "Magda would not know what that means. Please leave her alone," she cried out but regretted the outburst immediately and feared she had said too much. She sat back down and lowered her gaze. *I have to force myself to silence,* she thought.

"Quiet, Miss Dahl," the witch-finder said. "Let the old woman answer for herself. She knows what it means. She must have heard about the soul of a person and how important it is?"

It was better not to reveal that Magda was not a church-going woman. It did not strengthen her case. Clara moved to the edge of her seat and waited for Magda's reply. The room had an uncomfortable, hushed tension.

"Yes, I have," Magda answered. She looked straight at the witch-finder. "It is sold and I'm glad."

Angus walked in front of the audience, raised his eyebrows, bowed his head, and put his hands in the air, palms up. He then sat down, satisfied with the conclusion. The audience cheered and some of them clapped. A couple of young men in the back began chanting, "Witch, witch."

Clara could tell Old Magda was tired. Her arms were scratched where they had used a blunt knife on her skin to see if she bled like a witch. She had no shoes on, and her bare feet were both dirty and bloody. The variety of atrocities thrown at the innocent victims of the witch-hunt seemed to have no end. Clara's stomach tightened. She wished she could wake up and it was all a bad dream.

She closed her eyes as guards escorted Old Magda back to the waiting chamber and *not* acquitted of witch-craft, but awaiting further notice. *If only a heavy horse and large carriage ran over the witch-hunter so he could hunt no more,* Clara thought.

Angus got up and stood in the center of the room in front of the large table and looked at Clara as if to say, *I told you so.* Suddenly, he walked straight toward her and placed his clammy, white fingers on her shoulders. "Miss Dahl, you absolutely wanted trials in a courtroom. You are only a woman, a woman of little understanding when it comes to witch-trials. You have questioned my methods and requested court sessions for your so-called friends. Woman, in these matters it is necessary to supersede normal legal procedures."

His fingers were heavy on Clara's shoulders, and she felt the need to wash herself. She had to keep her mouth closed for fear she would mention something to worsen the situation. This was no game. He was in charge in a way that he had the council, the mayor, and the people in his sticky hands. His gaze penetrated, and Clara had to be watchful not to try his patience. She would be of no help to anyone if she was placed on trial for aiding witches.

"I appreciate the chance these women have to speak for themselves," Clara said quietly.

He snorted. "Yet here we are, Miss Dahl, and have we come any further with these witches? Not at all." He turned around and called out loud enough for everyone to hear, "Not at all, I say. Bring the next witch in."

It had been close to a fortnight since they stole Bess away from Frue Farm. Clara sat and watched as they brought her best friend into the room, the curly copper hair in a mess, but still more striking than any other woman in the room. She already looked thinner and paler, even sickly, and Clara worried about the unborn child.

Though worn down by her days in prison, Bess held her head high and walked like a noble woman into the middle of the room, then sat down on the wooden chair. The hem of her gown was torn and dirty, and she too, had no shoes on her feet. Clara was glad to see she was still the strong-willed, brave Bess.

Clara looked around at the men behind the long table. Mr. Hansen had his nose in his notebook, flipping the pages back and forth, stretching out his arm to read his own scribbling.

Dr. Bing-Olsen leaned over toward him and said loud enough for Clara to hear, "She only claims to cure people, you know. Look where she is today. She is such a false woman, not educated, not skilled like myself. She only professes knowledge of the workings of the human body."

"Yes, all that may be true," the innkeeper added, not looking up from his notebook. "But remember, we are here with more grave accusations than what kind of doctor the woman is."

It was a room filled with whisperings, loathing, and pity. Everyone behaved as if they had a piece of the situation in their own hand. The horror had become so profound, Clara felt feeble.

Angus Hill pulled out a root of chamomile from his pocket and held it in front of Bess, who rolled her eyes and said mockingly, "Do you think I will be less dangerous if you wag a root of a common herb in front of my face?" Looking over at the mayor, she added, "This is ridiculous. You cannot be serious in bringing me here. I am no more a witch than anyone else in this room. Knowing how to heal with herbs is knowledge, not witchcraft."

There was a murmur in the room. Bess looked back and forth at the people in the room. Most of them she knew. They had required her services and bought her delicacies at fairs or received her help when ill. Her eyes met Clara's who shook her head a little, to show Bess she thought it best to be still and not give too much information without being asked.

Angus Hill remained his calm self. *He knows she's different from the others, harder to break,* Clara thought.

"We all know this woman, Bess of Frue Farm," the witch-finder cried out with his thin voice, his interpreter repeating the words, making them comprehensible, even plausible. "Many of you have had dealings with her, health issues perhaps, purchases of fruits and wool or dried meat. Today we are addressing a far more serious matter, namely sorcery. There will be some of you who will say she is a good woman, but I ask you not to be deceived. Do you know what evil looks like? Not easy to tell, is it? Now, who will witness first?"

A man in ragged clothes whom Clara had never seen before, stood up and shouted in a hoarse voice, "I had an infection in my mouth and went to Bess for help."

The witch-finder from a distance tried to get him to elaborate. "Come, come, man, what more?"

"She told me to brew a tea with chamomile and sage and gargle, not drink it, just gargle."

"Did she heal you or did she hurt you?"

"My infection improved, but I lost another tooth."

Angus Hill did not see this allegation going anywhere and said leadingly, "So, you are saying she made your teeth fall out?"

"Yes, I guess that's what I am saying," the old man shook his shoulders even though people snickered and whispered behind his back.

"Hmm, interesting," Angus Hill said. "I would like to see for myself." Dr. Bing-Olsen and Innkeeper Hansen were right on his heels. They walked over to the insulted man who opened his jaws; hardly any teeth visible. A frightening stench streamed out, making the witch-finder and his crew back off. The old man did not seem miffed at their reaction but laughed loudly instead.

Behind the toothless man was Skipper Welam's widow. She raised her hand as she saw a chance to bring forth her complaint.

"Bess came to our home and fed my good husband herbs that killed him," she cried out.

The witch-finder looked at her to give her his complete attention while John Pywell translated.

"Very well," he said. "That's all well and good, excellent, excellent." He took a few steps in the other direction and called out, "Anyone else?"

Tilla, sitting straight-backed in a lavender-colored gown with large sleeves, lifted her lily-white hand. Angus Hill approached her with a straight smile, showing his teeth, but not his heart.

"Yes, sweet child, what do you want to say?"

Tilla stood up and walked a couple of paces into the center of the room. "Bess used spells on my sister, Taran," she said. She looked over at her twin, who gave her a reassuring look, then turned to face the front table again. "Bess poisoned my sister with a concoction that made her terribly ill, made her stay in bed for a fortnight…vomiting and in great pain. She could not move her legs."

"Go on, Miss Tilla." Angus Hill motioned with his hand in a circular way, all the while his glued-on grin almost stiffened in his cheeks.

"She put a hex on Laura's infant daughter," Tilla continued. She kept looking over at Taran, who stared straight back, clearly in agreement with her statement.

"How did she do that?" Angus Hill asked.

"She delivered the child and put her thumb on its leg, allowing an evil mark to be put there."

"Have you any proof?"

Tilla walked over to Laura, who stood up and brought the child forth. She removed the covers and held it up for everyone to see.

Angus Hill piously nodded his head back and forth. Empathy was important in the attempt of winning the approval of the masses.

"Anything else," he asked sweetly, patting the infant awkwardly on the head.

"She suffered from stomach cramps for several weeks after the birth," Laura explained.

"Who doesn't?" Bess asked out loud. "An infant's stomach cramps have nothing to do with anyone being a witch."

"Quiet, Bess of Frue Farm," the mayor said, showing he still had some authority. "You will have your say later on. Let the witness finish."

Laura gulped and squeezed her eyes to hold the tears back. Clara could tell she was uncomfortable being in the middle of a crowded room with everyone's eyes upon her. Angus decided to keep it going as every piece of evidence could be important in building his case.

"Ah, a sure sign of tampering," he said. "It is rough for a small child to be marked by evil. No wonder the infant reacted to it. Have you had the child blessed? Is it christened?"

Laura nodded.

"Then we hope it will be protected accordingly." He motioned for Laura to resume her seat and then turned to the younger twin. "Miss Tilla, anything else?"

"Oh, yes, your honor, Mr. Witch-finder, I mean…Hill." She walked over to the interpreter and whispered in John Pywell's ear.

Angus Hill grinned arrogantly when he heard the allegation in his own language, as if he had discovered a wicked truth to nail the copper-headed woman of nature. He hummed and clapped his fingertips lightly as he slowly strode back and forth in front of Bess. The audience was captivated. No one dared breathe a word. The only sound was the witch-finder's heels on the stone floor. Suddenly, he stopped and turned to face Bess.

"You have been observed dancing alone at dawn by the north forest lake in June of this year. Do you deny it?"

Bess looked surprised. She looked over at Clara, who nodded her head, suggesting Bess explain.

"No, I cannot deny it," she said calmly.

"You have been observed chanting at said place the same morning. Do you deny it?"

"No, I cannot deny it, but I wasn't chanting. I was sing—"

"So, you cannot deny it, you say." He turned to the audience. "Did you hear that? She admits to naked ritual dancing and chanting in the forest."

"No, I was certainly not naked." Bess protested louder. "I was in my night shift. It was early morning." She looked at Clara again. There was concern in her eyes now. "I was merely happy."

Again, there was a murmur in the crowd. Some were gasping with surprise. One elderly woman fell on the floor, as if she fainted. A man in the next seat, probably her husband, jumped up to tend to her.

He looked around the room, calling out, "What is happening? Please, someone, help her."

Dr. Bing-Olsen's long legs drew near but not all the way in fear that witchcraft caused people to fall unconscious without reason. He stood a few paces away from the woman, holding a handkerchief in front of his mouth.

"Protecting yourself, I see," Angus said. "Clever. With evil lurking around the premises, that's the only thing to do."

There was dead silence in the room as if everyone played a game of chess, waiting for the next move.

Clara glanced over at Taran and wondered what she and her sister could have been doing out at that time. The twin sat on a chair on the first row, gloating with a smirk on her face.

Good heavens, Clara thought, *how can someone so sweet on the outside be so wicked on the inside?*

Just then, a white dove landed on the sill of the open window on the west wall. In the midst of evil, misled thoughts of lies and revenge, the pureness of the dove brought a feeling of peace and serenity. Simultaneously, the sun peeked forth from behind a wooly cloud and sent rays of light, like beams, straight through the room and directly on Bess sitting alone on the chair in the middle of the room. The feeling was hushed, soundless.

Clara watched the witch-finder's expression. It looked like he found the pendant situation prickly and did not approve of the sudden mood change in his court session. He looked around the room at the stupefied faces. Clara wondered what he would say to adjust the unexplainable sweetness before it got out of hand. Suddenly, he stood up and pointed at the woman lying on the floor.

"There are evil spirits in this room," he shouted. "One has taken hold of this poor, old woman. She has lost her own strength."

"What is he saying? Pray, what is he saying?" people called out.

The tenseness was not eased by always having to wait for John Pywell to interpret. He had hardly finished the sentences before the reaction came, and uproar charged the courtroom. People were now talking loudly, some shouting, others fidgeting in their seats. They were frightened and looked around the room and up toward the ceiling, no doubt wondering if an evil spirit would appear out of nowhere and penetrate their skins also. Or did they expect the white dove to turn into a version of the Holy Ghost, magically more than spiritually, taking over the court session and influencing every mind in the room? Clara looked at Bess, beautiful in the white light, her copper hair glistening, as if golden strands were woven into the unruly curls. She looked tired, but peaceful.

The old woman came around and was helped back into her chair.

Tilla waved her arms and screamed, "I see it. I see the evil spirit go out of the old woman and it's moving toward Bess." Her voice became even louder, almost shrieking, and she pointed straight at Bess. "It's entering Bess."

By now, there was a mass of commotion and noise in the courtroom. The mayor hit his mallet several times as he called for order.

Angus stood up, lifted his hand to calm the uproar, and stated firmly, "The witch summoned it back. Let's continue the questioning." Then he sat back down again to give the town leader a chance to say a word or two.

The mayor looked around the room and glanced back down at his papers. Clearing his throat, he said hesitantly, "Well, there is the matter of the missing crucifix, but I don't know if it belongs in this court session."

He glanced over at the witch-finder, who, after having the words translated opened his eyes widely.

With enthusiasm Angus said, "But of course, very much so. This is absolutely the place and time to bring it up."

Clara watched how Tilla twitched nervously in her chair as if she sat on a family of porcupines. She looked around the room, her eyes wide open, her thumbs twiddling.

All of a sudden, the younger twin stood up again, shouting, "I have seen it. She has it."

The crowd was all ears again, and some started shouting. The mayor had to hit the mallet three times again.

"Order, order." he called. "What do you mean? What have you seen? Who has what? Come here, child."

Tilla straightened her dress and winked at her sister. She tilted her head back and walked up to the table to face the mayor and the witch-finder. She also took the time to look over at the jury of council members sitting on her right side.

18

The Waiting Chamber

~~~

"I have seen the crucifix", Tilla said. "Bess has it, and she has hidden it under a rock on her land."

Bess lifted her eyebrows and opened her mouth to speak, but the mayor interrupted her. "What are you saying, Miss Tilla?" he said. "How do you know of this? Do you know where to find it?"

Clara studied Tilla's face. The younger twin was clearly afraid of something, despite the confident conduct. What was she worried about? The sisters' eyes met and as Taran nodded, Clara realized the girl gave her approval to a sudden change of strategy. The twins had started a game they had to finish.

"We were picking flowers, my sister and I," Tilla said.

"Yes, yes." The witch-finder was clearly wound up about physical proof of witchery. "Finally, some tangible evidence, not hearsay or gossip" he mumbled. He rolled his hands in circles. "Continue, child, please, continue."
~~~

"We were close to Frue Farm and heard noises in the corner of the orchard, close to the path toward Rossby."

The witch-finder smiled encouragingly.

Tilla swallowed hard. "We put our baskets down and peeked through some bushes, afraid of what it could be."

"What did you see, Tilla?" the mayor asked, absurdly believing what the girl was saying.

"We saw Bess there. She had a shovel in her hand and dug a hole under a rock."

"Did you see the crucifix?" Angus Hill asked excitedly.

"Yes. It was the one from the church. We were so afraid she might hear something, and we thought if she saw us there, she would turn us to stone or into a toad."

"Oh, honestly," Bess burst out. "You cannot seriously believe in imaginary tales from young girls who have made it their leisure to gossip and make up stories about others."

"Quiet, you blasphemous woman." Angus stood up and put out his hand, motioning Bess to cease talking.

She looked at Clara again, who nodded, advising her to try to hold her tongue.

The mayor called out to the guards, "How long will it take to uncover this evidence?"

"A good twenty minutes, sir, even with a fast rider," a sentry answered.

"Have someone ride faster than the wind," the mayor commanded.

Clara had often appreciated his way of speech, though now was not the time to enjoy poetry. The sentry waved his hand toward a couple of guards by the door, who immediately exited the room.

Everyone waited. Clara wondered what would happen next. Why would the crucifix be hidden at Frue Farm?

The questioning continued in the court room of Town Hall as Angus Hill turned to face the older twin.

"Is there anything you want to add to these allegations, Miss Land?

Taran stood up and said loudly, "She murdered our brother."

Clara saw Bess lower her head and heard her say quietly, "Here we go again."

Angus stared intently at Taran. "Murdered, you say?" He looked intrigued by her assertion. "Pray, tell me more. What happened exactly?"

Mrs. Land put the back of her hand to her forehead. "I am falling, falling. The room is spinning. Ah…help me. Help me."

Mr. Land tried to support the weight of his wife as she leaned heavily against him. He looked around the room with a cry of help in his eyes.

"Please, enough of this," he pleaded. "My wife and daughters are suffering."

"This is much more than I had hoped for," Angus whispered to the mayor. "It's satisfactory indeed. Should I continue? I say that further testing of the redhead for witchcraft is redundant."

"Well, it will be a few more minutes before the guards return, perhaps we can give everyone a short pause, even stretch their legs for a minute?" the mayor answered.

"Yes, I agree. This must be hard on everyone. Poor people. To think, they have had this woman in their midst for years. It's a wonder that not more Rossbyans have come forth to make complaints."

Only a few scattered seats were filled as everyone was asked to take a breather, and go outside for some fresh air.

"The air in the presence of a witch is impure." The witch-finder managed to insult Bess, passing her on his way out.

Clara ran over and hugged Bess still on the chair. She must have smothered her. Bess seemed fragile already and asked Clara to be careful. Clara calmed down and kneeled on the floor next to the chair and gently wrapped both arms around her. Bess asked about Lucia and Uncle Samuel and wondered if Clara had heard from Mychel. Even Frue Farm was on her mind.

"How are *you*?" Clara managed to ask. "Are they being mean? Do they leave you alone?"

"It is bearable," Bess answered. "It's cold at night and the company is less than desirable. I am glad Lucia is not here to see this, even though I would love to hold my little girl and tell her how much I love her."

"I will let her know," Clara said. "Uncle Samuel wanted to be here, but we felt it was safer if he watched Lucia at the farm. This is no place for a small child."

Clara removed her shawl and placed it around Bess's shoulders. "How are you really holding up, Bess," she asked.

Bess shrugged. "They won't let you in to see me, will they?"

"No, I try every day, but they block us out for now."

Clara pulled a few strands of hair away from Bess's face and handed her a piece of bread she had kept hidden in her pocket. Bess devoured it before anyone had the chance to take it away.

"It is absurd. I stand accused of ludicrous and invented doings," Bess said.

"The stories are fabricated, Bess. They cannot truly believe all this nonsense coming out of Tilla's mouth."

"I know, but it seems the townspeople believe it, doesn't it? I have my back to them, but I hear their whisperings, and I sense their thoughts." She looked down at her hands in her lap, normally so diligent and hard-working, now they were shaking.

"I am not sure," Clara answered. "Maybe they don't dare to say their true opinion for fear that the witch-finder will accuse them of something."

Noises and talking by the door told them that in a few minutes the court would be in session again. Clara held Bess's hand for as long as possible, until a guard even younger than herself pushed her back into her seat.

The mayor sat down and banged his mallet on the table. A tall guard walked into the room with a dirty, cloth bundle in his hands. He placed it on the table in front of the mayor.

The witch-finder stood in front of the table, blocking the view. Clara could not see what was inside as he opened the bundle. The whispers were low and hushed as he returned to his seat.

The mayor cleared his voice and said, "The crucifix from the Rossby church has been recovered. Here it is."

Herr Christopher, who had held his head low during the session, now lifted his chin, his curious eyes wide as he looked at his lost crucifix.

With his hand high up in the air, the mayor showed everyone then addressed Bess.

"Bess of Frue Farm, this was found on your land."

"Well, someone must have planted it there. I know nothing about it."

"The evidence is presented, just as Miss Tilla gave testimony of. A fact is a fact."

"This is a conspiracy, Mr. Mayor, all lies. I never stole that crucifix. Why would I do that?"

"Why indeed? We desire to know that, too." He looked at the audience, asking for their approval.

The townspeople were mumbling. Some clearly wanted more.

Angus was more than contented. He stood up and walked over to face Bess. "Why don't you just admit it, witch?" he said.

"Admit to what? I have done nothing worth wasting everyone's time here in this court today."

"Why do you have to fight a higher, more righteous power than yourself?" Angus's voice sounded insolent and disrespectful.

"What?"

He turned to the audience and laughed. The sound caught fire like a flame in dry grass. Soon it seemed that most of the audience laughed with him, but it was the opposite of joyous, happy laughter. They were being cruel.

"She does not even understand what I mean," Angus yelled out. "Righteousness is our weapon. This woman is bewildered by the mention of her wicked ways. There's no need to question her any further."

He waved his hands in front of the audience to calm them down. He wanted to make his closing remarks.

"My observations are these," the witch-finder said, pacing with slow steps back and forth between the table and Bess on the chair. He tapped his lips with his pointing finger as he spoke, his forehead wrinkled in deep thought.

"No matter what, the cross is evidence. Stealing from the church is a crime larger than petty theft. It is a sacrilege."

He saw Bess lift her chin up, as if she was about to speak, but he hushed her severely.

"In closing, I have a few thoughts I want to share with you." He lifted his hand up in the air, holding the recipe book from Frue Farm.

Clara's jaw dropped and she saw Bess's eyes had a desperate look.

"I have here in my hand a book of spells," Angus said. "It is written in the language of a *witch*."

He accentuated the last word, looking around at the faces of his listeners. He thrived when he could say something to cause a reaction in people's faces, and he was rewarded.

"Witches are heretics, heretics to the Christian way of life, and that is the greatest sin of all. But not only that, they commit the greatest crime of all—irreverent sin added to sacrilegious crime. Well, think for yourselves, good people of Rossby. Think of all the proof you have heard today, like the testimony of a young girl." He pointed at Tilla, who sat holding Taran's hand, her mother's arm around her shoulder. "Think of how you felt when that poor woman fell on the floor. Think about the dove on the windowsill. Where on earth did it come from if the witch did not summon it here? Was it spectral evidence? Yes, clearly. Were you afraid? Yes. And fright is not a thing we welcome in this small town by the sea. You should be able to live without fear, without evil. She proved guilty when we tested her for witchcraft during the night. And then there's the crucifix." He smiled smugly, seemingly pleased with his arguments. "Good people, what more do we need? The evidence is overwhelming. Take her away."

People were nodding to each other, agreeing. Clara looked around the room. They seemed elated to have Angus Hill clarify a problem they had not even known existed in the first place.

Bess was pulled out of the chair by her arms and fought like a wild lynx. She scratched and showed her teeth while they placed a sack over her head. The witch-finder had said no one would be safe if they looked the witch in her eyes.

"I demand that you test me again and again," she shouted hoarsely from inside the sack. She screamed, kicked her legs, and fought with all her might to get free. "You will find me innocent. You will see that I am no witch."

"No, Bess," Clara yelled out, "don't." She turned to the guards. "Please be careful with her. She is with child."

Clara could not bear to have them torture Bess anymore. It did no good. Angus Hill had already made up his mind long before the trial and the rest of the people in the room just followed blindly along. She had to find another way.

Clara tried to get closer, but the guards were prepared for her reaction and held her back. Female strength was not worth much with two large men holding her arms. Frail and feeble, she fell on her knees, sobbing.

Angus Hill walked across the room to speak with the twins. He patted Tilla on the cheek, thanked her for her help, even blessed her. The girls curtsied politely and walked out with their parents, sweet, girlish smiles on their pale faces.

The mayor still sat on his chair shaking his head. "I would not have believed it, had I not seen it with my own eyes," he said. "Bess of Frue Farm? She was a good woman, was she not? Was she not?"

He looked both ways at the faces of the councilmen sitting next to him behind the table, but no one answered.

"She got what she deserved," the innkeeper stated and picked up his notebook from the table.

Dr. Bing-Olsen looked pleased that his competitor had been eliminated.

People cleared the room, chatting with each other about what had happened. As they stepped outside, the crispness in the air brought them back to reality. They nodded to each other and went on about their normal work. Some stayed behind to talk, and a few sauntered across the town square to the Watering House for something to drink.

~

Another week went by and still they did not let Clara in to see Bess, even though she tried every day. Early one morning she met Anna on Main Street on her way to work.

"Oh, Clara", she said compassionately and gave Clara a hug. "They still have Bess in the waiting chamber on the ground floor. Angus Hill seems to be collecting prisoners now. I have heard they are postponing the executions to save time. The guards talk about a great witch burning coming up."

"Anna, can you get me in to see her?" Clara asked. "Is there anything you can do?"

Anna pulled the large kerchief off her head and placed it on Clara's, tying it in a knot under her chin. "Here, walk behind my back, and keep your head down. I will try to get you in for a short visit."

The guards greeted her as she climbed the stairs. "My cousin," she announced and nodded toward Clara. "She's working with me today."

Clara held her breath as she walked through the blue double door. Town Hall had become a fortress since Angus Hill had arrived.

"The waiting chamber?" Clara asked Anna when they were safely inside, walking down the corridor. "Which room is that?"

"It is part of the prison, a larger room where prisoners are kept, awaiting trial or further punishment." Anna shook her head and looked at Clara with sad eyes.

They had known each other since childhood. Anna was a couple of summers older and friendly. Clara had always thought of her as neat and clean, which was probably the reason why she had employment as head housemaid of Town Hall. Her hair was always in place, not like Clara's, with strands of hair always getting loose, flying every which direction when she moved and getting in front of her eyes if she bent over. Anna's was at all times in a tight bun at the back of her head, making her look like she was in control.

"I am so sorry, Clara." Anna walked a pace ahead, showing the way. She turned and whispered, "I despise coming here now that the whole council has gone mad. What are they thinking? At least I get to check in on Bess and see how she's faring. Hopefully they will let her out soon. They've kept her in there for seven days now, and she has not been sent downstairs yet."

"What's downstairs?" Clara asked, dreading the answer.

"The holding chamber." Anna paused for a moment. "I have not been down there myself, but I hear prisoners taken there are left to die or are sentenced to death in one way or another. I have heard screams coming from down there. It's a horrible place, and the door is guarded night and day." Her face was solemn as she spoke of the frightful room. "Fortunately, Bess is not there. Come, I'll show you where she's kept."

Anna led Clara down the corridor to a back wing guarded by two tall and lanky guards. They nodded to Anna, who fortunately brought the announcement that Clara assisted her in cleaning out the buckets. One of them unlocked the iron-gate leading into another long corridor and walked in front to the waiting chamber.

Bess looked up when she heard the rustling of the keychain outside the cell door.

Anxious to see her, Clara peeped through the small, iron-barred window on the door, but the guard briskly shoved her away, mumbling something in a deep voice Clara could not hear.

Relatives or charitable souls had brought a blanket and nourishment to the prisoners. The less fortunate there had little, only the occasional bowl of pottage once a day.

Clara could see Bess was cold, sitting there shivering on a wooden bench. She had brought a blanket, a woolen cover made from Bess's own sheep, in threads of wool spun lovingly by her own hand. The days were not only colder, but shorter. The sun set earlier every day now. It was midday, and the light shone through the tiny window of the prison cell.

"My hair," she cried when she saw Clara. "They cut off my hair."

"Never mind the hair," Clara said and pulled the woolen cover around Bess's shoulders, tears running down her cheeks. "It will grow out again. You will have beautiful hair again. Your health is much more important. How's your stomach?"

"Oh, it's kicking and hiccupping and making me feel alive, when all else seems bleak." She leaned closer and put her lips close to Clara's ear. "Have you seen Lucia? Is she well? You have to make sure the council does not think of her."

Clara nodded and patted her arm, thinking it best not to speak about Lucia in there. No one could be trusted. There were guards close by. A prisoner said anything to get a favor or better treatment.

They did not need to speak. Clara and Bess had always been able to know each other's thoughts. When funny things had happened, they only looked at each other and laughed without having to say a word. They just knew. Now Bess looked at Clara, desolate, cold, and as if to say, "It's not really them. It's the time. It's the foolish firestorm of evil of our day." In the state she was in, she was still strong. She forgave, she understood, even when there was little hope. She tried a smile, a tired little grin.

Then she started coughing and her body shook even more than before. Clara pulled the woolen blanket tighter around Bess and asked a guard outside the gate if they could heat up the fireplace and put some candles in the sticks on the wall.

"Don't work for you, don't waste candles on prisoners," he exclaimed sourly.

Next time Clara would bring a wax candle and ask if she could give it to Bess.

There was a young woman standing against the far wall, and an old woman sat huddled in the corner of the room. Clara recognized the white hair, the small figure with the homemade shawl around her shoulders. It was Old Magda.

Clara kneeled down next to her old friend on the floor and tried to get her attention, but Magda did not respond. She looked at Clara with hollow, sad eyes. The smiling wrinkles were permanently engraved, although she did not smile. She looked tired and her soft curves were now bony. Her arms were bruised, and she still had no shoes on her feet.

How can I make her feel better? Clara wondered and stroked her white hair. "I don't have a blanket for you today, Magda, but I will try to bring one next time, I promise."

Still no response and Clara returned to Bess.

Just then there was a huge commotion in the hallway, and a guard pushed a large flamboyant woman, with long black hair entwined with beads and colored ribbons, into the prison room. She fell on her knees and screamed out in pain, causing a tirade of unmentionable names and accusations to stream out of her wide mouth.

"How dare you," she shrieked. "I curse you. I curse you. You will be sorry."

Bess and Clara sat on a wooden bench, flabbergasted, and watched the scene being played out only a few paces away. They did not know who the woman was, but Clara guessed she was one of the migrating gypsies who used tarot cards to tell someone's future.

Anna squatted down, leaned over, and whispered, "That's Francesca. She's a loud-mouthed, Rom vagabond, who steals and tricks people for a living. She speaks Romany with her family and has a fierce temper, which when released casts curses and spells on anyone who gets in her way."

"I met some of their people as I travelled through France on my way here," Clara spoke, almost in a whisper. "There they are hunted down as witches, as they are thought to have the ability to change themselves into crows. Some places have a gypsy residence ban."

"They are not much liked here either. For the most part they are a homeless and poor people with petty crimes on their conscience, but everywhere they go they are told to move on." Anna kept looking at the guards by the door, expecting them to tell them to leave, but they let the visitors stay a while longer.

"What are they doing here this far north?" Bess whispered.

"It's their way of life," Anna answered. "They drift without boundaries, without regulations. I have seen them on the field by the river on the east road. The women do their laundry there, and the children ride bareback on the horses in the field."

Anna paused for a moment. One of the guards stepped into the room and kicked Francesca, who tried to get up on her feet. She fell down again, and he laughed loudly as if he had conquered and was made king. The gypsy woman did not give up easily and wobbled on her knees then fell down again- Blood streaming down the side of her face was clear evidence of a struggle.

Francesca fought back and yelled a few non-decipherable words to the unfriendly guard, then she turned and glared at the women sitting as though they were watching a stage play.

"What are you staring at?"

Even with her rolling Rs and strong accent, Clara thought she must have spent some time in the area to have learned the language. The gypsy woman looked worn out and truly unhappy. They moved over, so she could have a seat on the bench.

Bess put an arm around the woman and pulled some of the woolen blanket around her.

"I have nothing to give you," Francesca whispered.

"No need," Bess answered. "No need."

Francesca seemed to have calmed down for the moment, and Clara remembered she had to get back to school. She hugged Bess goodbye and told her she would return the next day and bring her some food.

As Clara left the prison room, she told the guard she would be back to help empty the buckets the same time next day.

"Come back in a week," he said sternly.

"Pray for me," Bess said quietly as Clara left. "God listens to you."

19

The Luncheon on the Meadow

❧

"How do you actually know God is listening to you?" Bess asked Clara once.

"It's like the wind," Clara answered. "You cannot see the wind, but you can feel it on your face. You can see the effect it has on everything around you."

"I don't worry about what others are saying," she said. "We all need help from time to time. Neediness goes in circles, and next time, I may be the one who requires a helping hand or a friendly gesture."

Clara stared out the window of the small classroom. A spider's web clung to the corner of the woodwork, a fat fly caught in the threads of the net. She turned her head to look at the children writing. Their families must have heard about Bess and the other women. They were friends, neighbors, relatives.

"Where are those friends now?" Clara said. Where were those, who had received health, even life, from Bess?

Clara's father had not been an advocate for the Puritan Christendom that evolved in other areas of Europe. He told Clara about a group of people who, before she was born, had fled their country to avoid persecution caused by differences in beliefs and lifestyle. They were now established in colonies in Northern America, with a way of life that required strict boundaries and a narrow gaze at life itself. Her father did not agree with their religion as he thought it took the joy out of living.

"There's enough tribulation, enough hardships, enough long hours of physical labor and worries," her father said. "We need more kindness, more smiles in Rossby. If we perform noble deeds, we will be spreading the good word of God."

There were parishioners who preferred fire and brimstone, but Clara believed most folks enjoyed sermons about being a good neighbor as opposed to being told what loathsome sinners they were.

"Dance with me," a wagtail seemed to beckon as Clara walked across the path to the church the following Sunday. With light, little paces, as if he hardly carried any weight, his tiny feet jumped and skipped ahead on the path in front of her. The first sight of a wagtail from behind was a sign of spring. Now summer slowly came to an end, and Clara hoped for blessings.

Going to church was not the same as before. People were quieter in the pews, as if there was no need to say words out loud. Clara was certain she was not the only one whose thoughts were on the women taken prisoners and those already sentenced to death.

She sat alone, and preferred observing more than mingling these days. Uncle Samuel stayed home with Lucia, and there were no close friends to sit by. Anna sat in the back, and next to her Clara saw Lars with his hands folded in his lap. Behind the back pew, standing tall and looking somber, was Toomber.

Herr Christopher's sermon was short and thoroughly contemplated. His words from the scriptures about love and forgiveness comforted Clara a little. She decided to reread the verses when she returned home to the cottage. Forgiveness was a complicated word in her vocabulary these days, and she prayed for the strength to understand how to forgive.

Angus Hill did not attend the services.

"He is in his room with a slight fever," Herr Christopher told Clara.

She did not want to wish illness on anyone, but his absence was a blessing. Besides, she knew he was too keyed up to be away for long.

After the service, Herr Christopher and his wife arranged a meal on the small meadow behind the church. It was an unusual gesture but showed a parson, who in spite of shortcomings and outer helplessness, truly cared for the well-being of his beloved parishioners.

Clara was not surprised to see how more than a few showed up for a free meal, even with the nip in the air. It gave them an opportunity to rest and catch up on the latest gossip around town. There was homemade bread with butter, fresh berry pudding, and several kinds of meat and fish. The parson and Mrs. Sara had dug deep into their pantry and hearts to share some of their surplus, in the hopes that the gathering might lift the townspeople's spirits and encourage friendly thoughts and neighborly feelings. Just recently, Herr Christopher had brought Clara inside the *stabbur* at the parsonage and told her about his plans for the luncheon. Food items were plentiful, stocked with care by a forth-seeing man of God.

"I want to be prepared for storms and hard times," he told Clara. "Noah was prepared, and he did not get wet when the rain came. Look at what happened to the rest of the unbelievers around him. Preparedness is vital."

No matter how much food he stores, he misses out on vigilance for his parish, Clara thought. Innocent women were in danger. Clara could not help but wonder how her father would have handled the pending situation.

The mellow, noonday sun had dried up the morning dew, and Clara hoped to learn what the parishioners were thinking. Bess had healed them of everything from sore throats to near-death illnesses. She had birthed more children than anyone else in town and shared her food with the poor and needy. How many of them truly accused her?

It was all Clara could think about as she walked around and greeted the families, trying to make conversation. If someone thought gossiping about the imprisoned women as a jest, she was not amused. Clara observed and listened, as she slowly wandered around the meadow. She looked for guilty expressions—to see if anyone else had changed—and dreaded more finger pointing.

If she categorized the townspeople into good and bad, she could easily eliminate a few. But who was she to judge? Who was she to put the blame on anyone? Those Clara had previously looked upon as foolish or unable to perceive truth with their God-given sense, now took on the role as an enemy of some sort in her imaginary play of witch-hunt and accusation.

Out here in the fresh air, people relaxed more than inside the church. Some appeared unaffected by the events and rumors, laughing and even making witch-jokes. In a small community, where curiosity ruled and tongues were functional, it had not taken long before everybody knew about Angus Hill and his evil schemes.

Marcus, a middle aged farmer, was always good for a laugh no matter how grave the situation was. He bent forward and made a witty expression.

"Why does a witch go to church when nobody else is around?" He asked some of his friends.

They lifted their eyebrows and scratched their heads, but none could come up with a valid answer.

"She has meetings with the angels, asking them the regulations for flying."

The crowd around him roared with laughter. One fat woman chuckled so hard she fell backwards with her legs up and had to be helped back into a sitting position.

Had they always been unpredictable or had the inhabitants of Rossby changed? What had changed them and why? Catastrophe often changes someone's thoughts, and attitude could be contagious like the plague. Clara was not as gullible as before. She noticed herself becoming more skeptical every day.

She thought about brave Francesca, who did not bow down to conformity or even prejudice. None of the Roma appeared on the meadow, although they showed up on the back pews on Sundays. Even if Herr Christopher and Sara were hospitable, it seemed as if the people of Rossby turned their backs on the Roma. These roaming families would soon be on their way again. Forming long-lasting friendships and establishing trade relations was not their nature.

Clara picked up an apple from the large barrel and thanked Sara for the lovely meal. She placed her thumbs closely together by the apple stem and managed to pry it apart. She liked eating the halves one at a time and thought apples tasted better that way.

After the luncheon, Clara walked to Town Hall but was denied entry. When she was last there with Anna, the guard had told her to return after a week. Days had passed, but still they would not let Clara in to see Bess. She brought a woolen blanket for Old Magda one day and a candle for Bess and asked the guard to make sure they received the items. Every day she brought food for Bess and Magda, allowing enough for the guards to taste, still not knowing if the nourishment ever made it past the men at the door.

Clara met Anna again on the town square one day after she finished her shift. Anna embraced Clara.

"How are you, Clara? Will they still not let you back in?" She put her hand in her satchel and pulled out a small loaf of bread. "They won't let me give any of the leftovers to the prisoners, but I can give one to you. Maybe you can ask the guards to pass it on to Bess."

Clara nodded and thanked her. So far, any efforts had seemed wasted, but she did not give up.

"I will try," Clara said. "You would think they kept horrible murderers in Town Hall. It's fortified like a bastion during wartime."

Anna looked around to see if someone listened and leaned toward Clara. "Francesca was let out a few days ago," she said.

Clara opened her eyes in surprise, and a small glimmer of hope stretched forth in her mind like a sudden moonbeam on the ground on a pitch-black night.

"She was? Why? Did Angus Hill actually let her go?"

"Yes, he did. Francesca would not be tamed and was offended that he thought her a witch because of her background as Romany."

"But being accused as a witch offends any woman, don't you think?"

"Certainly, but she belongs to a people with ways and customs different from ours."

A young couple with eyes only for each other almost walked straight into the two women and they moved out of the way. Anna waited until the couple was a few paces further down the street before she continued.

"They use palm readings to foresee the future and cast curses when they are disrupted. Still, from what I have heard, they are seldom accused."

"What do you think made him change his mind about her? Did she have a proper trial?"

"I heard she was brought down to the room outside the holding chamber and tortured."

"What? What did they do to her?" Clara thought about her poor friends and how they were kept awake at night, cut with blunt knives, pricked with pins and needles, hair cut off, made to walk on cold and damp floors without shoes, and even drowned and burned. It was painful to know they were treated that way. She looked at Anna with sad eyes. "How is Francesca now?" she asked.

"They whipped her and made her lie on the ground with a board placed on her body. On top of the board they placed stones, one after another, all the while trying to make her confess to witchery. But, you saw what she was like, Clara. Francesca does not give up easily. She kept calling out menacing curses, and from what I heard, Angus Hill was afraid of her."

"Maybe he believed the curses and did not know how to lift them."

"That could be. Anyway, she is back with her people and it seems like they are packing up to leave again."

Clara held up the bread, thanked Anna again, and told her to be careful. It was important that the witch-finder's supporters did not know Anna shared sensitive information. His faithful could be anyone passing by on the street.

"There's one more thing, Clara." She quickly glanced to see if anyone was close enough to hear. "A few more women have been taken."

"What? No. Who has been victimized now?" Clara shook her head. It felt like she toppled over. She grabbed Anna's arm for support and stumbled to stairs nearby to sit down.

"Anna, who?" Clara asked again, looking intently at her friend.

"The woman Mari from behind the abbey, and Thea, a young foreign maid in the Land's kitchen. They were brought in yesterday. But that's not all. Thea has in turn accused two others, as well."

Anna leaned toward Clara and whispered their names as several men on their way to the Watering House walked closely by, making a spectacle of themselves, laughing, and pushing each other back and forth.

Clara's jaw dropped. She looked gravely at Anna and gave her a quick hug. "I have to go," she said and hurried down the last part of town and through the wooded area to Frue Farm. She ran through the thicket, and as she came into the clearing, she tripped on an old oak tree root, hidden under leaves and twigs. Her knee hit the sharp edge of a rock by the tree trunk. It tore up the material on her frock, and blood sieved through the stocking around the kneecap, but she barely noticed. She got up again and continued running. She had one thing in mind, and that was to find Uncle Samuel as fast as possible.

As Clara neared the fence around the orchard, she saw Uncle Samuel crossing the yard between the stables and the barn. He carried a large ball of hay on his back. Her first impression was he was a little more bent over, a little slower. As she approached him, she noticed how tired and worried he looked. He lifted his head when he saw Clara coming.

"Clara, have you been to see Bess? Have you heard anything? Are you hurt?"

He pointed to the blood on the front of Clara's frock, but she brushed his question aside and delivered the message.

"We need to get Lucia somewhere safe. This morning they brought in widow Doris and her daughter, Kari, who is only eight summers old. She's in the waiting chamber with her mother now. A child, Uncle Samuel. A child. We have to hide Lucia."

Uncle Samuel immediately dropped the ball of hay onto the ground and turned around in circles, looking desperate and furious at the same time. Then he looked straight at Clara, as if he had come to a decision.

"I'll take her somewhere today."

"But where? Where will you take her? It's cold outside, and I don't know who to trust anymore."

"It's better left unknown. They might question you and try to get information. No, I need to hide away from everyone, even you."

"What about the animals? I can come and feed them and take care of Frue Farm. I can return and bring Binna to my cottage."

"Yes, that's probably best. It will be easier without the dog, so leave Binna at the farm. She'll keep watch and sleep in the barn if we leave the door ajar. If you can check in once a day, it would be best."

"How long do you think we will have to do this?"

"There's no telling, right now. It just has to be done."

In her heart, Clara knew he was right. If she knew the whereabouts of Lucia, it could endanger the child's safety. Uncle Samuel's knowledge of the countryside around Frue Farm and Rossby came in handy now, and he was trained in survival from his military days. Even with his advanced age, his body was still strong and his mind sound.

Around the corner of the barn, the little, copper-headed sunbeam appeared and came running toward Clara, carrying her poppet. The dog trailed faithfully behind her. Clara lifted the child up, kissed her cheek and asked her if she was being good. She smiled and nodded, then told Uncle Samuel she was hungry.

Clara put her gently back down again and turned to Uncle Samuel. "We need to get her ready to go. Be quick about it. There's no time to spare."

A few minutes later, she knew she was out of time. "I have to run now," she said and threw her arms around Uncle Samuel's neck.

He bowed his head and said no more. Clara left with tears in her eyes, not knowing when, or if, she would ever see them again.

As she approached the town, she saw a commotion in front of Town Hall. Guards and horses were gathered. Innkeeper Hansen stood by a guard on horseback. He gave instructions and gesticulated broadly.

What now? Clara thought. She walked through the throng of people to the entrance of Town Hall. The blue double doors stood wide open, apparently no one had thought about closing them to keep out the cold. She hoped to find Anna, to ask her what was going on. Clara would request to see Bess, too, even if she had already tried once that same morning. She would not give up.

Rain poured down now, cleaning away dirt and grime but not people's thoughts and actions. Large drops of water landed on the ground at the town square, but that did not seem to bother the crowd who had already gathered.

As Clara was halfway up the stairs in front of the entrance, a guard poked her in the back with his spear.

"Where do you think you are going?" he roared.

Why did these men always think they needed to address people by trying to scare them? Clara thought.

She pretended as if she was actually having a civil conversation with a polite gentleman. There was too much at stake, and she could not afford any mistakes.

"Please, may I see Bess of Frue Farm this afternoon?" Clara smiled sweetly, trying to hide the frustration, fear, and anger welling up inside. She used all the acting skills that she could muster to give him the impression she was a well-balanced young woman. She felt as if she could topple over at any minute, but there was no chance she would let him know her motives were contrary to his orders.

"No visitors today." He grabbed her arm to bring her back down the stairs.

Clara tried to withstand the push and planted her feet firmly apart on the ground. "Wait. Is Anna here? May I go inside and see her for a few minutes? I will be quick about it."

He nodded and let go of her arm, and Clara proceeded up the rest of the stairs and through the open doors.

Two guards stood by the hallway leading to the waiting chamber and the other cells. She could forget about getting past them. After discreetly looking in different directions, trying to spot Anna, Clara finally peeked through the kitchen door, thinking she might be in there preparing a meal. A young maid did the dishes. She curtsied and told Clara that Anna had gone home for the day.

Clara was about to leave when the young maid came and whispered, "He's here, you know."

"Who is?" Clara asked.

"The witch-finder. He's having his meal in the mayor's office."

Clara nodded and backed out of the room, eager to get out of there. She could not let him see her, and she was certainly not up to answering any of his wicked questions.

She walked outside into the town square just in time to see the innkeeper pointing northward and the horsemen heading up the road. Her heart skipped a beat.

They cannot be going there already, she thought. She prayed fervently that Uncle Samuel and Lucia were on their way, and tried to listen for information from the people standing about. She had to pretend she was just a curious bystander like everybody else.

"They are off to Frue Farm," a woman with ragged hair said. She had a cane in her hand to support her limp left leg when she walked. "They're after the witch's bairn."

An old man nodded as if he consented to the fact that a posse was on their way to pick up an innocent little girl.

Had the world gone mad? She wanted to get away from there, afraid she would be discovered as an accomplice. She could not let them know she had just been to see the child. She carefully walked across the square, but it felt as if her feet were made of lead. Dreams from stormy nights came to mind. She knew she could run, run fast and easily, but her feet felt as if they were glued to the ground. It was as if she turned a key to lock the door, but every time she tried to turn the handle, it was always unlocked. It was like the ability to fly like a bird but not being able to take flight, heavy like a stone placed in the earth.

"Clala-san, dreams are you", her *mamasan* in Okinawa had said. "You feel you want to do things, but cannot find way to do. You afraid."

Hideko-san was always right. Her wisdom had helped Clara and comforted her when she was at a loss for what to do.

"Oh, Hideko-san, how do I go about this task now?" Clara whispered.

Whenever planning for something, Clara's brother, Nathanael, always asked, "What is your aim?" He was an excellent bowman and knew about targets, aiming precisely, and hitting the goal he set out for. Plans for his own life were made in a similar way. He set goals and diligently worked at reaching them. Oh, how she missed him, especially now when she truly needed him and his bravery.

What was her aim? Clara wanted to run after the horsemen who were heading for Frue Farm, but she could not jeopardize Uncle Samuel and Lucia's escape. People around the square were a group of know-it-alls, who had opinions about witches and punishments. A few whispered. She could not make out what they were saying, but there were others who loud and openly uttered their thoughts. They even bragged about having been to Sister Birgitta's execution. Some shook their heads and looked sad. Clara felt hope that not every person gathered there was in favor of witch-hunting.

She picked up bits and pieces of conversation as she walked away, an impression of how a change in the townspeople as a group took hold of the Rossbyans.

"He is so handsome, that Angus Hill, don't you think?" a young woman with braids and black front teeth said.

"He is God-sent," another with a wig full of bird feathers added. "We must be ever so grateful, that he has come here to save us from evil."

"The witch-finder will cleanse our poor town."

"I feel so much safer with him around. I hope he'll stay."

And maybe you'll be next, Clara thought. She did not want anyone to suffer by the hand of Angus Hill, but how could they all think they were exempt from his all-seeing eye. By now, he had spies around every corner.

Anxious and worried, Clara sat down on the stairs in front of Town hall. Thoughts twirled in her head. Uncle Samuel had told her he would leave the house and premises looking as though he was out on an errand. He did not want anyone to get the impression that he had taken the child and fled. A half-dozen guards out looking for him and Lucia was the last thing he needed right now, even though he had to be prepared for that.

Clara had helped him as he had rummaged through the house. Uncle Samuel had grabbed various items for their escape; woolen clothes and blankets for warmth, a second pair of woolen socks, leather shoe covers, a small shovel, dried meat and vegetables, a loaf of bread, a couple of candles and matches, rope, two sheep skins, and a few coins just in case. Hopefully, he would be able to return for more supplies later if they needed them. Clara had put cups and plates on the table and left tools and utensils spread around the room. These things, and a fire burning in the hearth, would give the impression that Uncle Samuel would soon return.

Fortunately, the family at Frue Farm was blessed with plenty of wool and skins for covers and blankets. Most families in Rossby only possessed a few blankets for cold winter's nights, and children often huddled together under a shared blanket for warmth. Clara knew

Uncle Samuel would make sure the things he removed would not easily be noticed as missing and leave additional blankets and clothes on the beds.

Lucia was good-tempered, quiet and shy, more calm-natured. Like her father, Clara assumed. That would be helpful with whatever Uncle Samuel planned now. The horsemen returned while Clara still sat on the stairs thinking, worrying. Lucia was not with them. Clara slipped down the stairs and stood behind the railing out of sight but strained her ears to hear the conversation. Angus Hill and his interpreter came out on the steps and approached the riders.

"Did you find the child?" John Pywell asked, the witch-finder standing close to hear the answer.

"No, Sir, we didn't," a sentry answered. "We rode out to the farm and checked the house and premises, but there was no one there, just a dog. The old man will be back. There was a fire that blazed in the kitchen and his tools were all over."

Angus Hill stepped forward and asked through his interpreter, "Did you burn the barn down? Or shoot the dog?"

Innkeeper Hansen dismounted. His nostrils flared as he breathed the crisp air. "No, not today." he said and lifted his chin. "We thought perhaps the old man and the child had heard us coming and were hiding. We scoured the barn and stables and saw that the animals were in place, fed and content. I believe they are out somewhere and will return. If we had burned something down, they would know we are after them and disappear for good."

Angus Hill turned to walk back up the stairs of Town Hall.

"We'll find the child," the innkeeper called after him and waved Lucia's small shawl in the air. "She won't get away."

Clara gulped a mouthful of air as she saw Lucia's shawl. She turned promptly to head for home. Tears ran down her face, and she slipped away from the crowd before Angus Hill could notice her. As she hurried back to the parsonage, an impression formed in her mind, first a gentle proposal—an inspiration that soon developed into a design she had to pursue. Her daily appearance on the steps of the Town Hall and the efforts in talking to anyone with connections to the witch-hunt had not changed the fact that Bess and several others were still in prison, accused of being witches.

”I have to go away for a few days, Ami,” Clara said as she picked up the cat and stroked his soft black fur. “I trust you to make sure no mice enter our pantry while I’m away.”

She packed a small bag with necessities, and sewed some extra coins into the lining of her frock. A small window was left open for Ami and she put out plenty of water for him. He would find mice and birds outside. Closing the door behind, Clara turned to run down the path to tell Herr Christopher she would be away for a few days, not offering any reason or explanation. She described the need for help at Frue Farm.

“I will return shortly,” she explained. “Please keep an eye on the cottage and my cat.”

Clara left a note for Uncle Samuel in the wooden box under the horses’ trough in the stables. This was their secret place of communication. Not expecting to hear much from him, she had asked him to let her know now and then that they were well and alive. No information, nothing to compromise their hiding place. But she simply had to know they were surviving. Otherwise, she felt her imagination would go wild and make her think of the most horrid things.

Her only hope was an answer to her prayers that Uncle Samuel would come and read the note, Lucia would be kept safe, and Bess would still be alive when Clara returned.

20

The Audience

A small sailboat headed for Bergen left the harbor of Rossby early that same evening. Onboard were the crew, a few merchants, a family of five, and Clara Dahl. She stood staring out at the open sea. In her pocket, she had a root of ginger from Bess' kitchen. She knew it would be helpful when the boat started moving along with the lively waves and encouraging wind.

Clara kept to herself for the few hours at sea, pausing only for a polite tête-à-tête with the mother of the family, as the youngest son climbed on Clara's lap to inspect the buttons on her frock.

She overheard the sailors as they discussed fishing methods, women, and witch-hunts. Most people knew someone, who in turn knew someone. Though it still made her sad to hear how easy it seemed to converse about the suffering of others.

Bergen, a trading town for hundreds of years, and the largest in these northern countries, was both beautiful and bustling—a town filled with culture and appealing happenings. Clara had been here several times with her father and Nathanael. No matter how much she wanted to relive those happy memories, she kept to her schedule and booked a room for the night, then bought a ticket on a ship sailing for Copenhagen the next morning. Her heart ached, but she could not just watch the atrocities in Rossby, feeling helpless and without progress. She had to turn the page and try something else.

The sea behaved most of the way there. Clara only emptied her stomach one time in the middle of the night, a few hours before they arrived the following morning. She often felt it unfair that someone who enjoyed seeing new places and journeying by coach or ship as much as she did should become ill from the voyage. The root of ginger in a cup of boiling water helped calm her stomach, and she concentrated on her plans.

The capitol was windy and gray this October morning. A few leaves still clinging to the branches of the trees were golden and brown; most had already blown away and lay on the ground in piles for her to shuffle through on her way from the harbor toward the town center.

The goal was to find her father's brother, Jacob Dahl. She hoped he could guide her through the next few days.

Clara clutched her hat as she rapidly walked the streets. She had to remember the house they stayed in when they visited her uncle many summers ago. She looked up at the houses on either side while she paced down the fifth road, trying to avoid bumping into others. A tall man with bolts of material under his right arm yelled at Clara for being in the way. She apologized, curtsied, and continued around the next corner, only to recognize the home of her uncle, just as she remembered it. It stood there in a small garden with a white picket fence in the front.

A small maid answered Clara's knock on the door. She wiped her hands on her apron, seemingly wet from working in the kitchen.

Clara explained who she was.

"Please enter," the maid said. "Herr Jacob will return for his meal at noon. You may come in and wait in the parlor. He should not be long."

She hung up Clara's coat in the hallway and showed her into a small parlor warmed by pleasant flames in the fireplace, burning briskly because of the wind outside drawing up air from the chimney.

It was not long until Clara heard the front door open. The maid ran into the hallway to explain Clara's presence in the house. She stood up as she saw her uncle with the friendly eyes under bushy eyebrows in the parlor doorway. He smiled and opened his long arms wide as Clara ran toward him, melting into his embrace. It was like coming home, seeing someone friendly she could trust.

"What a wonderful surprise, Clara. What on Earth are you doing here?"

Her uncle had questions, and Clara had much to tell. She had forgotten how famished she was and gratefully sat down to eat with him, all the while satisfying his queries with stories about her family, Okinawa, and work.

Uncle Jacob was her father's younger brother by two summers, and their likeness was especially pleasing now her own father was gone. Uncle Jacob listened intently as Clara told him about the last few months.

"I have come to ask you to help me be admitted to an audience with our king, Fredrik III. You have worked for him in his court for as long as I can remember. I am hoping you can use your influence and experience to get me inside the doors of the Royal Palace."

He scratched his head and asked the maid to refill their cups. Clara knew she asked for more than she should, but it was a risk she was willing to take. Her hope grew as he agreed to help then discussed how she should present herself with proper etiquette in the presence of a king and his court.

"I will go to court early tomorrow morning and present your case, Clara. Hopefully the king will have time to see you then."

As she walked back and forth in the guest room that night, Clara formulated clever words in her mind, wanting to be well prepared for a meeting at the Royal Palace. Her knowledge of state affair and politics would come in handy, but it was not an easy task she had chosen. She wished her father could be there to guide her presentation and support her views.

King Fredrik's interest in books and learning was widely known. Would he appreciate an educated woman or dismiss the thought of female intellect? With his inherited view of women and witchcraft had he perhaps read the "Book of Vengeance" Clara's uncle had talked about earlier that day? The document was endorsed by a papal bulla and royal proclamation. Religious leaders had given its content their blessing for more than a hundred and fifty years.

"It's meant as a guide for the clergy," her uncle had stated, "although, your father and I tried to use reason in our dealings with the subject."

"I never heard him talk much about witches," Clara said. "The parishioners still respect his memory, though they are easily caught in the winds changing direction."

"The Rossbyans are fortunate. Their solitary town by the sea is a distance away from large witch-hunts.

"Until now, Uncle Jacob."

He put out his hand to show her where to sit in the parlor and sat down in a chair opposite, leaned forward with his elbows on his knees, and folded his hands under his chin for support.

"Yes, Clara, until now," he stated sadly. "The time has come to stand up for what is right, even in the small town of Rossby."

Clara sighed. Desperate feelings of inadequacy had driven her to come to the capitol and speak with the highest authority. She knew in her heart how impossible it would be to change the opinion of a large group of people, but she had to try.

"I wish I had more townsfolk fighting with me. Times are unpredictable, and I have misgivings about most people there. I really don't know who to trust anymore, and my suspicions have left me alone in my struggles."

"You are brave to come here, and you fight for what you think is right. You don't give up easily, do you?"

"I guess not. Father said mother was the same way." Clara fingered with the coin purse in her lap, a little embarrassed at the compliment. She did not feel brave, only weak and small. "Uncle, what does this book or document do?" she asked. "How does it work as a guide?"

"The book is presented as a witch-hunter's manual. It discusses the demonic power of women and tells how to discover witches in your community. It is an almanac on how to punish the alleged witches."

"Does not sound encouraging for the female race, does it? Has it a name?"

"*Malleus Maleficarum.*"

"Ah, the hammer of witches."

Her uncle smiled briefly, knowing how much she enjoyed studying languages, even Latin. She looked out of the window and back at him.

"Uncle Jacob, what was the intention of a name like that?" she asked. "To nail poor women down, or hit them over the head with a hammer?"

"I don't know, Clara, but it's a serious document and still in use."

"Who wrote it?"

Uncle Jacob smiled again. "You have always been a curious child, Clara; I like that about you. Just be careful how you use your curiosity."

The maid came into the parlor with a porcelain plate of small cakes. Uncle Jacob handed Clara the plate and continued answering.

"The author was an Austrian inquisitor for the church at that time, called Heinrich Kramer."

"Do you think Angus Hill has a copy?" Clara asked, chewing the small cake with nuts and spices and enjoying the flavor.

"He has most likely read the book or parts of it. Any serious witch-hunter uses it avidly. A manual that claims witchcraft exists and explains how to rid the world of evil is an important tool."

"That's true, but he travels, and there are probably not many copies. I would not know if he has a book himself, but he certainly behaves as if he knows its contents by heart."

Clara thought about this conversation as she tried to go to sleep. Uncle Jacob had said that King Fredrik's large book collection contained a copy of the *Malleus Maleficarum*. It had been there since King Christian IV's reign. Tomorrow, she would try to get a chance to see it for herself. She hoped to be able to enter the king's vast library and see the abundance of books in one single room. She could begin by speaking with him about his interest in natural philosophies and education. Then they could discuss travel, theology, and languages, and when the time was right, she would present her purpose for requesting an audience. But she felt insecure about his decree about absolute monarchy. He was now more powerful than ever before, and she really did not know what to expect.

After a few hours of rest Clara awoke and prepared herself to go downstairs. Her uncle came energetically toward her in the dining room. The heels of his shoes made a click-clack sound as his long legs strode on the tile floor. His arms stretched out and he took hold of her hands.

"It is an excellent time to request an audience," he said optimistically. "I have been to the Royal Palace this morning and the king is in the best of moods."

"Why is that?" Clara asked as she sat down and put the napkin on her lap. The table exhibited boiled eggs, bread, and meats.

"He is, for the time being, the most admired man in the kingdom of Denmark and Norway."

Clara frowned and gave her uncle a doubtful look. "What has he done to deserve that?"

"His decision to stay in the Danish capitol to defend his people and fight the Swedish invasion proved him a wise and brave monarch." He rang the bell for the maid to bring some cheese.

"I am still skeptical," Clara said and lowered her eyes as she moved her feet nervously under the table, "although, I know everyone loves a leader who does not selfishly hide away, but fights for their freedom."

"That's true. There is also the recent annulment of a charter, reducing the influence of the nobles and granting increased power to the state council."

"What does that entail?"

Clara helped herself to another egg and nodded gratefully to the maid as she placed the plate with cheese on the table.

"The king is rich you know, dear Clara. The church used to hold the land, but now that the monarch is head of both state and church, he owns almost half of our country."

"Many men—and women for that matter—will do anything for power or money," Clara injected.

"True, that's been happening here lately, as well. We have experienced chaos and problems after the resent wars and struggles. Finances have been low and some sided with the king in order to protect their own monetary interests." He leaned back in the chair and stretched his long legs under the table.

"Will all this change politics for us?" Clara asked.

"No, it won't mean much for ordinary citizens. The state of affairs for both countries will still be conducted from Copenhagen, most of the men in leading positions will be Danish citizens. I expect for the most part, life will continue as before."

"Uncle Jacob, what can I expect?"

He looked at Clara for a few seconds, contemplating the answer. "Well, he is a strong leader, only eighteen summers old when he was made chief commandant. He rarely shows his feelings, does not laugh much, and is quite reserved. He is different from his father."

"Did you serve him as well?" Clara was fascinated by her uncle's position but more so by his knowledge and wisdom.

"Yes, I have been here for...including my studies..."

He gave a pondering look, counting the years with his fingers, and finally said, "It must be close to twenty years already. You were a little girl then. Fredrik's father, King Christian IV was outgoing and loved festivities and beautiful women." He looked at Clara with a crooked grin and lifted his eyebrows. "But he was fair and a good ruler, beloved by his people."

"My father spoke well of him."

"But Clara, having said that, you must remember both King Christian and his son Fredrik, agreed on witch-hunting, although the latter is not as possessed with the idea. King Christian made magic and devil worship illegal by law. As a result, hundreds of innocent women have been burned at the stake."

"How long has this law been in effect?"

"The law came into force about thirty to forty years ago. Clergymen are expected to fight witchcraft and evil at all cost, but your father and I saw beyond the law and observed the men and women behind the accusations. We did not believe in religion as a science but as a matter of faith and trust.

"Did you see anyone who deserved to be put to death for witchcraft?"

"I saw persons who were rude, ill behaved, loud-mouthed, and foul...but having made pacts with the devil? No, I think few go to that extreme."

Memories of Hilda and Birgitta came vividly to Clara's mind. The thoughts of these sweet women filled her eyes with tears and made her lip quiver.

Uncle Jacob came to her side of the table and put an arm around her shoulder. "Are you sure you want to go through with this?" he asked gently.

Clara nodded her head. "I have to. My best friend is in jail, accused of being a witch. I have to do what I can to help her."

"So be it. I will request an audience."

~~

The streets were already bustling as they sat in the carriage on their way to the palace. Uncle Jacob pointed out the university and enlightened Clara with memories of how he and her father had both studied there at the same time.

"There," he said and pointed out the window of the great school, "built in 1479, theology and worldly studies under one roof."

"I have often thought about cutting my hair and pretending my name is Niels just to be able to study there," Clara said with a smile.

It lifted her spirits to hear about her father and his younger days. Her uncle was cheerful as he recounted the story about Clara's parents' first meeting, and she felt her mind was at a place of rest for the first time in several months.

She waited in the carriage for half an hour before her uncle returned.

"I'm sorry, Clara," he said. "The king will see no one today. We have been kindly asked to return for a public audience tomorrow."

A refusal on the first try was not enough to discourage Clara but gave her more time to prepare for her audience with the king. The decision to come to Copenhagen had been made in haste, and the sea voyage had given her little chance to concentrate on her presentation.

"I need to do some things today, Clara, but feel free to use the carriage. Just tell my driver where you want to go, and take some time to see the beautiful sights of our capitol. Tomorrow will come soon enough."

The offer tempted her. She was far away from Rossby, and only prayers could help Bess and the other women now. The driver steered the horses through town as Clara comfortably sat in the carriage, watching life and people of the largest town in Denmark.

Women of all ages trailed through the busy streets. Most had spent their life bearing and rearing children, managing their households, spinning, cooking, preserving food, and brewing ale. But there were those who had to work outside the home as income was scarce. Perhaps they were widows or simply left alone, abandoned by their husbands. These women might find work in the textile companies, knitting and sewing for a living, while others served as maids, cooking and cleaning for the upper classes.

The roles women played intrigued Clara. Life was not all leisure and games if you were born to wear a gown. Though men ruled and made decisions, she saw how women formed their own groups, made relationships count, and used them to their advantage.

Clara returned to her uncle's home, more determined than ever to fight for the rights of the accused women in Rossby.

~

Next morning after the early meal, her uncle came back from a visit to the Royal Palace and told Clara a courier had been by with the message that the king was available for a private audience.

Clara dressed in her best gown, moss colored with an embroidered bodice. The jacket fit snugly around her waist and had lace at the bottom hem dyed in the same color. She paid special attention to her hair, making sure it was all in place in a soft and feminine style.

Uncle Jacob held her hand and gallantly assisted Clara into the black carriage. He sat down next to Clara and pulled his wide cloak across his lap so as not to cover her gown. It was a cold and damp morning, and she folded her arms and hugged herself to keep warm. She would not have minded if he had left his cloak to cover her legs but did not say anything. Uncle Jacob knocked on the front wall of the carriage to let the driver know they were ready to leave.

"Thank you, Uncle Jacob. Thank you for being here with me and helping me understand how to deliver my request," Clara said.

"We are family. I am pleased to be of assistance to you." He handed her a book bound with a ribbon. "Here, take this," he said.

"What is it?" Clara asked. She turned the book over and read *Astraea Redux* on the cover.

"It's a book by an English author named Dryden, published just recently. It glorifies monarchy and talks about how a king is the restorer of peace and order. King Fredrik enjoys gifts, and this will, hopefully, trigger his interest and make him pliable to talk."

"I should have thought about that. It's important I show my appreciation of being admitted. Thank you again, Uncle Jacob." Clara put the book on her lap and looked out the window.

Clara was a worrier, which was a waste of time. *One day I will realize I spend too much time agonizing and losing sleep over things beyond my own capacity and ability*, she thought. As long as she prepared well and did her best, it would have to be good enough under the circumstances.

Preparation would prove itself a vital weapon. Every word she said could be placed on the scale. She had to make the trip to Copenhagen worthwhile. Her heart leapt like a frog when she heard that not only were they granted a public audience but a private one. How grateful she felt at that time for an uncle respected for his time of faithful service and spotless conduct.

"You should know the king is a harsh ruler, and you being a woman may not incline his heart toward your plea," her uncle said as the carriage rolled across the bridge to the castle surrounded by a moat filled with dirty water. "Treason is a dangerous word, so choose your words carefully. Even the king's own family members are punished for uttering threatening words or behavior."

"I will be careful, Uncle, but I have to share the reason why I have come this long way."

"Of course, just be watchful and make sure your words are well thought out."

Clara stepped out of the carriage and into the courtyard encircled by white brick castle walls with red roofs on one side and dark towers and roof tiles on the other. Seeing the infamous Blue Tower where prisoners were kept gave her shivers as they walked toward the main entrance. She stopped for a second, feeling short of breath and heavy, but continued as her uncle put his hand on her back, gently pushing her forward.

Stay dignified and focused, she thought as they accompanied the royal guards down the decorated hallways with large portraits in heavy, gold-painted wooden frames on the walls and patterned red-and-brown carpet runners on the floor. She tried to look straight ahead and not gawk at the interior. A few more stairs and she would meet the monarch.

They were shown into a large room with windows facing the street, connecting Clara with the real world. There were large tapestries with biblical motifs on one wall and carved golden mirrors on another. A massive oak table on a brightly colored Persian rug was centered on the wood paneled floor. Matching chairs were randomly scattered around the room. Fredrik III and three other men stood by the table, pointing at maps and documents. She walked with her uncle across the room.

Clara had wondered if he wore his crown when he discussed plans and strategies for his kingdom or if he was more at ease in his home with his closest associates. But he wore no crown, appearing more like a distinguished noble man. His hair was darker than she had expected, and he had heavy eyebrows the same dark color and a thin mustache. Clara gathered he had not slept well, as he had shady circles below his eyes and a strong chin that looked like he had not yet shaven that morning.

His black coat with a white collar and lace tassels hanging from the neckline down, accompanied by a large plumed hat, as if he was ready to go out, looked familiar enough that her nerves were calmed. Clara hoped he would be as pleasant to talk with as he looked.

"My King," her uncle said and took off his hat. With a large hand movement he bowed deeply.

King Fredrik III turned around and nodded as he greeted Uncle Jacob, then he looked at Clara. "This must be your niece, the one who would like to meet her king today."

Clara curtsied and bowed her head, only to straighten up as she felt his hand pull her arm.

"There, child, let me see your face. Your eyes will tell me about your person."

A nervous smile unwillingly pulled the corners of Clara's mouth, and she looked into the eyes of the king.

"Lovely, yes, I am pleased," he said and looked at Clara's uncle.

Clara stretched out her hand with the book.

"A gift for me? Very nice. I will look at it later." He handed the book to a servant and invited them to see the maps on the table. "I am studying the boundaries of our countries," he said and placed both of his gentle white hands on the table. "Come, this is interesting, look at the way the borders are connected to other lands."

On Clara's part, this was a soothing way to get used to being in the royal chambers. She was allowed to answer questions and make conversation. The king spoke immediately in the Danish language, but throughout their discussion, he made comments in French and Latin, perhaps to test her knowledge of the languages or to put on a show of his own expertise.

Clara could speak when spoken to but was fully aware that King Fredrik controlled the conversation. She took care to moderate her opinions at the same time as she wrapped her message into sentences.

The king was in favor of education. He was a careful and self-controlled man who gladly discussed matters of studying and applying learning to life. Instead of revealing her desire to study at a university, where only men were admitted, Clara suggested the need for a university in Christiania, so the Norwegians would not have to travel so far to receive a proper education. He nodded but said nothing further, and she hoped she had not crossed the line. Clara only wished to open the curtains of his mind and plant seeds of good thoughts that might grow.

"Come, I will show you my library," he said all of a sudden, throwing out his hand in a majestic gesture.

Clara looked at Uncle Jacob, hopeful and excited as they followed the king through the palace to see his large collection of books.

Awestruck, Clara stood in the open doorway, the tall, wooden doors exquisitely carved and painted. She looked into the large library of His Majesty King Fredrik III, with wide-open eyes and stared at the shelves covering all four walls from floor to ceiling. It was filled with more books than she had ever seen in one place. She could spend weeks in that room. She had to concentrate on her purpose for being there so as not to become unfocused. There were several comfortable chairs in the middle of the library and seats under two of the windows for natural reading light.

"Miss Dahl, your uncle has told me about your love for books. How does my library suit you? Does it please you?"

"Indeed, it does. It is most beautiful and a proper place for knowledge and edification. You have a wonderful collection, my king."

"I do. And it gives me immense fulfillment." He stood close in front of Clara, pointing his finger in the air in front of her face, and said with a proud yet jovial countenance, as if speaking to a child, "Now, your uncle said you were interested in seeing my copy of the *Malleus Maleficarum*."

A servant with white gloves, knee breeches with silken ribbons, and elegant manners walked to the far corner of the library and picked out a book from the third shelf. Clara's heart leapt, not necessarily with joy for getting her way, but with horror and fear of what the book entailed and the fate it had sealed on a great amount of women in several countries. Her hands shook as the king put the book on a large table and gave her permission to turn the front page and see inside. He smiled and looked at Clara's uncle, bragging about how this book had in fact been a guide and a handbook in seeking out witches from countries from the Mediterranean Sea and northward, even to Denmark and its neighboring countries. Uncle Jacob said nothing, but behaved with grace and politeness.

Clara carefully turned the pages and read words written by a monk clearly under the influence of powers contrary to the kind God she believed in. King Fredrik looked over her shoulder, eager to show her pages he had noticed, finding them both interesting and true.

"I will not make excuses because you are a woman, Miss Dahl," he said. "I am the king; I don't need to excuse myself. But you will see that even though you are a woman, this book explains what a woman is really like, what she is capable of, if and when she cavorts with demons. Her weakness may take her down wrong paths in life and cause good Christian men to fall, even endangering families."

Clara looked at her uncle and understood that she should be cautious how she expressed herself. The king had admitted her to come to a private audience with her uncle and had discussed remarkable matters with them. She thought he admired the fact that she was an educated woman and possessed knowledge about his keen interest in natural philosophies and even religion. But she had to watch her tongue; the last statement from the king proved him to be fiercer than he had given her the impression of in the last hour she had spent with him.

"My King, what would you do if a woman was mistakenly accused and tried?"

"Mistakenly, is that possible?"

"Yes, my King." Clara explained the situation with Angus Hill and the women of Rossby and even dared to propose a few points on how she thought he could easily rescue those accused, those who still remained inside the prison walls of Town Hall in the small town of Rossby. It was one of many places and towns with similar problems, but it was where her heart was at the moment, and where with his help the suffering could be relieved.

He did not answer, but put the book away on the shelf himself and waved to one of the guards. "We are done here," he said and walked out of the room.

Clara followed him and said: "Please, my king, these women are wrongfully accused and convicted. I know you can help them."

At the same time as she said that, Clara felt she had been bolder than she ought to have been. King Fredrik turned around and looked at her and frowned. Clara lowered her gaze and bowed her head.

"Miss Dahl, I have other pressing matters to attend to. A guard will show out. Good day."

Uncle Jacob bowed before the king before they left.

"Please consider our discussion and give thought about these matters until tomorrow," he said. He backed up a step and bowed again, then put an arm on Clara's back and led her out of the room.

The conversation with the king had, after all, been enlightening. Clara had done her best to make sure he understood that every day was crucial, and that the unpredictable situation in Rossby was her main concern and reason for seeking his attention. But it was only polite and right to give him time to think about the matter.

When they returned the next day, the king was not there. He had embarked his royal ship early the same morning and would not be back for several weeks.

Devastated she had not accomplished what she came for, Clara walked back to the carriage and sat down. She buried her face in her hands and let her feelings out. There was no time to linger. She felt the need to return to Rossby as rapidly as possible. Nervous and wondering what had happened in her absence, she hoped and prayed she would not be too late.

"You have given the king something to think about. Don't give up," Uncle Jacob said and put his hands upon Clara's shoulders. "Be brave, and never give up an important cause. Continue to fight for what you know is right."

He sounded like her father, and Clara felt reassured she was doing the right thing, no matter how difficult or dangerous the struggle might be.

"Uncle Jacob, does it trouble you that we have a hereditary monarchy?" Clara asked in the carriage on the way to the Copenhagen Harbor the next morning. "What if the king proved to be an unjust ruler and brought up his son to be the same way, what then?"

"King Fredrik has promised all ranks a fair and just constitution, but we still have not seen any documentation of this. It's only words, so far, but as far as inheriting the throne from father to son, yes, that's what we have to live with for now."

A young man in a sailor's uniform approached them with rapid steps.

"Ah, there you are, Uncle Jacob said. "Clara, this is Jens. His parents are good friends of mine. He sails with this vessel, and I have asked him to make sure you arrive safely at your destination. I wanted to go myself, but I'm expected at the palace this afternoon. Promise to return soon."

Tears trickled down Clara's face as her uncle kissed her cheek and bid her farewell. He had comprehended her predicament and had taken her plea to heart. She was in need, and he had helped her. Clara hoped to return the favor one day.

There was plenty of time to think on the way home. Clara analyzed the events in Copenhagen and planned what to do upon her return to

Rossby. Her father quoted a Scripture once about the blind leading the blind, subsequently both fell into a ditch. Angus Hill guided the leaders and the inhabitants of Rossby off the road entirely. What more could she do to open their eyes and help them see how utterly mistaken he was?

The ship sailed into port late morning, and Rossby came into view like a fairy town materializing out of the mist. The closer they came, the more Clara saw how men, women, and children were on the go, working, talking, and playing. Young folks were occupied being youthful, thinking tribulations and death as improbable. Women with baskets on one arm and an infant in the other chatted with friends about their children, new clothes, and hairstyles. Men brought cod, haddock, sometimes tusk, ling and coalfish into the fishery for drying, while some of the fish were carried to the nearby market on the town square. Did anyone talk about witch-hunting and the fact that some of their neighbors suffered inside the four walls of the otherwise beautiful Town Hall building?

The witch-finder was certainly on their minds. Clara heard his name mentioned a few times as she walked toward Main Street. He obviously made the impression of being a powerful leader, a man of knowledge, and courageous in his quest for fighting evil. Clara would fight wickedness herself. In fact, this is what she was brought up to do, having a minister for a father and a well-read Bible on her table. She had watched blameless women drowned, burned to death, and imprisoned by a delusional man driven by greed and the prospect of having his name revered by simple folks. In his own words, these simple folks could not save themselves. If only the Rossbyans could see beyond the fake authority and impressive title. From what Clara found out, he was neither priest nor doctor. A witch-hunter? Well, yes, that title he could claim. And having been an apprentice to the notorious Matthew Hopkins? Yes, that was probably true as well, but there she drew the line. The way he had spoken about himself at the trial of Sister Birgitta, you would think he was God's apprentice.

Why were the parishioners not disheartened by the late events? Did they not fear what a witch-finder like Angus Hill was capable of doing to their own mothers and daughters?

Clara had her travel bag delivered to her cottage and walked down Main Street to see if she could get in to see Bess and Old Magda. On the way there, she passed the butcher, Mr. Land, and young Mathias. Nobody knew where she had been or why she had gone. It was not as if she had a supporting crowd. Herr Christopher had taught a couple of the school classes, and she was grateful for that. The children were probably happy to have the other days off.

The guards did not move aside to let her in the door at Town Hall. Clara provided them with gifts from Copenhagen but to no avail. She even asked to see Anna, but the guards offering nothing but one refusal after another. Bess was behind the cream-colored walls and Clara could not see her, comfort her, or help her.

Clara went by Frue Farm to see if the animals needed feeding. They seemed content and already fed that day; Uncle Samuel must have been by. The difference she noticed most of all was that the heart of the farm was gone. It felt like the memory of the night her mother had died. Even though Clara had been a little girl, the feeling her mother's passing had given her appeared now and then.

It was difficult to fall asleep that night. Outside, the wind blew fiercely, and noises from trees bending and creaking kept her awake. Clara finally dozed off and dreamed about a magpie caught inside a house, lonely and afraid, until a little boy befriended the bird and opened the window to freedom.

She woke up next morning drenched and fatigued. Her best friend had been put in a cage, not free to walk out when she pleased, not free to choose her own exit.

It was getting colder every day now. Clara decided to put up a bird feeder outside the cottage; that way, she could at least help the hungry little winged ones.

That same night when she was in her warm bed, struggling with dreams, Bess's infant was born in the Holding chamber in the basement of the Town Hall. The little girl arrived into the world in a cold, damp cellar, no midwife present, no clean sheets or warm crib. Clara heard about it when she tried to visit Bess the next morning.

"What happens to the infant," Clara asked the guard outside the blue double door.

"How should I know," he answered. "Get rid of it, take it out into the woods and leave it there, maybe give it to a family. Don't ask me; I don't make these decisions."

The mayor's carriage rolled up in front of Town Hall while Clara talked to the guard. The door of the coach opened and the mayor and his wife stepped out. Clara thought it more than fortunate, as good luck had not been her companion these last months. She silently said a prayer before approaching the town leader.

"Miss Clara, how are you today," the mayor asked first, trying to act friendly.

Clara's habitual skepticism kept her on guard. She knew she had to act polite and calm if she hoped to be heard at all.

"Mr. Mayor," she said, then nodded to his wife. "Thank you, my health is good. I have an important request."

"Clara, you know I cannot release your friend. She has been through trial and found guilty. I am sorry, but there is nothing I can do."

Clara clenched her fists, hoping he would not notice her frustration. "Mr. Mayor, I do not ask for Bess; I ask for the small child born last night."

"Yes," the mayor said slowly dragging the word. "I heard she was delivered during the night."

"The holding chamber is no place for an innocent child, Mr. Mayor. Please, may I ask at the parsonage if Sara, the parson's wife, can take the infant and nurse her for a period. She has a young one herself and plenty of milk." Clara boldly continued, thinking she had nothing to lose. "Mr. Mayor, surely you don't want a newborn on your conscience. Besides, Herr Christopher and his wife can bring the child up in a Christian faith."

Clara stood for a moment, worried she had spoken excessively forward. She did not know if she was courageous or foolish at the time; she only knew it had to be said.

The mayor's wife pulled his arm and smiled at him, having given birth to six children and having lost four, her heart softened. He looked at her and nodded, understanding her feelings. At that moment not all hope was lost in Rossby.

21

The Encaged

~

"Tomorrow. Come back tomorrow."

Clara had heard this often now but knew she could not give up.

Then one day as she approached the town prison, the yard guard opened the tall, heavy, blue double wooden door with the metal hinges and invited her in. It may have helped that she had brought him bribes of home-made cobblers and slices of meat every day for several weeks now. Clara walked behind the guard, straight ahead to the prison cells on the ground floor, but another guard in the hallway, who recognized her and knew who she wanted to see, pointed in another direction. He was a young man, not yet twenty.

"Down the stairs", he commanded. "We don't have witches up here. They are kept in the holding chamber."

The stone stairs going down were slippery and icy from the cold and damp. Clara had to hold on to the side of the wall to not fall and drop the food she had brought. At the bottom of the stairs was a small hallway with a lit torch on the wall. To the left was a room toward the back side of the building. The chamber housed five or six pigs and a few chickens. Clara quickly peeked into an open door of the room as the guard shoved her from behind. The swine grunted and waddled around in the mud, and the chickens had escaped up onto a wooden shelf on the wall, trying to keep warm by huddling together.

"Keep going," hissed the unfriendly caretaker.

He took hold of Clara's arm and pushed her into another small room on the right that contained peculiar tool-like instruments, thongs, and ropes on the back wall. An older guard wearing a winter hat and gloves sat on a stool but stood up as they entered the room.

"She's here to see the witch," the younger stated.

"Which one?"

"The pretty redhead," he sneered.

The ring with keys was taken from a nail high up on the wall, and the older guard turned the lock of a heavy-set door. An eerie squeak sounded as he swung the door open to let Clara enter. She felt sorry for someone whose job it was to sit in this dark and dreary hole—and to what avail—to guard innocents?

Clara bowed her head to enter. The holding chamber was no more than a low-ceilinged basement room. There was a tiny window high on the wall straight ahead, which let in a little daylight. The dirt floor had scattered piles of straw, and a bucket for human waste sat in the left corner. The place made Clara shiver. Indeed it was icy cold, but the chill of human abandonment penetrated her skin and went into her heart in a different way altogether. Clara's eyes had already adjusted to the dim light in the room, but the stench was harder to be oblivious to. It was a combination of the waste bucket in the corner and the pig sty next door, but also the unsanitary conditions and sickly smell of flesh.

Her eyes searched for Bess. She saw Thea, the maid from the Lands' residence, and next to her, widow Doris and her eight-summer-old daughter, Kari, huddled together on a small pile of dried grass. Clara saw Old Magda lying on the woolen blanket on the floor, now grimy and soiled. At least the guards had been kind enough to give it to her. Magda would probably die before Angus Hill killed her, Clara thought, watching her lying there as if there were no life left in her.

Then there was Bess. She sat on the floor in the corner of the cell, hugging her legs, her knees pulled up under her chin. She shivered, and her hair was still short, maybe raked with a knife. Perhaps that was just as well when Clara thought about the lice-infected place she was in. Bess did not even notice that Clara had entered the room. With her neck bent under the low ceiling, Clara slowly stepped across the floor, kneeled next to Bess on the cold, dirty ground and put her arms around her friend.

"Bess," Clara said. "I'm here."

Bess lifted her head slowly and forced a slight smile but said nothing.

"They did not let me see you until today. I'm so sorry. We are helpless pawns in this wicked display of arrogance and misunderstanding."

And as if being brought back into the reality of life and circumstances, Bess looked at Clara with the eyes of a concerned mother. "My baby, where is my baby?" she asked.

"She is well," Clara assured her, "safe with the family at the parsonage. She is being fed and loved."

"And Lucia?"

Clara nodded. "She is taken care of also."

Bess breathed a sigh of relief. Clara was glad she did not have to elaborate, considering how frail Bess was, so she continued talking about other things.

"Please, eat the soup. I put some of your dried herbs in it. It will do you good. And have some of the cheese and bread Sara baked this morning. She wanted you to have it."

But Bess was beyond hunger. She was weak and discouraged, not a good combination. The recent loss of blood during childbirth had drained the last bit of energy from her. Clara brought the soup to her lips and carefully fed her. Bess opened her mouth slowly and accepted the nourishment. Clara gave her some of the bread, but it was as if she fed someone half asleep.

"Tell me a story," Bess said, her voice shaking. "Take me away from here in thought."

Clara told her the dream about the magpie and the little boy, and when she finished tears were running down Bess's cheeks.

"We'll get you out of here, Bess," Clara whispered in her ear. "We'll find a way; I promise. Please be strong."

As Clara stood up to leave, she put the small cloth with bread and cheese under Bess's blanket. She turned her head to look at Bess one more time before exiting the holding chamber and saw her take the remaining food out of the cloth and share it with her cellmates.

Clara walked away feeling lonelier than ever before. For a while, she thought someone followed her, but it turned out he went in a different direction. Trust came at a dear price nowadays. Protection and safeguarding was nearly impossible with Angus Hill in town.

She thought about the dream in which she knew she could fly but could not get her feet off the ground. She remembered the crow on the road to Frue Farm and the recent reverie about the magpie who wished for warmth and safety without being locked up in a cage. The first dream reflected her insecurities, the fear of not completing her purposes or fulfilling vocational goals. The crow on the road reminded her to do everything within her power to get nourishment to Bess and the other women in the holding chamber, and the magpie was the epitome of the horrible situation. The deliberate essence of all three was that she had to work on a way to get back inside the basement of Town hall and free Bess.

Her feet felt limp and heavy as she trudged down the path to her cottage. Small puddles on the way had turned into miniature, icy lakes, making the world seem even colder than she felt inside. She stomped on one and listened to the thin ice crack and watched the water splat out on the toe of her shoe. A blackbird sat on one of the posts on the fence around the haddock, its head held high and the bright-orange beak wide open with important news. Clara had always seen the blackbirds in the wooded areas but not as much out in the open. It seemed like everyone emerged nowadays, showing themselves, talking about what went on in Rossby. No one was unaffected by the situation.

Suddenly, the bird closed its bright beak and flew off into the forest, just as Clara felt someone grab her from behind. A large hand held tightly over her mouth and she was pulled into the bushes. She could not scream and was not strong enough to fight against the sturdy arm around her waist.

Out of sight in the greenery, the person turned Clara around to face him, his hand still on her mouth.

"Will you stay quiet if I remove my hand?" he whispered.

She nodded, and he slowly took his hand away and stared into her eyes.

Clara recognized him from Bess's description—tall and muscular with blonde bangs pushed to the side and a bushy beard with a touch of the color of ripe strawberries. His eyes were blue as cornflowers, adorned with creases of wrinkles from smiling often. It was easy to understand why he had managed to charm Bess.

"You have come at the twelfth hour, Mychel." Clara said and embraced him. "We really need you right now."

"I know, I know."

Clara peeked out of the greenery to see if anyone was out and about and when she felt it was safe enough she brought him along to the cottage. Ami jumped onto his lap as she fetched something for Mychel to eat. He was famished and looked tired and worn. Through Bess it felt as though they were already acquainted.

"I have been here two days," he said and ate the food Clara placed in front of him like a hungry but grateful wolf. "I have tried to lay low and gather an understanding of what has happened here. A storm caught our fishing boat off the coast, and we were rescued by another vessel. The only problem was that they were headed in the opposite direction for the Faroe Islands and did not have the time to bring us back until now. We worked on the island to pay for our passage back here."

"It could not have happened at a worse time, I'm afraid." Clara poured him another cup of milk and added more bread and meat to his plate.

"I have knowledge of where Bess and the newborn are, and I heard you were here, but where are Uncle Samuel and Lucia?"

There was not much she could tell him but explained about her secret messages to Uncle Samuel, though they were few, and how she had noticed he regularly visited Frue Farm.

"In my heart, I know they are well," Clara said. "I have no other choice. I have to believe they are safe."

"Then I will trust in your belief." He took Clara's hand and thanked her for the meal. "We cannot let anyone know I am here, not yet. "

"I agree. Keep out of sight until we figure out what more we can do."

Mychel left, and Clara sat down on a chair, thanking God Bess's husband at length had returned home. Though prospects of a joyous family reunion were bleak, and Clara felt barren as the leafless trees after gusty autumn winds had toiled with them, she felt encouraged and twice as strong since Mychel now worked with her.

He returned to Clara's cottage late that same evening.

"Do you think anyone saw you coming?" she asked and poked her head out of the door and looked left and right. She had no idea what she would have done if she had actually seen someone lurking behind a tree, but fortunately the coast seemed clear.

"No, I am quite sure I was alone."

"Come in, quickly. It's cold tonight, and I don't want anyone to hear your voice."

She closed the door, pulled the curtains shut, and pointed at the chair in front of the fireplace, motioning for him to sit down.

"Would you like something warm to drink? I have some hot milk in a pot on the stove."

Mychel nodded and bent forward in the chair, holding out his hands toward the fire. He looked tired and cold. He had probably spent the whole day outside, trying to gather information and hiding from view. Clara could tell his heart ached for his family and the serious trouble they were in. She tried not to get emotional. She had to think straight as they had to save Bess. She handed him the warm cup and put a plate of bread and cheese on the small table.

"Mychel," she said, "there are pigs in the room next to the holding chamber. How do they get them in and out?"

"Maybe they bring them in as piglets and slaughter them down there."

"No, I don't think so. The stone steps going down are steep and narrow, and the room is crowded and dirty. A butcher would want more space and light to work in."

"Clara, can you draw me a room plan of Town Hall and the adjacent cells and chambers? I have seen some of the rooms, but that was a few summers ago. We need to know what we are working with."

"Yes, of course. I'll draw according to what I have seen. I will try to remember where the guards are placed and where the torches are on the walls."

"And remember the doors and windows." He carefully sipped the warm drink and held the cup to warm both hands. It must have hurt a little, as his hands were red from the low temperature outside.

Clara grabbed some paper and the pen and ink on her writing desk and started sketching. She made a rough draft, drawing up lines and scratching some out. Both were concentrating, trying to think of any details that could be helpful in bringing Bess safely and unnoticed out of the prison. They worked on the drawing for a while, sometimes staring out in space, trying to discover thoughts and ideas, sometimes talking simultaneously as the plan came along.

"We don't have much time. The execution will take place within the next few weeks," Clara said. "Anna told me earlier today that the town council is planning another witch burning."

Mychel clenched his fists as if he would beat someone. "They want to cleanse out all evil before they celebrate the birth of the Savior, do they?"

"Maybe they throw their consciences on the fire, as well. That way they don't have to feel bad." Clara's heart went out to him as he sat there angry, hurt, and afraid.

"What consciences?"

He put the empty cup on the table and she fetched more warm milk and refilled his cup.

"It has occurred to me, Clara, they actually believe in what they are doing," he said and scratched his head. "What makes God-fearing townspeople turn on their friends and neighbors?"

Clara shrugged. "I have wrung my mind trying to figure it out. I have thought about how fear makes people act in certain ways. I have had philosophical debates with myself, even religious conversations, thinking they are trapped in one way of thinking or another. It could even be by popular demand. But I think you are right. The witch-hunters seem to believe in what they are doing."

Mychel sipped the warm milk and honey and stared out into space with squinted eyes. Then the corners of his mouth stretched up into a little smile. You could tell his mind worked overtime. He put the cup down and said firmly, "Let's use the twins' wickedness to our own advantage."

"How's that?"

"They spread rumors for personal gain, and we can do the same. Fair is fair."

"You mean give them a taste of their own medicine? Interesting."

"Yes, but without knowing it, they will help us with our plan. It's time to put some flesh on the skeletons in their closet."

Just then, there was a loud knock on the door. Clara startled. She looked over at Mychel and whispered, "Who can that be? No one knows you're here."

He put a finger over his lips and walked behind Clara toward the front door and motioned for her to open it. With Mychel hiding to her right, Clara slowly turned the key and pushed the door open. Suddenly, something jumped down right in front of her eyes. She was so taken aback she almost fell backwards. It was Ami. He had jumped off the roof above and with a loud growl landed on the face of a tall man standing outside the door. The man took hold of the cat with two large hands and placed it gently on the ground. Then he straightened his back and stared her right in the face. It was Toomber.

Clara was shocked and had problems finding the right words. "What in the world? Ami, what are you doing?" She picked up the cat and held him tightly to her chest and stuttered, "Too—Toomber, why are you here?"

"I know where the old man has taken the child," he said.

22

The Strategy

In a split second, Mychel appeared in the doorway next to Clara. They both looked at Toomber, waiting for him to explain. What was a man like Toomber capable of doing with information like that?

They dreaded the worst, but the dirty giant looked directly in Clara's eyes and said, "I can help."

It felt right to let him inside the cottage. Ami slithered in next to their legs and ran over to find his supper. Toomber sat down with them, and Clara fetched him a mug of hot milk with honey. He seemed grateful, and for some reason, for the first time in her life, Clara felt like she could trust him. He had suggestions, and they had some thoughts, and together they made a plan.

"The weather here is unpredictable," Mychel said. "We should choose a night with no moon so as not to be seen. The ground is frozen now, which will leave fewer tracks. That's a good thing unless it snows, then our foot prints will be everywhere."

Toomber cleared his throat and mumbled in his deep, gruff voice, "The great ball at Town Hall is next Thursday. That's the time to do it."

"Why?" Clara protested. "There will be lots of people there. There will be lights and merry-making and dancing and—"

"True," Toomber said, staring straight at Clara. "They will be busy doing whatever merry-makers do."

Clara was curious about Toomber's change of heart. Why did he want to help them rescue Bess? She could not help herself and had to ask him.

"She saved my life once," he answered and walked out of the door.

And that was all. Clara could tell he was not ready to enlighten her with more details at that point. Amazingly enough, he had opened up and admitted to a kind deed. She would ask Bess to tell her what had happened later.

Clara kept telling herself things like that. *One day, Bess and I will go berry picking together,* she thought. *One day, we will sit in the evening and look at the stars together.* She could never give up hope. Not now.

She turned to Mychel. "How are you holding up?" she asked.

He fingered a small stone. It was round and smooth, shaped by weather and sand.

"Bess put this in my shoe one day. She said it would remind me of her every step I took." He smiled. "I have kept it in my pocket ever since; having it my shoe brought on more pain than loving thoughts."

"That is so typical of her," Clara said, "performing sweet acts in a humorous way."

Mychel sat with Ami on his lap. This rugged man with strong, working hands petted the cat with gentle strokes. He had the fight of his life ahead of him. His family was in danger. It must have been hard for him not to show his face, not to let anyone know he had returned.

～

The next morning a messenger boy came and asked Clara to report at Town Hall.

Her mind raced, worried. Her thoughts could not finish sentences properly. Had they found Lucia? Had something happened to Bess? Did anyone see Mychel and Toomber arrive at her cottage?

She entered the blue double door and a guard led her to the mayor's office. The appointment made for an easy entrance this time. The hallway that led to the holding chamber down the stairs was straight ahead and to the right. Lacking acting ability, she fought to pretend she did not think about Bess in that horrible room; hungry, cold, and sick.

To her surprise, the mayor was all alone in the room, pacing back and forth on the large carpet on the floor, hitting his forehead with the palms of his hands. He stopped as Clara entered, came forward, and pulled her arm to set her down on a chair by his desk.

Clara looked at him, expecting him to speak first. He said nothing, but held his hands at his back and walked over to glare out the window facing Main Street. She waited, perplexed.

"She's no witch." he stated, affirming an undoubted assumption.

"Pardon me, Mr. Mayor, who is not a witch?"

"My sister." He turned around and faced her.

"Your sister?"

"Yes, my younger sister, Cornelia. Miss Taran Land claims to have proof that my sister has engaged in—I can hardly say it—devilish acts. The town council is convinced it is so, and my protests have fallen on deaf ears. The innkeeper and Angus Hill are going to make their charges today, and I have not even been able to warn her."

The dark rings under his eyes showed lack of sleep, and his meal lay untouched on a pewter plate on the large, oak desk. Parallel thoughts galloped through Clara's head, but most of all she wanted to say, "I told you so." Nonetheless, she tried nonetheless to maintain enough dignity and wisdom to say something worthwhile and productive, for Bess's sake. Even though he had been part of the witch-hunt in Rossby, she had felt his sympathy and uncertainty at times.

But how could she trust him? Perhaps he had someone hiding behind the long curtains, waiting for her to reveal information about Lucia, or someone waiting outside the door, ready to interrogate her about Bess. She could not let her guard down, or behave without caution.

"Clara, this has gone too far." He finally walked back to sit on the large chair behind the desk. "I don't know how to stop it. My sister is innocent." He paused and swallowed hard. "And maybe some of the other women are as well," he admitted dejectedly.

For the first time, Clara felt a trace of hope but not enough to let the thought linger.

"What do you suggest can be done, and what can I do to help?" she asked. She thought it best to let him feel he was still in charge, which he was. Collaborating might be helpful, under the circumstances. Not knowing his sister seemed beside the point.

"What reasons have been given?" Clara continued. "Is there any substance to Taran's accusations?" She needed him to keep opening up in order to understand which strategy she should play.

"Angus Hill has a royal permission to roam our country. Did you know?" The mayor avoided any questions and pulled a document from his desk drawer and placed it in front of Clara.

She watched her speech and made sure she did not step into his personal realm.

Clara looked at the document. "No, Mr. Mayor. I did not know. How can this paper give him that power?"

"It gives him authority to seek out witches and deal with the problems."

"But you are the mayor."

"I am, but by royal decree Angus Hill can carry out the hunt, and he has the council backing him. His decree is law, even here on the northern coast, far away from Copenhagen."

There was no need to explain about her recent travel to the capitol. What good would it do? She had not returned with any charter banning witch-hunting. She had tried, but even now, she did not know if she had stirred up more interest for the hunt or calmed it down by her pleas for justice.

Clara put the document back down on the desk and said calmly, "King Fredrik is an avid combatant of witchery, just like his father and predecessor, Christian IV. That is what we need to worry about."

"There's not much we can do about that."

She racked her mind, trying to come up with something useful to say, any proposal to be of assistance to the mayor's plea for help.

"The king fights witchcraft in the name of natural philosophy."

"How?"

She struggled to get eye contact while she told him in a few short sentences about the king's interest in new ideas and discoveries. Without sounding blasphemous or committing treason, she carefully explained her point of view on how laws were made without considering the worth of a person and punishment easily distributed by men of power. "You are the mayor and know the law. You can use them to your own benefit."

"What do you mean? I don't understand." He scratched his head and looked at Clara. "I have worked this through in my mind over and over again. Now that my sister is accused, I thought I could speak to you about it. I would have done so with your father, Clara. You are a woman, but I—"

"It's all well, Mr. Mayor."

Clara's opinions about the difference between men and woman had no room in this discussion. Keeping the conversation in line, she said, "Listen, Mr. Mayor, thus far, Cornelia has not been apprehended. She has neither been taken into custody nor to trial. If they bring her in, suggest they banish her from the country. That is one of the punishments for witchcraft and a way she might avoid physical chastisement and an eventual death penalty."

"But she's my sister." His voice was sad and cracking.

"It could save her life, Mr. Mayor. That is worth the risk. Gentler times will come, and then you may bring her back. You have the authority to do so."

The mayor nodded and fingered with a candlestick on his desk. "My sister has a beautiful soprano voice," he said. "She was to entertain at the town ball in a few days. I must say I am not in a festive mood anymore."

Like window shutters that open up to welcome the light of a new morning into a sleepy room, it dawned on Clara what Cornelia's accusers were up to. The twins were jealous of a competitor. Their desire for attention had no limits. It was time to fight back, as Mychel had said, by using their schemes, their own sly methods.

"Might I suggest you ask the twins to sing at the ball, Mr. Mayor?"

"The twins? They do have lovely voices and they sing in harmony, but after what they have done, I don't know."

"Your sister will probably be exhausted after today's events. If the twins prepare for a performance at Town Hall, they will not have as much time to pester others.

"Keep them busy, you say?"

"Yes, flatter them, and give them the assignment as soon as possible."

"An excellent suggestion. Yes, I will do that. I am still mayor of this town, and I can still make some decisions without my council," he responded defiantly.

***

Meanwhile, Angus Hill prepared in his room at the Rossby Inn. Innkeeper Hansen had showed Angus particular attention by giving him the largest room with a view of Main Street, the best meals, and updates on happenings by messenger twice a day. The witch-finder made his bed meticulously every morning and folded his clothes neatly across the back of a chair. Comb, soap, and a knife for raking were lined up next to the basin of warm water.

Before leaving his room to seek out the next witch, there was a matter of formal procedure to go through, performed every morning before his essential duties as a witch-finder. This procedure was also followed at the end of every day. He sat down on a chair by the desk with his traveling bag next to him on the floor. Out of the bag he pulled a linen pouch, one among several, deftly placed between the folds of a small coverlet. One by one, he took trinkets out of the pouch and placed them methodically on the desk. Among them were the ring from old Magda, the cross Sister Birgitta had worn around her neck, the knife from Hilda's cottage, and the recipe book of the women of Frue Farm. Embellished trinkets, small treasures, and personal belongings of each woman he had accused and tried. This ritual was executed ceremonially, like partaking of a holy sacrament.

The witch-finder ran his long and cold white fingers across each item, smiling a thin, crooked grin, shuttering with pleasure and satisfaction. Then lighting a candle, he uttered, "I will get you. I will get you all. Glory be, where glory is deserved."

23

The Gravedigger's Choice

~~~

Outside the Land residence, Toomber waited for the twins. When they appeared in the doorway, he grabbed both of them and pulled them aside.

"Not a word," he mumbled, as he hauled them around the corner of the house behind a shed.

"I'll scream," Taran said, trying to pull her arm out of the giant's grasp.

"No you won't. You're interested in why I want to speak with you. Now, I have a few questions. You will answer them truthfully, then I will let you go."

"And if we don't?"

"I will take you to the cemetery, tie you to a tree, and let you stay there until after dark." Toomber was surprised at his own imagination but kept the menacing mannerism and hit a clenched fist in the air toward the girls.
~~~

The twins looked at each other and nodded. The prospect of being alone with Toomber at the graveyard after dark did not tempt them.

"What do you want to know?" Tilla asked.

"I have been watching the two of you." He frowned and a growl came out of the left corner of his mouth. "I have seen how you have persecuted women in Rossby. I have noticed your scheming and lying ways and I want to know why."

"What's in it for us?"

"What's in it for—" Toomber rolled his eyes without finishing the sentence. "You are the most annoying females I have ever met. I'll tell you what is in it for you: I will let you go and not tell your father what I know. I will not throw you into the sea on a stormy day."

The gravedigger lifted them up on a large rock next to the shed. "Now, stay. Tell me, why Hilda?"

"She smelled."

"She smelled?" Toomber snorted. "That's all? She smelled?"

The twins nodded. "She was dense, you know. Did not understand what people said to her, probably under some evil spell."

Toomber let out a long breath and shook his head in disbelief.

"What about Birgitta?"

"We didn't like her. She was too precious, too perfect."

"Old Magda?"

"Oh, her, she was so old anyway; but she's not dead yet, or is she?" Taran looked over at Tilla, who shrugged and lifted her eyebrows.

"But why her?" Toomber continued.

"She did strange things. She was, or is, a witch, you know. We asked her to hex us once, just for fun. She refused."

"I see. And you don't like to be refused. And Francesca?"

"Oh, we did not have anything to do with her. We never go into the gypsy camp. They are filthy."

"Filthy? Well, well."

Toomber did not have a social life, nor did he know how to associate with people on friendly terms. He had stayed away, threatening both young and old in order to be left alone, but the girls had actually gone to the extreme of hurting others, even causing their death. It was appalling to him, but he did not want to scare them off, not just yet. Jealousy seemed to permeate their beings.

They had a reason for each woman accused; Thea, the willful and outspoken servant's maid in the Lands' kitchen, who had not been afraid and had dared speak her mind in their presence; the woman Mari from behind the abbey who had borrowed money from their father and never paid it back; the mayor's sister, Cornelia, whose beautiful soprano voice was a true competitor and needed to be eliminated. Doris and her daughter Kari were innocent bystanders, framed by a furious Thea. The twins did not know why but did not mind.

"And Bess?" Toomber asked, appalled at what he had heard so far.

"Bess is the worst. That witch murdered our brother."

The gravedigger believed them, in the same way he believed they thought they were speaking the truth, even though the facts were horrid and twisted. He stood and stared at the twins sitting on the rock. They were only fourteen summers old. What would become of them? Who would be safe around them?

"Now can we go?" Taran got impatient and moved off the rock. She took her sister's hand to help her down.

Toomber nodded. He had heard enough. "Breathe a word of this to anyone and I will come and get you." He showed his yellowed teeth and hissed. "You know I will, and it is better for you not to find out what I would do to you then."

He watched the twins walk warily back to the entrance of the Lands' residence, then he returned to Clara's cottage, contemplating his life in Rossby. He had been alone for most of his life, but now and then a kind person had connected with him. Even though he did not know how to show it, he appreciated a few trustworthy relationships. Someone who did not judge him or put him down. He had felt that way with the minister. He had felt it as Bess brought him back to health two summers earlier, and now he did not doubt that Clara, being the minister's daughter, and Bess's husband Mychel were true and reliable acquaintances. Friends? Maybe. It was not a word he kept in his vocabulary, but it felt good thinking they might be his friends.

When he arrived in Rossby on a small boat with his mother, he was only seven. She never spoke about his father but struggled to make a living for her son and to be safe without violence. He had already seen enough in his short life, and his mother thought hiding away in a smaller town would save them both. But she was sickly and spent more time in bed than she did working as a maid at the parsonage. A couple of summers later, she passed away, and Toomber was left alone in the cottage, but he already knew how to take care of himself in spite of his young age.

The minister let him work as an assistant to the old gravedigger, a mean and ruthless man who never had a kind or encouraging word to say to the young boy. One evening, the old gravedigger was found dead in the corner of the graveyard with a bottle of strong drink in his hand. Toomber became the master of the cemetery at only sixteen summers old.

Taran turned her heads a couple of times, in hope that Toomber did not follow them. He stood there by the rock, staring. They walked fast to get away from him. As they came to the stairs by the entrance, the maid stood in the doorway holding a basket, looking left and right on Main Street.

"What do you have there?" Taran grabbed the basket tied with pretty ribbons on the handle. Before the maid had time to answer, Taran continued, "You stupid girl. It has a note: *For Taran and Tilla*. It's a gift for us. You didn't take anything, did you? Did you?" Taran screamed.

The maid shook her head. She curtsied and ran inside.

Taran and Tilla went to their room, sat down on their bed, and emptied the contents of the basket on the downy cover. They could never get enough gifts and eagerly started rummaging the items— small, cloth pouches tied with string and with notes attached to each one.

"Who do you think it's from?" Tilla asked and picked up one of the pouches and started reading the note.

"It says, *Dried Flowers for Protection against Evil Spirits*," Tilla read out loud. She looked over at her sister with a puzzled face. She emptied the bag in her lap, dried flowers spreading on her gown. "What is this? Who has sent us this gift?" she asked, bewildered.

Taran picked up another pouch and read: "*Oregano—Protection against Wytches*." She tilted her head. All the pouches were similar. There were seeds of sweet fennel to put in the keyhole to prohibit anything evil entering the room, some dried fennel to hang over the door for safety, dried estragon for snake bites, dried nightshade as a shield against the *huldra*, and lady's bedstraw to keep witchcraft and witches at a distance. There were five or six more pouches with the same message.

Taran threw the basket on the floor and leaned back to move away from the cloth bags, sweeping the dried flowers off her lap. "Who is trying to scare us? Why does anyone think we need this?"

"Bess? Old Magda?" Tilla picked up the basket and put the pouches back in. She scooped the dried flowers off the bed along with any other dried remedy left there.

"No, they are both in prison."

"How about Hilda by the Sea?"

"My goodness, Tilla, she is dead. Remember?" Taran thought for a minute. "You don't think she has come back to haunt us, do you?"

"I don't know, sister. Those witches are capable of curious things, maybe even visits from the realm of the dead. I'm scared, Taran."

"I know. Me, too."

Taran put an arm around her sister, and there they sat for a while, huddled together, not knowing what to think about the gift and its contents. Finally, Taran pushed Tilla away and got up.

"Let's go practice our song," she said. "First Toomber and now this basket. I don't know what's happening, but they won't get to us, whoever it is."

In front of the parlor door, a maid dusted paintings on the wall. Taran pushed her aside as they passed and said, "Go clean up the mess in our room, and throw it far away."

24

The Ball

～

Toomber rounded the path around the paddock fence and walked through the door of Clara's cottage as she and Mychel were arranging all the planned items on the table, counting and double-checking to make sure they had everything under control. They looked at the gravedigger who nodded with a satisfied look, telling them the encounter with the twins had been successful. Clara's basket had hopefully scared them as well.

"Angus Hill is a worm," Clara said as she put the hammer next to the crowbar.

"I have not had the pleasure of meeting him, Clara, but if you say so."

Clara gazed at Mychel with a dejected look. She had come to know him a little over the last couple of days, and knew he was as good as Bess had described him. She blamed herself for being low in spirits when he needed her support.

"Yes, I say so," Clara persisted, trying not to sound maudlin. "He wiggles and squirms. He digs holes in the ground. He hides and only comes out on rainy days."

"That I believe," Mychel agreed.

"Sounds like me," Toomber said and placed a shovel next to a chair.

Clara smiled. "Not quite the same, Toomber, but I see what you are saying."

Mychel turned to him. "What do you think, Toomber?"

"The witch-finder believes in his obsession," Toomber said, winding a long piece of rope around his wrist and shoulder before he placed it neatly on the table with the rest of the items. "When a child is taught which way to go, he trusts his teacher. He will accept his principles as true because his teacher said so. I believed every word Clara's father said. He took good care of me."

That brute had a heart and more wisdom than Clara had ever given him credit for, and she wondered how he could have been so misunderstood.

"Toomber, I know now is perhaps not the time, but I wish to get to know you better. I am sorry I did not know you before."

He smiled at her. Clara had not thought he was equipped with muscles to move his lips upwards, but that's how narrow-minded she had become.

He handed her a piece of old paper, folded in half and torn in places. "This will explain some," he said. "You can read it later."

"Thank you, Toomber, I will," she said and put her hand on his arm. "I will read it after we are done."

They went through their plan one last time, making sure they all remembered the details and adjusted questionable elements.

"If this works, we'll have a good head start before anyone notices what has happened," Mychel said and threw the rope across his shoulder. He looked like a miner carrying his equipment to work. "It's getting dark. The guests should be arriving at Town Hall within the hour. Toomber, we will see you in a little while."

The gravedigger nodded and left. He knew what his task was. Clara put on her warmest coat, hat, and gloves. She walked the path to the parsonage to speak with Herr Christopher and Sara about the infant, then continued to town to meet Mychel.

The wind from the ocean blew wintry cold toward the back wall of Town Hall. Because of the slanted hill by the ocean, the basement wall was half uncovered, and a small door to the pigpen was bolted from the outside but unguarded. Clara held her breath as she hid to watch Mychel creep behind a dung of waste. He checked to see if the coast was clear, slunk toward the door, and put his equipment quietly on the ground. With the crowbar, he was able to pry open the bolts and lock.

She had seen many well-dressed people approach Town Hall on her way there. By now, the ballroom on the main floor was probably full of merry, cheerful guests.

Someone opened one of the back windows in the ballroom. The music and noise of people talking and laughing spread gracefully into the dark night, disturbing a couple of cats out on their nightly prowl.

Clara put a hand to her chest and breathed out. She saw Mychel cling to the wall by the pigpen and hoped no one had hung their head far enough out the window to see him. She waited for a minute or two until she heard the window shut. Nothing to be alarmed about so far; it was only someone who threw the waste out. Now she had to remain out of sight until most of the guests had arrived. She waved to Mychel before she walked around the front of the building to present her invitation to the guard by the blue double door. The card requesting her presence at the mayor's town ball had come as a surprise, and an opportunity.

The mayor and his wife stood by the entrance to the ballroom, greeting the guests from far and near. Clara peeked into the ballroom. The Land family had arrived. The twins, in identical gowns and their hair styled in a grown-up fashion for the occasion, were surrounded by four or five young men who seemed eager to make their acquaintance. Dr. Bing-Olsen and the innkeeper stood in the middle of the room speaking with Angus Hill, via his interpreter. Festive decoration adorned the ballroom and a small orchestra was seated in a corner playing music.

Clara greeted the mayor and his wife, then lingered in the hallway for a while, talking to acquaintances and taking time pretending she needed to hang her winter coat in the wardrobe. There were several guards on the premises; some walked in and out of the ballroom, while others were posted in various areas of Town Hall.

Knowing Anna was on duty for the ball, Clara walked toward the kitchen to look for her friend. Suddenly, she came out, carrying a large tray with a stuffed pheasant surrounded by boiled vegetables. Several younger maids followed, also carrying trays with colorful food.

"Anna, I brought a couple of bottles of wine for the guards. May I just put them in the kitchen so they may serve themselves?"

"Yes, that's a nice gesture. They will probably enjoy that. We'll be back in a few minutes; just put the bottles on the center table."

Clara placed them in the kitchen then walked down the hallway toward the guard.

"You again?" He could not be pleasant, even on the evening of the grand ball.

"Yes, I know we have met before, many times. I am enjoying the ball. Isn't it a lovely night?"

He obviously did not sense anything lovely about being on duty whilst others indulged in nice food and drink.

"I know it will be a long evening for you and I wanted to thank you for giving Old Magda the blanket. I brought a couple of bottles of wine to show my appreciation. They are in the kitchen; please share with the others and help yourselves."

He seemed pleased with the chance to take a small part in the festivities that evening. As he went to the kitchen, Clara ran through the gateway farther down the corridor and hid behind the corner of the passage leading to the stairs descending to the holding chamber.

She stood with her back to the wall and put the right hand to her chest, trying not to breathe so hard. The chill in the air coming from below gave a cloudy sense to every breath. She told herself to calm down and to concentrate on the following move. In the other hand, she held the bag with one more bottle of strong drink.

Before long, Clara heard cheerful whistling and a thump as a cork of a wine bottle popped out. *He must be back with his bottle of red*, Clara thought. *I hope he thinks I have joined the celebration in the ballroom.* Little did the guard know that she had added root of valeriana to the drink to make him and his companions drowsy.

Clara slunk down the stairs one step at a time, feeling the tension build, the closer she came to the chamber where Bess and the other women were held. She almost tripped and made a noise which alerted the guard a little sooner than she had hoped.

"Who's there?" he called out and poked his head out of the door in the small room outside the holding chamber. He stared straight at Clara as she tried not to fall and break the valuable bottle in her bag.

"Oh, good evening, I have been asked to bring you this."

Lying had never been her forte. She stuck her hand inside the bag, then handed him the bottle of wine, gently blended with a touch of belladonna, taken from a jar in Bess's top kitchen cupboard. The foreign plant had a bitter flavor and unpleasant odor, and Clara had carefully warmed some honey and added that to the drink, hoping it would go down easily. He grinned and greedily grabbed the bottle out of her hand.

"Finally someone thinks about us poor guards," he said. He opened the bottle and started gulping down the beverage.

He mumbled while he drank, and wet red drops trickled down into his beard.

"Who told you to give me this?" he asked.

"The guard upstairs; I don't remember his name. They were given a few bottles as the town is celebrating tonight. Lucky you."

"Well, a welcoming sight this be on a cold night in a place like this." He held out the bottle toward Clara. "You want a swig?" he asked. "I could do with some female company."

She backed up a little. "No, thank you, I have already had my share. Enjoy."

She pretended to walk up the stairs but lingered around the edge where the staircase turned a corner, trusting it would not be long before he passed out. She hoped with all her heart she had administered just the right amount of the poisonous extract. She did not want to commit manslaughter, only put him out of consciousness for a short while. Clara heard him finish the bottle and throw it on the floor. The glass shattered on the cold stones, and she heard him mumble and topple over, bringing with him the chair and other things on the table.

"Oh, can't you just fall asleep quietly," Clara whispered. She peeked around the corner to see if anyone had heard the noises from outside the holding chamber. But the hallways were long, and the merry ball with music and laughter drowned out any clamor from downstairs.

Regardless of our current state, there is hope for us. Clara was reminded of the words from a sermon her father had given. He spoke of God's love for His children on Earth. She could barely manage to keep herself from opening the door of the holding chamber to see if Bess was still there. Patience was a virtue, according to her father, and at this moment, she practiced being virtuous at the peril of her life.

When she felt all was safe and the old guard had passed out, Clara hurried back down. Relieved to find he still breathed, she grabbed the ring with keys hanging on a nail by the entrance of the chamber, then must tried three keys before the door opened. She pushed the small door aside and stepped inside. The stench was more horrid than last time, and she thought there were more women huddled on the floor. She searched for Bess and found her lying down in the same place as before.

"Bess, Bess."

Clara shook her shoulders, but Bess did not respond. Clara tried again and wanted to scream out to get her attention. She was terrified it was too late, but then Bess slowly moved her legs, lifted her head, and looked up at Clara in the darkness.

"Clara?"

"Yes, Bess, I'm here. Please be quiet."

Clara looked around and saw the others were awake. She put a finger to her lips.

"Shh, be still. I will try to get you out of here."

"Magda died today," Bess said sadly.

Clara looked over and saw Magda's lifeless body still lying on the cold floor in a fetal position. Why had nobody come to feed or check on the prisoners that day? Her heart went out to these poor women. How they had suffered…

She hurried out of the room and across to the animal shelter. She waded through dirt, pushing a hog that stood in her way. It grunted and would not move easily. She pushed again and managed to reach the small door in the back of Town Hall. Hopefully, Mychel waited. Clara opened the iron bar lever that kept the door locked from the inside and pushed it open. Mychel jumped inside and rushed through the muddy pigsty and into the holding chamber, where he found Bess on the floor. He picked her up and, half bent over, tenderly held her close for a moment then carried her away from there—away from the cold, the sinful dark, and the wickedness.

Clara squatted down in front of the other women. "There's an open door on the far wall in the pigsty," she explained. "Make your way out now, try to get as far away as possible, and don't go in the front of the hall or on Main Street. Stay away from people. Good luck." She knew they were frail and weak, but hopefully, they could escape the dungeon before anyone noticed.

Clara scurried back to the small, open door toward the ocean. Mychel was on his way out with Bess, and Clara followed. They stuck their necks out to see if anyone watched from the windows of the ballroom. When they felt the coast was clear, they hurried uphill and into the thicket of woods on the north side of Town Hall. Bess said nothing, just stared at her husband with tired eyes. She lifted her hand and touched his face.

Clara found her bag by a large birch tree in the murky grove. It was packed with a fresh set of shoes and clean gown like the one she already wore. The plan was for her to go back into the ball not smelling like pigs and death. She had been gone long enough, and even though there were guests at the ball, she could not risk that the mayor, Innkeeper Hansen, or even Angus might wonder where she was.

She changed her gown and bid them adieu. Tears filled her eyes, and she sniffled and wiped her nose.

"I don't like to say goodbye." She put her arms around Bess. "Welcome greetings are better."

Mychel put a hand on Clara's back. "We need to continue," he said.

Clara swallowed hard. "I know. You need a head start. It's just so hard to part."

The strong fisherman lifted Bess up and took a few steps before he turned around and mouthed a thank you then disappeared into the woods. Though this was the worst farewell of Clara's life, it had to be done. She straightened her clean frock and lifted her head. Now to muster her performance, and act as if nothing had happened. She walked back to Town Hall.

25

The Downtrodden

～

That night, Toomber fetched Bess's infant from the parsonage. Sara held the child close to her chest. "Take care of her. Keep her warm. She likes being held. She likes to be sung to."

Herr Christopher took the small child out of his wife's firm arms and handed her to Toomber. He put his arm around Sara and gently wiped her wet cheeks. The young babe was well-fed, swaddled in warm blankets, and had a woolen hood with embroidered ribbons around her small head. A sheep's stomach filled with warm goat's milk provided enough nourishment for the first hours. If they waited too long to use it, it would curdle and become too solid for the infant to drink. Additionally, Sara handed Toomber a rag to soak the milk in for the child to suckle and some bread softened in water in a small jar. Even with Sara as a wet nurse, they hoped Bess's milk returned, so she could nurse her own child. It was still possible to bring back a full milk supply.

Toomber had never held a small child before, but his large, working hands cupped gently around the infant. He gazed at her and smiled, then looked at the parson's wife and nodded as he saw the concern in her eyes.

"I will be careful," he said in a curiously confident manner. "She is sleeping well now. I will meet with Samuel and give him the instructions."

Tears still rolled down Sara's cheeks as her husband came behind her and put his hands tenderly on her shoulders.

"Thank you, Toomber," Herr Christopher said. "Take her safely to her parents. May God bless you."

Toomber walked with long, rapid paces on the path east of the main part of town, out of sight of curious townspeople or meddlesome folks. Not that he had a problem with that, as people did not usually speak to him. As long as the infant quietly slept in the bundle tied on his back, no one would ever guess he actually carried a child.

Up on the road past Hilda and Lars's cottage by the sea, Toomber stopped and looked around. The infant still snuggled asleep on his back, and the only person he had met on the path had walked by without even so much as a "good evening".

Startled, he turned his head in the direction of sounds coming from the bushes next to the road. He saw a man's hand poking out from the bushes, motioning him to approach.

"Toomber," a voice whispered. "We're here. Come away from the road."

Behind large rocks, mounds of earth, and evergreen pine trees, he found the family—Uncle Samuel, Mychel holding Bess, and little Lucia leaning on her mother's lap with her poppet in her hand. Toomber treaded carefully and kneeled down with one knee on the ground. He fondly lifted the precious bundle from his back and handed it to Bess, whose eyes lit up as she saw what he had brought. Even though her thin body was weak and frail, her motherly instincts gave her strength, and she stretched out her arms toward the bundle, swaddled in a warm blanket. The tender reunion of the family was more touching than anything Toomber had witnessed.

"How can we ever thank you, Toomber?" Mychel asked.

Toomber just smiled.

Uncle Samuel broke the silence. "We need to continue."

He picked up Lucia and helped Mychel bring Bess into a standing position.

"I will carry Bess," Mychel said and lifted up his wife, carrying the little infant. "Toomber, we are so grateful for what you have done. I don't know when we will see you again, but I hope it won't be long. Take care."

Water filled Toomber's eyes as he kissed Bess's cheek, patted Mychel on the shoulder, then turned around and stepped back onto the road toward Rossby.

〜

Uncle Samuel guided the way and brought his family to a cliff where a steep, stony path led to a small provisory dock. A boat with provisions of food, blankets, and clothing bobbed up and down on the cold waves, secured with strong ropes and a dropped anchor. Access to the dock and tying the boat had been difficult but manageable. However, it was a much more ardent task to take Bess and the children safely down the cliff-face.

The firm trunk of a tall fir tree became the base where Mychel tied the end of the rope and threw the rest of the coiled up line off the cliff. Uncle Samuel went first. He held onto the rope and managed to climb down just as he had done many times already. Mychel pulled the rope back up and tied it around Bess. He swaddled the babe with a long piece of soft cloth and tied her on Bess's back before he carefully lowered both down the path of the cliff. Her weak steps helped the burden only a little; mostly, he had to use his strength alone to get her down. Holding the babe was strenuous enough for the weak mother, and at one point, she slipped on the wet moss and let out a cry. She looked up at Mychel, who motioned for her to continue, hoping the sound of her voice had not been carried on the wind to suspicious ears. As her feet were placed safely on the rocks and sand below, Mychel hauled the cord back up and tied it around Lucia. The little girl was tired and whined, asking for food. Mychel kissed his daughter and told her to close her eyes—and when she opened them, she would be with her mother and get something to eat.

"Just stay still, and I will help you," the father said. "Close your eyes, Lucia. Don't look down."

Lucia squeezed her eyes shut as Mychel slowly lowered her off the stony cliff. The narrow and steep path was a hindrance to the little girl. Rocks and bushes clinging to the hill were in the way, and she did not know how to push away from the cliff. She started whimpering as her face brushed against a twig sticking out, and she dropped her poppet. The doll plunged down toward the seashore, and Lucia cried louder when she opened her eyes and saw how far it was down to where her mother sat. Uncle Samuel leaped forward and caught the doll before it hit the ground. He waved at Lucia and told her to close her eyes again and to be brave. The little sunbeam was obedient, and Mychel continued lowering the rope until she safely landed on the ground below. Then, finally, he followed.

"Quick, hurry," Uncle Samuel said as he helped them into the boat. "Just go, please, no long goodbyes. There's no time for it, and I cannot do it. Please, hurry now."

He shoved the boat as Mychel pushed away from the shoreline with a large oar to get out into the sea and away from the rocks.

Bess looked at her uncle on the shore as the boat floated on the waves. She stretched out her hand cried, "We cannot leave him behind; we cannot."

Mychel tried to calm her sobs. "It's not forever, my dear," he said. "We need to get you and the children to safety. Hopefully, we may return one day."

They looked at the old man climbing the rope back up the cliff. The last thing they saw was the rope being pulled up, and Uncle Samuel disappeared from sight.

<center>~~~</center>

In the decorated ballroom of Town Hall, Clara rejoined the merry guests just as the twins were about to perform their musical number. She nodded to people both left and right to make sure they noticed her presence and had no reason to expect foul play.

The twins in their exquisite peach-colored gowns looked both beautiful and mature, and young men's eyes followed them as they made their way in front of the audience to sing. Had Clara not known better, she, too, would have been mesmerized by their looks and talent and had to give her lacking acting ability the utmost attention and concentration so as not to give anything away.

After the rendition, Clara noticed Angus Hill approaching. She nodded courteously and gave him her hand when he asked her to dance. Under any other circumstances, she would never have even looked at the man. She felt nauseated and angry but knew dancing with him kept him occupied.

"Miss, Dahl, you look well tonight," he said in a flattering manner. His mouth drew into a thin horizontal line to resemble a smile.

"Thank you. It's a wonderful ball." Clara concentrated on remembering the steps and variations to the formal dance, weaving in and out between other couples and curtsying in the right places.

"Indeed, indeed. I was thinking, Miss Dahl, we are the same, you and I. We both fight for righteousness and goodness in the world. So beneficial for you to spend more time with me. You would like that, wouldn't you?"

He swirled around another couple but returned too swiftly then said, "I know you are not the most beautiful woman I have seen, but I am considering you as a future wife."

Shocked at the unexpected proposal, Clara fervently prayed for God to grant her a clever answer and help her not reveal her true feelings. How on Earth could he think they were a right match or that she was even remotely interested in sharing her life with him? They did not agree on anything. Besides, he managed to both suggest marriage and insult her in the same sentence. The man was insufferable.

"Thank you, Mr. Hill, I will consider it," she answered. "Please let me have a few days to think about the matter."

He jerked his head back, and his mouth fell open, apparently surprised at her answer. She managed to wiggle out of his clammy white hands, curtsied, and walked toward the bottles of apple cider for a refreshing change of taste and scenery. The twins were there, drinking cider, laughing, and enjoying compliments from men of all ages.

By the virtue of all that was good and important, Clara had managed to keep Angus away from Bess a little while longer. She had not been able to decline his offer to dance but would never accept his offer of marriage.

The music was pleasant, and all around people seemed to be enjoying the festivities, but Clara had picked the worst time of her life for merry-making, and her thoughts were constantly on her friends and how they were faring.

As she gulped down the third glass of apple cider, she saw a seemingly frustrated innkeeper approach Angus with long strides. She carefully shuffled her feet closer to hear.

"The guards are lacking in concentration," the innkeeper said. He put his hands on his hips and frowned. "When they changed guards in the dungeon by the holding chamber, the guard was fast asleep. They found an open door and empty chamber."

"What?" the witch-finder bellowed. "How could you let this happen?"

The innkeeper stepped aside as Angus pushed his way forward. Panic arose among the council members and guards, but it was bleak in comparison to what went on inside Clara. She could not stand idly behind, and she blended in with the group of curious guests who followed the men into the hallway.

"What's the meaning of this?" Angus cried out as he saw one of the guards on a chair yawning by the corridor leading to the stairs going down to the dungeon.

John Pywell interpreted as lively as he could.

"You are on duty. No time to sleep." The witch-finder kicked the guard's legs.

The man almost fell over but caught himself with one hand on the floor then got up on his feet and saluted his superior.

"Show me the chamber," Angus roared and led the way down the corridor.

The bystanders, including Clara, followed to the top of the stairs, where a guard stopped them from following any farther. Everyone stretched their necks to get a glimpse into the abyss downstairs and hear what was going on.

"There's a guard asleep on the floor, and the door to the holding chamber is open," the innkeeper called out. "Wait, there's someone in there. Bring a torch, so we can see."

"What a ghastly smell. Who is it?" Angus sounded as if he had problems breathing. "Ah, it's the old witch who lived by herself in the woods. Disgusting."

"Remove that body," the innkeeper said. "The stench of filth and rotted flesh is unbearable."

Back upstairs, Angus paced the room. "Where are the rest of the witches? How many were down here? How many have we lost?"

Innkeeper Hansen shook his head. "I am not certain." He put his hand up in front of his chest, looking at his fingers, counting. "Let's see, there was Old Magda—she is dead—then there was Hilda...no, not Hilda, I mean Mari...then—"

Angus was fuming. "Enough. How did they get out? Where are they? We cannot let wicked witches roam free."

Clara and guests of the ball stood perplexed and moved aside as the witch-finder pushed his way through the crowd.

"Who knows what these women are up to?" he called out. "Who can tell where they are?"

Innkeeper Hansen called together a group of men to go out and look for the *witches*, who, in the words of Angus, had magically removed themselves from the premises.

The crowd followed to the open blue double door to watch the men mount their horses and get ready to leave. Outside, the town square teemed with people who celebrated the ball in their own way in the streets. Any excuse to make merry on an otherwise dark and cold autumn evening was enough to keep both young and old out and about.

A few young women stood on the stairs, flirting with one of the guards.

"Please, let me through," Clara pleaded. She had to keep an eye on the company on horseback in the town square but mingled inconspicuously among other guests and interested townspeople.

She saw Angus Hill pointing in different directions as he circled around on horseback.

They don't know where to go, Clara thought. *They don't know what has happened. But for how long? When will someone figure out which direction they need to go to search for Bess?*

Just as she thought about Bess, Clara heard Angus's voice.

"Bess of Frue Farm," he said to the guards, "concentrate on finding her first. It's most imperative that she is found."

Clara watched the horsemen as they rode away, only to come to a standstill at the northern end of the crowded square.

"Halt."

Angus lifted his hand. On the narrow dirt road going out of town, a person came walking into sight. The light from the torches showed a silhouette of a rather large stature of a man. Angus Hill looked at the figure and narrowed his eyes.

"The gravedigger," he mumbled in a disparaging voice. "What is he doing there at this time of night?"

He rode toward the large man with John Pywell, the innkeeper, and guards following closely behind. As they drew nearer, Toomber stopped in the narrow gate at the end of the square and stood as a giant sculpture. He opened up his arms wide in order to stop anyone from passing.

"Hmm, interesting." Angus retorted. "He must have a reason for trying to prohibit us from going up the northern road." He flung his arm in the air and pointed at Toomber. "Make him move. I want to search in that direction."

The guards on horseback pulled and pushed, but Toomber did not budge.

"We don't have time for this. Shoot him," the witch-finder commanded. "We need him out of the way."

A guard in front dismounted and pulled his musket out of the belt on the horse's side. He poured gun powder from a powder horn in the saddle bag into the muzzle of the musket and shoved it down the barrel, then placed a lead bullet on top. Finer powder was put into the pan before he placed his firearm into position and pulled the hammer back.

Angus held the reins tightly as his horse impatiently stomped the cold ground, snorting damp steam and nodding.

"Get to it. We don't have all night," he said. "We have no time at all to spare."

The shot fired. Like a large tree chopped down in the dark woods, the gravedigger fell to the ground, dead.

Horses' hooves straddled the gravedigger, and Angus Hill and his men rode on.

Screams shot across the square. A murder in Rossby? And at the night of the grand ball. People ran toward the giant on the ground who lay there with his eyes open. They gawked at the body, and one man kicked the gravedigger's side to see if moved.

Clara put her head on Toomber's chest and sobbed, not caring what others might think or do.

"He never did one good thing in his life," she heard a woman say.

"He was a horrible man, greedy and mean. Good riddance to him," another said.

Clara closed Toomber's eyes. The life he had found had ended, and the lead bullet in his chest poisoned his already silenced heart.

The townfolks had no idea. *A man who gives his life for another, will have eternal life.* Words from another of her father's sermons came to mind, reminding her that in the end, serving others is what is vital.

"Someone help." she cried out. "Please, someone help me get him away from here."

An old man with a pot belly and a much-too-large mustache said he could fetch his horse and carriage and help Clara bring the gravedigger to the parsonage. He had placed his horse by the Watering House on the opposite side of the town square.

A few minutes later the possy returned.

"There's nothing out there. Split up in groups and continue the search." The witch-finder stood in the stirrups and yelled at the men. "I refuse to be defeated, nor will I give up. Find the witches, especially Bess."

Sitting next to Toomber on the ground, Clara heard horses' hooves galloping into the square from the opposite direction. Six cavalry troopers dismounted in front of the steps of Town Hall. They were well equipped with swords and buff carbine belts with steel hooks. Most of them had one or two waist pistols tucked into their belts. She looked at them and thought for a moment, she could have used the help of those men once or twice during the last few months.

"Toomber, I will return," she said, even though she knew he was not there anymore. "I'll make sure you are brought home, I just have to see what is happening here." She leaned toward his ear and whispered, "I have to make sure Bess is safe." Then she ran back to the hall.

One of the visiting soldiers steadfastly ascended the steps of Town Hall. His black-spurred boots sounded heavy as he stomped up to the blue double door. His uniform was a coat and breeches made of leather and a large black hat with feathers and colored ribbons. A colored sash draped from his left shoulder to his right hip identified him as one of their own.

The soldier seemed determined and purposeful as he marched straight into the ballroom and called out for the mayor. Angus dismounted and followed, obviously intrigued.

Clara thought it looked as if the mayor was drowning his worries. He looked out of control, devouring a leg of lamb that he swallowed down with gulps of cider. He arose as one of his own guards announced the visitor.

"May I help you?" he said in a shaky voice.

"I come from Christiania with a royal proclamation concerning the town of Rossby and its inhabitants."

Angus pushed his way in front of all the bystanders until he stood next to the messenger. He seemed eager to find out what was more important than his witch-hunt. He tried to grab the document out of the hands of the soldier, who pushed him aside and held it up in the air.

The mayor looked at Angus in dismay. "You are forgetting yourself, Mr. Hill. This man is an emissary from our king."

Angus bowed and stepped back, still impatiently staring at the document in the soldier's hand.

"As I said," the soldier continued, "I come with a royal proclamation naming a certain Englishman named Angus Hill."

"Yes, I am he." The witch-finder keenly stepped next to the mayor, and his pride melted into a broad grin on his face.

"Mr. Angus Hill is hereby banned from Rossby and its territories and will never practice here in the future."

The soldier lowered his arm and handed the document to the mayor, who verified that the royal signature and bulla were visible at the bottom of the page.

The grin on Angus Hill's face dropped hastily, and he tried to get the document out of the hands of the mayor.

"Let me see that," he cried. "This must be a mistake. Banned? I have never heard of such a thing. This is an outrage. We are in the middle of a crucial operation here. I cannot leave until I have finished."

"You *are* finished." The mayor drew a long breath.

The look on his face let Clara feel that his burdens had been lifted, and there was hope once again for Rossby.

The soldier took a long look at the witch-finder and stated, "So you are the notorious witch-finder? You are to pack your bags immediately, and be on your way. We will escort you to the next ship bound for other shores. King Fredrik III will not have you in Rossby."

It was a downtrodden witch-finder who passed Clara in the doorway to the great ballroom.

"Miss Dahl," he said as he passed her.

She looked at him, feeling nothing at the time, but knew the reaction would come later.

The innkeeper walked with short steps behind the witch-finder, trying to connect, speaking continuously.

"What are we going to do? We have to finish our work. Where are you going?"

The witch-finder stopped and turned to face his former assistant. "The King of Denmark and Norway has noticed me," he said. "Me." His nose turned up and he watched the innkeeper through a crack below his eyelids. "He has heard of my reputation. You are nothing, Innkeeper Hansen. You are a small sea-weed in a large ocean. I am the one they are after, and I am the master of this grand vocation."

Even when his fortress has been broken down, even when the enemy has marched across his borders and crucified him, he still thinks himself superior, Clara thought.

The soldiers gathered to accompany Angus to the inn. Clara watched them go but noticed that one was different and did not have the proper uniform of a soldier. She tilted her head and stared at the man to see his features under the hat's brim. Suddenly, her face broke into a smile, and she to hug him.

"Oh, Peter, it's you."

He hugged her back. "I came back to see you and on the way I met the soldiers heading for Rossby. It seemed like an excellent cause to support, so I decided to aid."

Clara looked into his eyes. In her heart, she felt a change. In her mind, she imagined a small boat drifting on the gentle waves of the sea—moonbeams shining on the deck—a little family close together, singing tender songs of love and good days.

26

The Repair

~~~

"I never believed Angus Hill was inspired from on high," Clara said. She handed Peter a cup of warm drink and sat down on a chair. They had returned to the cottage exhausted but hopeful. The soldiers took care of Angus Hill, and Toomber's body had been brought to the cemetery. Ami jumped on Peter's lap and purred as the Irishman gently stroked him.

"They came, Peter. The king actually listened and sent his soldiers." Peter looked at her as she explained about her trip to Copenhagen.

"You courageous, willful woman. What a perilous journey to make—and all on your own." Peter put Ami down and took hold of her hand.

"Well, we are finally rid of Angus Hill but there's still the innkeeper to worry about, not to mention the superstitions and accusations still floating in the air around Rossby," Clara said.

"Changing an attitude takes time, Clara. The question is how an English witch-finder could capture a small town here in the north."
~~~

Clara leaned back in the chair. "He was neither gifted nor knowledgeable about human nature," she said. "As a witch-finder, he had already made up his mind before he received an invitation to come to Rossby. He had a reputation to uphold and could not leave before causing a stir."

"He has probably accumulated wealth at every place he has been," Peter said.

Clara nodded. "I am sure when he left, his coffers were a little fuller with the treasures he had confiscated and his pockets a little heavier with blood coins and stolen trinkets. He still has Bess's recipe book."

"Did he justify the hunt in any way?"

"He said he claimed the right to rid the world from evil and that it was his calling and vocation to continue a work of great magnitude." Clara pulled her hand back and folded her arms tightly.

"You have lost loved ones?"

"I have, and it's been difficult. Part of me wishes Old Magda's spells on him had come true. He ridiculed her homemade rituals and the hex she cast on him. Innocent women were no threat to him. He worried more about Francesca's curses. Who is Angus Hill to decide they were not to live anymore? My father taught me to forgive everyone, Peter. I am still working on it but it's no easy task."

"I know. We are all in that same boat."

Clara leaned forward again and stretched out her hand. "I have been so afraid, Peter. It means the world to me that you are here now."

He stroked her cheek and got up to leave. A rooster announced the morning from the barn at the parsonage. They had talked all night.

~~

Toomber's funeral that day was simple. In the fog encircling the cemetery, Uncle Samuel appeared, walking his work horse toward the open grave. Clara ran to meet him. Together with Herr Christopher and Peter they sang hymns and remembered the man who had given his life for Bess.

Clara's thoughts kept going back to the last days she spent with Toomber. Her heart ached for him as he had spent most of his life misunderstood and unloved. She had no problem with being perceived as a maudlin woman. Toomber became her friend. She only wished he had been sooner.

Clara pulled the worn piece of paper Toomber had given her from her pocket. It was a birth certificate. It said: *Elsie Juel's son Thomas born in Christiania, Norway. Father unknown.*

A record of Toomber's work experience at the cemetery of Rossby Church, the cottage he lived in by the marsh, and uplifting insight into Toomber's personality traits had been added. Maybe her father thought the certificate useful if Toomber ever sought employment elsewhere. On the back of the document, her father had written a few personal notes about Toomber, and it helped Clara understand why he had become the town's gravedigger and also why her father had cared for him.

The next week, Clara spent with the woman Mari from behind the abbey. She had been found with Doris and little Kari in the woods and brought home. The council saw no reason to keep them locked away after the culprit was gone. Wounds heal, but Clara knew scars remained, reminders of the fight. Mari suffered from nightmares, and Clara held her shaking body and comforted her when she cried. Her sensitive soul took longer to heal than most.

Why Thea, the maid from the Lands' kitchen, accused Doris and her daughter seemed a mystery to Clara. Mrs. Land whipped the maid fiercely when she returned. Thea ran away and was never heard of again.

Uncle Samuel invited Clara and Peter to Frue Farm for supper one evening before the New Year.

"I have heard news," he said. "Fishermen in the harbor brought greetings from Mychel. They are well, Clara. They are well."

Clara hugged him then twirled around on the kitchen floor. "One day, they will return," she sang. "Mychel and the children are her life, Uncle Samuel, but you and Frue Farm are her heritage. Having both will make her whole."

Uncle Samuel looked at her. "What will you do, meanwhile?" He knew already Clara would not stay in Rossby forever.

Clara stopped twirling and became serious. "I will be back," she said. "Bess will need support when she returns. Some may be troubled and even threatened by her homecoming. I pray they will ask for her services again."

They sat down at the table to eat. Clara felt at peace. Here were two men she trusted. She knew they would not try to talk her out of her plan.

"It's scary how easily thoughts and ideas are planted into someone's mind and how we become like sheep," she said. "We follow the flock leader and never question why. I can never again sit idly on a chair and watch blameless people suffer."

"What will you do?" Uncle Samuel said.

Clara saw a disapproving frown forming on Peter's forehead. She ignored it, took a deep breath and said, "I have made a decision. I will find Angus Hill. Wherever he goes, I will fight his influence. Where on earth he works his horror, I will go and stand up for the innocent. Whenever he enters the stage, I will be behind the curtains. He has to be stopped."

She paused for a moment and looked at the two men.

Uncle Samuel was silent for a while then asked, "I suppose there's no stopping you?"

She shook her head, and he put his hands together and clapped.

THE EPILOGUE

Clara put the pen in the ink bottle and flicked her wrinkled left hand. It trembled and dozed off, but so did she. Her life reminded her of a book with many chapters. Some parts were joyous, some sad. But every word was a part of her time.

She thought about the book she had given Bess all those summers ago.

"I will treasure it for life," Bess said when Clara had brought her the volume with notes about herbs from Okinawa. Neither of them knew at the time she nearly would.

"Books, books," Clara said to herself. She had devoured the written word with an appetite. Isaac Newton's writings were among her favorites. She gazed at the prism hanging in the window and admired how it revealed the light.

"My reflections are true in my eyes," she said, "my story bold and full of memories."

ABOUT THE AUTHOR

Heidi Eljarbo grew up in a home filled with books and artwork and she never truly imagined she would do anything other than write and paint. She studied art, languages, and history, all of which have come in handy when working as a freelance writer, magazine journalist, and painter.

After living in Canada, six US states, Japan, Switzerland, and Austria, Heidi now calls Norway home. She and her husband have a total of nine children, ten grandchildren—so far—in addition to a bouncy Wheaten Terrier and a bird. They love to have the munchkins come and visit at the Duck and Cherry, their family dwelling.

Their favorite retreat is a mountain cabin, where they hike in the summertime and ski the vast, white terrain during winter.

Heidi's favorites are family, God's beautiful nature, and the word *whimsical.*

If you would like to know more, please visit:

Website: **www.heidieljarbo.com**

Facebook: **www.facebook.com/authorheidieljarbo**

Pinterest: **www.pinterest.com/heidieljarbo**

Twitter: **www.twitter.com/heidieljarbo**

AUTHOR'S NOTE

I have always loved history. While studying the seventeenth century's witch-hunting processes in Norway and the Salem Witch Trials, I became fascinated by the impact of mass suggestion. How could a person—or even groups of people—lose their independent reasoning due to outer influence? Even though many were reliant on someone with knowledge of healing and folk medicine, they were more than ready to judge that person as evil, eager to sentence the person to death. This is not the only time in history that the blind follow the blind.

In this story, the witch-finder, Angus Hill, is the instigator. Even though he is a fictional character, his teacher, Matthew Hopkins, was a notorious witch-finder general during the English Civil Wars.

The scenes and dialogues with historical characters are invented. The Danish-Norwegian kings, Fredrik III and his father, Christian IV, both believed that evil witchcraft had to be conquered. King Fredrik III enjoyed books as much as Clara does. He was well read and interested in the theology and science of his day. King Fredrik III had a substantial book collection and founded the Royal Library in Copenhagen. I have only guessed that he had a copy of Heinrich Kramer's *Malleus Maleficarum* (The Hammer of Witches).

Wyllem Coucheron, whose wine the mayor and Angus Hill enjoy, was my ninth great-grandfather. His story is real, though if he had his own wine label, I would not know.

Clara's background as part of a missionary family in Okinawa is a play with history. There were Christians in the Far East in the seventeenth century, but Christianity was also forbidden by the Japanese shogun. Persecution and executions made it a dangerous way of life.

Clara grew up with the shamanistic wisdom of the Okinawans. That the Dahl family lived on the island of Okinawa was more of a humanitarian or anthropologian effort than a purely proselyting practice.

Even though this is a work of fiction, witch-hunting was a real and horrible part of history and, unfortunately, is still a threat in some parts of the world.

I honor the women and men who were innocently accused and tried as witches.

PERMISSION TO USE
BIBLE QUOTES

Extracts from the Authorized Version of the Bible (The King James Bible), the rights in which are vested in the Crown, are reproduced by permission of the Crown's Patentee, Cambridge University Press.

GET SPECIAL DEALS ON MORE BEST SELLING BOOKS

Get discounts and special deals on our best selling books at

www.tckpublishing.com/bookdeals